The Citadel of Fear

The Citadel of Fear

Francis Stevens

MINT EDITIONS

The Citadel of Fear was first published in 1918.

This edition published by Mint Editions 2021.

ISBN 9781513297002 | E-ISBN 9781513298504

Published by Mint Editions®

MINT
EDITIONS

minteditionbooks.com

Publishing Director: Jennifer Newens
Design & Production: Rachel Lopez Metzger
Project Manager: Micaela Clark
Typesetting: Westchester Publishing Services

Contents

PART I

I

Hidden in the Hills

Don't leave me—All—in—" The words were barely distinguishable, but the tall figure in the lead, striding heavily through the soft, impeding sand, heard the mutter of them and paused without turning. He stood with drooped head and shoulders, as if the oppression of the cruel, naked sun were an actual weight that pressed him earthward. His companion, plowing forward with an ultimate effort, sagged from the hips and fell face downward in the sand.

Apathetically the tall man looked at the twitching heap beside him. Then he raised his head and stared through a reddening film at the vast, encircling torture pen in which they both were trapped.

The sun, he thought, had grown monstrous and swallowed all the sky. No blue was anywhere. Brass above, soft, white-hot iron beneath, and all tinged to redness by the film of blood over sand-tormented eyes. Beyond a radius of thirty yards his vision blurred and ceased, but into that radius something flapped down and came tilting awkwardly across the sand, long wings half-spread, yellow head lowered, bold with an avid and loathsome curiosity.

"You!" whispered the man hoarsely, and shook one great, red fist at the thing. "You'll not get your dinner off me nor him while my one foot can follow the other!"

And with that he knelt down by the prostrate one, drew the limp arms about his own neck, bowed powerful shoulders to support the body, and heaved himself up again. Swaying, he stood for a moment with feet spread, then began a new and staggering progress. The king-vulture flapped lazily from his path and upward to renew its circling patience.

After years in hell, where he was doomed forever to bear an intolerable burden across seas of smoking fire, the tall man regained a glimmering of reason. It came with the discovery that he was lying flat on his stomach, arms and breast immersed in liquid coolness, and that he was gulping water as fast and as greedily as swollen tongue and lips would permit.

With a self-control that saved two lives, he forced himself to cease drinking, but laved in the water, played in it with his hands, could scarcely believe in it, and at the same time thanked God for its reality. So sanity came closely back, and with clearing vision he saw the stream that meant salvation to sundrained tissues.

It was a deep, narrow, rapid flood, rushing darkly by and tugging at his arms with the force of its turbulent current. Flowing out from a rocky gorge, it lost itself again round a curving height of rocks.

What of the white-hot torture-pit? He was in shadow now, blessed, cool, revivifying. But—alone.

Dragging himself by sheer will-power from the water, the tall man wiped at his eyes and stared about. There close by lay a motionless heap of brown, coated with sand in dusty patches, white sand in the tumble of black hair at one end of it.

Very cautiously the tall man got to his feet and took an uncertain step toward the huddled figure. Then he shook one dripping red fist toward a wide, shimmering expanse that lay beyond the shadow of the rocks.

"You missed us," he muttered with a chuckle almost childishly triumphant, "and you'll never get us—not while—my one foot can follow the other!"

Then he set himself to revive the companion he had carried through torment on his shoulders, bathing the face, administering salvation by cautious driblets on the blackened, leather-dry lips and tongue. He himself had drunk more and faster. His already painful stomach and chest told him that.

But this other man, having a friend to minister, need take no such chance with his life. From his face the sand was washed in little white rivulets; his throat muscles began to move in convulsive twitches of swallowing.

As he worked, the tall man cast an occasional glance at the gorge from which flowed the stream. Below was the desert; above, craggy heaps and barren stretches of stone towered skyward. Blind and senseless, led by some inner guidance, say instinct rather than sense, he had dragged himself and his fellow-prospector from the desert's hot, dry clutch. Would the hills prove kinder? Water was here, but what of food?

He glanced again up the gorge and saw that beside the swift water there was room for a man to walk. And downstream drifted a green, leafy branch, hurrying and twisting with the current.

As LIQUID IRON COOLS, WITHDRAWN from the fire, so the desert cooled with the setting of the sun, its furnace. Intolerable whiteness

FRANCIS STEVENS

became purple mystery, overhung by a vault of soft and tender blue, that deepened, darkened, became set with a million flashing jewels.

And under the stars cool night-winds roved, like stealthy, invisible prowlers. Up among the rocks they came, stirring the hair of two escaped prisoners of the sun as if with curious fingers.

As their chill, stealthy breath struck through to his heated body the smaller man shivered in his sleep. His companion rolled over and took the unblanketed form in his arms; to share with it his own warmth and unconquerable vitality.

Dawn came, a hint of dun light. The stars faded and fled in a moment, and saffron glory smote the desert into transitory gold. One man had slept little and the other much, but it was the first who rose strongly from the bare rock and roused the second to action.

"We're our own men again," he asserted with confident optimism. "'Tis time we were proving it, and though cold water's a poor breakfast, that's but encouragement to find a better. Come, now. Stand up on your own two feet, Mr. Kennedy, the way we may be seeking it."

Unwillingly the other raised himself. His face, save for the dark stubble of a three days' divorce from the razor, was clean-shaven, and his black hair, dark, alert eyes, and the tan inflicted by a Mexican sun, gave him almost the look of an Indian.

His companion, on the other hand, was of that blond, freckled type which burns, but hardly tans at all, and his young, homely face flamed red beneath a thatch of hair nearly as ruddy.

Well over six fit in height, lean, tough, with great loose-moving shoulders and slim waist, Colin O'Hara looked what he was, a stalwart young Irishman whose full power was yet to come with years, but who even at twenty excelled most men in strength and stamina. Under his worn flannel shirt the muscles played, not in lumpy hillocks, but in those long, easy curves that promise endless endurance.

"Come along," he repeated. "They'll be waiting breakfast for us up the arroyo."

"Who will? Oh—just some more of your nonsense, eh? Can't we even starve to death without your joking over it?"

"And for why should we starve; little man? Take the edge off your temper with this, then."

He tossed over something which Kennedy caught with eager hands, and bit through its gray-green skin almost before looking at it.

"A lechera pear, eh?" He gulped and bit again. "Where did you get it?" The other pointed at the rushing stream. "It came floating down last night and I saved it, thinking you might need a bit of encouragement the morn."

"Only one?" demanded Kennedy with a quick, greedily suspicious glance.

"Only one."

Finishing the milky pulp hurriedly, the dark man washed its sticky juice from face and hands and turned with a grin.

"You're a fool to have given it all away then—too big a fool for me to believe in. How many did you eat, really?"

The Irishman's red brows drew together. He turned away.

"I gave you it all that I might be saved the carrying of you," he flung back. "I'd enough o' that yesterday."

He was striding upstream now, and Kennedy followed, scowling at his swinging back.

"I say, Boots," he called in a moment. "You know I meant nothing. You saved my life, I admit, and—thanks for the pear."

"Boots" (the nickname being probably derived from the enormous pair of cowhides in which the young Irishman had essayed desert travel) flung back a brief: "It's all right," and tramped steadily on. He was not the man to quarrel over so trifling a matter.

As for their present goal, the best that even optimistic Boots hoped for was some uncultivated valley where they might precariously sustain life on wild fruit and such game as they could take without weapons.

Barren, unpopulated, forsaken even of the Indians, this region had an evil reputation. "Collados del Demonio," Hills of the Fiend, the Mexicans called it. So far as Cuachictin at the desert's rim the prospectors had come without trouble. Those were the days when Porfirio Diaz still kept his iron grip on the throat of Mexico, and by consequence even a "*puerco gringo*" might travel through it in safety.

But Cuachictin offered them no encouragement to further progress. Kennedy had tried in vain to persuade some native of that Indian settlement to accompany them as a guide. Gold? Ah, yes, there was gold in the hills. Gold in nuggets as big as your closed fist—so. But also devils.

Was it not known that in ancient days all Anahuac was inhabited by giants? Even now, in turning new fields, a man was likely to uncover their enormous bones. Their terrible white ghosts overran the hills. They hunted the hills with the ghosts of white cougars for companions. They would twist off the head of a man and swallow it and his soul like melon seeds. No, no! Blanket was not woven nor knife forged that would pay a man for being eaten, soul and all, by devils!

In the huge, half-rotted brown thing like a strange log which they finally dragged forth to support their story of giants, Kennedy recognized the thigh-bone of a mastodon! The prospectors yielded hope of conquering a superstition rooted in the prehistoric past, and set out alone.

It was true that they had reached their goal, the hills, but with their own bare hands for sole remaining equipment, and for provision the hope of what the country itself might offer.

Shadowed from above by beetling cliffs, the curving path of the torrent led them on. The gorge widened. They reached a sharp bend of the walls and rounded it.

"Saints above!" came Boots' sharp exclamation. "Mr. Kennedy, did you ever see the like o' that?"

Mr. Kennedy made no reply. Had the gorge opened out upon a pit of flaming brimstone, neither man could have halted more abruptly nor stared with a greater amazement.

Their emotion, however, was the opposite of dismay. To eyes sand-tortured and sun-weary, the vista before them seemed hardly less blessed than paradise.

On either hand steep, thickly wooded bluffs ran parallel to the reach of a gorgeously flowering and fruitful ravine. Through its midst meandered the stream, broadly shallow between pleasant banks, till it reached the rocks and swirled to a somber turmoil of revolt.

But better than flower, or fruit, or sparkling river, the scene held a certain homelier significance. The groves of fruit trees were set in orderly ranks. *Pina noñas* raised their sharp spikes in rows of military alinement. Along the stream a brown path trended toward that which confirmed the meaning of all the rest—a gleam of white walls near the upper end of the ravine.

"A plantation!" cried Kennedy at last. "A plantation in the Collados del Demonio! And by report there isn't a square foot of cultivated land within a hundred and fifty miles of this spot."

Boots grinned cheerfully.

"Report's a liar. Maybe it's the house of the old hill devil himself we've blundered upon. So be, he owes us a breakfast for hunting him out!"

With the direct purpose of hungry men, they headed straight for those patches of shining white which betokended, as they supposed, the dobe house of a rancher.

In the orange groves, blossom and full golden sphere flourished side by side. Sapodillas, milk-pears, and ciruelas, hung with a million reddening globes, offered proof of generous soil and a kindly climate. Flocks of butterflies, crimson, blue, and metallic green, shared the air with humming birds whose plumage put the sailwings to shame for brightness. Musical-voiced blue sparrows, wild canaries and gaudy little parrakeets filled the trees with rainbow-hued vivacity.

"It's Eden without the—" began Boots, when *whir-r-r-r!* came a sharp warning from the long grass that bordered the path. Boots bowed in mock salutation toward the sound. "Asking your pardon, Mr. Rattler! Eden, serpent and all, is what I'd meant to be saying."

"Don't crack any of your fool jokes when we reach the house," growled Kennedy. "Some of these Mexicans are as touchy as the devil."

"Ah, now, you'd soon soothe 'em down with a scowl or so," laughed Boots. "But—well, don't you admire the look o' that, Mr. Kennedy? It's no ranch-house they have, but a full-fledged hacienda no less!"

It was true. Instead of the common dobe-plastered casa of a small rancher, the thinning trees revealed an establishment far more imposing. Wide-spread, flat-roofed, its walls even yet showing only in patches through rioting rose-vines, here was such a residence as might be owned by any wealthy gentleman of Mexico. To find it in these hills, however, was as surprising as to discover a Fifth Avenue mansion at the heart of a Bornean jungle.

From one chimney, presumably over the kitchen, a thin curl of smoke was rising. This was the only visible sign of life within. And now it struck them that in the whole length of the ravine they had not seen so much as one peon at work among the plantations.

The hacienda seemed very silent. Behind the walls of its courtyard no dog barked nor cock crowed. Save for the musical tumult of birds, they might, have wandered into a valley of magic stillness.

"Smoke spells fire and fire spells food," asserted Boots. "The cook's awake, and 'tis shame if the rest be sleeping with the sun up these two hours. Will we walk in or knock, Mr. Kennedy? You've the better knowledge of what's considered fitting in these parts."

"Knocks," came the curt advice of his companion. He was eying the hacienda suspiciously, but as suspicion was Kennedy's normal attitude toward the world, Boots paid that no attention.

He boldly advanced toward the wooden outer gates that stood open, yielding a pleasant glimpse through two archways to the inner patio, with its palms, gay oleanders, and tinkling fountain. His fist smote loudly on a leaf of the open gates.

Almost immediately, the summons brought response. On pattering bare feet a child came flying out from among the palms, only to pull up abruptly when she perceived that the visitors were strangers. She was a pretty enough youngster, between three and four years old, with curling black hair, bright, solemn, dark eyes, and a skin surprisingly pink and white for a Mexican child. Her dress was a single slip of brown agave fiber, clean, however, and painstakingly embroidered.

"*Buenos dias, chiquita*," greeted Boots, whose Spanish, though atrociously accented, generally served the purpose. "*Esta usted solo en la casa?*" (Are you alone in the house?)

The curly black head shook in solemn negation. Then the round face dimpled into laughter, and running straight to her giant questioner she put up chubby arms in an unmistakable plea. With an answering laugh the Irishman caught the baby up and set her on the towering height of his shoulder.

Kennedy frowned weary irritation.

"Are we to stand here all day?" he queried.

Leaning forward, the child peered down at him around the ruddy head of her swiftly chosen friend.

"Do 'way," she commanded calmly. "Red man nice—tum in. Black man do 'way—'way, 'way off!" She emphasized the order in her unexpected baby English by a generous wave of her hand toward infinite outside spaces.

Boots' shout of mirth at this summary choice and dismissal produced two results. Kennedy's annoyance was increased, and a man came out from some door which the first archway concealed, and strode quickly toward them. Dressed in immaculate white, well-groomed and confident of bearing, here seemed the probable master of the hacienda.

"What is this? Put that child down, sir! Who are you, and how did you come here?"

THE IRISHMAN SHRUGGED A TRIFLE resentfully.

"The little maid's in no danger," he protested. "We're seeking the common kindness of food and shelter; for the which we'll gladly pay and get on our journey again."

Without replying the man advanced, took the girl from her lofty perch and set her down. "Run in, the house, little daughter," he commanded briefly.

But with a wail of rebellion she flung both short arms around the Irishman's dusty boot. Foreseeing trouble for the young lady, he stooped and gently disengaged her.

"I've a little sister at home, colleen," he said, "that's the spit and image of yourself, save she's the eyes like blue corn-flowers. Don't you be crying, now. We'll see each other again."

As she still clung, her father stooped, lifted her and faced her about in the desired direction. "Go—in!" he commanded, with a gentle sternness that this time won obedience.

Boots looked at her regretfully, for he liked children. He was, indeed, to see her again, as he had promised; but not to know her—not though that recognition would have saved him terrible and bitter pain. But now she was to him only a small girl-child, who went at her father's insistence, and going turned to wave a chubby and reluctant farewell.

Upon her disappearance the fathers manner relaxed.

"You took me by surprise," he explained. "We are seldom favored with guests here, but I meant no inhospitality. You come from—"

"The desert." Boots' brevity was indignant. Did the fellow think him a child-eating ogre that he snatched away his daughter so anxiously?

But Kennedy was more voluble. He plunged into an instant and piteous account of their recent sufferings, or, to speak more correctly, of his own, and before the tale was half finished, their unwilling host's last trace of hostility seemed to have completely vanished.

"Come in—come in!" he exclaimed. "You shan't tell me that sort of story standing out here. Come in and I'll find you something or other worth eating, though I can't promise what it will be. My people—" He paused and seemed to hesitate rather strangely. "My servants are off for the day," he at last concluded. "I'll do my best, and ask you to put up with any lacks due to their absence."

Both men offered willing though surprised assent.

"Off for the day!" thought Boots. "And where off to, I wonder? Does he give picnics to his peons? He's a different master, then, to any I've met in this slave-driver's country."

Having seated them in a great, cool, high-ceilinged and galleried dining-room, their host disappeared to return presently bearing a piled trayful of plunder from his own deserted kitchen.

The food, which included chicken, the inevitable tortilla, sweet potatoes crystallised in sugar, bananas and other fruits, was as typically Mexican as the hacienda. Yet all signs failed if their host were of Spanish blood.

No Spanish-American speaks English as if it were quite native to his tongue, and moreover, though his eyes were dark, and his hair save where it was liberally shot with gray, almost black, there was something about his keen, clean-cut face which spoke of some more northern race. "You're from the U.S.A.?" questioned Kennedy. The question was too blunt for courtesy, but the man nodded.

"Yes, I am an American. A Californian, though my parents were born on the Christiania Fiord."

"Ah, a Norseman, is it?" Boots' eyes lighted appreciatively. He had known a Norwegian or two, and thought them fine, upstanding, hard-hitting men of their hands. "I'm very glad to know you, Mr.—"

"My name is Svend Biornson!" The tone was so challengingly abrupt that his guests involuntarily stared. If he had expected, however, to amuse another sort of surprise, he was disappointed. He saw it instantly and laughed as if to cover some odd embarrassment.

"Pardon my not presenting myself earlier. One forgets civilized forms in this, out-of-the-way place. And now I fancy you'd welcome a chance to wash and change to fresh garments. Will you follow me, gentlemen?"

THE COOL, AIRY CHAMBER TO which he escorted them opened off one of the two galleries surrounding the dining-room. Its three windows overlooked the patio, and through them one could step out upon another long, open gallery. There were two beds, draped with elaborate lace work, furniture of woven grass and wicker, and a bathroom with great, porous jars of cool water.

In his first glance about, Kennedy's eye was caught by a thing that stood on a bracket over one of the beds. Without apology he lifted the object down and examined it curiously.

It was an image, some ten inches high, done in brilliantly polished but unglazed porcelain. The face, though flat, bore a peculiarly genial and benignant expression. On the head was a sort of miter, adorned with black spots. A tunic, on which embroidery was simulated in red, blue and gilt enamel; a golden collar, gaiters spotted like the headdress, and dead-black sandals completed the costume.

On the left arm a round shield was carried. The right hand grasped a stag, terminating at the top in the curved neck and head of a snake, springing out of a collar or circlet of feathers.

It was a very beautiful piece of potter's art, but Kennedy had another reason for appreciation and interest.

"Quetzalcoatl, eh?" he said. "From Cholula, or did you find it around these parts?"

Biornson, who had not observed Kennedy's act, whirled like a flash. To the amazement of both men, his face had gone dead white, as if at receiving some intolerable shock.

"Quetzalcoatl!" he exclaimed in a quivering voice. "Sir, what do you know of Quetzalcoatl?"

Kennedy stared back in blank astonishment.

"Why—this." He held up the image. "I didn't suppose that one of these existed, outside the museum at Mexico City. Don't you know its value?"

Slowly the pallor vanished from Biornison's countenance, and his nervous hands unclenched. With another of those queer, embarrassed laughs, he took the porcelain godling from Kennedy's hands.

"I had forgot the thing was in here," he muttered. "It belongs to my wife. She would be greatly annoyed if it were broken. Lucky piece, you understand. Superstition, of course, but no worse than throwing salt over your shoulder, or not walking under a ladder—all that kind of nonsense. I'll put it in her room if you don't mind. Got everything you want? Then I'll leave you. Better sleep out the day—nothing like siesta—dinner whenever you desire to have it—"

Still muttering detached phrases of hospitality, and with the image clutched firmly to his bosom, Biornson fairly escaped from the presence of his guests.

"What ails the poor man?" queried Boots. "Did they think we'd steal his china manikin, do you suppose?"

Kennedy scowled and shrugged.

"I suppose," he retorted, "that this Biornson, if that's his real name, is a rather queer sort, and that while w are in this house his eccentricities will bear watching."

WEARY THOUGH BOTH WERE, THEY did not find it easy to fall asleep. There was something oppressive about this vast, silent hacienda. The mystery of its emptiness, the mystery of its very existence, combined with the odd manners of their host to fill their brains with riddles. They lay silent, uneasy, while outside the drowsy heat increased and even, the vociferous bird-life ceased its clamor.

Out of the silence, however, rest was born at last, and it was late in the afternoon when they woke.

"By the way, Mr. Kennedy," Boots said, "if you'll forgive changing the subject to something more recent, what was the bit of bric-a-brac that Biornson snatched out of your hand? Quetz—Quetz—what was the name of it?"

"Quetzalcoatl. A piece of old Aztec work. Down in Yucatan one can pick up all sorts of stone and terra-cotta images among the ruins, but not like that."

"And this Quetz—what's-his-name—who was he? One o' the poor heathens idols, maybe?"

"The lord of the air. The fathered serpent." Kennedy was generally willing to talk, when he could air some superior knowledge. "By tradition he was a man, a priest, who was afterward deified for his beneficent acts and character. It is said that he ruled Mexico in its Golden Age— Anahuac they called it then—and when he left his people he promised to return at the head of a race of men as white as himself.

"He was a white god, you must understand. For that reason, when the Spaniards first landed the natives believed the lost god's promise had been kept. Images of him are common enough, but not in porcelain of that quality. Biornson surprised me into giving away its real value, like a fool, but at that I could pay him a good price for the thing and still make a profit. It would bring almost any sum from a New York collector."

"Don't deceive yourself that he didn't know its value! You could see in his eye that he did."

"What do you think of Biornson, anyway?"

"A fine, soft-spoken man—after the first minute."

"Did you notice how he boggled over his name? Svend Biornson! I dare swear he has another, and one he has reason to conceal."

But the other's retort was cold and to the point.

"We Irish do hate an informer. Are you ready yet to go down?"

Save for a look of black resentment, Kennedy made no reply. However, as their briefest discussions generally ended in a clash, Boots ignored the glance and passed out to the dining-room gallery. There was yet no sound of life in the house, but on descending and finding their way out into the patio, they discovered Biornson there and he was not alone.

Seated on a stone bench by the fountain was a woman. She was a tall, slender person, of unusual beauty, and Boots thought her dark eyes and hair and peculiarly roselike complexion reminiscent of the child who had first greeted them. She was dressed in a simple gown of some silky, leaf-green material, and as she talked with Biornson her hand fondled the long, soft ears of a white hound, whose head rested on her knee.

None of the three seemed at first aware of the guests' approach, but as they came nearer the woman's face lifted with a quick, startled attention. She sprang to her feet, and the dog, as if in imitation, reared up beside her. On its hind legs the brute stood nearly as tall as she; and an ominous rumble issued from its throat.

"Quiet!" cried Biornson sharply. He laid a hand on beast's neck, pushing it downward. "Gentlemen, I had hardly expected you to awaken so early."

He had grasped the hound by its silky white fur, for it wore no collar, and under that insecure hold the animal surged disobediently forward. Its eyes flamed in a menace more savage than the bared fangs beneath; and as the dog seemed about to spring, Biornson flung his arms about its neck. In a flash it turned and tried to reach his face with snapping jaws.

At that the woman, whose dark, startled eyes had been fixed on the strangers, seemed for the first time to become aware of her pet's misbehavior. She spoke to it in a murmur of soft, indistinguishable syllables, and the hound, which had so resented Biornson's interference, subsided instantly. A moment later it was flat on the ground at her feet.

"That's a fine dog," approved Boots, "and you've a finer command over him, madam. May I ask what breed he is?"

Before the woman could reply, Biornson intervened.

"Just a hound of the hills," he said quickly. "Astrid, these gentlemen are those of whom I told you." He presented them more formally and, as Boots had expected, introduced the lady as his wife.

The name "Astrid" had a Scandinavian sound, and her beauty might well be as Norse as her husband's ancestry, but they had little time to study her. After murmuring a few shy words of welcome, she excused herself and left the guests to Biornson's entertainment.

As her green-clad form, with the white hound pressing close beside, receded into the inner shadows, the eyes of one man followed with a gleam of interest not aroused by her beauty.

Her accent was the thing that troubled Archer Kennedy. That it was neither American, Norwegian, nor Spanish he was ready to take oath. Her appearance, too, had a vague hint of something different from any white woman he had ever seen. Yet surely no dark blood flowed in those pink-nailed hands, nor behind such rose-leaf cheeks.

Dismissing the problem as immaterial, he returned to his host.

II

The Moth Girl

"Mr. Kennedy, we should go early to bed, for I think we'll be leaving the morn just so soon as we can barrow or buy means of travel."

Rising, Boots cast away his brown leaf-cigarette with an impatient gesture.

It was now nine in the evening, and for half an hour, following another picked-up meal eaten by the three men alone together, they had sat in silence.

During that afternoon and evening Biornson's embarrassment had taken refuge in a distinct coldness and reserve. Their questions he put aside, or calmly left unanswered, but there was a worried line between his brows and he had developed a speculative, tight-tipped and narrow-eyed way of watching his guests which made it clear to him they were a Problem with a capital P.

Boots, who possessed more worldly knowledge than his years or careless manner would indicate, began to look speculative himself. Men with secrets to keep sometimes dispose of their Problems in an unpleasantly summary manner, and certainly this ravine was secret.

To believe that such a vivid jewel in the barren Collados del Demonio had been kept from knowledge of the world by accident was folly. In the common course of events, the plantation would have been famed if only for its isolation.

By what means and for what reason had Biornson prevented the spreading of its repute? From the first they had sensed something wrong in the ravine. As time passed, and their host's peculiar manner became more and more emphatic, they began to believe that nothing was right.

At Boots' half-irritated suggestion, Biornson rose with suspicious alacrity, and Kennedy could do less than follow suit, though he scowled in the darkness. For hours he had been waiting with the patience of a cat at a rat-hole for their host to let slip some careless word or phrase that would give him the key to a possibly profitable mystery. But he and young Boots were an ill-matched couple, and he was more annoyed than surprised that his watch should be put an end to by the latter's impatience.

Having for the second time escorted them to their gallery beds, Biornson handed the small triple candelabra he had brought to Boots and bade them a brief good night. Then he closed the heavy door behind them and a second later there came certain unmistakable sounds from outside, followed by the unhurried footsteps of their departing host.

With an oath Kennedy sprang for the door and wrenched vainly at the handle. As his ears had already informed him, it was locked and not only that but bolted.

With the sudden frenzy of the trapped, he kicked it, beat at it with his hands; then, with the same furious and futile energy, sprang across the room and attacked the solid wooden shutters which, though he had not at first observed them, were closed when they entered.

Still holding the candelabra, Boots stood near the middle of the room and watched his companion from under drawn, troubled brows. After a moment he set down the candles, took one stride forward, and grasping Kennedy by the shoulder forced him away and into a wicker armchair.

"That's no way to behave," he said reprovingly. "D'ye want to be frightening Mrs. Biornson with your bangings and your yells like a he banshee? Your throat's not cut yet, nor like to be."

"You young fool!" snarled the other. "Shall we sit here quiet till they do it? Use that big body of yours to some purpose and help me break out before that cursed brigand comes back!"

"He'll not come back."

"How do you know?"

"'Tis not reasonable he should. For why would he entertain us all day, herd us off alone with himself for watchman, keep his wife and bit child from our company lest they drop some word to betray them, and he plotting to murder us the night? All the hours we lay sleeping here—why, a bit of a knife-thrust would have just as well settled the business then. Better, for he's put us on guard now with this foolishness of locked doors and barred shutters."

"Murderers are not logical." Kennedy's first flurry of rage and fear was past, and a cold hatred for the man who had imprisoned them was replacing it. "You were fool enough to let him know we have money in our belts. You may wait if you choose to be pig-stuck and robbed, but my motto is—strike first and strike hard. Help me out of here and I'll show you how to deal with this Biornson's sort."

"Will you so? Now hear me, Mr. Kennedy, and just remember that, though you're older nor me and of perhaps more refined education, yet in the last showing and betwixt the two of us 'tis myself has the upper hand. You'll make no more disturbance, but you'll lay down, or sit there in your chair, till such time as I see fit to act. Then you'll do as I say and no otherwise. Dye understand all that?"

Kennedy glowered blackly up at him, making no reply, but Boots seemed content to take his obedience for granted. Turning away, he made a brief, careless inspection of door and shutters, then flung himself on the bed and lay quiet.

TIME PASSED. THE CANDLES BURNED down toward their sockets and the closed room grew swelteringly hot, but still neither man spoke to the other.

Once or twice Kennedy rose and paced up and down the floor, or drank from a clay water-jar on the table. But the giant figure on the bed did not stir. The iron muscles of a hibernating bear were never less restless than the Irishman's when he had no occasion for their use.

Yet at last he yawned, stretched, and sat up. "We'll go now;" he coolly announced. "Now blow out the candles!"

He caught at the edge of the shutter as the hinges gave way. Pushing it a little further outward he worked the bolts loose and eased it carefully down on the balcony outside.

Sullenly the other followed, as the dominant Irishman stepped out on the balcony. Around them the inner walls of the hacienda rose dark and silent. Not a light showed anywhere.

"A poor jailer who trusts to doors and shutters alone," thought Boots. "It speaks well for his lack of practice that he's set not even the dog to watch us—or we'll hope he's not set the dog!"

With his boots slung about his neck, he cautiously climbed the railing; a moment later he was hanging by his fingers to the edge of the balcony floor, whence he dropped, to land with scarcely any sound, for all his weight, on the hard clay that paved the patio.

Again Kennedy followed, but not caring to risk a broken leg he improvised a rope from the bedding, slid down it, and at that made more noise than the Irishman.

No one, however, seemed to have been aroused, and in three minutes they stood together safe outside the hacienda. Once clear of their room, there had been nothing to hinder escape, for the wooden gates were merely shut to, and neither locked, barred nor guarded.

About them night lay so black, so oppressively breathless, that it gave almost the impression of a solid, surrounding substance. They were in a region where rain, when it does fall, comes always between two suns. This night the world was roofed with thick cloud, like a lid shut down on the air, compressing it to the earth, making it heavy and unsatisfying to the lungs.

"We're in for a storm," whispered Boots. "I'd not reckoned on a night like this."

"Reckoned on it for what?" Kennedy's tone was keenly unpleasant. "To go after another sand-bath? If you are too cowardly to settle with Biornson, let me go back alone. I'll engage to find him, and by the time I'm through he'll be glad enough to let us have supplies or anything else—if he's still alive."

"Time enough for all that tomorrow. Body o' me, little man, have you no curiosity? I brought you out here to find the secret Biornson's so set on concealing, and all you can think of is retaliation and general blood-letting! This ravine isn't all the plantation. 'Tis a grand big hacienda. He's not crops enough in the ravine to support it, and I've a notion that the upper end leads to the place or the thing he wants hidden.

"We'll find out what it is, and then go leave the poor man in peace, since he's so afeared of us. But see it I will, if only to make clear to him his mistake in locking us up so uncourteously."

The other swore, as he realized that Boots' curiosity was a thing cherished purely for its own sake. Boots steered him away from the hacienda, down to the stream, and along the narrow path that followed it.

Kennedy was cursing again, for he had stumbled against the spike-tipped leaves of an agave with direful results, and then blundered into the water before he knew they had reached it, but Boots was cheerful.

An occasional flare of distant lightning gave them twilight glimpses of the way, but otherwise they stumbled through breathless blackness, their only guide the feel of the trodden trail to their feet and the soft rush and gurgle of water beside it. The path grew steeper and more difficult, as it left the stream to flow between rapidly heightening banks.

Came another flare of lightning, brighter and nearer. Boots halted so abruptly that Kennedy trod on his heels.

A forest Of giant ferns had leaped into existence on their right, and immediately before them, almost upon them, it appeared, was an enormous, grayish figure, huge, flat-faced, that leered and grinned.

Like the flick of a camera shutter the light had come and gone. They were blind again, but flee leader flang out his hands and touched the thing he had glimpsed.

"Stone!" Boots' voice was distinctly relieved. "It's just a big image by the path." Boots struck a match and held it high,

Six feet above his head the gray face leered downward. Its grin seemed alive in the wavering light—alive and menacing, but Boots grinned back more good-naturedly. "You poor heathen idol! You gave me a start, you did. Aztec, do you think, Mr. Kennedy?"

"Of course. Tlaloc, God of the Hills and the Rain. Unless I'm mistaken. Yes, there is the cross of the Tlalocs carved at the foot. Where are you going now?"

"On, to be sure. We're coming to the pass I surmised was here that leads from the ravine into the hills beyond. It's the beyond I've a wish to investigate."

THE PATH WAS INDEED VERY narrow, and the sound of water came up as a low and distant murmur. On that side was blackness and the sense of space. On the other, an occasional brushing against face or hand told of the great ferns that stretched thin frond-fingers across the way.

Then abruptly the path ended, or seemed to end. Their feet sank in moss or soft turf, and Boots collided with an unexpected tree trunk. Both men halted and for a moment stood hesitant.

The silence was uncanny. Not a whisper among the ferns, not the call of a night-bird. Even the usual insect-hum was stifled and repressed to a key so low that it seemed only part of the stillness. The cloud-lid was heavy above earth. The dense air pressed on the ear drums, as on first descent into a deep mine or well.

Then, as they stared ahead through blackness, the attention of both men was suddenly attracted by a faint, purplish glowing. It was quite near the ground and a short distance ahead of them. There was grass there, straight, slender stems of it, growing in delicate silhouette against that low, mysterious light.

Advancing, Boots peered in puzzled question. As he neared it the light flashed brighter with a more decided tinge of purple, and out of the grass a wonder soared up to float away on iridescent wings.

It was a huge, mothlike insect, fully ten inches from wing-tip to wing-tip, and the glowing came from its luminous body, in color pale amethyst, coldly afire within. The broad wings, transparent as a globular walls of a bubble, refracted the creature's own radiance in a network of shimmering color.

Boots gasped sheer delight, but Kennedy's comment was as usual eminently practical.

"Sa-a-y! That beauty would bring a fortune from any museum. Do you suppose there are any more about?"

The moth had settled in the long grass, where a dim glowing again marked its presence. Cautiously the two men moved in that direction.

They seemed to have come upon a sort of high meadow, though what might be its extent or general contour was impossible to say. As they went, another and yet another of the moths glowed, shimmered and rose, flushed up by their swishing progress through the grass.

"Like a dream of live soap bubbles," murmured Boots. "Wouldn't it be a shame now to catch one of those beauties and smother out the flaming life of him?"

"For a young man of your size you have the least practical sense— hel-lo!"

There was cause for the astonished exclamation.

He had glanced to one side and there, standing between two slender trees with a hand on each, appeared a figure so exquisitely, startlingly appropriate that it was no wonder if for a moment both men questioned its reality.

The form was that of a young girl of fifteen or sixteen years—if she reckoned her age by mortal standards, which Boots for his part seriously doubted. But elf or human maiden, she was very beautiful. Her skin was white as that of Astrid, the wife of Biornson, and she watched them with wonderful, dark eyes, not in fear, but with a startled curiosity that matched their own.

All about the black mist of her hair the luminous moths were hovering. One, with slowly waving pinions, clung to her bare arm.

Recovering instantly from his first amazement, Kennedy surmised that the insects were tethered by fine threads, as women of the tropics fasten fireflies in their hair. To Boots, however, she seemed no less than the carnified spirit of the creatures, who held them to her by bond of their mutual natures.

Indeed, the garment in which she was draped had about its soft green folds a suggestion of the downy feathering of a moth's body, and the necklace about her slim throat seemed itself alive with soft fires. Its jewels, smooth and oval in shape, glimmered and glowed with the gentle motion of her breathing.

Under his roughness, big, homely, redheaded Boots concealed all the romance, all the capacity for worship of his Celtic forebears. He stood at gaze, almost afraid to breathe lest the vision float up against the heavy background of night and go drifting away across the grass.

But Kennedy had other thoughts in his head. To him the girl was a girl, the wonder-moths no more than convenient lanterns by which he saw something greatly to be desired.

"What opals!" he cried softly. "Look at them, man! Why, that Indian girl has a fortune round her neck. By Jupiter, here's where we square accounts with Biornson! There are opal-mines in these hills, and for some reason he doesn't want his holdings known. You went right for once, boy! We've stumbled straight upon his precious secret!"

III

The Guardians of the Hills

Before Boots had grasped his companion's meaning, or guessed his purpose, Kennedy had crossed the short space between them and the lovely apparition. Like a child that has never been frightened by brutality, she watched his approach in grave, wide-eyed curiosity.

When, however, with one hand he grasped, her shoulder and with, the other snatched at the necklace, she gave a little cry and attempted to draw back. The moths fluttered wildly, dazzling Kennedy with then flashing bodies, beating their iridescent, panic-stricken wings in his very face. He released the necklace to strike at them, brush them aside.

Then at last Boots ran forward, but before he could reach them a sharp report shattered the heavy stillness and a bullet whined by so close to Kennedy's head that he jumped back and instinctively flung up his hands.

"Keep them there!" commanded a stern voice.

Boots, who had halted at the shot, saw a dim, white figure striding toward them. Before it more moths flickered up, and by their ghostly light the newcomer was revealed as Biornson.

His guests' informal departure had not, after all, gone undiscovered, and by the still smoking rifle he held at ready, and the brusk determination of his manner, the man intended an immediate resumption of his role as jailer.

At sight of him the moth-girl gave a low, birdlike thrill of pleasure. She began talking in soft, low tones, using a language strange to two of her hearers, but full of liquid, musical sounds.

Biornson answered her in the same tongue, though his accent was harsher and more forced. All the while he kept his rifle and his eyes trained on Kennedy. He finished speaking and the girl answered him briefly. Then Biornson deviated the threatening muzzle toward Boots, who had stood inactive since his coming.

"Stand over here, you! There, by your friend."

Boots obeyed He understood exactly how the scene had appeared—one man ravishing the girl of her jewels, the other rushing to aid in the contemptible thievery.

"Mr. Biornson," he began, "I had no wish at all to—"

"Silence! You big, red-headed bully, I have eyes and I saw what was going on here. Not that it surprises me. I took your measure when I first saw you in my gates. Now turn around, both of you. Do you see that stable lantern?"

They did. It was one which Biornson had brought to find his way by, and he had left it set on the path beyond the field of grass.

"March very straight and carefully toward that lantern. Remember that if I kill you it will only save me trouble."

Kennedy was shaking with futile rage, but Boots was less angry than disturbed. He found himself in the position of many another innocent, careless man—condemned by the act of a rascally companion. But argument must wait. Just now there seemed nothing for either of them but obedience.

A little way from the spot where the girl stood looking wonderingly after, Kennedy struck his foot on a hidden stone, stumbled, and dropped to his knees. Seeing him fall, Biornson surmised the cause and waited for him to get up. He did, and in his hand was the stone he had tripped over.

Whirling with the nervous quickness of his anger and temperament, Kennedy flung the stone straight at the armed man behind them. More by good luck than aim it struck Biornson fairly between the eyes, so that he threw out his arms and reeled back and downward into the grass.

With a cry more like a wildcat's voice than a man's, Kennedy rushed to the fallen figure, snatched up the rifle and set its muzzle against Biornson's temple. His finger curled to the trigger.

Another moment would have seen the scattering of Biornson's brains, had not a hand intervened and snatched the gun aside.

"You—interfering—booby!" gritted Kennedy, as he wrestled for possession of the weapon. "Let me have it—let me have it, I say!"

Stumbling over the victim's body, Boots lost his grip, and with a triumphant snarl the other sprang back and flung the rifle to his shoulder. But even as he took aim the sky above them ripped open in one jagged crevice of blinding fire.

The bolt shot across the clouds with a rattling, firecracker-like sound, splitting them asunder and releasing the pent-up deluge which all this while had hung above the earth. With the terrific explosion following that rattle and thrust of electricity, the clouds emptied themselves.

Startled and disconcerted, Kennedy had not fired and Boots again leaped in to close with him.

About them trees, meadow, and hills flickered through sheets of rain like scenes in an old-time moving picture.

Drenched, deafened by the incessant roar of rain and thunder, the two swayed stumblingly about. In that hampering turmoil Boots could not at first wrench the rifle from his antagonist, and though he might have easily killed the smaller man, bare-handed, this was far from his desire.

Then came an interruption more sudden and terrible than the storm, in whose tumult any warning noise there may have been was drowned.

Out of the curtaining rain a horde of ghost-white forms hurtled upon them. They were beasts; great snarling, white brutes, with slavering jaws and wolflike fangs.

Swept down by the rush, the human combatants were instantly buried under a piled, writhing heap of animal ferocity.

In the stress of that utterly unexpected attack, Boots did not try to analyze its nature. In the back of his mind there was a dim feeling of wonder that the elfin stillness and beauty of a few moments before should have culminated in such a series of cataclysms. For the rest, he knew that innumerable jaws and claws were tearing at his body, and that he was engaged in a mad, unequal fight to save his own life and Kennedy's.

In some rare men the protective instinct is ineradicable. Because Archer Kennedy was his mate and weaker than he, in spite of all that had taken place Boots was as ready to give up life for him now as he had ever been.

They had fallen so that his body shielded the other man. That was accident. But the effort which throughout that delirious battle kept their positions the same was no accident, and Boots paid dearly for acting as a shield.

Had he been willing to fight his way to his feet again, he might have had a better chance. Flat down, the best he could do was to throttle any furry throat within reach and keep his own neck free from the tearing, furious fangs.

For a full two minutes the struggle continued.

Boots had one white demon squeezed tight to his chest, the smothering weight of its flank protecting his face. His fingers were buried in the throat of a second But he could not breathe wet fur, and the jaws of a third enemy were worrying at his right arm muscles. From shoulder to heel he felt them tearing and biting.

Taken at a tremendous disadvantage, blind, smothered and over-matched, Boots was in a very fair way to be torn to pieces when, suddenly, another rush of feet came plunging through the rain.

He did not hear them come. The first Boots knew of a change in conditions was that most of his snarling, growling tormentors had inexplicably ceased to either snarl, growl or bite. Then he realized that the weight of them also was off him.

The dirty cowards! They had given up the fight and run!

That left only the pair in his actual grip. With a gasp of fierce joy, Boots tightened his hold, rolled off from Kennedy—who, he greatly feared, was by this time smothered in the mud—and got his knees under him. Incidentally, he clamped the head of one kicking, white monster under the knees. The one whose throat he had been squeezing had ceased to struggle and he dropped it.

With his face free at last of the blinding fur, Boots knelt up straight and looked for the rest of the pack.

Though rain still fell in torrents, the lightning's illumination was becoming more spasmodic, and Boots was hardly sure that what he saw was real.

Was he actually surrounded by a circle of strange, tall, white men? At each recurrent flash he seemed to see them. Tall men—inhumanly tall—the rain sluiced off bare, gleaming shoulders—the rounded muscles shone wet and white—their faces were stern, pallid, eyes fixed on him—their hands waved—they were pointing at him.

Through his Celtic brain flashed a wild suspicion that there stood the very beasts which had attacked him. Werewolves—creatures neither man nor brute, but able to take the form of either.

Under his knee, the white thing he held there wriggled feebly. He had already strangled one. Here was another whose diabolical tricks he could stop.

Dropping his hands, Boots shifted to find its throat and keeled over quietly in the squelching, trampled grass. His last conscious emotion was self-scorn that he hadn't finished the "manwolf" before, like any common weakling, he died of his many wounds.

"CHEER UP, OR I'LL THINK you hard to content. 'Tis the wonder of wonders, Mr. Kennedy, that they've let us live at all, and Biornson's face fair ruined by the rock you hove at him."

Swathed in bandages, lying on a grass-stuffed pallet in the cubical,

FRANCIS STEVENS

brick-walled chamber which for three days had been their prison, Boots looked kindly reproof at his fellow captive.

Biornson himself had just paid them a brief call, and after his leaving, Kennedy's sullen countenance appeared more somber than usual. Now he stared at the Irishman with the shadow of some strange dread in his eyes.

"Tlapallan!" he muttered softly. "Tlapallan! Did he really say Tlapallan, or did I dream it?"

"He did that," the other confirmed. "And why, may I ask, should his saying it fill you with despair? It's a fine, hard word, I'll admit, but I'd never get it off my tongue like Biornson did, or you either, but—"

"Tlapallan!" Kennedy repeated it as if the other had not spoken. "He called this place Tlapallan—and if that is true—but it can't be! Quetzalcoatl—Tlapallan—no, no; one can't believe the impossible—and yet—"

His head drooped and his voice lowered to an indistinguishable mutter.

Here was a phase of the older man's character entirely new to Boots, who eyed him with an amazement bordering on alarm. Their position was puzzling enough in all conscience, but Kennedy's manner and speech of the last few minutes hinted of some new riddle, some potentiality for harm in a mere word which Boots found vaguely disturbing.

For three days they had been held close prisoners. The cell of their confinement, bare, built of yellow polished bricks, or rather tiles, was in the daytime lighted to a golden gloom by one small, round window, offering a barren view across a brick-paved alley to a wall of highly polished white stone. As for what that alley might lead to, or what might lie beyond the wall, they knew practically nothing.

This place was no part of the hacienda. The experience of Kennedy, who had been in his senses when brought here, told them that. They were, it was almost equally sure, somewhere beyond that pass which Boots had so eagerly desired to explore. Here ended their certainties and began a mystery beside which that of the ravine faded to commonplace insignificance.

After the calling off of the white hounds—in sober sense, and remembering the beast they had seen in the patio, Boots dismissed his thought of "werewolves" as nonsense—Kennedy had staggered to his feet. Though half-strangled from being crushed in the mud, he was otherwise unhurt.

No sooner was he up, however, than his arms were seized, a bandage was whipped over his eyes, and, the grip of those so much stronger than he that struggle was futile, he was dragged helplessly away.

Like a child between two grown folk, he could hear the men who held him murmuring together over his head. "Great lumbering louts!" he said viciously, in describing the affair. "They must have been even larger than you are, Boots, and goodness knows you're big' enough. They went muttering along like a couple of silly fools—talked the same gibberish as that girl with the opals. When I tried to ask a question, one of the brutes struck me in the face."

He had expected to be taken back to the ravine, and when, having walked a considerable distance, mostly down-hill, they came to a place where his feet found hard pavement under them, he at first took it for the courtyard of the hacienda.

As the march continued, however, turning corners, descending interminable flights of stairs, passing through covered ways—he knew them by the echoes and the fact that they were out of the rain—down yet more open stairs, and still onward, he became hopelessly bewildered.

At last, when he had began to believe the downward march would last forever, his arms were released and he was given a push that sent him headlong.

There was the closing of a door, and silence. He tore the bandage from his eyes. Darkness was, all around. Fearing to move, lest he fall into some chain, Kennedy remained crouched for another seemingly endless period, till dawn light replaced his imaginary chasms with the desolate, bare cell they still inhabited.

He was then alone, but later Boots joined him, being carried in on a stretcher, one mass of bandages from head to foot. Had he come from the operating-room of a city hospital, these dressings could have been no more skillfully adjusted, but the stretcher-bearers differed somewhat from the orderlies of such an establishment.

Boots, being then and for several hours afterward unconscious, did not see them, but Kennedy described them after his own characteristic fashion. Savages, he said, plumed, beaded, half-clad, and barbarous. Let their skin be as white as they pleased, they couldn't fool him. Nothing but buck Indians of a particularly muscular and light-hued type, but Indians and no better.

His tone inferred that an Indian was a kind of subhuman creature, whose pretensions to equality with himself should be firmly suppressed. But, though their physical proportions were not comparable to those of the giants who had called off the hounds, they were sufficiently stalwart, and Kennedy reserved his opinion of them for Boots' ears.

One who spoke fairly intelligible English instructed him to care for the "big red man," and informed him that if the patient failed to recover the fault would be his, Kennedy's, since the "sons of Tlapotlazenan" had done their part. He hinted, moreover, that these same offspring of an alphabetical progenitor would regard losing the patient as a personal affront, and probably take it out of the one responsible in a very painful manner.

The stretcher-bearers then departed, and, with one exception, that cell had received no visible callers since. Food and drink were set inside the door at night by a jailer whom they never saw. Refuse of the previous twenty-four hours was removed in the same manner.

Such conditions might not, one would think, be conducive to the rapid recovery of a man whose flesh had been ripped to shreds in a dozen places. But Boots seemed to be doing rather well. He awoke clear-headed, had developed no fever, and, though practically unable to move, he insisted that this was due more to a superfluity of bandages than the wounds they covered. Kennedy, however, perhaps recalling the stretcher-bearer's warning, would allow none of them to be displaced, and waited on his companion with a solicitude that astonished the recipient.

Late in the afternoon of the third day they heard a trampling of feet on the bricks outside. The door opened, and from his pallet Boots caught one glimpse of waving plumes and barbarically splendid figures before it closed again. The man who had entered, however, was of far more commonplace appearance, save for his head, which in the matter of bandages matched Boots' body.

It was not until he spoke that the latter recognized him as Svend Biornson.

Pointedly ignoring Kennedy, he walked over and stood looking down at the swathed figure on the pallet.

"You seem to have had a little more than enough, my man," he greeted Boots.

Because there was truth in that statement, and because he felt at a great disadvantage, Boots managed a particularly happy smile.

"Ah, now," protested he, "'twas a very amusing frolic while it lasted! Leave me try it again with me two feet under me and I'll engage to tame a few of those lap-dogs for you. And how is your face the day, Mr. Biornson?"

"It's still a face." The tone was rather grim. "It would have been less than that if your friend had got his way with the rifle, so I shan't complain."

"Mr. Kennedy is a bit quick-tempered," conceded Boots, "but sure, you're never the sort to hold against a man the deed done in hot blood, more especially when the worst of it was never done at all, but just thought of?"

The other laughed.

"That is an unusual plea. I'll consider it, and meantime let me thank you for having diverted the rife-muzzle from my head. I learned of your act from the daughter of Quetzalcoatl, whom your friend would have robed—another, deed I suppose you place in the excusable 'just-thought-of' class!"

"The daughter of—you can't mean the lass from fairyland, with the fire-moths in her hair? Don't tell me she has years enough to be the child of an old, dead heathen god like that!"

Biornson cast a nervous glance toward the closed door.

"Be careful! Never call Quetzalcoatl a dead god in Tlapallan! The Guardians of the Hills are inclined in your favor. They admire strength and courage, and it is seldom indeed that a hound of Nacoc-Yaotl's has been killed by a man bare-handed. But to speak against Quetzalcoatl is a cardinal crime. Only your life could ever wipe out that insult."

"Would you believe it now!" Boots' curiosity was immense, but he held back his questions, thinking Biornson might be more communicative if merely led on to talk. "And there I might have hurt the feelings of them by a slip of the tongue, had you not warned me! Fine, large, handsome men they are, too, with a spirit of fair play that matches your own, Mr. Biornson."

"It is good of you to say so." The other's voice was grave, but between the bandages his eyes were twinkling. "And fair speech matches fair play in Killarney, eh?"

"Kerry," corrected Boots. "But I meant my words."

"I believe you did. They are true enough, too, of the Tlapallans. I can't say exactly what will be done about you and your friend, but Astrid has promised to speak for you, and I'll do what I can. As for your wounds, the Tlapotlazenan gild are wonderful healers, and I shall expect to see you on your feet in a week or so. You have reason to be thankful that the Guardians of the Hilts called off their hounds when they did. A little more and it would have been scarcely worth while trying to piece you together."

"Guardians of the Hills," repeated Boots thoughtfully. "There was more truth than fancy, then, in the tales we heard of white giants, though the ghost-cougars they hunt with are just dogs, and there's little of the fantom about any of them. 'Tis all a most interesting discovery. An adventure after my own heart, though so far the head and the tail of it are well hid, and the middle past all understanding!"

The patient angler for information paused tentatively, but Biornson shook his head.

"For your own sake," he said, "it is better that you should not understand. I tell you frankly that there is a truth in these hills which no man has ever been allowed to carry beyond them. When you first came to my house, it happened that none of the folk were in the lower valley. It was the time of the Feast of Tlaloc, and they were all gathered in Tlapallan. As men of my own race, I would have done much to save you, but you know how my efforts resulted."

"I do not," Boots retorted. "Betwixt one mystery and the next my head is fair swimming!"

"Better perish of curiosity than meet the fate I am still trying to avert from you."

He looked pityingly down at the homely, good-humored Irish face, with its danger-careless eyes and smiling mouth.

"I told you there was a secret in these hills. I tell you now that there is also a horror—a—a—thing—a way they have—"

In a spasm of inexplicable emotion he broke off, and it was a moment before he could control his voice to continue. "When I say that you are housed now, in the seat of Nacoc-Yaotl it means nothing to you, but to me it means threat of a terror that I never think of when I can avoid it! When I was first here, a prisoner, I, who had never given much thought to religion, used to spend whole nights in prayer, entreating God to make it untrue—or let me forget!

"And yet when I could have escaped I did not go. Though by staying I not only risked my soul, but betrayed a trust, I did not go! I knew by your faces at the house that you had never heard of Svend Biornson. Perhaps conscience exaggerated my fame in the world, and my dropping out of it left hardly a ripple. And yet I know that in some circles that could not have been so. But it was all so many years ago!"

He paused again.

"Very like," said Colin. "If 'twas so very many years ago I must have been a small, ignorant spalpeen in Kerry when it happened. 'Tis no wonder I never heard of you."

"I was younger myself," the other answered reflectively. He might almost have been talking to himself, instead of Colin—arguing that old case that every man argues eternally before the inner tribunal "Young and impetuous. For all the standing I had achieved in the archeological field—I know now how young I was! Very proud, too. Twenty-five, and set at the head of a scientific expedition! I wonder who has since done in Yucatan the things I set out to accomplish?

"And our party! Did any one of them survive to carry back a report? Wiped out by the Yaquis, and poor young Biornson, too! I can see the dear old gray-beards who sent me out shaking their heads and sighing for another young promise lost—and sighing, too, for the work that had not been done. And I, who had been chosen, could have later taken them news whose confirmation would have made the university world-famous—I—fell in love and cast in my lot with Tlapallan! A trust betrayed and youth served! It isn't the biography that was prophesied for Svend Biornson!"

"If that's all you have on your conscience," consoled Boots, "it's lighter than most men's! Sure, to carry tales for the world is an interesting occupation, but I cannot see how you were damned in neglecting it. By your manner, I had thought you left a trail of murder and arson behind you!"

Biornson stirred impatiently and seemed ill at ease. "I'm a fool!" he said. "What is science or a scientific reputation to an ignorant boy like you? Of course you can't understand! But—it isn't only, that! They are my friends, these folk. Sometimes I think they are the last remnant of a forgotten race, older than Toltec or Mayan, or even the Olmecs, who have left nothing to archeology but a memory.

"And sometimes—I have other thoughts of them, thoughts that I can't put into words, for there are no words to express them. I know that they speak the Aztec tongue in all its ancient purity, and yet they are surely not of Aztec blood. However it be, they are good, true comrades, and my own wife is one of them, but I sometimes wonder if I have not—have not lost my soul in living here! I am saying too much—you can't understand and you must not. You shall go back to your own people and your own God—"

Stooping unexpectedly Biornson seized the surprised Irishman's hand and gripped it hard.

"Boy," and his voice was a harsh whisper, "never bow your head to the gods of a strange race! Never! Not for our nor love, nor wealth, nor friendship! Not for wonders, nor miracles! You speak of mysteries. There is a mystery I could tell you of—but your soul would be sick afterward—sick—you might even desert your Christ—as I did, God help me!"

"I am a good Catholic," said Boots, gravely and simply.

"Then stay so! You are in a city where mercy and kindness excel, and their roots are set in a monstrous cruelty. Where beauty springs out of horror, and they worship benignant gods with the powers of devils! Don't seek to know the heart of Tlapallan! Go, if they'll let you—and once away forget that you ever set foot in the Collados del Demonio!"

With no farewell but a final squeeze of the hand Biornson was gone.

A memory flashed across the mind of Kennedy. Tlapallan! The White People of Tlapallan! Grant that myth to be true, he thought, and anything was possible—anything!

For the rest of the afternoon the materialist sat with his head in his hands, silent and glum, till Boots, who could accept miracles, gave up trying to get at the cause of the other man's perturbation, and fell peacefully asleep.

IV

Tlapallan or—

A re we to rot here forever?"

Jerking to his feet, Kennedy glared as if it were some contumacious obstinacy of his companion which still kept them prisoners.

Six days had passed since Biornson's visit, and brought no increase of knowledge nor change in their condition.

Boots, whose wounds had closed with a rapidity that did credit to either an unusual constitution or the medicaments originally used, sat up lazily and stretched his arms.

"A few hours yet till night. Dye ever notice how still it all is, Mr. Kennedy?"

"Still as the tomb. Silent as the desert. I've thought of nothing but that silence for days. I wondered how long it would be before a glimmer of its meaning reached you."

"You've the unfortunate disposition to hold your thoughts till they sour on you. Never mind how thick my head is. Be kind to me, and say out the meaning, if you know it."

"I will if you'll shut up a minute yourself. The meaning is clear enough. It is simply that your dear friend Biornson is a particularly effective and artistic liar. That all his talk of Quetzalcoatl and Tlapallan is so much empty rubbish. I told you in the beginning that there were mines in these hills. I'm doubly sure of it now.

"Let us suppose, what is probably true, that Biornson is a man well and unfavorably known by the *rurales*, and in consequence a man who doesn't dare apply to the government for a mining concession. Suppose, then, that he sees a certain opportunity in the current superstitions about these hills. What would be simpler than to strengthen them with the aid of a few white followers and a pack of hounds, and proceed therewith to make his fortune in safe secrecy?"

"I can think of a lot of *simpler* things," said Boots reflectively, "though I'll not say you're wrong. But what's that then?" He pointed to the polished white wall opposite the window. "The back of a mining shack, maybe? It must be a magnificent fine one to be built of white marble!"

"That," Kennedy retorted, "is part of the same ruins that his men brought me down through blindfolded that first night. I'll grant you that we are in a city of the Aztecs, or possibly of the Mayas. But it is a city as dead as the bygone civilizations of those races. Once out of this cell, and I promise you the sight of empty ruins, and no more."

"You've got a good head on your shoulders," conceded Boots rather sadly. "I misdoubt you're right. And here I'd hoped to be seeing the strange wild city of a tale, with its priests and its multitudes bowing down to their poor false gods, and maybe a bloody sacrifice or so to make it the more interesting!"

For once the older man laughed, but it was a contemptuous merriment.

"From the curiosity of children and fools, good Lord deliver us! Biornson conjures up a frightful dream, and here you are ready to weep because it isn't real! Do you, know the meaning of Tlapallan?"

"I've been trying to wring it out of you for a week," was Boots' bitter reply.

"In the old mythology of Anahuac, Tlapallan was a city of white wizards. It was to rule this fanciful Community that Quetzalcoatl deserted the Chollulans. In Yucatan they still expect him to return leading the magic race of white giants who are to restore all Mexico to the Aztecs. It was clever in Biornson to use that legend as a kind of scarecrow. His men are costumed to the part, and I dare say more than one Indian or greaser has been well frightened by them and the pack of hounds in their trail.

"What I appreciate, though, is his nerve in trying to put the illusion over on *me*. He didn't want to do it. He was deathly afraid we'd run across some of his stage settings before he got rid of us. When we did, he decided to take the bull by the horns and try to victimize us through our imaginations, just as he's done for years with the Indians."

"But what's he to gain by cooping us here, and—what of the queer language they all speak?"

"Aztec. You've heard it spoken in half a dozen Indian villages, but they give a queer twist to it here which I'll admit deceived even me. They are some white hill tribe over whom Biornson has got a hold, but take my word, the whole affair is a kind of elaborate hoax.

"For the rest, he has us here, and he doesn't exactly know what to do with us. I suppose some remnant of decency makes him hesitate at murder, and on the other hand, he's afraid to let us go. If you had only allowed me to kill him when I had the chance we should be free men today. What are you grinning over now?"

"Nothing—or just the astonishing difference betwixt a murder and a killing. If we leave here tonight, will y'be content to do it without bloodshed?"

Kennedy brightened a trifle.

"You have a plan?"

"I've me muscle," was the placid retort. "If that fine actorman, Mr. Biornson, believes me disabled entirely by a few small scratches, 'tis deceiving himself, he is. I do hope the jailer he sends to feed us is an upstanding lad, for 'twould be shame to waste the returned strength of me on a man of contemptible proportions!"

As Boots had once pointed out, the fact that they were given no light after sundown was no great deprivation, since they had nothing to look at but each other, and the long, empty day was more than sufficient for that.

Tonight, however, it was a positive advantage. If they could not see their jailer, neither could he see them.

On these occasions the door was never opened wide. There was a chain outside, restricting the aperture to a matter of a dozen inches. Through this the invisible one passed his burden; fruit always, corn-cakes, boiled beans, or, more rarely, podrida of chopped chicken and peppers—a plain but plentiful diet. For drink there was water and a kind of thin, sweetish beer, contained in the porous clay ollas that kept it cool.

Kennedy had never made any effort to attack this provision-bearing visitor. For one thing there was the chain, and for another, except in the fury of being cornered, or with an overwhelming force to back him, he had not to any great degree the spirit that attacks.

With Boots on his feet again, the situation changed, and it was a pity for the jailer's sake that he could not know this. Nine times had he approached that door, done his benevolent duty and departed unmolested, but on this tenth visit he met a different reception.

Playing second part willingly for once, Kennedy received his instructions, and around ten o'clock the unsuspecting one came slapping along, the alley on sandaled feet.

Setting down his basket he slid back the great bolt of solid copper, gave a warning rap, and pushed in the door to the length of the restraining links.

As was his custom, before taking the fresh provisions Kennedy thrust out the containers of the previous day, and this time he began with a water-jug, large and heavy, which he started to place in the waiting hands outside just as the groping fingers touched it, Kennedy let go. It was very neatly done. The jar, insecurely grasped, slipped, and instinctively the hands made a downward dive to catch it.

As the guard stooped, a long arm shot out, an elbow crooked about his lowered neck, and for one astonished moment he was helpless.

But Boots had got his wish. He had an adversary of no contemptible proportions, and that cramped grip through the doorway did not, could not hold. Even more quickly than Boots had expected the man broke away, but meantime Kennedy's part was accomplished.

Their hope had been set on the fastening of that chain. If it locked, failure was certain. It did not. The end was a great hook, caught over a ring-bolt in the wall. Kennedy's arm flashed out at the same moment with his ally's, felt along the links, found the hook—the ring—his finger-tips barely reached it—and just as the enemy jerked free with an angry grunt, the chain rattled and fell.

When an Irishman charges he flings himself, muscle and mind and spirit, in one furious projectile.

The guard had scarcely straightened when his towering form crashed back, clean to the wall behind.

It was all in the dark, of course. Whether he thought himself attacked by a man or a raging demon cannot be known, but though the breath had been knocked from his body by Boots' first rush, he rallied magnificently.

The Irishman found himself caught in a clinch that was like the grip of a grizzly bear, and though his ribs were not pasteboard they felt that awful pressure. His right forearm came up beneath the other's chin, jolting it back, and he tore himself free by main force. When the other giant lunged after him, he was caught in a cross-buttock that sent him crashing down on the bricks.

But he was up with a resilience that Boots envied. For all his boast, the scarcely healed wounds he bore, coupled with nine days of inaction, had left the Irishman a good deal less than fit. And this jailer of theirs was a vast, dim, silent, forceful creature—a pale shadow that, chest to chest, overtopped him by a good two inches; a terribly solid shadow, of iron-hard muscles and a spirit as great as his own.

For almost the first time in his life, Boots tried to dodge an adversary's rush. That grip on his ribs had warned him.

It was too dark for good foot-work. Tripping over the basket of fruit, he fell, and straightway an avalanche of human flesh descended upon him. Over and over they rolled, amid squelching oranges and bursting melons. Welded as in one figure, they rose and fell to rise again.

Boots' ribs were cracking, and his breath came in hoarse gasps.

Then one braced foot of the man he fought slipped in the mess of smashed fruit, and the slide of it flung him sideways. He recovered instantly, but no longer erect.

Boots' left arm was locked tight around the small of his back, the right was beneath his chin. Gasping, choking, his back curved in an ever-increasing arc, he yielded to that relentless pressure on his throat. Back and back, sweat poured down the Irishman's face, and the blood from opened wounds ran over his body, but he had his foe now where he knew that nothing could save him.

Bent almost double at last, the huge form suddenly relaxed. It was that or a broken back. A second later, Boots' knees were crushing the jailer's chest, his hands squeezing the last gasp out of his windpipe.

"That's the way, boy! Kill him—kill him—kill him!"

The whispered snarl at his shoulder brought the Irishman to his senses like a douche of cold water. There was something about it so base—so bestial—as if the very lowest depths of himself, the depths that a real man treads under and keeps there, had been suddenly externalized and had spoken with the voice of Kennedy.

He snatched his hands from the helpless throat. He rose, swift and silent. For one moment Kennedy was as near death as a man has a right to be, who whispers murder in a victor's ear.

Then Boots remembered the poor thing Archer Kennedy was, and his great hands dropped.

"Get back in the cell," he said quietly. "Two *men* have been fighting here, and the airs not safe for the likes of you to breathe *Go!*"

And Kennedy went.

AGAIN THE GRASS PALLET IN the corner was filled by a giant, bandaged figure. This time, however, the mouth too was swathed, and the coarse, strong strips bound arms and legs in a manner to preclude any possibility of movement. A stifled groan rasped through the dark, but no one was there to hear.

Beside the dim white wall outside, two other forms walked cautiously along.

"It's a scanty outfit of garments I got from that lad," grumbled a deep voice. "I'd feel more decent to be strolling with a blanket to my back, as was my original intention."

A grunt was the only comment elicited.

"Feathers," continued Boots, "are fine in their place. For the decorating of hats, and for dusters, and for the wing of the bird they grew on, there's nothing more appropriate than feathers. But to string a few of them together and hang them here and there on a person of good proportions, like myself—why, to cell it a complete costume is no less than exaggeration!

"Here's an end to our going, unless—yes, a gate there is, and praise be, no lock on it, either. Now for your city of tombs and ruins. A pity it's so dark we won't see them," Boots finished.

The alley, which had run straight between two high walls, ended in another as high. However, as Boots' words indicated, there was a gateway. The door that filled it, though not fastened, was astonishingly heavy. He had to put the strength of his shoulders to the pull before it swung slowly inward.

"Good heavens!" breathed Kennedy.

Boots said nothing at all. He was entirely occupied with gazing.

In the very first moment, he knew that it was Kennedy's dead city of tombs and ruins which had been the dream; Tlapallan, living and wonderful, the reality.

But—a city! Surely, here was the strangest city that ever mortal eyes beheld.

They had expected to emerge from that gate on or near the floor of a valley. Instead, a straight drop of some hundred feet was below them. They had come out on a railed balcony, from whose built-up stairs of stone slanted down the face of an immense facade of sheer, black cliff.

They had thought to find night close and dark about them. But their view for miles was clear, and the base of the cliff was lapped by the pale ripples of a lake of light.

Wide and far extended that strange white sea. Its waters, if waters they could be called, were set with scores of islands. About it, like the rounded, enormous shoulders of sleeping giants, loomed the somber hills.

The light of the lake was not glaring It was more as if, when night swallowed the sun, Tlapallan had held the day imprisoned in its depths. Every painted temple and palace of its islands, every gorgeous, many-oared barge and galley gliding across its surface, showed clear and distinct of hue as though the hour were high noon, instead of close to midnight.

Clear and strange. For one thing, there were no reflections. For another, the shadows were wrong. It was the under side of things that was brightest, the upper that melted into shade. The light was upside down. The sky, as it were, was beneath instead of above.

Over all brooded that great stillness which they had felt in their cell, and interpreted as the silence of desolation. And yet it was not quite the perfect stillness they had thought, for a low murmur came up through it, like the rustle of leaves in a distant forest, or the murmur of waves on a far-off shore.

On the many islands, amid gardens and beneath flowering trees, moved the forms of Tlapallan's people. But no separate voice raised in speech or song floated up toward the watchers on the cliff.

The vessels of its traffic went to and fro, rowed by striped white oarsmen, who labored in an endless quiet. What lading did they bear, across an inverted sky, between islands as splendidly colored as sunset clouds?

A midnight traffic in dreams, one-would think, through the floating city of a vision.

Kennedy turned from the rail. Far up on the cliff there, they stood in a kind of spectral twilight. He saw his companion but dimly, a grotesque, gigantic figure, its huge limbs sketchily draped in a mantle made of strings of parrot feathers, that hid them none the better for having been through a wrestling match. Its height was increased by a helmet, shaped like the head of an enormous parrot and standing well out over the face. The golden beak of it curved down over the forehead, gaping, duel, lending its sinister shadow to the face behind.

And it stood so oddly motionless, that figure.

Kennedy's glance traveled to the unearthly scene below and back again. He was swept by a horrible sense of unreality, of doubt.

Was this his homely, tiresomely light-humored mate of the camp and trail? Or was it the thing it seemed the specter of some old Toltec warrior, massive, terrible, with folded, gory arms, gazing out to the fabled home of its blood-stained gods?

The broad chest heaved in a sigh that sent a menacing quiver to the golden beak. From the shadow of the parrot-head there issued a solemn voice.

"Priests, did I say, and processions, and the poor commonplace of gilt idols? To the devil with them all! Here's a sight worth owning two eyes for! Why, Shan McManus never saw the like o' this, when he spent twelve months in Blake Hill with the Little People!"

"Boots!" exclaimed the other, with a rather curious emphasis.

"Well?"

"Oh, nothing. I wish you'd shed that helmet, though. It's absurd."

"I will not," answered Boots firmly. "I do not know what it looks like, having seen it only in the dark, but I feel that it lends me an air of becoming dignity, . and moreover it is a part of me in disguise. Would you have us embark in one of those elegant boats we see, and myself with me bare red head shouting 'Irish' to every beholder?

"Ask what you like, but not for one string of these feathers I was slandering, and which I now perceive will enable me to move in the ranks of fashion. Dye see that boatload yonder? Not a gentleman passenger but is feathered like a bird o' the jungle. You'll notice, though, that the oarsmen are less particular. If you can't get a feather suit for yourself, Mr. Kennedy, you can shed what you've got and row."

"Are you actually insane enough to propose our hailing one of those vessels? Why, you great fool, they'd find you out in an instant. You can't even speak the language:"

"I can shut me mouth," was the placid answer. "I've all the right plumage of a citizen. Should they discover me true identity, I'll grant you that a shindy may follow. But what of that? Come or stay here, Mr. Kennedy. 'Tis a matter of indifference to myself."

A glance of mingled anger and despair was the sole reply, and when Boots set foot on the long stairs slanting lakeward, the older man made no motion to follow him.

V

GOLD

Archer Kennedy had two good reasons for failing to accompany Boots on his hare-brained expedition. One was the perfectly rational objection he had advanced that they would be found out and recaptured almost instantly.

The other, though less rational was far more powerful. It dragged him back through the gate before Boots had half accomplished his downward journey.

Kennedy was afraid. He was afraid as he had never been afraid in his life before, though he had experienced a warning thrill of it when Biornson visited their cell and spoke of the gods and Tlapallan.

A mythical city, set in a lake of cold fire, where fantom galleys moved in majestic silence, had no place in his conception of the universe. He had no curiosity about it. He desired no more intimate knowledge. It was simply without a place. He was seized with a desperate desire to escape, not only from Tlapallan, but from the very idea of Tlapallan.

As he plunged back through the valley, even the desert seemed a preferable memory to what he had just seen. Somehow he must make his way back to the ravine. Somehow he must provide himself with food, water, and a means to carry them, reach the gorge and, by no matter how painful a journey, return to a sane and credible world.

Coming to the cell of their recent confinement, he paused only to make sure by faint sounds through the window that the jailer was still a prisoner, then hurried on. In this direction also, he found that the alley terminated in a wall and gate. The latter he opened with some difficulty, to find himself in a covered passage, dark as the pit and coldly dank as a cellar. As it extended in only one direction, at right angles to the alley, he had no trouble in choosing his way.

Presently his foot shuck on what proved to be the first step of a flight of stone stairs. This was encouraging. On that first night he had been led down many stairs.

Very softly he crept up them, for silence could no longer deceive him with the assurance of being alone. He reached the top. It was blocked by a door—a wooden door, that opened easily at a touch.

Beyond it there was a light. Stepping through, he came into a bare, rectangular chamber, paved and walled with stone, empty, and opening through an arch to some place from which light blazed, warm and golden, though from where Kennedy stood he could not see its source.

In his mind he cursed it. Man or beast, your fugitive fears light, as its revealing enemy.

Yet behind him there lay only the cell, with its outraged and doubtless furious occupant—and that lakeward gateway which he longed to forget.

Treading softly, he crossed the flagstones and crept along the wall. Very cautiously he thrust forward till his eyes just cleared the edge of the arch.

Then indeed did he forget the uncomfortable weirdness of Tlapallan. With his soul in his eyes Kennedy gazed and gazed. Here was that which might wipe out a thousand unadjustable memories. Here was that which Kennedy understood and loved with a great and passionate affection.

Here was *gold*.

Tons of it. Though the worshipped metal was cast and carved in many shapes, it was not the workmanship that appealed to Kennedy. It was the stuff itself—the delightful, yellow-orange surface, the rich look of weight and body, the feeling of warmth behind the eyes that reveled in it.

Transcendent boldness welled up in Kennedy's heart, and Boot's himself could have crossed that threshold with no greater a carelessness for danger.

The room was lighted by four lamps, themselves suspended by massive yellow links, and beneath their radiance the place was one of splendor and glory polished metal. The walls themselves were sheeted wit beaten plates of it.

Ranged on a stone shelf; running clear around the chamber, stood dozens of urns, vessels and vases of massive size and crude but effective design. Set about the floor were various larger objects—a thing like a baptismal font, where the basin, as long as the body of a man; was supported on the back of three nearly life-size cougars; a throne-like chair; two or three chests, of various shapes and sizes; some half-dozen five-branched candelabra, each one taller than a man and weighing more than any man could carry.

All of gold. All of the metal itself, pure, divine, beautiful, without alloy, so soft in its purity that Kennedy could mar the stuff with a reverent finger-nail.

There was a curious lack of care in the arrangement of these treasures. They were set about anywhere, anyhow, and the worn stone flags of the floor, the unbarred road he had come by, seemed to show that the chamber which held them was common thoroughfare for any feet that chose to pass.

It was like the lumber-room of some public edifice, into which furnishings not in use are carelessly thrust till required. A lumber-room— for gold!

Kennedy's eyes glistened. Such cavalier treatment of the world's desire argued an astounding wealth behind it.

At one end of the room was a second doorway. Before it there hung two curtains, black, straight, made of heavy cotton stuff without ornament, austere in their splendid setting as the cassock of a Trappist monk at the court of a king.

What lay beyond? What manner of building was this that stood on the cliff, high and far from the island palaces of the lake? A store-house, perhaps? It seemed possible—probable. And this was only one room, and an outer room at that.

What wealth—what incredible stores of jewels might the other rooms reveal! More gold, of course—and jewels—

There was no sound anywhere. The curtains fascinated him.

On venturous tiptoes, Kennedy reached them, parted them, hesitated a moment only—and passed through.

Behind him the curtains fell together and hung straight as before, black and shabbily sinister—austere in their splendid setting as the robe of some inquisitor of old Spain.

The confident security in his borrowed plumage displayed by Boots was more jest than earnest. Before quitting their prison he had washed and rebound two deep gashes which the combat had opened in thigh and shoulder. But since, barring helmet and mantle, the only garment worn by the jailer had been a sort of kilt, made from soft cloth woven of cotton and feather-down, the white bandages, not to mention his other scars, seemed perilously conspicuous. Strings of parrot plumage were an inadequate concealment.

Of course, there might be other wounded heroes mingling with the society of Tlapallan. But Boots had a dark suspicion that gentlemen of his exact complexion and appearance were scarce enough there to arouse dangerous comment.

For these reasons he meant to take a long and careful survey of the scene before attracting attention from any of the boatmen. Beside the larger vessels, a few small craft were visible, canoes of one or more occupants, which darted and dodged here and there across the silver flood. A lone canoe-man, now, should be more easily deceived—or overcome—than a whole bargeload.

As he approached lake-level, however, he met an unexpected hindrance to his purpose. The nearer he drew to that glittering expanse, the more difficult it became for him to see it.

From above the view had been no more dazzling than is any common sheet of still water, just following sunset when the sky seems less bright above than in its mirrored reflection. But standing at the edge, as he presently did, the whole varied scene resolved itself into a molten glow that forced shut his lids and made him realize that the Tlapallans must be possessed of optic organs as unusual as their habitat—unless they wore smoked glasses, a practice he had not noted.

"'Twould better be dark," thought Boots disgustedly, "than a sight so bright you can't see it. Now what am I to do?"—

The stairs had ended at a broad floating stage, made of barked logs fastened together. As he stood on it, hesitating whether to wait till his eyes became more accustomed to the general brilliance, or to give up the adventure as impossible, a slight thudding sound to the right reached his ears.

By squinting desperately he could just make out the shape of a small boat of some kind. Then a low, clear voice murmured a sentence in the bird-like tongue of the Tlapallans.

Boots, taking emergency full face as was his custom, turned and walked boldly toward the voice. Dubious though he knew his position to be, there was no hesitation in either his manner or his stride.

Boldness is often a saving quality, but in this case it was a mistake.

Misled by that first thud, he had taken it for granted that boat and stage were in immediate juxtaposition. They were not. A good four-foot clearance intervened, and heading for the dark blur, which was all he could see, Boots carried his confident bearing straight over the edge and down into the glittering flood beyond.

An unexpected plunge bath is always startling. But a plunge bath in Tlapallan proved to have qualities of shock so far beyond the ordinary that Boots forgot every consideration in the world except an overwhelming desire to climb out again.

The instant his body touched the water, it was as if his skin were being lanced by a million red-hot needles. A dip in boiling oil could hardly have been more painful.

Straight down he went, to rise again so sick with agony that he could only clutch futilely at the air, and if left to himself his debut in Tlapallan would have meant an exit from life.

But the blade of a wooden paddle was thrust into his excited grasp, and he retained just sense enough to hang onto it. Swirled rapidly through the tormenting quid, his chest struck on something hard, and a second later he found his arms drawn up and over a rounded edge. It was the landing stage.

Somehow he dragged himself out upon it. Though dripping wet and so weak that he lay prone for more than a minute, he realized that the pain had eased off at once. Maybe, he thought, once thoroughly boiled, a man's capacity for suffering ceases.

Then he was gently prodded by a foot.

"Stand—up!" The voice of the invisible speaker lent a musical softness to the harsh English words. Also if was the voice of a woman, and a young woman, too, or Boots had never heard a young girl speak.

Although in doubt if there were a whole square inch of skin left on him, he tried to obey. It proved astonishingly easy. The pain had entirely departed, and now he felt little worse than before the plunge. Some other quality of the water than heat must have caused his torture, and indeed it had been more like a highly electrified bath than anything else.

Except as a formless blur he could make out nothing of his rescuer, and he prayed, though not hopefully, that she could see him no better. The parrot head-dress was lost, and his borrowed feathers clung in bedraggled strings. Twenty is a self-conscious age where the opposite sex is concerned, and Boots felt that he cut a remarkably inglorious figure.

Something was thrust into his hands. It was the lost helmet.

"Cover your head," said the voice, which seemed to have taken command of him and the situation with the utmost coolness. "Your hair is beautiful, but it is a wrong color. Among us no man's hair is so—so gay. Only Tlatlanhquetezatlipoca. He is red, like you, but he is a god who has no sons in Tlapallan. Tell me, did you paint your hair so red because you are a son of Tlatanhquetezatlipoca?"

"Me father's name was O'Hara," blurted Boots, rather desperate.

"O'Hara?" She pronounced it like two distinct words. "He has no seat in Tlapallan. You shall bring him here, and we will build him a red house, finer than the seat of Tlatlanhquetezatlipoca, who has no children."

"It's kindness' self you are," protested the bewildered one, "but the poor man's dead."

"Then he was not a true god," asserted the voice disapprovingly. "The true gods never die. You should forget him and serve another. Tlaloc is strong. Let your hair your hair grow black again and become a son of Tlaloc. And why do you shut your eyes? Is it because the eyes of O'Hara are closed in death? Think no more of a dead god, but open your eyes and look at me."

He grasped at the last arbitrary command as slightly more intelligible than the rest.

"With them open or shut, the beauty of you is equally hid from me. 'Tis the light that's to blame, not my will. 'Tis too glaring entirely!"

That truthful statement seemed to puzzle his new acquaintance as greatly as her remarks had bewildered him. It was some moments before she could be convinced that superfluity of light was really blinding to this stranger from the outer world.

That she knew him for a stranger had been evident from the first, and her calm acceptance, together with the excellent though slightly accented English she spoke, were as surprising as every other experience he had met in this home of surprises.

"If you really cannot see me," she said at last, "I will take you where the glory of Tonathiu (the Sun God) is not so great. Tonathiu sits in the roots of Tonathiutl to rest from his day's journey. His spirit flows out through the waters, and is brightest where it touches the shores of the land he loves. Around Tonathiutl itself the spirit is not so bright as here. I wonder if my lord Svend's eyes are as weak as yours? I must find out from Astrid. It is very interesting and curious. Come."

Willingly enough Boots accepted a guiding hand from this mysterious young person, and a few moments later was safely ensconced in the bottom of a fair-sized canoe, made of skins stretched over a bamboo frame. Had her words been a thousand times more incomprehensible, the risks involved incomparably greater, still Boots would have taken his chance and embarked in that canoe.

But though he could make little of what she said, the girl seemed amazingly friendly, and altogether he felt that the adventure was going rather well.

VI

The Black Eidolon

A vast, circular chamber, lofty as the rotunda of some mighty cathedral, vaporous with ever-rising whirls of pale mist, made visible only by the livid effulgence which sprang from a strange luminous expanse that was its floor.

Having reached this place in his quest for carelessly stored wealth, Archer Kennedy halted—and shrank back.

Through the black curtains he had come into a series of passages, lighted by hanging lamps like those in that outer room. In the polished white walls of these passages there had been no doors, and he had followed on, growing more doubtful with each step, yet driven still by that powerful desire of his, till he came down a flight of stairs that led to a lofty arch where he now stood, peering into the far loftier chamber to which it was the entrance.

He had been seeking gold and jewels. Gold and jewels were here. Round the outer rim of the rotunda at floor level ran a ledge or walk, set at brief intervals with throne-like chairs, and every chair of them carved from virgin gold. In the white, curving wall behind them their reflections gleamed, like gold drowned in milk.

High above the wall lifted an enormous dome, and through the vapors its vault glowed with sullen fires, scarlet, green, and azure—the glowing eyes of a million jewels set there—opals all, those most living and unfortunate of gems.

But Kennedy, lover of gold and seeker of jewels, gave their splendors hardly a glance. Wealth is very well, but a man must have life to enjoy it. There was that here which might well rend Kennedy's from him.

The place was shaped like a cathedral rotunda, but it was floored like—like nothing on earth that he had ever seen.

A sort of unnatural marsh, or fen it was, where pale, slimy rushes grew thick out of steaming mire, and globular fungi shone with a livid, phosphorescent light. From its surface mist-wraiths rose continually, in twisting whirls and spirals, and the breath of it was dank in Kennedy's nostrils.

Like a marsh in a dream it was, and its reality was the reality of a nightmare. But it was not that which Kennedy thought of in the first moment.

Let a man, walking through the corridors of a public building, come suddenly upon the open gate of hell, alive with its demons, and his first emotion may well be dread of those demons, rather than wonder that hell should open there.

The pale rushes and luminous globes were strange and repulsive as some new, dank circle of the inferno. But among them moved living shapes that crept and lurked—wolf-like, savage shapes that would have been snow-white save for the mire that plastered their silk fur. He had met shapes like those before. On that first night in the pass only chance and his companion's stubborn effort at protection had saved him from being torn to pieces by such as these.

"The white hounds of the Guardians—here!" muttered Kennedy, and saw that around the marsh where they prowled there was no barrier.

Like any common dogs, they had been instantly aware of his presence. Three of them came splashing and floundering to the very edge of the reeds, and meeting the savage hunger of their eyes, he expected the rush that would end him. But it did not come. He stood quiet, not from courage, but because he feared that at the first sign of flight the beasts would pursue.

But as seconds passed and the white brutes kept inside the marsh's boundaries, nor made any effort to cross them, physical terror was engulfed by another sort fear. The intolerable *strangeness* of his discovery swept Kennedy like a flood.

What place in Nature had this domed-in, coldly steaming marsh, with its pale growth of rushes, its luminous fungoids, and wallowing wolf-like inhabitants?

The very character of the beasts was an anomaly. Had they been reptiles, saurians, creatures of mire by birthright—they might have been terrible but in a comprehensive manner. But—dogs! White hounds. In a sane world hounds are neither bred nor kenneled in a marsh!

Yet there they splashed and prowled, swaying the rushes, emerging to glare with fierce, unfriendly eyes, or wallowing their silky coats anew in the softer mire around some giant, isolated fungus, that was like a pale sphere of light.

And those thrones! What inhuman sort of spectators were wont to sit there, and for the enaction of what incredible spectacle?

Taken by themselves one can tolerate a white dog, a white reed, or a phosphorescent fungus. Assemble them in mire, multiply them, surround them with golden thrones, and roof them with a jewel-lined dome, and the combination becomes—suspiciously weird.

Suddenly the man knew that he had seen too much.

He had feared the hounds and not dared to run from them. Now once more he feared a *thought*, and from that inescapable pursuer he did run, though not very far.

Half way up the stairs he halted and crouched, listening intently.

From beyond the arch came only an occasional splash or swishing of the reeds.

Yet somewhere a sound dissimilar to those had begun—the first he had heard since leaving the alley of their former prison.

It was a kind of *slap, slap, shuffle, slap*—a blurred, commingled noise, that to Kennedy was anything but welcome. It meant that along these passages he had so stealthily traversed, many sandaled feet were approaching.

He straightened stiffly, elbows bent, hands clenched, and trembling like a man with the ague. He was caught. What would be the penalty he did not know—something vague and terrible—those folk were no longer to him "just buck Indians of a particularly light-hued type." They were the white people of Tlapallan—the mystic people who in a sane material universe had no place.

Crushed between two dreads, Kennedy stood still and shivered.

SLAP—SLAP—SHUFFLE. THEY WERE very near now. They were coming, solemn and slow. The very leisureliness of their approach seemed inimical They knew he was here! They knew that he could not escape them! They knew—

Turning suddenly he plunged back down the stairs. His one instinct was to hide.

Back through the arch he sprang. This side of the marsh there was no possible concealment, unless he should have chosen to join the wallowing hounds among the rushes. That scarcely appealed to him, and he ran on round the curving rim, following the narrow path that intervened between the line of thrones and the mire.

To his dismay several of the marsh-hounds tried to follow. Had they leaped out on the stone rim, they could have outrun him easily enough, but not one attempted to do that. Floundering, splashing they pursued in heavy, mud-hindered bounds, with ferocious eyes fixed always on the fugitive.

He could not doubt that those silent, snarling jaws longed to rend his flesh. There seemed no barrier to prevent their reaching him. And yet his flight had half-encircled the rotunda and still not a paw had been set on the path he followed.

Though seeking a place to hide, the terror of those lurching pursuers had kept his attention on the marsh. In consequence he collided heavily with some large object that blocked the way, and the breath was so thoroughly knocked out of him that he clung there a moment, gasping. Then he saw what from the rotunda's far side had been obscured by the vapors.

Here the white marble ledge broadened before what seemed to be a deep, narrow niche. On the broadened ledge outside this recess, ranged not carelessly but in a decorous regularity of order, were many more such golden vessels as he had seen in the outer room. The thing he had run against was another golden font, with its three nearly life-size cougars, and its basin long as the body of a man. Two other fonts, identical in appearance with the first, stood, just beyond, and beyond them again the line of thrones was renewed and continued.

On either side of the niche itself two great candelabra raised their golden branches, five to each, that bore tall candles like those set to burn by the bier of the dead. The candles, however, were not lighted, and the depths of the niche they guarded were very dark. The rotunda was walled with blank, white marble, but this recess in it had been built of stone, dead-black as unpolished ebony. The radiance of the fungi, diffused and made uncertain by mist wreaths, hardly penetrated the black niche at all.

Now, having looked for a place to hide, it seemed possible that he had found one, and yet he shrank oddly from exploring those dead-black depths.

Without reason he felt convinced that there was something in there—*something that lived.*

As has been hinted earlier, curiosity in Archer Kennedy was, as a rule, sternly subordinated to more practical considerations. Curiosity about a living *something* that lurked darkly behind a livid, unnatural marsh, he found so easy to suppress that not even panic could at first drive him to investigation.

The white hounds had ceased to give him any attention, and looking for them he found that he had this side of the marsh to himself. The

FRANCIS STEVENS

uncertain light and the vapors prevented his seeing across it, but he heard the brutes splashing around beyond. They were making back toward the entrance and he guessed why. Dogs ignore neither enemy nor friend, and even from where he stood there was audible again the steady shuffle of many approaching sandals.

Again the fugitive looked to the niche, vainly trying to pierce its impenetrable gloom. As on the stairway, fear was driving him whither fear had shrunk from going, and—after all, how could there be anything *alive* in that niche? No sound of motion or breathing came out of it.

Cursing himself for an imaginative fool, Kenny tautened his nerves and made the forward step that set one foot on the black floor where it joined the ledge's whiteness. Then he stopped dead.

No light was reflected from the depths. He had been very sure of that, and yet, in the instant when his foot crossed the line, *he began to see.* Unless there is black light as well as white, perceive may be the better term, but whatever the faculty so abruptly acquired, it at least gave the sense of vision and after an extremely vivid fashion. By it he learned that he had cursed his imagination unjustly, for something did really lurk in the narrow niche. It was a face.

Though, black as its environing gloom, it appeared to reflect no light, to Kennedy every feature of that dark countenance grew unforgettably distinct.

It was not a good face. No evil, indeed, could have been too vile for its ugliness to grin at. A toad's mouth is wide, ugly—and rather funny. The mouth of this face was toad-like in width and narrowness of lip, but the grin of it was in no sense funny. A tense, cruel grin it was, that had never heard of humor. Cruel and monstrously alert. Alert stealth was in the very distention of the nostrils above it. The eyes were slits, but they were watchful slits.

The whole face gave the impression of being thrust forward by a neck strained with eagerness, but the threat of it was not the clean threat of death. Had it witnessed torture, not the victim but the tormentor would have held its avid attention. Not pain, but cruelty, not vice but viciousness—and the corruption of all mankind could hardly have sated its ambition, nor the evil of a world-wide race of demons have quenched the desire behind its narrowed lids.

Poised rigid, Kennedy confronted it eye to eye. His gaze seemed so fixed that it might never waver through eternity, and yet, without glancing downward, he became gradually aware that beneath the face was a body. He knew that the thing squatted naked, and that the fingers clasped about its drawn-up knees were long, and stealthy, and treacherous.

But for once Archer Kennedy felt neither dread nor the impulse to flee. Of what the face meant those fingers were only another adequate symbol—*and the face drew him.*

In the natures of different men there are, as one might say, certain empty spaces. Voids that long to be filled. So one craves beauty, and another love, a third goodness, and a fourth, perhaps, mere lust of the senses.

Meeting these, the emptiness is filled and the man is happy. So, Kennedy. He had craved gold, but bade of that desire was another and deeper lack—an emptiness unknown and unacknowledged, even by himself. The face filled it.

Like a devout Buddhist, withdrawing his soul from earthly distractions, absorbed in contemplation of the mystic jewel in the lotus, so Archer Kennedy would have wished to stand there a long, long time, content, while the unguessed emptiness of him was filled at last.

But following the rotunda's marble rim many feet were approaching, and in another moment the vapors would no longer shield him from discovery.

VII

The Cloak of Xolotl

'T is the little lady of the fire moths." Boots knelt up straight and beamed upon his *vis-à-vis* like one who welcomes an old acquaintance. Impelled by a deft and vigorous paddle, the canoe had swiftly left the landing float, shot across what seemed a wide band of blinding fire, and now, some hundred yards from shore, Boots found the radiance much less intolerable. In fact, he could see very well, and his first glance was not for the islands nor the island craft, but toward the girl who had apparently taken him under authoritative protection.

"If you jump about so, we shall be upset," she admonished him.

"I'll not move a finger more," cried Boots, "for I can think of nothing more misfortunate than to end an acquaintance before it is fairly begun. Did you know me at first sight then, as I knew you?"

She tried to look serious and demure, but the effort ended in irrepressible merriment.

"Oh," she cried softly, "how could one help but know you? You are—you are so different to look at from my brothers of Tlapallan!"

Self-consciousness claimed him again, and if his face was red before it was flaming now.

"The costume of your country is a fine, handsome selection, but maybe it's not so becoming to an Irishman."

"But I like you different! I would have you tell how it is, though, that you are wearing Xolotl's head and his cloak of honor. Did he give them to you for friendship?"

"You might say so." Boots surmised that Xolotl was the vanquished jailer, and caution seemed advisable. Then a gleam in those amused, dark eyes warned him. "You know otherwise!" he accused.

"I hope you did not kill him," she answered reflectively. "If you killed him, being a stranger, they may give you to Nacoc-Yaotl. Did you kill him?"

Had she been asking the time of night the question could have been no more indifferent.

"No," said Boots, shocked into curtness.

The mischievous smile flashed across her lips again.

"Then I shall laugh at him! Xolotl is a boaster. He thinks he should run the hills with the guardians. But he is only a small boy, grown tall and large. Some day, since he is not dead, and when he has finished his novitiate to Nacoc-Yaotl, I shall—what is my lord Svend's word?—I shall marry him; but I shall always laugh because you took away his cloak of honor."

With another mental gasp, Boots attempted changing the subject.

"It's fine English you speak. You maybe learned from Mr. Biornson?"

"Oh; all of my gild speak English. When I was only a little baby, my lord Svend came. Though he was a stranger, they spared him because of his wisdom and his knowledge of the gods. It had been thought that the gods were forgotten save in Tlapallan. But he spoke our tongue, and later he mated—married with a daughter of Quetzalcoatl. That brought him into our gild, though for some strange reason he will not live in Tlapallan, but built him a house in the lower valley. Very soon it became—what was that phrase of Astrid's—oh, yes, all the rage, to use English. The other gilds have picked up a little, too, but we never encourage them. Don't you think it sounds much more distinguished than the old-fashioned tongue?"

"Maybe; but when you speak your own language it sounds like a bird singing."

"But birds are so common, aren't they? See! There is Tonathiutl. If you do not care to serve Tlaloc, become the son of Tonathiu, who is sometimes as red as your beautiful, painted hair. Then perhaps I shall marry you instead of Xolotl!"

She said it with the air of one bestowing some incredible hope of favor, but things were moving a little fast for Boots. Lovely though she was, here cold-blooded reference to poor Xolotl's demise, and her equally cold-blooded annexation of himself, went clean outside the Irishman's notions of propriety.

"I'll think of it," he muttered, and for the first time really gave heed to his surroundings outside the canoe.

They had come well out on the liquid silver shield beneath which, according to the faith of Tlapallan, Tonathiu, the sun-god lurked throughout those hours when the rest of the world was dark and deserted of his spirit. Therefore at night and through night only they gleamed like Mezkli, the moon, and were terrible to touch as the superheated body of Mictlanteuctli, lord of hell.

So Boots was informed, as he gazed with great curiosity at the god's house. It was the first "heathen temple" he had ever seen where the worship was living, and not a mere dusty memory of the past.

Tonathiutl, smallest of the islands, was also nearest to the shore they had recently quitted. Unlike the others, it was low and flat, and the round structure which almost filled its circumference stood scarcely ten feet high. Nothing showed above the walls, and Boots, who had noted it from the cliff, recalled that the roof was flat as a pancake.

It was all built of something that he took for brass, though Kennedy, had he been present, would have better judged the metal's value. Doors and windows there were none, save one low arched aperture, and altogether it did not in the least fit with Boots' idea of a temple.

"It goes down," explained the girl. "What you see is only the top. It goes far down, and there, below, Tonathiu slumbers in the midst of a circle of his priests. Should one, even one, of his sons sleep in these hours, Tonathiu would never climb the heavens again. He would die. Then Tlapallan and all Anahuac (Mexico) would perish in a darkness having no end. Is that not terrible fear? If you become a son of Tonathiu, you must never sleep at night. Do you ever sleep when you shouldn't?"

"More often than not," Boots hastily assured her. Whatever force it was that charged the waters, even his elementary knowledge of astronomy sensed a discrepancy between her version of "Tonathiu's" habits and the actual facts. But he could see no profit in arguing the matter, and just so he kept clear of any promise likely to involve him in strange religions, he was content to accept her statements as they were made.

"Here come Topiltzen, Nacoc-Yaotl's master priests," she suddenly announced, pointing to a galley of twenty oars which at this moment surged majestically past. "Look! There he stands near the bow, with the others crouched down around him. Tell me, is he not a fat, ugly, disagreeable old man?"

THE INDIVIDUAL IN QUESTION, WHO stood pompously erect in the midst of an adoring circle on the quarter-deck, his fat paunch covered by a white and black emblem, draped in a feathered mantle of black, white, and green, might almost have heard the girl's remark. He whirled sharply and glared toward their canoe with pudgy mouth pursed and scowling brows.

"Are you not afeared to speak of your priests so disrespectfully?" queried Boots.

She shrugged high disdain.

"I am a daughter of Quetzalcoatl. My head need not bow to those of the lesser gilds. Did you see him look at you? He knew you for a stranger. If he dared he would take you for the mysteries; but fear nothing. You are with me and Quetzalcoatl guards his own. Even Nacoc-Yaotl cannot take you from me—or I think he could not!"

She looked back toward the cliff they had left, and Boots' eyes followed hers. Now he saw what nearness had before shut from him. The dead-black rock was topped by a long, even wall of white stone. Above it rose the pale heights of a stupendous building.

In that building he and his mate had been imprisoned, and it seemed strange now to Boots that this had been so—well nigh impossible that for nine days they had dwelt in that vast place, and remained as unconscious of its vastness as are coral insects of the mighty reef they inhabit.

It was a structure so large, so ruggedly massive, as to suggest one of nature's rock castles, though its lines were too regular for that. Like the temple of the sun, it was blank of windows, but unlike that smaller temple it was neither round nor flat-roofed A hundred turrets crowned it, and out of the very midst of them there curved a titanic white dome.

The dome form is one of the glories of architecture, but this one distinctly failed of beauty. It was squat—ugly. It was as though the round top of an incredibly large white fungus had sprouted among the turrets and been allowed to remain because of its bulls and inaccessibility.

But the whole structure was in some indefinable way—oppressive.

It had not been for fear's sake that Boots had left it and descended to the lake, but now, without knowing why, he felt sure that his course had been wiser as well as more reckless than Kennedy's.

Kennedy had returned into those blind, white depths. That foolish, protective instinct of Boots rose up at the thought. No matter what else Kennedy was, he was a poor, weak thing—and Boots' mate. Should he go after him? Better get the good of some information, first.

He asked the building's purpose.

"That is the seat of Nacoc-Yaotl." A somber look shadowed the girl's mischievous face. "Nacoc-Yaotl, the black maker of hatreds, who would destroy mankind if he could. Some day they say that he will destroy Tlapallan, but I do not believe it. Our lord of the air, Quetzalcoatl, who was once human and is noblest of all the gods, is stronger than he. How they must hate each other, those great, strong gods! Would you not like to watch a battle between gods?"

"'Twould be a destructive spectacle. Watch yourself! Watch—out!"

His shout of warning came barely in time. With two swift thrusts of her paddle, the girl shot them out of the path of a galley of twenty oars. It swept on by, and from near the bow glared Nacoc-Yaotl's master priest, thwarted malice in every line of his fat, furious face.

"He *did* hear you!" cried Boots. "And the old devil tried to run us down!"

The girl's face was sternly calm, but her eyes blazed with a rage more deadly than the priest's.

"I meant he should hear me," she said quietly. "Topiltzen is the mortal father of Xolotl, whom I despise!"

The galley had wheeled again and was heading back toward them.

"Paddle!" urged Boots desperately. "Paddle—or let me!"

He stretched a hand, but the girl only shook her head and watched the oncoming galley with quiet scorn.

"Now you will hear him apologize," she said. "It was an accident for which the poor steersman will suffer. I am a daughter of Quetzalcoatl, who guards his own, and even Topiltzen will not dare admit that attack was intended. But had we been cut in two, as was meant, you would have died and I would have been let suffer the pain of Tonathiu's spirit for more than a little before they picked me up. Oh, I hate Xolotl and all the black god's cruel gild! Son of O'Hara, I *wish* that you had slain Xolotl!"

"Faith, I'm beginning to think you've cause to wish it. Look at the old fat villain bowing there!"

THE GALLEY'S ROWERS WERE RESTING on their oars. Every face on board was turned toward them, and the master priest himself had crossed the quarterdeck and bent his head with a respect rather mocking, under the circumstances.

This was Boots' first view at close range of any of the men of Tlapallan. They were all white men—whiter than himself, to speak the truth—and yet, by certain subtle differences, Boots was quite sure they were not "white men" in the generally accepted sense. Whether or not Kennedy was right to call them "Indians," they were certainly of another than the Caucasian race.

Straight, black hair fell to their shoulders from beneath various fantastic head-dresses, fashioned to represent brightly colored beasts and birds. Such garments as they wore were of gaily hued cotton cloth, or the same downy, feathery stuff that the moth-girl was dressed in. Feather mantles like the one Boots had borrowed were worn by all save the rowers, whose attire was restricted to a broad girdle or a kilt.

Black-browed, straight-nosed, broad of shoulder and well muscled, they were as fine looking a set as Boots had ever set eyes on, and no more comparable to the common Indian tribes of Mexico than a Japanese of the "Sumurai" caste to a low-class Kolarian.

In the matter of athleticism, however, Topiltzen was an exception. He was a short, fat, pudgy little person, and the black scowl he wore now did not add to his beauty.

When he spoke it was in that hushed tone used by all in Tlapallan, as if it were some vast hospital in which the patients must on no account be awakened.

"Speak English," the girl interrupted curtly. "My friend here, the son of that great and powerful god, O'Hara, does not use our tongue."

The priest straightened and stared balefully at the "son of O'Hara," more balefully at the girl. His English was bad, and she knew it—a petty embarrassment to put on her future father-in-law, but everything counts in war.

"Where," said the priest, slowly and painfully, "Xolotl—thee head—thee cloak—I see—look hard—no Xolotl—"

Breaking off in despair, he waved expressive hands toward Boots.

"You mean, I suppose," the girl was loftily superior "that you would have run us down in order to see if my friend here was Xolotl. Yes, it is the head of Xolotl. It is the cloak of Xolotl. But my friend is not Xolotl. He is a man much stronger and more courageous, and that is why he wears Xolotl's cloak of honor. Look very close indeed. You quite see, do you not?"

But that insolence was too much for Xolotl's father, who understood English better than he spoke it. With a snort of rage he whirled and addressed a hushed command to someone behind him.

Instantly, a man sprang to the side. The girl dipped her paddle in earnest now, but too late to avoid the fling of a small grappling iron, which fairly caught their bow.

Hand over hand they were hauled ignominiously in, while Topiltzen, no longer obsequious, grinned at them in obese triumph.

It occurred to Boots that the might of his arms was going to be of more immediate service than any protection Quetzalcoatl, or any other of Tlapallan's numerous gods, seemed likely to offer.

VIII

Before the Black Shrine

Archer Kennedy was, as Boots had once observed, "a man of more refined education" than the Irish lad. Moreover, he had a quick, furtive mind, that snatched at whatever came its way and hoarded it as a jackdaw hoards its stealings, on a bare chance that it might some day prove practically useful. Stored among many such smatterings was a fair knowledge of Aztec antiquities, picked up partly in his college days, partly at close range in Yucatan and Campeche.

When Biornson had said: "You are housed in the seat of Nacoc-Yaotl," the words had not been quite meaningless to him.

In the tangled mazes of old Aztec theology, many a god possessed not only two or more names, but as many personalities, some of them as divergent from one another as black from white.

So Tezcatlipoca, "shining mirror," who descended from heaven at the end of a spider's thread, was a being of most virtuous and commendable qualities. Justice and mercy were his to administer, and if his enshrined eidolons sometimes presided from judgment seats made of piled human bones, this was in accordance with the rather grim ideas of a grim and bloody people.

But like the well-known Dr. Jekyll, Tezcatlipoca had a double nature, and a nature, moreover, of which the second and darker phase might have caused even Mr. Hyde to cover his reprehensible head in shame and jealousy.

As Nacoc-Yaotl, creator of hatreds, the virtuous Tezcatlipoca was accustomed to steal, invisible, through the streets, and in every Aztec city there were seats placed for his convenience—seats in which no mortal man was allowed to seek repose. It seems improbable that any man would care to, considering who might be his companion there.

A temple consecrated to Nacoc-Yaotl as an individual deity, however, was an innovation of which Kennedy had never heard.

On encountering a dark face in a darker niche, he did not promptly comment: "Here is exactly what I would have expected to find—the carved black image of Nacoc-Yaotl, an idol which these pale-hued and foolishly superstitious Indians are no doubt silly enough to worship."

Instead of making this sensible remark, he not only failed to identify the face, but unconsciously yielded to it a more sincere and whole-hearted worship than had probably come its way in many centuries.

His much-prized reasoning faculty went to sleep, as it were, while whatever Kennedy had for a soul basked in fascinated contemplation of its unacknowledged ideal. Alert—stealthy—desirous—ruthless—all that the secret soul would be, the face was, and raised, moreover to the nth and ultimate power.

But rapture, in this decidedly imperfect world, is proverbially of short duration.

The minor priests and acolytes of Nacoc-Yaotl, entering the rotunda with solemn tread, could not know that their deity was receiving the perfect worship of a real devotee. They themselves were rather shy of offering that perfect worship. In fact, the countenance of Nacoc-Yaotl, or rather of his eidolon, was seldom looked upon by his cautious "sons".

But, like other men, they had some inescapable duties. The affair before them now was of minor importance—the captive being only a poor little specimen of a Yaqui Indian, strayed north in the hills and half-witted from fright—but none the less must be gone through with.

Topiltzen, head of the gild and chief priest of the mysteries, had not deigned to attend. In consequence some fancier touches of ceremony might be dispensed with, and Marcazuma, officiating as Topiltzen's understudy, rather hoped to be through with it in time to attend a banquet given that night by the sons of Tlapotlazenan, mother of healing.

Like members of that gild the world over, the men of medicine were a pleasant lot, with a goodly collection of amusing jests and tales at their tongue-tips. Under his breath Marcazuma cursed his superior for shoving all the drudgery onto his shoulders so that he had little time for pleasure.

He cursed again and more earnestly when the staff of the standard-like insignia he bore caught behind the golden claw-foot of a throne, and wrenched the standard fairly out of his hand.

Such an accident in the temple's very sanctum was an omen of direst import. As the standard clattered to the pavement, a shudder and muttering ran the length of the plumed line behind him, and as if in sympathy the hounds of the marsh, silent hitherto, set up a low, concerted howling.

With a nervous glance for them, Marcazuma recovered his standard. To his increased dismay the white and black feathers at its tip had dipped in the mire of the marsh, and become seriously draggled. They were sacred feathers, not to be touched by bare human fingers, and he had to carry them on as they were, dripping slow black drops that ran down on his hand and arm.

He resumed his dignified pacing toward the shrine, but with thoughts effectually distracted from the banquet. He was a very young man to have reached the position he held, and Topiltzen had of late showed a disposition to find fault on that score, and because of a certain impediment in his assistant's speech, two defects which Marcazuma certainly could not help.

But when his chief heard of this night's carelessness, he guessed what might happen. Sidewise, he glanced at the hounds again—and shivered.

The clatter of the standard, however, had brought dismay to another heart than his.

It woke Kennedy as from a dream. He started, looked over his shoulder and caught a glimpse through the mist of nodding plumes. Fear came back with a rush, reason roused, and all his brief content was gone in an instant.

Not only were the people almost upon him, but he realized that he had been perceiving without light. The walls of his universe shook again at a thought, and though still drawn by the face he was also unutterably afraid of it.

He actually considered diving head foremost among the reeds and hiding there, in preference to the niche. But a wolf-like head thrust out from between two clumps of bushes promised such instant disaster that he took the second of two bad choices, shut his eyes tight and lunged forward into the recess.

ONE STEP—TWO STEPS—THREE—and his outstretched hands came in contact with other hands. They neither yielded nor grasped at him. They were cold, smooth, polished as the marble walls outside. They were clasped around two rounded, polished knees.

A statue. The thing in the niche was only a statue! He opened his eyes and discovered that he could see with them—with his eyes, not his soul. Just *see!* The niche was not half so dark as he had thought. What a fool he had been to let that idea of perception without light get a grip on him! This was a statue—an idol, of course—and though black, the highly polished surface had caught gleams from the marsh.

True, the face of it was not one tenth as clear to him now as it had been, but doubtless that could be laid to the change in their relative positions.

Outside the feet were still coming on, slow, ominous, inevitable as the tread of Fate, but Kennedy found himself smiling. He felt the relief of one who has snatched victory from defeat. Having been deceived into thinking he saw a demon by its own dark light why might not the other apparently irreconcilable ideas he had of this place its people turn out to be equally deceptive?

Finding a narrow space behind the statue, he slid hastily into it and crouched there.

"Good old idol!" he muttered, and patted Nacoc-Yaotl's adamantine, polished shoulder.

Into his range of vision very slowly there stalked a tall figure, plumed headdress nodding to each step. Its feather mantle was long and gorgeous. It bore a staff crowned with a human skull, above which a bedraggled spray of feathers dripped miry water into the skull's hollow sockets.

The face of the standard-bearer was more hideous than the skull, for it was extravagantly beast-like and striped with bars of white, black, and gold. But again the hidden man smiled. He had seen devil masks like that before. They were common enough at every Indian ceremony. This leading figure he placed easily in his universe—a priest of the sacrifice. An *Indian priest*. He must remember that and never let fancy play tricks on his keen intelligence.

Now the priest halted and set up his standard in a socket prepared for that purpose in the floor by the central font. Kennedy, peering over the idol's shoulder, observed that not once did the man so much as glance into the niche, but kept his back consistently toward it.

Two torch-bearers, dressed like the first-comer, but a bit less splendidly, were next to appear. They, too, presented only their backs to the shrine, and having lighted the ten candles before it they passed on out of sight. Marcazuma knew, what Kennedy could not, that they went to take their places on two of the thrones. All the thrones must be filled before the ceremony might proceed, but Marcazuma was no longer impatient.

Another pair of his followers advanced, escorting the captive. That unfortunate, whose naked brown hide was marked with scarcely healed wounds very similar to those borne by Kennedy's trail-mate, was then lifted, laid in the basin of the central font, and secured there with ropes of agave fiber.

Marcazuma watched through the eye-holes of his wooden mask. When the Yaqui writhed, moaning through his gag, the young priest shivered with sympathy. The sympathy was for himself, not the Yaqui. His prophetic eye saw the form of Marcazuma lying in that identical basin. Topiltzen was not a tolerant chief, and when he learned of that very bad omen—

The captive's escort had left him and gone on. Several pairs of figures stalked solemnly past the niche without stopping. Then one lone acolyte, a boy by his stature, clothed in white and wearing a white mask, came and took his stand opposite to the officiating priest. With that the procession ceased to march, for all the others who formed it had enthroned themselves, and the circle being complete, Marcazuma might take up his duties.

OF ALL THE CEREMONIES THAT Kennedy had ever witnessed, and he had seen quite a number, that was the strangest. In the first place there was none of the singing, chanting or dancing inseparably connected with barbaric ritual elsewhere.

In the second, the thrones being out of Kennedy's range, the only audience visible to him was formed of the marshhounds. All told there were probably a dozen of the great white dogs, and they came out of their radiant jungle to the curb's very edge. Eyes fixed on the central font, they crouched with quivering flanks, in an eagerness which to Kennedy seemed well understandable.

"Here," he thought, "we learn how the hounds of Tlapallan are fed," and he was very glad to crouch safely behind the old black idol.

Well-trained brutes, those dogs, though. Man-eaters, he was sure now, they had allowed a possible dinner in his own person to pass them safely. Having their masters' command, doubtless, to stay within the marsh's boundaries, there they had remained, hungry or not.

The body of the little Yaqui would hardly go round among that ravenous-looking dozen. He wondered if it would be tossed to them living, or slain first. He recalled that in the Aztecs' time of glory, when human sacrifices were made by thousands, the victim's living heart was invariably cut out with an obsidian knife and offered to the god.

So far, however, save in the matter of costume, nothing of the present ceremony conformed to those old customs. The fonts themselves did not remotely resemble the curved sacrificial stone over which a victim was bent conveniently backward, exposing his chest to the knife.

Having stood motionless for at least five minutes, the priest and his young acolyte stirred at last. The smaller figure sidled backward toward the presiding eidolon. Because of the candles, the niche was by no means so dark as it had been and Kennedy promptly ducked out of sight. For several minutes he dared not peer out again. He heard a low mumbling voice, that blurred the musical accents of the native language rather as if the speaker had no teeth. It mumbled on and on, till at last Kennedy peered cautiously round Nacoc-Yaotl's protruding marble ribs.

He needn't have hidden. The acolyte had barely crossed the dividing line between black floor and white ledge, his back was still turned and he stood with arms rigidly outstretched like a human cross. He gave an odd impression of being set there as a guard—as a guard to *withhold something from coming out of that niche.*

But the black god never stirred—how may stone move of its own volition?—and the man behind it smiled sneeringly. *He* wasn't afraid of the old black thing. He patted its ribs. The high polish of them felt almost like live skin that writhed a little under his fingers, but he could never be deceived again. Stone was stone.

Peering under the acolytes out-stretched arm he could see the officiating priest, who stood before the font with its captive and was speaking across it. His mumbled remarks might have been addressed to the attentive canine audience in the marsh, but more likely he was speaking to no one in particular—just going through some silly, empty ritual.

Ending at last, he stooped to a great golden vessel and withdrew from its depths several smaller vessels, also of gold. One of them was flask-shaped, carved all over with writhing, lizard-like forms, and fitted with a crystal stopper. The others were small jars of plain gold.

The officiating priest set them out on a kind of ledge that projected behind the font's basin. Then he stood motionless, hands stretched above the captive as if in blessing or consecration.

Silence settled in the rotunda, so that Kennedy could hear his own heart beating, and also a faint gasping sound that came from the gagged victim.

Then the priest's hands dropped with startling suddenness, he wheeled—made one lightning-swift genuflection toward the niche and had his back to it again before Kennedy could even think of dodging from sight.

When was this mummery to be done with?

Immediately, it appeared. With the air of a man who gets down to business at last, the priest drew on a gauntleted glove he had carried in his girdle—a glove that gleamed yellow as flexible, soft gold—opened one of the golden jars, sniffed its contents testingly, dipped his gloved fingers in the stuff, whatever it was, and began swiftly anointing the Yaqui's naked body. The man writhed in his bonds, but whether from pain or fright Kennedy had no means of knowing—and, to do him justice, did not particularly care.

THE PRIEST WORKED SWIFTLY. HE might be too young, as Topiltzen hinted; he might be possessed of faulty vocal organs, and of a not quite pleasant personal appearance; but none could deny him a deftness unequalled by any man of the gild. Would Topiltzen consider that? He set the empty jar aside and took up the flask.

As at a signal, the dogs that watched him pointed their noses straight upward and once more a long, doleful howl ascended to the opal-lined dome and was echoed dully back.

Marcazuma started nervously. Twice now had the white hounds howled—the white, silent hounds, whose loudest utterance had ever been a low snarling, and that only in heat of combat. Unlucky indeed was the night! Flask in hand, he hesitated, wondering if Topiltzen would blame him more for continuing the ceremony, or breaking off in the middle. Then he shrugged. In either case, as he saw it, his doom was sealed. Two such omens, in one night!

He tugged at the flask's stopper, which stuck; but it always did, so that could hardly be counted as a third sign. He got it out at last and without further pause poured forth the contents in a glittering stream over the writhing form of the living man in the font.

It was a violet-tinted liquid, with a strong odor like bitter almonds, and as it touched the Yaqui's quivering skin it spread out thinly. It spread as oil does on water, swiftly, almost, one would have said, intelligently, so that in less than a minute the Indian's brown hide was entirely coated with a thin, purplish film.

This seemed a novel way of preparing a man to be torn in pieces by beasts. Kennedy watched intently.

The ceremony proceeded

Omens or no omens, Marcazuma was an expert at this task and he carried it through unfalteringly, without a slip from start to finish.

But near the rite's completion a scandalous interruption occurred, for a man—a gasping, pallid, fear-sick wreck of a man—plunged shudderingly out of the niche with its hidden god, brushed the acolyte aside, and began to run staggeringly along the curved edge of the marsh.

He was caught and held by the astonished occupant of the first throne he tried to pass, while for the third time that night the white hounds howled dolefully. But Marcazuma, startled beyond measure, nevertheless sent up a silent prayer of gratitude.

No wonder that there had been signs and omens in the temple!

Even Topiltzen could hardly blame him now. The mystery of mystery had been spied upon, the very shrine desecrated, and—Marcazuma almost swelled visibly with the story that he had for Topiltzen's ear!

But Archer Kennedy, who had for once done a fellow-being a very good turn, would have scarcely appreciated the fact had he known it.

A sign and an omen there had been indeed for him that night!

He had seen the thing that Biornson, in the first days of his captivity, had prayed God to make not so, or at least to let him forget. Kennedy did not pray, but had his captors slain him forthwith he would have welcomed the stroke.

The walls of his universe had crashed down at last, and when, with blows and curses, he was dragged from the rotunda, he cared not at all whither they were taking him, just so it was away from that which now lay quivering in the font before Nacoc-Yaotl's somber den.

IX

Maxatla Speaks

Though unobserved by Boots, when the canoe was dragged to the galley's side, two other events took place simultaneously with its capture.

Far away at the end of the black cliff a boat rushed out of some invisible harbor, propelled by six oarsmen of such unusual muscle that the heavy vessel seemed fairly to leap from the water at every stroke.

And nearer at hand another galley, heading leisurely toward Tonathiutl, suddenly diverted its course and swept down toward the master priest's craft.

The prow of this second galley bore a strange figurehead—the reared body of a gigantic serpent, crested with feathers like a heron, a collar of plumes about its golden neck.

Boots looked straight up into Topiltzen's leering face. The lesser priestlings had left their postures of adoration and crowded to the side, threatening hands outstretched to drag on board the insulters of their chief.

The Irishman did not wait to be dragged. A kneeling position in a light canoe is impossible to spring from, but, reaching up, he got handhold on some massive carving under the galley's bulwark. That was enough. He came over the side, agile as a sailor, leaving the girl in a madly rocking but uncapsized canoe.

Topiltzen, confronted by an unexpectedly aggressive foe, tried to retreat, tripped over his own flowing mantle, and a moment later was clasped tight to Boots' breast. It had all happened too quickly for interference. But now the under-priests closed in, and down the vessel's length the stalwart rowers dropped their blades and came surging toward the bow in a jostling mob.

Boots swung the fat, kicking little man in his arms toward the side. A stout girdle held the white and black emblem about Topiltzen's middle and it offered a grip.

The master priest of Nacoc-Yaotl suddenly found himself dangling in mid-air above the silver flood, while a great voice shattered the hushed quiet of Tlapallan:

"Get back! Get back, the whole pack of you—or down he goes!"

Even to those who could not understand the words, Boots' meaning was unmistakable. It brought them all to a stand.

Topiltzen squeaked like a rabbit. Though the girdle had cut off his wind, he prayed that it might hold. Swimming was little good to a man when Tonathiu charged the waters with heatless fire.

"Cast off that iron!" Boots indicated the canoe with a bob of his parrot-crested head. The man who grasped the light cable attached to the grappling iron hesitated and looked toward the priests for orders. One of them shook his head slightly.

"Cast off!" roared Boots, and lowered his captive a foot nearer the water.

The threat should have been effective, but it wasn't. Not a man stirred or spoke, and Boots had a sudden creepy doubt that he had been shouting at fantoms. The shadows were all wrong—the sky was under him—he faced a throng of weird, silent, feather-decked ghosts and threatened to drop the chief of them into the sky! No, that was no ghost in his hands—it was too heavy. But why did none of them move or answer him? Boots blinked and cast a wild glance outward, seeking the solidity of the hills to restore his mental balance.

Then the loop of a rope dropped over his head and shoulders.

That little event had been what they were waiting for. No bodiless fantoms ever rushed in on a victim with such a weight of flesh and strength of brawn.

Unfortunately for Topiltzen, however, the caster of that rope had miscalculated. He had meant to jerk the stranger so suddenly inboard that the master priest would come with him; but quick though a man may be, it is easier to relax muscles than to flex them.

As the rope touched his chest, Boots let go, and with one gurgling cry the priest splashed and vanished in the light beneath.

But on the quarter-deck poor Boots was hopelessly outnumbered. Underman to start with, his arms encumbered by the rope, he had not the shadow of a chance, and at the end of a brief struggle he rose, a bound and battered prisoner, grasped on either side by one of the stalwart crew.

Worse still, as the press cleared away from about him, he saw a bedraggled figure hauled over the bulwark by a dozen solicitous hands. It was Topiltzen, and though he promptly subsided on the deck, he was unquestionably alive.

IN THE MIDST OF DEFEAT, Boots grinned. He knew from personal experience that the master priest had at least endured a punishment he would not forget in a hurry.

And just at that moment, while the attention of all was focused on the prisoner, and on the limp and furious Topiltzen, there came one long, splintering crash.

Every oar in the starboard bank smashed to flinders, as the galley of the Feathered Serpent plowed ruthlessly alongside.

Nacoc-Yaotl's followers turned to meet the rush of a wave of silent assailants. They came leaping across the bulwark, leaving the serpent-headed craft to drift or stay as it might, and fell upon the startled defenders so suddenly that the latter were almost driven over the side in a body. Two or three did go over, but no one was bothering to offer a rescue then.

Battle swept up and down the galley, among the rowers' seats, in the open way between them; an indiscriminate whirl of interlocked limbs, flying plumes, and fierce white faces.

Boots' two guards were lost in the mêlée, and he made frantic efforts to break his bonds. Though unable to distinguish attackers from attacked, it was a most glorious shindy, and he longed to plunge into it.

But for once in his life he found he must watch a fight and take no part in it. In despair of freedom, he at last resigned himself to look on in silent admiration.

Silent! It suddenly struck him that here was the most remarkable battle ever fought. They were all silent. Save for the thud of blows, the crash of broken boat seats, or an occasional splash when some unfortunate descended into the spirit of Tonathiu, there was not a sound.

No yells, no groans, no battle-cries. And no weapons, either. It was hand to throat and fist to body, with never a sword or spear to grace it.

But they were men, the Tlapallans! Surrender was not in them. Until hammered into insensibility, or driven over the side, they would fight, and since both galleys had carried about the same complement, and they equally matched in sinew and stubbornness, the combat promised an indefinite duration.

And so it might have been, save for an unexpected intervention from without.

Up over the stern they came, white, stark, and terrible. They wore no plumes, those six. Their height required no headdress to increase it.

Towering head and shoulders above the tallest fighter there, the galley warriors were as children before them.

Some, blind with rage, attempted to face that mighty onset, but the majority knew better. When the giant Guardians of the Hills took the field, lesser men stood out of their path or perished.

In this case short work was made of the resisters. Where a man was struck down, there he lay, and in a very few minutes peace reigned aboard the galley of Nacoc-Yaotl.

Then, and not till then, Boots remembered the girl. In the press of exciting events she had clean slipped from his mind, and when with a start of self-reproach he at last turned to look for her, the canoe was gone.

Moreover he discovered that the battle had been by no means without spectators. Very much as in more ordinary cities the crowds will gather to watch a fight, so the lake craft had swarmed in, until the contending galleys were almost entirely surrounded.

They were very quiet about it, though. There was something almost stealthy in the silent, eager, curiosity of those innumerable faces that thronged the decks and peered from every available vantage point.

In that still water, the serpent galley had drifted only a few feet from her victim, and by the time Boots' attention returned to them most of her crew who were able had sprung lightly back aboard.

The six gigantic peacemakers were advancing toward the quarterdeck, followed by a limping and disheveled crowd, and among them were three figures which Boots immediately recognized.

The group which presently gathered about the Irishman was a curiously assorted one.

There was Topiltzen, still a survivor, but one mass of cuts and bruises and with none of his finery left save the white-and-black emblem.

There were six white giants of proportions which Boots could only view with envious admiration.

There was the moth-girl, who with two of the others had come aboard in the peacemakers' wake. She had picked her way daintily through the wreckage, and now beamed upon her red-haired protégé from the arm of a tall, stern young man, whose head-dress of a crested serpent proclaimed him one of the invaders.

There was also Svend Biornson, his neat modern clothes giving a touch of the theatrical to all the rest; and last there was the gentleman who had returned into Nacoc-Yaotl's temple for dread of the white lake.

Coatless, shirt half torn off, and his arms bound behind him, Archer Kennedy looked as if he had been through the wars himself. But his spirit seemed to have suffered the worst shock. His lips twitched continually, his whole body shook in spasms of trembling like a nervous horse, and he met Boots' half-amused, half-resigned: "You, too, Mr. Kennedy!" with a blank, unrecognizing stare.

"Well," began Biornson, his marred face grim and angry. "I see that you have recovered from your wounds enough to be about, O'Hara."

"I've had the evening of me life! Did you find Xolotl?"

"We did," was the stern retort. But before he could say more, the wreck which had been Topiltzen broke in with a torrent of low-voiced accusation. At least, Boots judged it to be accusation, though to him it was no more intelligible than the scolding of an angry sparrow.

Presently he said something that the Moth-Girl appeared to resent. With flushed cheeks and flashing eyes, she broke into the stream with a few remarks of her own; the young man beside her took it up, and they all talked at once with the energy and indifference to polite usage common among very angry people the world over.

The only word Boots understood was "Xolotl," and, that was tossed from mouth to mouth with significant frequency.

BIORNSON BEGAN CUTTING IN WITH placative intent, but his sole success was in diverting a large share of the indignation to himself. At last, as he threw up his hands in despair, one of the six giants who had been grinning in the background with distinctly human amusement, strode forward and uttered a curt sentence.

Argument ceased. Even Topiltzen, who, red with fury, had been shaking his fist in Biornson's very face, subsided instantly. As an arbiter, Boots thought the giant admirably successful, but Biornson did not seem to share the opinion. He turned away with an air of dejection which flared into bitterness as he came face to face with the Irishman.

"*You* are responsible for this!" he accused. "In two hours, O'Hara, you have wrecked the consummation of five years of faithful effort!"

"Why, Mr. Biornson, what harm did I do?" protested Boots. "The jailer-lad wasn't hurt to speak of, except maybe in his feelings, and as for the little lady, we only took a bit of a ride on the lake. You can ask herself—"

"I don't need to ask herself. If civil war is the result of tonight's work, you are the one primarily responsible. Quetzalcoatl rules the lake; Nacoc-Yaotl, the surrounding shores. There has always been an undercurrent of rivalry and hard feeling. Why, in past years the guardians, who are chosen from all the gilds and are neutral by oath, have shed more blood policing Tlapallan than in keeping the hills free of invasion.

"For years I have been trying to patch up the quarrel. I thought that I had succeeded, when the Gild of Quetzalcoatl consented that the daughter of their master priest should marry the son of Topiltzen, priest of Nacoc-Yaotl. But naturally, when she appeared on the lake with a stranger who wore Xolotl's garments of honor, Topiltzen was wild.

"Wasn't it enough for you to half-kill the boy, without disgracing him? He swears he will never show his face on the lake again! And to crown the insult you dropped his father overboard, and for reasons best known to herself the young lady signaled a galley of Quetzalcoatl to offer you a violent rescue. Now she declares her intention to marry my lord Maxatla, the captain of that galley, and Topiltzen is willing that she should.

"He says that Xolotl has been dishonored, and no child of his shall ever mate with a daughter of the Feathered Serpent. He says that reconciliation is impossible, and I very much fear he is right. That is the sum total of your evening's pleasure, young man, and I hope you are satisfied with it!"

Boots, who was trying to look properly overcome, just then caught the Moth-Girl's eye. There was a twinkle in it that he found irresistible.

"Yes, grin!" Biornson's exasperation was complete. "Trust an Irishman to think civil war delightfully amusing! confound you! I might have known by the color of your hair—"

"But Mr. Biornson—"

Boots stopped. A certain lovely young trouble-maker had used him ruthlessly for her own ends, and he was not too stupid to see it. He rather suspected that this sudden affair with "my lord Maxatla" was not half so sudden at it seemed. That careless offer of hers to marry Boots—perhaps—had been mere bait to keep interested one in whom she foresaw a glorious *casus belli* with her loathed fiancé's entire gild.

Well, she had got her wish—and her love as well, for Maxatla did not look the man to give up his sweetheart lightly, once promised.

But Boots could not defend himself on those lines. The inbred chivalry of him forbade it.

"You saved my life," snapped Biornson, as if that were an added grievance. "I tried to help you in return, but this night's work is too much. You and Kennedy are a pair. You are both forfeit to Nacoc-Yaotl—he because he was caught prying into the most sacred of mysteries, you for offering violence to the body of Topiltzen. Let them take you! My intervention is finished."

A gleam of satisfaction came into the master-priest's small eyes, but the Moth-Girl whispered a word to her young captain. He nodded, then with a slight bow to the guardians came forward and laid a hand on the bound Irishman's shoulder.

"My lord Svend," he said with stern dignity, "I believe that the Feathered Serpent is still supreme in Tlapallan. I claim this man in his name. He was wrongfully made prisoner while defending a daughter of Quetzalcoatl from the insults and violence of those who have no place on these waters save by tolerance. Under their oath to uphold the law, I call upon the guardians to support my intention. This man is Quetzalcoatl's. Let any son of Nacoc-Yaotl lay hand on him at his peril!"

Biornson frowned, but anxiety again had the upper hand of irritation. It had not been revealed to Boots exactly what position the man held in this unusual community, where the most common passions and rivalries of the human race were enacted against a background so weird and strange that it seemed only to be accounted for on a basis of the supernatural. But whatever his influence, it was sufficient in this case to avert the hostilities which Maxatla's challenge had threatened to reopen.

"Lord Maxatla," he answered, "no man has a higher respect for the Feathered Serpent than I. I spoke too hastily out of anger, but this is not a matter to be settled here. Will it satisfy you if both prisoners are held, and their cases decided before the council of gilds, as was first intended?"

"Held in the power of Nacoc-Yaotl?" demanded the other scornfully. "No!"

"Held in personal charge by the guardians," substituted Biornson patiently. "They will do this thing, I believe, for the sake of peace in Tlapallan."

"You are right, my lord Svend." The giant who had spoken before pushed Maxatla gently but firmly aside and laid his own enormous hand on Boots. "This is for the council to decide. We, Guardians of the Hills, and Keepers of the Peace of Tlapallan, take these two prisoners in our keeping. Do I speak well, my brothers?"

"You speak well," confirmed his five companions, and their voices, soft and murmurous as the night-wind, carried a decision that no man there dared question.

IN A FOLD OF THE hills, a dim, twilight valley, where the verdure grew scant and starved between scattered boulders, a group of men had halted.

Though the sky was black above, the valley was grayly visible in what seemed a perpetual and never-growing dawn. It was the light of invisible Tlapallan, reflected and diffused from the rocks at the valley's entrance.

Scarcely an hour had elapsed since the prisoners passed into the guardians' charge. Carried ashore in the latter's low black boat, instead of being escorted to another prison, they were brought here. After disembarking, the whole company turned their faces to the hills, and only halted again when shut from the glittering lake by the walls of this desolate valley.

There was a foreboding of secret evil in the manner of all their keepers.

By Biornson's first words, the suspicion was no idle one.

"You saved my life, O'Hara, but I would rather have died than seen this feud reopened. You think it a light matter. A few lives lost, perhaps, and a few heads broken—the sort of riot-play you Irish delight in. But Donnybrook Fair is not so far from Tlapallan as the ways of its people from your ways.

"Nacoc-Yaotl has horrors in command beyond all thinking by one who has not seen his power. The Feathered Serpent will fight fire with fire, and even the lesser gilds control forces that, if turned loose on the world, might almost wreck civilization. Only the delicate counterbalance of power and certain religious traditions have kept Tlapallan from long ago destroying itself. But I know that Nacoc-Yaotl grows restive—

"Nacoc-Yaotl," continued Biornson in a changed voice, "would dwell in peace with the other gods, and to drive him into anger is folly. Therefore you, O'Hara, must leave Tlapallan. Quetzalcoatl has no possible claim on your mate, and the council will give him up to the priests whose mysteries he has pried into. But over you there would surely be fighting. Young Maxatla stands high in our gild, and having once claimed you he will never draw back. So you must—escape tonight, friend O'Hara.

"Will you believe me when I say that to save these adopted people of mine—and to prevent another possible thing I can't speak of—I would condemn myself as readily as you?

"You will be taken blindfold far out into the desert, left so bound that by effort you may free yourself, and the rest—will be between you and the drifting sands."

"Food and drink?"

"If you can find them. Goodby, O'Hara, and though you won't believe it—I am sorry."

"Goodby," said Boots curtly, and as he felt himself gripped by two of his warders, he turned to go without another word of farewell.

But at that Kennedy came to life with a sudden vain leap against the hands that instantly restrained him. Struggling desperately, he called after his mate as he had called in the desert, his voice like a wailing cry:

"Don't leave me, Boots! Don't leave me with these fiends! If you leave me it will be worse than murder—worse, do you understand? I will tell you what I saw—I will tell you—"

The cry died as a heavy hand closed over his mouth, and he could only watch with agonized eyes as his mate was led helplessly away.

X

The First Visitation

C liona, my dear, 'tis a quaint-looking present I've brought you, but they do say it's worth a power of money for its rarity. The value I put on it, though, is another sort. There's a tale behind it so wild I'd not tell it to even you, little sister, lest you think me a liar of outrageous imaginations."

Colin O'Hara passed his fingers reflectively over the polished bit of colored porcelain in his hand. Fifteen years had elapsed since first he set eyes on it, when his trail-mate had lifted it down from the bracket in Biornson's hacienda.

Those years had left no mark on the porcelain godling but they had wrought their inevitable changes in the man. The face that at twenty was broadly good-humored was good-humored still. But the blurred lines of youth had set to a deeper firmness, the lips could be stern as well as smiling, and the light-blue, kindly eyes were capable of flaring into anger as intolerant as was promised by the red thatch of hair above them. In both size and appearance the contrast between the man and the girl he had just addressed was striking to the point of absurdity.

Colin's height missed the seven-foot mark by a bare four inches, while Cliona O'Hara Rhodes, his young married sister, measured no more than five feet five. Her raven's-wing hair shadowed eyes that were wonderfully blue; from beneath straight, fine brows the lashes curved thick and long, and her skin had the tint of one of those small seashells that are like smooth, new ivory shading a to a center so delicate that to call it pink is almost desecration—say, rather, angel-color.

Yet a resemblance to her brother might have been traced in the girl's generous forehead, the carriage of her head, and certain inbred mannerisms of speech and gesture.

Since the death of her parents, when Cliona was a very small child, this huge, rugged man had been her whole family and sole guardian. Many of those years he had spent world-wandering; yet he had ever kept in touch with his little sister, given her a convent education, and to this day she had all the love of his great, affectionate heart.

Now they sat together on a stone bench in the gardens that surrounded her bungalow home at Carpentier, a small suburb just within the wide-flung boundary line of a city in the eastern part of the United States.

As he fell silent she tapped an impatient foot on the gravel path.

"Had I guessed where you were off to when you left me six months ago, Colin, I should have kept you here or gone after you!"

"Ah, now," he protested, "am I not back safe and sound? 'Twas for that very reason I said nothing of it. With you just married and all, would I be spoiling your honeymoon with anxieties? Not that the danger was worth speaking of, but I guessed how you'd fret. And this journey was one I've had in the back of my head a-many years. Always there's been one thing or another risen to prevent. It seemed like fate was set against in ever learning the truth of the matter, and now—now I'm less sure than before I went if 'twas all a dream and a fevered vision or a sober reality!"

"Tell me the story." Cliona took the porcelain Quetzalcoatl in her hands and examined it curiously. Though about it there was an indefinable look of age, its unglazed, polished enamel might have left the potter's hands but yesterday. From the delicately indicated embroidery of the tunic to the minute scaling of the serpent-headed staff it held, it was an exquisite bit of craftsmanship. The flat, benignant face eyed her with a kind of patient stoicism that brought a smile to Cliona's lips.

"Poor little idol-man!" she said whimsically. "Are all your worshipers dead and gone? Tell me the story, Colin."

"If I do, you'll neither repeat it to another nor think it a fabrication?"

"Colin!"

"I know, but when I've finished you may 'Colin' me in another tone, my dear! It strains my own belief to think of it, and I'm not sure—not sure at all—to go back and find naught but a lake so deep there was no fathoming it; to find but the ruins of the hacienda, and they so overgrown one could scarce identify them, and only certain scars I bear to this day and the bit of image you hold in your hands as an evidence that 'twas not quite all a delusion! They and the name of Svend Biornson.

"*He* was once living, for I looked up the history of him. Sometimes I do think that I was sickening for the fever when we came to that valley; that poor Kennedy died of it there in the Norseman's house, and myself

FRANCIS STEVENS

escaped Biornson's care to stray back to the desert, naked and raving, as I was, when some friendly Mayas found me and took me to their village.

"'Twas many a week before I was a man again, and then I was in the hospital at Vera Cruz. I'd never have known how I got there had not Richards, the American ornithologist who brought me in with his party, left word with the hospital authorities before he took ship for home.

And I had no money and no friends. I worked in the streets at cleaning and the like to keep body and soul together, and was so ate up with worry for you, who was but a babe and me with naught but an empty blessing to send those who had care of you, that I nigh went crazy before I got a paying job.

"Could I go back then, I ask you? I never left a mate in trouble before nor since, but poor Kennedy; may the saints have helped him, must have been a dead man long before I was on me feet again! That is, if the heft of it happened at all. Like a dream it was to me—and yet with a differ betwixt it and the dreams of the delirium. 'Twas all so clear and bright-colored and—and *bright* like. The little man in your hands is no clearer to your eyes than was the sight of Tlapallan to mine."

"Tlapallan?"

"Tlapallan! Ah, you strange, bright city, do you really lie ruined at the bottom of that black lake—or were you the fancy of a fever?"

"Colin, that's no way at all to tell a story! Begin at the first, not the last. Now who was this Svend Biornson—and who was Kennedy?"

"For the last, a man I picked up, in Campeche, on the Gulf. The both of us were on the gold trail. At least, I thought I was ready for it, though I was a raw, green boy then—all this happened a matter of fifteen years ago, you must understand. I knew little then of the tricks of that hunt, and the half of what I knew being false information.

"But this Mr. Kennedy, he was a man of fine education, and with some dozen years the better of me in age and experience. He was wanting a mate for a desperate hard trip, with the yellow stuff to be picked up off the ground, so he said at the end of it—be off there, Snookums, dog! You've untied my shoe-lace again!"

He paused to kick very gently at Cliona's bull-pup which retaliated by dashing upon the other shoe with great enthusiasm. Cliona caught the pup in her arms and gave him an admonitory pat.

As she set him down again the puppy tore off up the path to fling himself recklessly against the legs of a young man advancing along it. The newcomer swept Cliona into his arms with an abandoned disregard for O'Hara's presence, which caused that gentleman to frown disapprovingly.

"Tony, my lad, I can see you've no more idea of the behavior of a dignified husband than you had when I left ye!"

Anthony Rhodes released his wife, and turned a delighted countenance to her brother.

"When Cliona phoned me I dropped everything and made for the train!" His hand met Colin's in a long, friendly pressure. "We thought you had dropped clean off the earth, old man, till we had that postal from Texas."

On this afternoon in June luncheon was served in the glass and screen enclosed veranda, a place of yellow light and many comfortable chairs. Thence one could look out to a prospect of green lawns, flowering bushes, and between the trees, down and across Llewellyn Creek to delectable vistas, part forest, part open meadows beyond.

The bungalow itself stood on the crest of a hill, and was so surrounded by trees that only in winter could one hope for any general view of its outer architecture.

"Cliona," said Rhodes while they lingered over the coffee cups, "would you and Colin care for a trip to the capital tomorrow?"

He had given up trying to extract any satisfactory account of his brother-in-law's recent journeyings, and, surmising that he might have some good reason for reticence, had good-naturedly dropped the subject.

"I am to have a talk with Senator Dobson in connection with a new insurance law he is pushing through in the special session. He has promised me an interview as representative of my firm and several others. It's a business trip, of course, but when I heard Colin was back I thought we might run over in the car, all three of us, and make a sort of pleasure-jaunt of it."

His wife hesitated, then shook her head.

"Do you and Colin go. Later I'll drive with you all you please, but I've had enough of chasing the moon for awhile, and my house is not yet in order."

They would start the following morning. Colin's luggage had been brought up from the station, and while Cliona insisted on personally packing her two men's suitcases, the men in question sallied forth to give the car a thorough overhauling, dubiously assisted by David, man-of-all-work.

And so Colin's story remained untold, and the afternoon which Cliona had planned to drain with her returned wanderer like a cup of sunshine and summery wine was wasted after the commonplace way of the unforeseeing human kind.

How could she know that this was the last such cup this place would offer her, or guess the dark, strange cloud that was so soon to overshadow their pleasant bungalow home?

IT WAS 3 P.M. OF the day following when Mary, the trim and obliging maid whom Cliona justly regarded as "a treasure," approached that young housewife with the unmistakable air of one about to ask a favor.

"Please, Mrs. Rhodes, are you havin' any company this evening?"

"I am expecting none. Why do you ask?"

"You promised I might go spend the night with me sister in Chester some day this week, ma'am, and, seein' as Mr. Rhodes and Mr. OHara is both away an' you not doin' no entertainin like, I thought—"

"That this would a good time for your visit? You may go, Mary, but try and be back tomorrow afternoon. I'll be needing your help then in work I have planned."

"Yes'm. I'll certain sure be here by lunch time—and thank you, ma'am."

Cliona smiled after the maid's retreating figure. The girl had been with them since they had come to live in the bungalow, and this was the first favor she had asked.

Rhodes and Colin had departed early that morning, but the voluntarily deserted one had kept herself too busy to think much of how lonely she was going to be for practically the first time since her marriage. True, she might phone in to the city and persuade one or another of her women friends to come out and spend a night at the bungalow, but this she hardly expected to do. With books and fancy work she believed the evening would pass pleasantly enough.

The maid's defection, however, was followed an hour later by a more serious interruption to household affairs. The phone rang and a woman's voice asked for Mr. David King. Cliona sent the cook to look for David, who, besides being gardener and garage-man was, *ex officio*, the cook's husband. A few minutes later he was at the telephone, from which he turned with a very white face.

"What is it, David? Has anything happened?"

"Mrs. Rhodes—" The man stopped, took a deep breath and continued. "It's my son, George. That—that woman on the phone is a nurse at the City Hospital, ma'am. He has fell off a pole, and—he's bad hurt she says—"

He was interrupted by a scream, as Marjory, the cook, fairly flung her husband aside and grasped at the receiver; but the other party had hung up.

Cliona had intervened.

"Never mind the phone. David, get your hat. You've just three minutes to catch the four-fifteen—there's the whistle now! Run, David! Marjory, you may take the next train if you like."

For she well knew how dear to the couple was their son, who was a hard-working young wireman in the employ of an electrical contractor.

David did run and caught the train, for the Carpentier station was almost at the foot of the hill which the bungalow crowned. Then Cliona had her hands full in offering what solace she might to her stricken cook.

There was another train at six, and in the meantime David called up, urging his wife to take it and come. He was alarmingly indefinite, but the very fact that the hospital authorities had suggested that the boy's mother be sent for told its own story.

Marjory King, good soul, able to consider another even in the midst of grief, urged her young mistress to accompany her and spend the night in town. The bungalow was too lonely. But Cliona hurried her off, assuring her that if she felt in the least nervous she could go and beg the hospitality of a neighbor. As a matter of fact, being as yet only slightly acquainted in the locality, she intended doing nothing of the sort.

Left alone, she reflected for a time on the sadness of losing an only son, thanked her stars in innocent selfishness that the hurt man was neither her husband nor brother, and proceeded to get her own supper.

By the time the dishes were cleared away and washed it was after eight and quite dark. Having first turned on all the lights in the front of the house, Cliona seated herself in the living-room beside Rhodes' own particular table with its brown-shaded reading lamp, and took up the knitting on which she was then engaged.

The living room was itself of a comforting and companionable appearance. Even alone in it, Cliona had a pleasant sense that its walls offered a sort of conscious protection.

Not that she was really nervous, but this was her first experience of that queer feeling of emptiness that pervades a house at night when deserted by all its customary occupants except one. And the bungalow was entirely isolated, in a practical sense, standing as it did among trees at the summit of a quite high hill. Until one came close to it, it could not even be seen.

About ten o'clock she rose, put away her work, and went through the house making sure that doors and windows were secure and the burglar-alarm system, so far as she could determine, properly set.

Outside the night was very still, frosted white by the radiance of a brilliant moon.

On an impulse she passed through the enclosed veranda, opened the door and stepped out. The air was pleasant, neither cold nor warm, and scented with the breath of flowers.

Slowly she walked around the house, Snookums, her bulldog, bouncing and wriggling before her. In the black shade of the trees the dog was a white shadow, but in the general paleness where the moon struck full he seemed almost to disappear. Indeed, it was as if only the ink-black shadows preserved the world from melting into invisibility. The open meadows overlooked by the hill were pale, wide pools of light.

On the path beneath Cliona's feet the moon, peering through foliage, wrought embroideries of black and white more intricate than any needle had ever traced.

The night was absolutely still—so still that the gentle ripple of water reached her ears from Llewellyn Creek, flowing past the foot of the hill.

Presently a little wind came and shook the branches over Cliona's head with a sound strangely startling and mysterious, like feet running through the night far away.

It is true that there was a great peace upon the world, but it was a peace too coldly colored for Cliona's lonely ease. There was nothing human in it. When she presently returned into the bungalow, she was glad of its friendly walls and kindly rooms.

Having put Snookums in the kitchen and half reluctantly turned out the lights, she retired to her bedroom which, with three others, opened directly off the living-room. The servants' empty quarters were located in a small wing leading by a passage to the kitchen.

Shutting and locking her door, she began to brush her hair. And then at last the loneliness that had been creeping up on her all evening made its final spring. Cliona stopped suddenly, brush poised in the. air. What if—what if—

"Well, what if what?" she demanded aloud, staring at her mirrored reflection as if expecting a reply. "Cliona O'Hara Rhodes, shame upon you for a little, sniveling coward! What is it you're afraid of? Tell me that now."

The reflection looked back with big, indignant eyes. But the indignation was a sham, roused there to hide a less comfortable emotion, and well she knew it.

Unlocking her door, she went to the kitchen and called Snookums, who bounded joyfully from his basket in the corner and dashed ahead of her. On returning through the living-room, Cliona caught up a small, brightly colored object in passing, and with a whimsical smile set it beside Rhodes' automatic pistol on the table by her bed. Let it represent the giver, in whose protecting strength she had such perfect faith.

So the eyes of that little "heathen god" Quetzalcoatl, lord of the air, looked benignantly on as Cliona said her orisons before the shrine of another faith.

Snookums had been "put to bed" on the rug, but once his mistress had definitely retired he improved on the arrangement by jumping on the bed itself and curling up over her feet. Twice she put him off, then yielded to the pup's particular form of bulldog tenacity and let him remain.

The house was very empty—she could feel it even through her closed door—and the warmth of the small, live body through the sheet was comforting. Because she knew her nervousness to be mere folly, Cliona drifted off to sleep at last.

And all outdoors was drenched in its pallid moon bath.

At the foot of the hill Llewellyn Creek ran ripples of ebony and white fire, and where at one point there was a wide slope of treeless lawn, it was as if the turf were powdered with snow.

The natural voice of the creek became merged with a distant splashing. That second sound grew louder—nearer. Presently from the little stream something came out and up—something almost invisible in that false lucidity of moonlight.

Crossing the unshaded turf it was a vague largeness, wallowing clumsily upward. In the black shade of the trees it was a white shadow—a white, frightful shadow, too terrible for the right to existence, even in a bad dream.

Cliona's sleep was untroubled by dreams, bad or good, but from it she was awakened by a frantic sound of barking, and realized that Snookums was bouncing about on the bed like a pup gone mad. He was tugging at the sheet with his teeth, and making racket enough for a dog twice his size.

Roused to that temporary superwakefulness which follows such a nightalarm, Cliona sat up. There was in her mind a notion, too, that the pup's barking had been preceded by some other and far different sound.

As his mistress roused, Snookums bounded off the bed, rushed to the door and scratched furiously at the crack beneath it, as if trying to dig under it through the floor. To Cliona but one explanation occurred. Someone had broken into the house, and for a ten months' pup Snookums was proving himself a pre good watchdog.

Cliona snapped on the electric light, picked up the pistol and— hesitated She was no coward, but neither was she rashly indiscreet. To unlock that door at which the pup was still tearing would be to place herself in the power of whatever night prowler had entered.

If the dog's yapping ha not scared the supposititious burglar from the premises, then he would be a burglar on guard, and probably a burglar at least as well-armed as herself.

All their genuine plate and most of Cliona s jewelry were safe in the city. Was it worth while, would Tony thank her, to expose her own person to unknown danger in order to protect what valuables were in the bungalow?

Abruptly she received notice that an intruder was really present, and that he had been by no means frightened to the extent of leaving.

As has been said, four bedrooms, of which Cliona's was one, opened upon the living-room, and between that and the dining-room was an open archway hung with portieres. After clearing away her supper dishes, Cliona had set the table for breakfast.

Now she heard a great crash and jingle, as if someone had deliberately tipped up the heavy dining-table, allowing silver and dishes to slide to the floor. The bang of its mahogany legs as it fell back confirmed the supposition.

With all her heart she wished that there had been a branch telephone in her bedroom, but there was not. To phone she must go outside her door.

It sounded to her as if every piece of furniture in the dining-room was being violently flung from one side of the room to the other. Now the intruder's attentions had been advanced to the living-room. She heard a smash and tinkle that told of the destruction of the brown-shaded reading-lamp of which her husband was so fond.

She was trembling, not so much with fear as because of her inability to cope with the situation. Her ears conveyed warning that the inside of their dear bungalow was being literally wrecked; yet she still hesitated at opening the door and trying to stop the destructive work.

Then Cliona became conscious of a new thing. It was an odor, and every moment it was growing stronger—a penetrating, almost overpowering smell of musk.

Something whimpered about her feet. Looking down she saw Snookums writhing there in agonies of puppyish supplication. He was the valiant watch-dog no more, for his nose informed him of a terror unfit for his tender years to meet.

The intruder's noisy operations had ceased at last. Cliona had a moment's wild hope that he might have smashed his way clear outside, but it was a hope quickly dissipated. Something was being dragged now, or was dragging itself, across the floor of the living-room. It reached her door and paused.

She crept into bed and sat with the covers pulled up, eyes fixed on the door in an agony of anticipation. There followed a snuffing noise, much the same as Snookums had been making, only louder. Then something reared up and came rasping down the whole length of the door and she could hear the wood follow in great splinters.

Snookums squealed like a young pig and scuttled abjectly beneath the bed.

"Get away from that door or I'll fire!"

Cliona's voice was so hoarse that she scarcely knew it for her own. She had the pistol beside her.

The only reply was a sort of snort through the keyhole, and the knob was violently shaken. The rattling was accompanied by a low snarling sound of bestial rage, as if something were chewing at the knob and resented its hardness and refusal to part from the door.

The odor of musk became nauseating. A moment later the claws rasped down the door again. This time Cliona knew beyond chance of doubt that they were claws, no less.

In one place, where the wood was thinnest between panels, it was pushed out in a long splinter and for a single instant one great, whitish talon gleamed through, curved, needle-pointed, appalling in its vicious menace.

And at that sight Cliona for the first time really lost her head. What she should have done was to climb out the window, an easy thing since it was only a matter of a few feet above the ground, run down the hill and raise an alarm in Carpentier. That might have been course had the burglar turned out to be a burglar.

But this—this *thing* of the midnight that thrashed snarled and ripped clean through a door with its pale, enormous claw—it had robbed her of capacity to think or reason.

She screamed, jumped out of bed, and raised Rhodes' pistol. Without taking aim she loosed its ten shots in the general direction of the door.

The crashing rattle of the automatic was drowned in the tumult that answered from without. Shrieks like the scream of a mad stallion, and a furious thrashing against the weakened door mingled with the splintering sounds of wood ripped up by chisel talons.

The gun was empty. Cliona saw the door bulging inward, and she did what many a woman would have done nearer the beginning—fainted and dropped to the floor, a pathetic heap of pretty silk and soft, dark hair, one white arm flung out with fingers extended, as if grasping again at the useless pistol they had just released.

PART II

XI

The Red-Black Trail

A deep swoon is the anesthetic that Mother Nature offers her children when horror or pain becomes too great for bearing. Cliona's faint of terror passed into natural sleep, and when she at last opened her eyes the goblin-be-friendly moon had been ousted by the honest sun, and the room was yellow-bright with reflected light from a morning all cheer and sunshine.

She became aware that a small tongue was licking at her face, and that someone was pounding lustily on the locked door. For a moment her brain refused any explanation of why she should be crouching there on the rug, with a joyful puppy wriggling beside her.

"Mrs. Rhodes! Mrs. Rhodes, ma'am! Oh, my God, are you killed?"

The veil lifted from Cliona's memory, and shaking off Snookums she struggled to rise ** in doing so, one hand fell on some hard, irregular object, and looking she saw that it was the bright-colored image that had been brought her from Mexico. In her fall she must have brushed it from the table.

The godling's flat face smiled up as benignly as ever, but the serpent-headed crook it had grasped was gone. Only a thin fragment of porcelain standing out on either side of the clenched fist showed where the staff had been broken off.

In a dull, detached way Cliona regretted this damage to Colin's gift. She even thought of searching for the shattered pieces, with an idea that they might be cemented together again.

But the hammering on the door was too insistent. Staggering up, she went to unlock it.

By the condition of that door the events of the night had been no dream. The lock and one hinge held it partly shut, but the upper hinge had been torn out, splitting a long piece off the jamb; the door itself was split half-way down from the top, and—yes, there was the very place where the white claw had pierced through, and the round, neat holes drilled by her bullets.

Cliona had time to observe these things, for at first the key refused to turn. Finally, however, the strained lock yielded and with some trouble she got the door open.

There stood Marjory King, gasping with terror and anxiety. As soon as Cliona could entangle herself from the large embrace in which she was received, she stepped past, took one look about the living-room, and sat down with a gasp on the side of an overturned chair.

As might have been expected, the place was no more than a spoiled wreck of the cozy, homelike room she had left the night before. But the disorder and breakage were by no means all.

On the floor just outside her room was a great pool of black, half coagulated blood, and from that pool a line of similiar dark blotches led through the arch into the dining-room.

Cliona could not conceive how any creature that had bled so profusely could have lived even to drag itself from sight. The outer side of her door was literally ripped to flinders, and the door itself gashed and torn as though some mad carpenter had been at work there. The furniture was all upset, and most of it hopelessly smashed.

"Mrs. Rhodes," questioned Marjory, "who was here last night?"

Cliona shook her head. It ached, and she felt very dull and stupid. That odor of musk still permeated the air, though faintly.

"I don't know. Snookums, come here!"

The pup had emerged from the bedroom and was sniffing cautiously at the horrible, blackening stuff on the floor. He wore a very chastened expression, quite unlike his usual devil-may-care cocksureness. Cliona took him in her lap and looked wistfully at the cook.

"I wish I'd minded you and gone in to the city, Marjory. Tell me, have you looked about the place at all?"

"Indeed, no, Mrs. Rhodes. I had the key you give me and I come in through the front door and the veranda. Everything was right there, but when I seen this room, and when I seen that blood and that door, thinks I, 'Mrs. Rhodes has been murdered!'"

"It's the mercy of Heaven I wasn't," conceded Cliona simply. "Where is David?"

"At the station. They have a big crate down there that must be the sun-dial Mr. Rhodes was ordering. And they operated on our boy last night, ma'am, and they do say he'll get well, after all. But, oh, ma'am, if you should see him it would bring the tears to your eyes. So white, and—and—he knew me, ma'am—and—"

She was wiping her eyes with the black cotton gloves she carried, and Cliona realized that others than herself had been under a heavy strain the previous night, though of a different sort.

FRANCIS STEVENS

"Poor, poor Marjory!" she cried impulsively. "Forgive me, my dear, for a selfish, heedless little cat that I never asked you for the word of your son! Would you not like to return to the city that you may be near the poor lad?"

"No, indeed, ma'am!" Marjory swallowed her sobs with sudden heroism. "Leavin' you alone last night was bad enough in all conscience, though Lord knows what happened here. I'm sure you ain't told me nothing yet. But right by you I stick now till Mr. Rhodes and your brother gets back. My goodness, they'll be wild when they know!"

Cliona slipped on a kimono and slippers, started for the dining room. The cook followed Both women stepped carefully to avoid setting foot in the blood.

The dining-room was worse than the other, if possible, and still the trail led on, through the pantry, the kitchen, the summer-kitchen, and out the back door. That was clawed like Cliona's, and burst entirely from its fastenings so that it lay flat. She reflected that the crashing in of that door must have been the sound that was ringing through her brain when the dog awakened her in the night.

Over it the creature had evidently passed on its outward way, still shedding its gore with incredible generosity, out into the yard, past the garage, across green lawns, and down the hill, and still Cliona followed the ghastly trail.

She forgot that she was attired only in a nightgown, kimono and bedroom slippers. She was conscious of nothing but a horrible and growing curiosity as to what possible or impossible beast might lie at the trail's end.

That it was dead seemed certain. No known creature could shed such gallons of blood and live long. The bare fact that no known creature could shed such gallons of blood, whether it continued to live or no, had not yet become apparent to her mind. Her usually acute brain was fogged by terror and the nerve-strain of a shock whose full effects she was yet to feel.

Marjory knew it, however, with a certainty that was rapidly turning her mind to all the horrors of the supernatural. But her best efforts to induce her mistress to return to the house were vain. Cliona told the cook to go back if she pleased. For herself, she was going right along now until she found—it. At last the two women came to the foot of the hill and the boundary line of Rhodes' estate—Llewellyn Creek.

And there the trail ended in a muck of crimson-streaked mud, as if the creature had rolled and splashed therein the ultimate convulsions of death.

But of the creature itself there was no other sign.

The far bank was green, peaceful, undisturbed The trail simply ended in the creek-bed, and the little stream flowed happily along, sparkling and chuckling as though it could have told an astonishing thing or two, had it felt at all inclined.

It suddenly occurred to Cliona that she had stood staring blankly at the crimson mud for a long, long time. She turned dull, troubled eyes upon Marjory.

"Send—"

She stopped Her throat was oddly constricted, as by an agony of unfelt grief. Mentally she was conscious of no emotion, but she experienced that feeling which overtakes a fever patient, as though mind and body were wholly detached from one another, or connected only by threads of gossamer, and those threads swiftly breaking. Again she tried to speak:

"Send—Tony—"

Then the green and gold world swirled into blackness, and had Marjory not caught her she would have subsided into the brook. But the cook was a big, strong woman. Lifting Cliona like a child, she bore the small, unconscious form up the hill and into the house.

There was David, agape at the wreckage.

"Never mind staring!" she cried at him sharply. "Go back down the hill as fast as ever you can. Have a doctor here and phone in a telegram to Mr. Rhodes. You'll get him at the Hotel Metropole. I heard him tell that to this poor child yesterday. Tell him he's wanted at home as quick as he can get here. Move, now!"

David, though burning up with curiosity, deemed it wise to obey the keen urge in his wife's voice. He knew her for a capable woman, better able than he to meet emergencies, and as Marjory laid her burden gently on the bed she heard him go out of the door and down the steps in two long strides.

"Lord knows what will be the end of this," she muttered as she removed Cliona's slippers, "or what Mr. Rhodes will say or do when he comes home. It was the devil himself that was here last night, I'll swear to it. Not any creature that God ever made—no! The poor child! And her all alone here to meet it!"

FRANCIS STEVENS

"Come home quick," read the wire. "Mrs. Rhodes bad hurt—burglars or something. David B. King."

David was not a person of tact. His message had been kept within the ten words he knew to be a telegram's proper length, and it fairly covered the situation as he knew it. But it drove the unlucky recipients into torments of speculative dread.

The telegram was handed to Rhodes at the Hotel Metropole two hours after its receipt there, when the two men returned to the hotel for luncheon, and not bothering with the car, they caught the first fast express for home.

At Carpentier they dropped from the train while it was still moving and made straight for the hill.

To their amazement, as they ascended the winding, tree-shaded road, they began to pass people, men, women, and children. The road was private, and what they were doing here its owner could not conceive. Most of the faces seemed unfamiliar, and they were too many by far to be only the inhabitants of Carpentier.

Rhodes stopped to make no inquiries, though had he and Colin not been too preoccupied to buy a paper on the train, the head-lines would have offered an explanation.

It was then mid-afternoon. David had notified the central police-station early that morning, and the reporters had allowed no grass to grow under them nor waited for details. The bare story, as it stood, had been sufficient to attract every idle, horror-loving mortal who had the price of the half-hour's railroad journey to Carpentier.

Glancing back, Rhodes and O'Hara perceived that more chattering, curious folk, who had arrived on the same train with themselves, were following.

But the two asked no questions, even of each other. Shouldering their way through the throng, they at last reached the bungalow, only to be barred from its door by the blue-uniformed figure of a policeman on guard there.

"Get out of this!" His tone was that of an officer sorely tried. "Can't you reporter fellows get enough copy without tryin' to butt into the house itself? Mrs. Rhodes can't see nobody."

"She can see me," said Rhodes between his teeth "I am her husband. What has happened here?"

"Never mind what's happened," growled O'Hara. "We've years to find that out, and—Cliona may be wanting us!"

Rhodes obeyed his orders dumbly. He felt suddenly very ill, and as he passed through the veranda he had to support himself by grasping at the chairs.

Colin followed him into the living-room, where they received a vague impression of wrecked furniture, restored to some semblance of order or stacked in a corner, heaped over with a ruined pile of beautiful, blood-stained rugs.

But their real attention was focused on the strange lady in a white uniform who met them with raised brows and inquiring, hostile eyes. In the back of his mind Rhodes knew that none of this was real. This was some other man's home, not his. His home was a quiet, untroubled place, with Cliona waiting there to smile a welcome; with no throngs of strangers trampling its lawns, no police at the door, nor strange, white-capped women in uniform to meet him in a wrecked room stained with blood.

And through the thought he heard his own voice asking:

"For God's sake, what has happened to my wife?"

XII

The Opinion of Mr. MacClellan

The hostile look faded from the white-clad woman's eyes and her face brightened.

"Oh, are you Mr. Rhodes? And the lady's brother? I'm so glad you've come! Dr. Glynn is with her now, and I am sure he will permit you to see her at once, for she is still unconscious."—

Cliona was sunk in the depths of a deathlike coma in which she might remain for many hours; and to rouse her from it by the use of powerful restoratives would mean probable insanity, possible death. This was Dr. Glynn's verdict, and it was confirmed by the specialist called into consultation that evening at Glynn's request.

In the meantime Rhodes and Colin had learned all that could be known until Cliona's own story should be told—if that time were destined to come. They had talked with Marjory and David; they had followed the same grim trail that Cliona had traced, somewhat overtrodden now, to the deep disgust of both detectives and themselves. By this time the crowd had dispersed and the place was lonely again.

Cliona's men folks had returned, then, to talk over the wreckage of furniture, and the splintered doors and floor. The bullet-holes and the empty pistol formed a phase of the silent tale that Blake and MacClellan, the detectives, enlarged upon to the utmost.

MacClellan, the elder of the two plainclothesmen, was a large, stolid, matter-of-fact man, and he delivered his verdict in the tone of an ultimatum.

"Now then, the possibilities are these." He ticked them off on the stubby fingers of his left hand. "Number One, burglars. Nothing has been stolen, but that don't do away with the intent to steal. There may have been a gang of hoboes; and they may have got in a fight, torn up the place, knifed each other, and finally been scared off by the pistol.

"Number two, a lunatic. I say one lunatic, because that sort don't generally hunt in couples.

"Number three (and number three, I may as well tell you, is the number I'm banking on as the most probable and the one that fits best), that this whole business was done in the nature of a particularly horrid and vicious practical joke, carried out with elaborate care and directed not at Mrs. Rhodes, who they couldn't have known was alone here—"

"A joke, is it?" snarled O'Hara, eyeing the stolid detective with intense disgust. "A pretty joke it would be for a man to shed his blood by the bucketful and then vanish into thin air! Is it crazy you are?"

MacClellan flushed angrily.

"No, I ain't crazy. As for blood, how do you know all this red stuff is blood and not some kind of red paint or something?"

THE DETECTIVE CONTINUED, "I SENT a sample of it in to be analyzed, but I don't believe it is blood at all. Crazy? Why, what kind of man or animal do you think could spill that much blood, anyway? It would take an elephant with wings to get away afterward.

"A while ago, Mr. O'Hara, you suggested that some tiger or other wild beast might have escaped from a menagerie and broken its way in. There is nothing to bear that out except the claw marks, or rather the apparent claw marks. Anyway, the beast that could bleed like that would be too large to get in an ordinary doorway."

"You've the right of it there," conceded O'Hara regretfully, for he had taken an instinctive dislike to the man and his cocksure way of speaking. By the very look of him he was a man of no imagination, and the type had no appeal for Colin.

"You say," objected Rhodes, "that the brute would have needed wings to disappear so completely. Mightn't it have gone up of down the creek bed?"

"Blake and me followed the creek pretty nearly a mile in both directions. There wasn't a sign on either bank. How far do you think a beast bleeding like that could get? It ain't even worth while to put dogs on it, though of course if you say so we might try bloodhounds. It won't be a particle of good, though. Whoever done this was human, and with all the other tracks that's been tracked around here, the bloodhounds ain't born that could pick up the trail.

"I tell you, this job was done by some crazy fool or fools with a grudge against Mr. Rhodes here. Why didn't the burglar-alarm work?"

"I couldn't say," answered Rhodes. "The company who installed it must tell that."

"I know it. And when they do, you'll find it was put out of commission in some darned clever way. No beast could have done that, could they? Another thing, there ain't any tracks, except man tracks there. I'll admit that fool gardener of yours let the crowd tramp all over everything before we got here, though the chief warned him over the phone not to do that very thing.

"When we came in he was gassing away to a couple of reporters in the house. Spilling everything he'd ever known about the whole family and showing 'em a china image he said had been right in the room with Mrs. Rhodes when this thing happened, and got busted when she fell— as if that gave it the biggest kind of news value!

"The man's a fool! If he'd tended to business, instead of letting those reporters jolly him along, Blake and me would have had some show. But even with all the tramping, if the thing was an animal there ought to some trace left."

"There is," put in Rhodes quietly. "There is a broad track, trodden over as you say, but still evident."

"Where?"

"Before your eyes." Rhodes pointed at to turf in front of them.

The four men were standing where the trail left the macadamized drive and led off across the grass down the hill.

Blake leaned forward and stared keenly at the place Rhodes indicated. Then he rose with a shake of the head.

"I don't see anything."

"You don't? Why, the grass is laid flat in a long swat."

"Oh, that! I didn't know what you meant. That ain't tracks. Somebody's dragged something heavy over the ground."

"Sure," put in MacClellan scornfully. "I saw that long ago. That's what I mean when I say this is all the work of some vicious practical joker. Whatever tub or can or thing he used to hold all that red stuff, he dragged it after him as he went along."

"The marks on the doors?"

MacClellan shrugged "How do I know? A chisel, maybe. This fellow was clean bughouse, perhaps, with just the infernal cleverness and devilish sense of humor that some lunatics have. Or else it's a scheme of some sort in connection with something I don't know about."

He looked keenly from Rhodes to O'Hara, a flash of suspicion in his eyes. It was not the first hint he had given that he thought they were keeping something from him.

"Ah, now, don't start that again," snapped Colin. "You've already asked us every question in the world, man. What is it you think? That Tony here and myself ran home from the capital yesterday night and raised all this devilment just to destroy his house and the happiness of both of us?"

"Certainly not! What I am looking for and what you haven't helped me find, is the possible motive that lies behind. In our business—even you must know this—half the time to find the motive is to find the criminal. You ought to understand that, Mr. Rhodes, you being a lawyer."

"If I were the district attorney," observed that young man thoughtfully, "it might be worth while to review my record in search of some desperate criminal who had taken a vow of vengeance against me. But since my only cases have been in the civil courts, and those cases, I must admit, most obscure and unimportant ones, such a review seems hardly worth while."

He looked up with a faintly boyish smile.

"So far as I know, I haven't a personal enemy in the world!"

"Well," said the detective sulkily, "the analysis will show whether it's blood or not, and if you can't tell me anything else you—won't, that's all. Blake and I must be getting back to town."

"Sorry we can't help you out," said Rhodes stiffly.

"So am I. Well, I'll let you know what the analysis tells us about this stuff that's been spilled around here, and we'll keep right on the job till we get to the bottom of it. By the way, do you want me to send another man out to relieve Morgan for the night?"

Morgan was the officer still on guard at the front entrance. But Rhodes shook his head and O'Hara volunteered gloomily: "No need. The harm's done. They'll not come back, whoever they are—though by all the powers, 'tis the one wish of my soul that they might do just that!"

XIII

THE BUNGALOW SOLD

"Mr. O'Hara, is it really true that you are going down into South America to find a gold-mine?"

The speaker's sister, a tall, dignified girl, frowned slightly and wished again that she had left Alberta, better known as "Bert", at home. The child was nearly fifteen, but her frank curiosity was a trait for which her sorrowing family had yet to find means of restraint.

Colin, however, rather liked "Bert" Fanning, and he smiled upon her pleasantly enough.

"That's my intention. Though," he added whimsically "if I don't find it, 'twill not be the first mine I've dropped the gold into instead of taking it out."

"How could you drop it in a mine you couldn't find?" inquired Bert, the matter-of-fact.

"Ah, the mine you don't find is an Irish mine—a bit of a bull like that never troubles it at all!"

Everyone laughed, and O'Hara beamed, amiably at their appreciation.

Again he was seated on a stone bench in Cliona's garden. But the luxuriant growth of Virginia rambler that covered the arbor above him was blossomless and with reddening leaves, for the season was mid-September. Nor was this the hilltop garden at Carpentier.

A short distance off rose the gray walls and moss-colored roofs of Green Gables, the new home purchased by Rhodes when it became evident that his wife should be removed to other surroundings than the unlucky bungalow.

By the time that Cliona's condition permitted her to be moved, he had acquired this house in a suburb many miles from Carpentier and working together, he and Colin had labored to furnish it in as different a style from the bungalow as be could.

On this day, which heralded her return to the freedom of the outer world, Cliona was holding a sort of miniature court in the rose garden. Her throne, a great invalid's chair, gave her more than ever the look of a little girl, and the day being cool though sunny she was half buried in a fluffy tumble of blue-and-white wool wraps.

Comfortably cuddled on the foot-rest sound asleep, lay the only memento of her terrible experience for which she had ever expressed a desire—the bull-pup, Snookums.

For some minutes Cliona had been sunk in silent reflections. At last, breaking into her brother's conversation with Bert Fanning, she inquired irrelevantly:

"Have you heard anything lately from Mr. MacClellan, Colin?"

"I have not." He shrugged a trifle contemptuously.

"Has he dropped the case, then?"

"It's still in his hands."

"Those chaps are not an overly brilliant lot, are they?" put in young Stockton Repplier. He was a fresh-faced, intelligent-looking boy, a distant relative of old Elbert Marcus, another guest. "As I understand it, they simply ignored your story, Mrs. Rhodes, and went off on a blind lead. Now any reasonable person must concede that the thing was some sort of wild beast and not—"

The young man suddenly broke off and subsided, with a scared glance at his hostess. Rhodes had caught his eye.

But the invalid only laughed.

"Come round here, Tony—and don't alarm poor Mr. Repplier like that! I know the doctor has told you that I am not to talk of that night, but really, I'm long past the hysterical stage. I was foolish about it for a while, but not any more. Are you perfectly sure, Tony, that this Mr. Brandon is going to buy the bungalow?"

"Perfectly. I am to meet him tomorrow at the office of his lawyers to conclude the deal. In another twenty-four hours the last thread of connection will be severed between ourselves and poor Cousin Roberts' bungalow. Are you glad, Cliona?"

She pondered, as if not sure of her reply, then said slowly:

"Yes, I am glad. Forgive me, people, for bringing up so unpleasant a subject, but—you don't know how I think and think about it! And whenever the picture of the place rises in my mind, it is as if a horrible red shadow had been laid on the house.

"Don't laugh—had you been there that night you'd not even smile, Tony dear! I tell you there's a red, red shadow hangs over it—and there's a thing that waits and hides watching for us three to come back there. I couldn't bear that any one of us should walk under the edge of that red shadow again!"

FRANCIS STEVENS

She was sitting straight up in her chair, her eyes shining and her lately pale face burning with a dangerous color.

"I am sure," said old Mr. Marcus earnestly, "that it would be far better if you could put the whole affair out of your mind, Mrs. Rhodes."

"Yes," agreed Colin with elaborate carelessness, "the place is sold now, so Tony will have no business there. And for myself, there'll soon be a few thousand miles' curve of the earth betwixt me and Carpentier. You've no cause to fret any more, Cliona."

His sister regarded him with puzzled, troubled eyes. Slowly the color faded and she sank back wearily, still with her gaze fixed on him.

"You said you'd not leave till I was well again," she reminded, in the tone of one renewing some former discussion.

"Nor do I—the doctor himself told me yesterday that all danger is past and gone."

"And—and you said you would not go till you'd got at the true secret of all that happened!"

Sensing a certain strain in the atmosphere, the two Fanning girls and young Repplier drifted off into conversation with Marcus on a different subject.

"I showed you Finn's letter," Colin said. "A good man he is, Charley Finn. I learned him well in the Klondike. When he says he's on the trail of a big find, you may reckon on the weight of his word. And it doesn't seem we'll solve our mystery now."

"And so your foot to the stirrup and off you go!"

"But surely, Cliona, you'd not ask me to live my whole life out like a cat at a rat-hole, and maybe the rat dead or gone on his travels?"

"N-no—oh-no, Colin. If you really feel so about it, and as Mr. Finn is expecting you, in Buenos Aires, then go by all means."

But as she finished Cliona turned away her face and bit at a trembling lower lip. She was yet very weak, and this was the first time in her life that her big brother had turned from her when her need actually called to him.

A little later, all the guests save Marcus had departed, and the convalescent, complaining of weariness, had been wheeled into the house by the trained nurse still in attendance.

"It's a darned shame!" exclaimed Marcus, and Colin started guiltily. But as the old man continued he realized that the remark was not intended to apply to him. "If we had any detectives worthy of the name the scoundrel, responsible for that outrage would not go unpunished!"

"What can one do?" inquired Rhodes resignedly. "MacClellan is firmly convinced, I know, that we have withheld some information that would have helped solve the problem. It has seemed to me that in consequence his work was very half-hearted. He believes, too, that Cliona's memories were confused with subsequent delirium and thereby robbed of value.

"It is true that the analysis showed real blood to have been shed, and that it was the blood of another animal than man. But he contends that it would have been easy to bring the stuff from a slaughter-house. The alarm wires had not been interfered with. The trouble lay in the insulation where a leaking drain had rotted it. I'll admit the fault as my own, since I had not tested the system for a week.

"But though that does away with one of MacClellan's objections to the beast theory, nothing will shake his conviction that the affair was one of revenge, and that I know a cause for it. It may be that he hides behind that as an excuse for not solving the problem. I don't know. I spent some time over it, myself, but every clue I could find ended, like that red-black trail down the hill, in emptiness and air."

"Well, if a lawyer and a detective can't find the answer, I suppose it is useless for a layman like myself to attempt it. I hope you will have the best of fortune in Argentina, Mr. O'Hara. Since you are leaving in a few hours, I shall say goodby, now," said Marcus.

"Thanks. Doubtless I'll have the fortune I deserve—they say every man gets that in the end. Goodby and good luck to yourself, also."

But when Marcus had gone, Colin spoke somewhat uneasily.

"Tell me, Tony, do you think Cliona will fret herself at my going—enough to harm her, I mean?"

"Why should she? Don't worry, old man. I'll take care of her, and when you return, believe me, you'll find the warmest welcome a man ever had. By Heaven, I hate to see you go! I shall miss you as I never thought I'd miss the company of any man!"

O'Hara's freckled face darkened with an embarrassed flood of color.

"That's a kindly thing to say, Tony, and it's not just any man I'd have trusted Cliona to in marriage. As for coming back, the trip may not take so long after all. But think little of it if you hear nothing from me in long whiles. I'm a bad correspondent, and where I'm going I may not care to write from, lest the message be traced. This is rather a secret expedition, you must understand!"

Exactly how secret it was, and how easily a message might have led to discovery, Rhodes would have more readily comprehended had he stood at O'Hara's side two days later.

Colin's surroundings did not remotely resemble the decks of the passenger steamer on which he was supposed to be then en route for the distant South American republic. In fact, he had just descended from a fussy, self-important little local train, and the sign that stared him in the face above the door of the tiny station would have explained to his sister in one word all the mystery of his seeming indifference to her welfare. That was "Carpentier."

"No man or beast," said Colin to himself, "can frighten my little sister out of her five wits, and me to take no proper heed of it! Charley Finn will forward her the letters I have sent him from Buenos Aires, and the place where I am need make no difference, just so she believes me elsewhere.

"Now we'll see if the job of that poor fool MacClellan cannot be improved on, even though the trail is so old and stale! Cliona has the seeing eye, and I know she felt sure that if any of us three should live here there would be another visitation. One O'Hara gave them the welcome of a few friendly bullets. Now let them call on the other! Maybe he'll do yet better. 'Tis my own house now, that I've paid Tony well for, though of that the lad has no notion, and here I'll receive whom I please and Cliona be none the wiser or more worried!"

XIV

The Second Visitation

M r. Cosmo Stackfield, rounding a sharp curve with no warning hornblast, swerved, swore, and bringing his car to a halt, turned in his seat.

"I say," he called back, "I wasn't trying to run you down, O'Hara!"

"Oh! I thought you were."

"Are you people back at the bungalow?" inquired Stackfield. "I trust Mrs. Rhodes is recovered from the results of her fright."

"She is," retorted the other with intentional briefness. "She's not here. I came out by myself for the solitude. When a man's used to the open, he wearies of just hearing people chatter. So I'm living alone for a while. Good day to you, sir."

Colin's rudeness was too gross and too obviously intentional for Stackfield to ignore longer. A slow flush tinged his flabby cheeks, and with a muttered word that sounded less like "good day" than some term not so polite, he sped past on his road to the city.

O'Hara smiled grimly after his defeated interrogator, but the incident gave him food for thought. Had he too greatly relied on not being acquainted with people is this neighborhood? Having arrived only yesterday, Stackfield was the second man who had greeted him on his early morning stroll. Secrecy promised to be a difficult achievement.

Laying the matter aside as one that must be left to chance, O'Hara turned back toward Carpentier.

Having no particular fancy for housekeeping, he had engaged a middle-aged woman to come up by the day, cook his meals, and keep the bungalow in order. Luncheon that day proved one sad fact conclusively. Promising of all housewifely virtues as had been the neat vine-covered cottage from which Colin had wrested her to his own service, Mrs. Bollinger could not cook.

The house had been thoroughly repaired, even to the laying of new planks in the scarred living-room floor, and the furniture left undamaged was plenty for his needs.

Four days he spent, reading—an occupation of which he was always fond—and wandering about the now-neglected gardens.

Ten o'clock of the fifth evening found him going about his usual preparations for the night. They were painstaking, though of a sort which would have astonished Mrs. Bollinger. Most people expecting an undesirable caller do not leave doors and windows unlocked—certainly not invitingly ajar. Nor does the burglar-expecting householder prefer his home to be in utter darkness from ten o'clock on throughout the night.

Having little use for the police at any time, Colin had disconnected the burglar alarm. Now he sought the kitchen and returned, his arms laden with tin aluminum utensils, to be stacked in high tottery piles behind the doors opening inward upon the living-room from the veranda and from the pantry into the dining-room, placing them so, rather than at the outer doors, lest the intruder be frightened away too early for successful pursuit.

As he carried out this simple and homely expedient for providing noise when noise should be least welcome, he whistled quite cheerfully for a man expecting so very strange a visitation.

Then he lay down fully dressed, in the room that had been his sister's.

FOUR NIGHTS HIS LIGHT SLUMBER had been unbroken, but on this fifth night he suddenly awakened, every sense alert in the black darkness.

Something, he knew, was imminent. Something had telegraphed a warning to his sleeping brain. A sound? He listened keenly, intently. From far away came the faint whistle of a locomotive. Against his window he heard a slight tapping sound—then a flutter, accompanied by a mouselike squeaking. A wind-blown vine tapping the pane—the squeak of a bat. Those sounds should not have roused him.

With stealthy noiselessness, O'Hara slid from his bed and stole across the floor. The night was moonless, with an overcast sky, and save for the dim, oblong shapes of the windows the darkness within the bungalow was absolute. But O'Hara saw the location of every piece of furniture in the light of a carefully schooled memory, and he made no blunders.

Every sense quivering with a vivid expectation, he peered into the living-room.

What had awakened him? A dream? He had not been dreaming. Sheer nervousness? He knew himself too well for that to receive consideration. He heard no sound, felt no vibration. He had fallen asleep in a house empty save for himself. It was not empty now. He knew it, felt it, yet could give himself no reason for the assurance.

As noiselessly as he had crossed the bedroom he passed through the living-room. From the portièred arch he stared on into further silent blackness. On turning back, however, O'Hara became aware that a change had befallen the space behind him.

Vaguely he could now perceive dark masses—chairs, a table; even, though faintly, the rug on which he stood.

It was some seconds before he perceived the source of this illumination, which was, by infinitesimal degrees, growing steadily brighter. Between living-room and veranda the partition was pierced by two windows, glazed and hung with thin, ivory-yellow curtains. Three other windows, similarly draped, opened upon a lawn beyond the angle formed by the veranda's end wall.

On sunny days nearly as much light was reflected through one set of windows as the other, for the veranda was finished in yellow spruce and faced south. Now, however, the windows toward the lawn were invisible behind their curtains, while those opening upon the veranda had become faintly glowing rectangles of yellowish light.

It was not a steady light. It throbbed, first dim, then brighter, in a long, regular pulsation.

O'Hara's first impulse was to spring across the room and sweep the curtains aside. His second was better. A view through the window might gratify his curiosity, but he wanted a more practical satisfaction than that. He would take no chance of giving a premature alarm by spying between curtains.

The light, which until now had continually increased, ceased to grow, but continued to throb.

Still no sound came from the other side of the partition, nor could he see anything through the translucent window draperies. He stood there in the dim twilight of the living-room and the two windows hung like yellow, oblong Chinese lanterns, pulsing between light and shadow, but giving no other hint of the presence that must be back of them.

At last Colin moved. Crouchingly he stole toward the door, body half bent, ready at any moment to leave creeping and spring. Even to him the stillness had become somewhat ghastly. If enemies were there, why did they make no move? What could be the object of this ghostly and silent illumination? They did not, could not know that he was aware of their presence. What was there in the veranda to hold their attention for so long a time?

Then Colin committed a folly for which he never afterward quite

FRANCIS STEVENS

forgave himself. In the intensity of his desire to reach the door, fling it wide and take the enemy unaware, he forgot his own precautions against its noiseless opening. As his hand closed on the knob one foot grazed the little pile of precariously balanced tinware. Over it went, clashing and clattering, a most satisfactory alarm—had he not been the one to spring it!

XV

THE THIRD VISITATION

The racket so startled its originator that he leaped backward, collided with a taboret, and sent that over. The oblongs of light in the southern wall vanished abruptly. Further stealth was absurdly useless. Colin flung himself at the door, wrenched it open and, reaching upward, snapped on the general light switch of the veranda. It sprang into dazzling visibility, but no one was there.

Colin made sure of its emptiness in one swift look that included the space beneath a large table and a wicker divan, snapped off the light—he had no desire to form a mark for bullets—and was at the outer door.

It stood ajar as he had left it. Outside, the darkness was nearly as impenetrable as within the house, but for that there was a remedy. Opening a concealed steel switch-box, Colin pulled a lever and sprang down the steps. The lever completed the circuit for several powerful lamps about the grounds, and by their aid he began a search which he felt in the beginning would be fruitless.

He had only himself to blame. The unknown foe had walked into the trap, so he told himself, and his own careless foot had kicked it open.

Raging, he darted from tree-shadow to tree-shadow, cautious even in his fury, but lawns, gardens, and outbuildings were empty as the veranda itself. For any signs to the contrary, that dim irradiation of the windows might have been a product of his over-stimulated imagination.

"The cowards—the sneaking, crawling cowards!" he muttered angrily. "Afraid of the noise of a tin pot or so! 'Tis myself has a notion to give them no further attention!"

But as he flung himself into a chair in the living-room he knew that he would sit there the balance of the night, nourishing the hope that again those two windows might slowly, uncannily illuminate themselves. They did, but it was by the matter-of-fact light of a desolate dawn.

Disgustedly Colin replaced his too-efficient burglar-alarms in the kitchen, undressed, got into bed, and slept soundly until nearly noon.

"It's busted, but I didn't do it, Mr. O'Hara. It was laying broke on the floor when I come in!"

"That? Where were you finding it?"

Colin's brows knit as he took from his housekeeper the shattered object of her protestation.

"I tell you it was laying on the veranda floor when I come in. Honest, I never even seen it before, Mr. O'Hara!"

Mrs. Bollinger's lean, corded hands twisted themselves nervously in her apron. Though no ceramic expert, there was a quaint beauty about the broken manikin that warned her of possible value.

"H-m!" exclaimed Colin. "It must have been left here with the rest of the furniture when we took Cliona away—though I can't remember seeing it about. All right, Mrs. Bollinger, I likely knocked it down myself last night."

When she had gone he stood for some minutes eyeing the image in his hands. The poor little "Lord of the Air" had certainly found bad fortune in the alien land to which Colin had brought him.

First he had lost his serpent crook, and now the round, feather-trimmed shield on the other arm had been broken off, arm and all. Yet still he smiled patient benignity.

"'Tis odd," muttered Colin, "that I never saw you standing about in the veranda, little man. It's a wonderful faculty you have for being broke in the midst of a mystery! Well, your bit of staff is gone for good, but the shield and arm here can be restored to you, and shall be for the sake of the dream you will always bring to memory. Smile away, little man! Cement will work miracles!"

With a whimsical smile he set the image and its broken part on a shelf and promptly forgot them both. That there could be any actual connection between the Lord of the Air and their troubles at the bungalow never once occurred to him. How should it? Dream or reality, that strange night of so long ago had held nothing for him that could have led him to suspect the truth—a nightmare, dreadful truth for whose discovery he was at the last to pay a heavy price.

When a full fortnight had slipped by, its monotony unrelieved, Colin's patience wore decidedly threadbare. He did not at all like this game of waiting and watching.

He dared make no new acquaintances, and rebuffed what advances were offered him. Afternoons and evenings he spent in reading, or in taking long tramps through the autumn woods, while at all times he kept a sharp lookout for any clue, small or large, that might serve to simplify his problem.

But September passed, and October struck the woods to sharp reds and gold, and still he had discovered nothing. The time began to drag intolerably. What people he met looked at him with irritating curiosity, born of his unusual appearance and solitary habits.

The last week of October crept in. The thick foliage that hid the bungalow was beginning to thin in places, and the lawns were a-rustle with bright leaves, when that occurred which led Colin to take renewed hope of his long vigil.

The sun had set, a blood-red ball behind the purple autumn haze, and Colin stepped out of his front door to take a few long breaths of the crispy cool night air. Then he would go in to the lonely and ill-cooked dinner which Mrs. Bollinger had laid out before departing for the night.

That good woman glanced back through the twilight at the dark mass of screening foliage that still concealed the bungalow, and went her way with many shakes of the head and a hastening step. It was already night beneath the trees that overhung her road.

"The poor man will have to get some one else to wait on him," she reflected as she hurried along, "or else I must leave earlier. It's all right for him to live in a house that the devil visited, if he likes that sort of thing. But goodness knows, Mr. O'Hara is big enough to thrash even Satan himself, but I'll never stay in that house again after dark, no matter how bad we need the money. And I'll tell him so tomorrow morning, first thing. There was that rustling in the trees last night as I went home, and I was a perfect fool to stay so late—oh!"

The woman suddenly picked up her skirts and fled like a rheumatic but badly frightened deer. A little distance from the road there had begun a great rustling and crackling of fallen leaves, and at the same time something whizzed through the air and struck her a painful blow on the cheek.

The missile was only a chestnut burr, but its sharp prickles more than made up for its light weight. Poor Mrs. Bollinger dashed into Carpentier at a gallop, under the firm impression that she had been shot in the face by a rifle bullet.

Her story, however, was somewhat skeptically met. A bullet is supposed to leave some visible mark of its passage, and anyway no neighbor of hers was quite neighborly enough to care for investigating those dark woods with their evil reputation. So the injured lady retrieved her children from the care of a friend and retired to her home, nursing a stung face and the firm resolve that not even daylight should tempt her to return to the bungalow on the hill.

Colin strode up and down the macadamized drive, beneath the arching trees. He had that day received his first letter from Cliona, which had gone the long route to Buenos Aires and back, remailed by the faithful Charles Finn.

She was much better, it seemed, in fact practically well, but Tony babied her dreadfully, and they were going down to St. Augustine the first of December. They missed him, Colin, very much indeed, but she presumed and hoped that he was happy and having a good time.

She supposed by now he must be well on his way across the Pampas. In that case this letter might never reach him, but she hoped it would so that he might know how well she was and enjoy his chosen road untroubled by care for her. Tony sent his love with hers, and Snookums had caught a rat, but it bit him and got away. She hoped he would think of her sometimes, and remember that she was always his faithfully loving sister, Cliona Rhodes.

"Now, why," said Colin as he paused beneath a spreading oak and kicked at the dry leaves with an impatient foot, "why Cliona Rhodes? That's the first time she was ever any other than just Cliona, or maybe Cli, to her poor runabout brother. And I wonder, have I left Buenos Aires or no? If I have not, 'twould be an easy matter to lay up poor Charley with a broken leg and postpone the expedition; or myself with a fever requiring immediate return that I be cured of it.

"I'm thinking the O'Hara has made a fool of himself. Now, will he be the bigger fool to stay here, or to throw up the whole business and return for a pleasant reconciliation with this Cliona Rhodes that's so formal of a sudden with her only born brother?"

He pondered a while longer, then threw back his red head in a gesture of decision. What that decision may have been is immaterial, for just then something rustled the boughs above him with a violent, crashing motion, and two enormous, hairy hands closed in a strangling grip about the Irishman's throat.

Colin had so, nearly resigned any hope of being attacked, and had so little reason to expect attack to descend upon him out of a tree and at that early hour of the night, that he came near to being strangled before he could realize what was taking place.

The hands that had gripped him were unnaturally long and sinewy. The fingers overlapped on his by-no-means slender throat as his own might have twined about the neck of a child. And as they squeezed inward they pulled upward. Colin's two hundred and thirty pounds of bone and muscle actually rose into the air, till only his toes touched the ground.

He enjoyed all the sensations of a man being unexpectedly hanged, and as such a man would grasp at the rope over his head, so his hands flew up to seize the thing above him.

His fingers closed on shaggy hair over iron-hard muscles. The blood was pounding in his ears, and the transparent darkness brightened to a red, star-spangled mist. If it had been a rope about his neck, his effort to raise himself might have relieved the strain, but in this case the rope was alive and squeezing inward with murderous intent.

Fortunately for Colin, though his assailant was strong enough to raise his victim clean off the ground, the tree limb which supported the operation was less efficient. As Colin struggled there came a sharp, loud crack. Next instant he was down on the macadam, part of a frantic, writhing tangle of legs, arms, and the dry bough that had saved his life by breaking.

The fall loosened his assailant's hold and they met on equal terms. Over and over they rolled, the Irishman breathing in great gasps as he at first strove only to keep those terrible hands from regaining their grip on his throat.

Devil or man or monkey, it was the strongest, most thoroughly energetic antagonist he had ever encountered. It had been silent, but now it was snarling in a slobbering, avid sort of way that made Colin's gorge rise in disgust even as he fought.

But his own strength was fast returning, and with one mighty effort he tore the great thing loose, flung it back off his body, and got to his feet, half crouched and straining his eyes through the gloom.

A pale bulk rose at him in a long leap, its grasping arms outstretched. With the quickness of a trained wrestler Colin caught one of the wrists in both his hands, turned his back, and with the arm over one shoulder bore down with all his force.

There was a cracking noise, as when the branch snapped off, but not so loud, accompanied by a snarl of pain. The white thing came flying over Colin's head and landed with a heavy thud on the macadam before him.

Releasing his hold on the arm, he grasped at the body of his victim, but the creature evaded him. Showing remarkable activity, in view of its broken arm and the bad fall it had sustained, the thing was on its feet in an instant, rustling and pattering across the leaf-strewn lawn with Colin in furious pursuit.

The latter was unarmed. Though he had brought with him to the bungalow a large-caliber pistol whose bullets would pierce a four-inch hardwood plank, he had, quite characteristically, never even removed it from his suitcase. Each night he had sat watchful, content in the confidence of his own great strength, but now he wished with all his heart that he had the weapon with him.

Had the season been summer, the fugitive might have easily escaped. Beneath the scattered trees it was dark as a cellar, and only the creature's own whiteness made it dimly visible in the starlit open spaces. But the dry leaves of autumn traced its progress, and though Colin ran against more than one tree-trunk and had to stop occasionally to distinguish the noise of its flight from his own he managed to follow down the hill, across Llewellyn Creek, and into some denser woods beyond.

There began an increased rustling and a crashing of boughs ahead. Colin realized that his former assailant had left the ground and was swinging itself from bough to bough through the forest.

To follow farther seemed folly. Nevertheless, the Irishman kept doggedly on, following the trail of noise and never getting very far behind it. Perhaps its broken arm retarded the creature's speed. At any rate, though he stumbled among vines, tore his clothes and flesh on briers, climbed fences, fell headlong over rotting logs, and generally suffered great personal inconvenience, the pursuer kept always within hearing distance of the pursued.

It was heart-breaking work. Only a man of supernal strength, stamina, and stubbornness could have held to that mad hunt, mile after mile, as did Colin O'Hara.

The fugitive avoided houses, and for that reason they by no means went as the crow flies. Several times they crossed roads, and once Colin dashed across a turnpike just in front of a whizzing automobile. The driver slowed to look back and swear, but Colin had neither time nor attention to spare for his grievance. On, on, on, and still ahead of him the October foliage betrayed that wild flight from tree-top to leaf-strewn glade, and up to the branches again.

Colin had lost all sense of direction. Save for the occasional roads and fences they crossed, and judged by the route they had come, this section of suburbia one vast and trackless forest. Colin was no mean woodsman, but never before had he explored such an apparent wilderness, through black night and at so breathless a pace.

He had begun to believe that the chase would never end, and that so long as he followed the untiring thing ahead would flee, when the noise ceased. Stopping in his tracks he listened intently. Only the small, usual sounds of night broke the stillness, the chirp of a late cricket, the thud of a ripe chestnut burr falling to the ground and far away a honking auto horn.

Had his quarry taken counsel of common sense and hidden itself in a treetop? If so, then the chase was indeed ended. In that darkness, without dogs or torches, he could not hope to find its hiding place.

Again Colin began to move forward as silently and swiftly as he might, still listening for any significant rustle before or above him. He came to a deep ditch, just missed falling into it, leaped across and found himself on a broad, smooth road, electrically illuminated at wide intervals.

An explanation of the silence occurred to him. This road was practically bare of the telltale leaves. Was it possible that the fugitive had left the false protection of the trees and taken to the road? If so, in which direction had it gone?

To the right, far down the way, a pale, squat bulk glided into view, slinking on short-bowed legs—into the light of a lamp and out again like a fleeting white shadow.

Colin gave vent to a wild hallo and dashed in pursuit. He caught occasional glimpses of the thing ahead as it passed beneath the road-lamps, and thought that he was at last gaining ground. In a foot-race, over smooth going, the creature of the trees had the worst of it. The road curved, crossed a stream, and a high stone wall replaced the forest on the left-hand side.

Scarcely the length of a city square now separated the Irishman from his quarry. Then he saw it pause directly beneath a lamp, a semihuman shape, and shake one long, thin arm at him, as if in defiance. The other hung limp at its side.

Colin shouted again and increased his speed. His feet pounded over the hard oiled road in giant strides, but again the creature flitted from the circle of light, this time to one side.

FRANCIS STEVENS

Colin pulled up and came on more slowly, for a shrill bell was ringing somewhere behind the wall. There followed a rattle, a clang as of iron, and then the creaking of hinges. A voice spoke, mumbling indistinctly, and Colin arrived at a pair of wrought-iron gates just in time to have them shut in his face with a vicious clang.

XVI

Admitted

O'Hara stepped up and, grasping the elaborate iron scroll-work, shook the gate angrily.

"Here, you," he cried, "if this is the city zoo, what do you mean by letting your ferocious baboons and gorillas roam the country at large?"

The guardian of the gate, he who had opened it for the ape's entrance and closed it in the face of its pursuer, made no reply, unless an incoherent mutter could be so accounted.

He seemed a tall, thin man, dressed in rough corduroys, and his narrow, triangular face peered out at Colin through the floral scrolls with a curiously furtive looks. Colin could see him very well by the light of the road-lamp, and thought that his face had a whiteness, as if the man had been badly frightened, or was just risen from a sick bed.

"What's that?" demanded Colin, his indignation growing as he recalled the difficulties and discomforts of his long run and the unpleasant combat preceding it. "You need make no excuses to me! I saw the brute come in here, though I do not see him now, and I wish to come in myself and talk with the man who has charge of this place and takes in raging gorillas like they were invited guests at a parish lawn party! Will you admit me, or will I break down this fancy gate of yours?"

He gave it so violent a shake that the man inside jumped back.

"Stop!" he cried excitedly. "Stop it instantly! You are making a noise—a big noise! Stop it!"

The man's voice came out of his lips as if there were no teeth behind them, in a kind of hushed and mumbling shriek. But he had teeth, for as Colin loosened his grasp and the man again thrust his face against the scroll, they were bared in an animal snarl. His glaring eyes reflected the lamplight with a reddish gleam. A little shiver of cold crept down the Irishman's spine. Almost involuntarily he retreated a step.

But Colin O'Hara was not the one to be done out of satisfaction for his wrongs by a white-faced, red-eyed, silly-mouthed booby hiding behind a gate, and so he intimated in very positive terms.

"And," he concluded, "you will now permit me to speak with the gentleman who has the bad taste to keep you and your brother that you just let in for household pets! And if you do not, I'll come in, whether or no. We'll see if the O'Hara must chase wild apes over bog and ditch and win his pains for his trouble!"

At that the keeper of the gate moved sulkily away, mumbling over his shoulder:

"You must wait, then, till I go to the master."

"I'll wait, but don't try my patience too far now!"

The figure vanished into the darkness that lay beyond the wall. O'Hara, peering after him, could see only a few square yards of leaf-matted gravel, on which the pattern of the gate was laid in shadow by the lamp behind him.

Beside it rose a roughly peaked cubic mound of reddening ivy, which he took to be either a much-neglected gate-lodge or a monument of some sort. Probably the latter, for there was no sign of door or window. Beyond only dark tree masses loomed against the starry sky. No lights gleamed through the branches, nor did any sound come out save when the night-breeze faintly rustled the dry leaves.

"A queer place and no mistake," muttered Colin; "and I'm thinking that once in the O'Hara may wish himself out again. I wonder has this beast I've chased here anything at all to do with the other matters? Could a monkey, however knowing, have done the things that were performed at the bungalow? No, likely this is an occurrence by itself, and I'll just give the beast's owner a piece of my mind and go home again."

Having reached this conclusion, Colin began to weary of such long waiting. The gate-keeper had now been absent at least a quarter of an hour, and for any evidence of life the Irishman might have been the only human being within miles. Not even a car had passed on the pike behind him. He shifted from one foot to the other and swore softly.

"The white-faced fool has played me some trick!" he grumbled. "Very like 'twas through his fault that the beast got loose, and he's never gone near his precious master."

Well, there was a bell connected with this gate. He had heard it sing. Searching for a moment he located a push-button and set his thumb firmly against it. The bell rang; but it rang inside the ivy-covered heap beside the gate. It was a lodge, then. The shrill clamor sounded so startlingly near and out of place in the silence that Colin hesitated a moment before ringing again.

Was that vague rustling sound from inside the lodge, or was it the wind among the leaves? It ceased after a moment. Colin waited, then as no one came he rang again. For fully five minutes he continued to ring, first steadily, then in long and short assaults on the bell-push. But the noise he made was his sole reward.

Disgusted, and at last really angry, O'Hara drew back from the gate and contemplated the wall. Fully ten feet high it extended right and left in an unbroken barrier.

"My coat to the wall," said Colin, proceeding to take it off, "and I'll soon be over."

The garment with which he intended padding the sharp, wicked-looking spikes was in his hand, and he was about to fling it upward when he arrested his arm and hastily slipped the coat on again. A sound had reached his ear from beyond the gate. Either the gatekeeper was returning or the bell had at last roused someone else to action.

AGAIN HE, PEERED INTO THE grounds. Out of the darkness a figure emerged, walking with a brisk, firm tread, and close behind glimmered the white face and red eyes of his first acquaintance, the gate-keeper. As the newcomer advanced, Colin could perceive, even in the dim, shadow-streaked light, that he was a bearded man, that he wore a pair of round glasses with tortoise rims, and that he was frowning angrily.

"Are you the ruffian who broke that poor brute's arm? Marco, open the gate and have him come in!"

O'Hara was so taken aback by this forestalling of his own complaint that Marco, he of the white face, had time to unlock and swing wide the portals before he could think of any fit reply. But he had no hesitation about entering. In he stalked and confronted the newcomer, while behind him the gates shut, clanging.

"I am the man your beast would have strangled," he began indignantly; "and for why do you let him run wild at night, the way he might have killed me had I been a small, weak man? Strangling at the throat of me when I am meditating in my own dooryard! Or is it that you are training the handsome creature for murder?"

At that the bearded man laughed. His tone was low, amused, with just the faintest hint of a sneer somewhere about it.

"Pray, my dear sir, don't carry your accusation to the point of absurdity. If, as you hint, it was Khan who attacked you first, I owe you an apology.

Perhaps we had best go to the house and discuss this quietly. Will you follow me, sir?"

O'Hara hesitated, but only momentarily. He was possessed of a dubious feeling, scarcely amounting to suspicion, that wisdom would carry his feet elsewhere than inward. To O'Hara, however, discretion was ever an uninteresting virtue. When the bearded man led the way into the dark shadows of the trees, after him went Colin.

He was still conscious of a sense of repulsion toward the white-faced gate-keeper, following close at his heels, and of a generally eerie and disagreeable impression. But no doubt this was folly, and no man, not even such a one as this gate-keeper, can help the looks he is born with. As for the ungainly monster he had chased here, it was most likely a valuable pet, whose ferocity might or might not be known to its master.

Barely able to see his way, Colin was not aware that they had approached a house until the drive curved sharply aside and they arrived at an entrance, the light of whose open door was shielded by a deep stone porch and a *porte-cochère*, arching above the driveway.

From the look of these he judged the mansion to be one of considerable size and dignity, but whether a private residence or a public institute of some kind, he was not yet able to determine. The three men ascended the steps, passed through the porch, and came into a square, old-fashioned reception hall.

Within the door the master of the house turned to his guest. He was an older man than the latter had at first supposed, for the carefully trimmed Vandyke beard was thickly streaked with gray. But the dark eyes behind the great, round lenses were very bright, his expression was keenly intelligent, and these characteristics, together with his quick, alert way of moving, lent him a deceptive look of youth.

As he stood, Colin noticed that he kept his left hand in the pocket of his coat. He noticed it, because that hand had been in that pocket since the first moment of their meeting. Colin had seen other men's left or right hands concealed in the same consistent manner, and it generally meant one thing.

He himself was unarmed.

"Will you be seated, sir?" inquired the man courteously enough. "I must ask you to excuse me while I give Marco some directions for the setting of Khan's arm. The poor brute is suffering."

O'Hara acquiesced. As Marco passed across the room in his master's wake, the visitor received one quick, full view of him and of his face. The man's singular pallor was explained, for Marco was an albino. He had removed his cap and disclosed a smooth, oval skull, sparsely covered with bristling white hairs.

By this more revealing light, his eyes, that had gleamed red in the shadow-shot gloom, were a reddish pink, and in that one clear glimpse of them O'Hara had a sickening notion that those eyes saw not out but inward. The pupils were like black pin-points.

The effect was as if the man had literally reversed his vision and contemplated not his outer surroundings but the secrets of his own stealthy soul. A childish and an unjust idea, for what had he against Marco save his unfortunate appearance?

Alone in the hall O'Hara looked about with a judging, curious eye. His first impression had been pleasant. The room was agreeably lighted by a hanging fixture, whose translucent, cream-colored globe diffused a mellow radiance. A log glowed in the depths of a fireplace of black dignity and size. The furniture, while severely plain, was good. There was certainly no hint of mystery or danger in that well-lighted, well-ordered, empty hall.

And yet as he stood there, O'Hara was again keenly conscious of the feeling he had experienced on entering the gate. It was as though the very atmosphere were charged with discomfort and some incomprehensible warning. It was indubitably charged beside with a faint but unpleasant odor. Very like it was that which troubled him. He wondered again if Reed kept other beasts than Khan on the premises, and if the bungalow mystery were not indeed near its solution.

A door opened and his host reentered.

"What? Still standing?" began the man, but Colin broke in on his hospitable protestations—which might have seemed more friendly had not that left hand remained in ambiguous concealment.

"I will not sit down. I am not fit to be seated on a decent chair, for I am mud and mold from the head to the feet of me."

"And for that it seems that we—or rather Khan, is responsible. You must let me make amends, Mr.—"

"O'Hara," supplied the other.

"My own name is Chester Reed. When you first came here, Mr. O'Hara, and from Marco's account, I believed that you had met Khan on the road and broken his arm with a club or bullet in an effort to capture him. Now I am inclined to believe that an explanation is due you. Before I offer it, would you give me an outline of exactly what occurred?"

Something about the man, or the tones of his voice, struck O'Hara as faintly familiar. Disagreeably familiar, too, as if the former association, if there had really been one, was of a distinctly unpleasant nature. Yet the name was new to him and the face called up no recollections. Doubtless the familiarity was no more than a resemblance to someone he had once known.

He began his narrative, but not until Reed had insisted that he be seated, mud or no mud, and had brought out a decanter, glasses, and a humidor of strong but good cigars.

For this service he used his right hand only. The left was still in his pocket. Colin began to believe his suspicions unjustified. Perhaps the man's hand was in some way deformed, and thus a mere personal habit, because he scowled over the inconvenience of his one-handed hospitality, and two or three times very obviously overcame an impulse to bring the left hand to the aid of its mate.

The tale ended, Reed shook his head with a frown of annoyance.

"This is the result of Marco's carelessness. He is an excellent trainer, but he will persist in regarding Genghis Khan as a human being rather than a monkey. I myself had no idea that Khan had a trace of viciousness. He is as gentle and tractable as a child, eats his meals at table, dresses himself in the morning, helps Marco with the other animals—in fact does everything human except read, write and talk. I suppose that in the woods Khan cast aside his clothes and his gentility together. I must congratulate you, Mr. O'Hara. I should not myself care to try a fall with Genghis Khan."

"Have we met before, Mr. Reed?"

The irrelevant question took his host by surprise. For just an instant Colin thought that the lids behind the round lenses flickered curiously. Then he replied with a quietness tinged by natural surprise. "I am sure we have not, Mr. O'Hara. You are not the sort of person whom one forgets."

Colin met his quizzical smile and glanced down at himself ruefully.

"You may say so—but I'm not always the wild barbarian I do look just now. Your pet led me a wild dance and that's the truth. You spoke of other animals. Will you tell me this—what kind of beasts do you keep, and did one other of them break loose early in the summer?"

"Never!" Reed put a strong emphasis on the word which he seemed to regret, for he qualified it instantly. "Never, that is, that I am aware of. I have a rather queer assortment, I'll admit. By methods of my own I breed and raise animals which I intend later to dispose of to menageries, museums, and the like. That is my business.

"But all precautions are taken, and there is no more danger than there might be in connection with any ordinary menagerie or breeding farm. That is what this place really is—a stock farm. Only, instead of cows and sheep we handle—more peculiar beasts. But there are none of them large enough or savage enough to do any particular harm if they did break loose—and they are all shut behind bars and strong fences."

"Genghis Khan?" suggested O'Hara, with a lift of his red brows.

"I have explained that. Hereafter Khan will not be given so much liberty. Some time, if you care to come around by daylight, I shall be glad to show you over my place. It is a privilege I extend to few, but—"

Breaking off in the midst of speech, Reed grasped the arm of his chair with his free hand and half rose with an indistinct exclamation.

Somewhere—though it was hard to say from what direction—there had begun a peculiar groaning sound. The very floor quivered to its vibration, and Colin was momentarily conscious of a strange feeling of nausea. The sound persisted for perhaps ten seconds, then ceased as abruptly as it had begun.

There followed a sudden patter of feet across the floor of the room over their heads, a faint scream—that was a woman's voice. Colin sprang to his feet, bewildered, but with an innate conviction that something had gone very much wrong somewhere. Reed, however, laid a staying hand on his arm.

"Do not disturb yourself, I beg. That voice—I may as well tell you, as you will hear of it perhaps from other sources. I live here alone with Marco and—my daughter. She is—deranged. There! It is a painful subject, and the great sorrow of my life, but such things are given us to endure by God, or Providence, or whatever arbitrary force rules the universe. She cannot bear my poor animals, and will often scream like that at a noise from the cages or yards."

As he spoke, the expression of almost savage impatience which twisted Reed's features had faded and smoothed into one of deep and painful sadness.

Colin stared.

"Was that first noise made by one of your beasts, then? 'Twould be a queer animal with a voice like that. I'd like to see the creature."

"That noise?" Reed looked oddly uneasy. "I really couldn't say, Mr. O'Hara. It might have been Marco dragging around one of the small cages—or a box. Yes," he continued with more assurance, "he probably dragged some heavy box across the floor. But my poor daughter takes alarm at the most innocent sounds."

It was on O'Hara's tongue to ask why, if the proximity of the beasts so distressed his daughter, Reed did not send her away to a sanatorium or asylum. But he repressed the question. After all, it was no affair of his. Instead, he said gravely:

"You have my sympathy, sir, and I understand your feelings entirely. But as to the invitation, 'twould give me pleasure to visit you on some other day and in a manner more formal."

"If you feel yourself to have been injured by Genghis Khan, or if he damaged your property in any way, I shall be glad to—"

"Nothing of the sort. I more than squared accounts with the poor ape in person. To tell the truth, there's a deal of time on my hands now, and I've a fancy for animals. Would it trouble you should I run over tomorrow afternoon?"

"Not at all. Do so, by all means." Reed spoke with a great appearance of cordiality. "Come at any time, and ring the bell at the gate. Marco will let you in."

"Then thank you, and I'll be going. By the way—" He broke off with a laugh—then explained: "Your Genghis Khan knows the country hereabouts better than myself. He led me about and about, the way I've no notion at all what part of America I'm in now."

"This house is only a short walk from Undine," smiled his host, "and Carpentier, where I suppose you wish to return, is the next station up the line. I keep no car, or I would send you back that way, but at least Marco can show you the road to the station. If you would care to—er—straighten your attire—"

"And wash off the mud and the blood," put in Colin. "'Tis a fine idea, for I doubt they'd take me onboard in my present condition. But no need to trouble your man. I can find my own way, if you'll point it and thanks to you."

"As you like."

REED LED THE WAY UPSTAIRS and introduced him to a well-appointed bathroom.

"Here is a clothes-brush, and help yourself to the soap and clean towels. I will wait for you in the hall below. You have half an hour for there is a train at ten five. Sorry I can't offer you the services of a valet, but we live very simply, and Marco and Genghis Khan are my only servants."

"I've already been valeted by Genghis Khan," jested O'Hara, "and do not care to repeat the performance. I'll be with you in ten minutes, Mr. Reed."

Alone, as he brushed at his clothes, Colin reflected on the singular make-up of this household.

"A mad daughter and a menagerie to care for, and he keeps one servant! Yet is it poverty that ails him? The one room I've seen is well-furnished enough, and here he has an elegant bath-room—clean towels by the dozen. And himself is not poorly dressed. Strange he'd not have one woman at least to be company for the unfortunate girl. And he says his beasts could not break loose! And that noise was the dragging of a cage! It would be a heavy cage that shook the house like that, though I myself find it hard to account for by any other cause. Nevertheless, had MacClellan a head on his shoulders he'd have found out this place and explored it. But no, he would not believe that Cliona's wild beast was aught but human."

Having done the best possible by his clothes, he began cleansing his face and hands.

"An odd thing, now I think of it, that the people hereabout kept quiet. So close to Carpentier, and the papers so full of it and all. How Mr. Chester Reed was not dragged into our business, man-monkey, stock-farm, and all, is a bigger puzzle than the other. I'll be kind to the poor man and courteous, and perhaps tomorrow I'll step on the tail of the whole mystery. There, I'm decent to pass in a crowd—and three minutes of the ten yet to spare."

He passed out toward the stair. As he did so a door opened at the end of the hall behind him, and hearing the soft click of its latch, he glanced around.

There, framed in the doorway, stood the most melancholy and at the same time the most oddly beautiful figure that Colin had ever seen. She could be none other than Reed's mad daughter, but the Irishman forgot that in amazement at her loveliness.

What she thought of him O'Hara could not know. The slight parting of her lips and her wide eyes might have expressed either amazement, alarm, or expectation. Curiously enough O'Hara was convinced, both then and afterward, that her emotion was really the last named, though what she could expect of him, whom she had never before set eyes on, seemed hard to surmise. He was also convinced—and this belief was as lacking in practical foundation as the other—that she had some information to impart—something which it was highly important that he should know and which concerned them both.

Heretofore O'Hara had compared all women with Cliona, to their disparagement, but here was one who could be compared to no one. She was herself alone and utterly a creature apart, almost unearthly, and who yet suggested in an odd way all the natural beauties of earth. So the darkness of her hair and eyes hinted at mystery of dusk and the recurring miracle of starshine.

She was tall and slender, and her height and slim, bare arms made one think of dryads that live in willow-trees and come out to dance at moonrise. Her hair hung down in rippling, dark curls over the green gown she was dressed in, and Colin saw the beauty of her hair and did not perceive that the gown was so worn and old that it hung in tatters about her bare ankles, and so threadbare in places that her white limbs shone through it.

Her face was long and oval, and her large eyes were too bright, as if suffused with unshed tears. She had the loveliness of night, and the sorrowful beauty of forest pools that hold the stars and the trees in their bosoms.

That was the wonder which appeared to Colin O'Hara.

But had he not been Colin O'Hara, or had he ever loved any other woman save his sister, then it may be that the wonder would not have appeared to him. So he might have seen only a slim girl in a torn, green gown; beautiful, perhaps,—but thin and very melancholy.

And how should either of them guess of a former meeting? Fifteen years are a gulf to swallow memories, and in fifteen years a girl-baby finds magic indeed to change her. Their first glance for each other was of recognition; but it was not a recognition to save suffering. Being not of the flesh and earthly it spared them no after pain.

Colin had no idea of how long he had stood there, staring at the girl and waiting for the message she had for him. But it could hardly have been more than a few moments until Reed's voice floated up to him from below.

"Is that you, O'Hara? You haven't long to catch that train."

Colin roused with a start, and the girl, who had seemed on the very edge of speaking, laid two slim fingers on her lips in a gesture of silence and slipped back into her room.

O'Hara went down the stairs like a man descending out of a dream. He did not know what had happened to him, but that something had happened he was gloriously aware. Every nerve and fiber of his giant body tingled with vivid life, and had she not made that gesture of silence and warning, he would have gone to the girl, not to Reed.

The latter met him at the stair-foot with a glance sharply suspicious.

"I heard you stop there on the floor above. Did my daughter speak to you? Poor child, she is as ready to address a stranger as her own father!"

Colin came to earth with a jolt. That, then, had been the mad girl, Reed's daughter! And he had—he had—Why, he had done nothing; only life had for him turned a somersault and seemed right-sideup for the first time. But mad! Was it madness that gave her that elfin look, that made her so differently, so marvelously beautiful?

"I had no word from your daughter, sir," he replied gravely and sadly, for he was wishing he had. "Will you show me the road to the station?"

"You will have no trouble in finding it. Go out the gate, turn to your right, and keep straight on by the wall. From where it ends you can see the lights at the station. Good night, sir!"

The door closed with needless sharpness as Colin went down the steps. Then it opened again.

"If you want any further directions," Reed called, and there was a strange hint of laughter in his voice, "ask the gatekeeper!"

And once more he banged the door.

Colin had turned at the first word, had seen Reed standing in the lighted doorway, and had caught an odd impression of some trifling difference in his appearance. He stood stock-still on the drive, staring at the shut dooor. Then he scratched his bare head reflectively.

"Ask—the—gatekeeper!" he muttered. "Now, what in the devil did the fool mean by that—and him laughing when he said it? And what was it about him now—oh, his hand!"

That hand had been out of its pocket at last, and it had been large—white—furry.

"To keep a glove on one's hand is not strange," thought Colin, "but why the like o' that white fur one? Mr. Reed, Mr. Reed, 'tis a man of mysteries you are, both small and large, and I do not like you! But your daughter—"

It was hard enough to follow the path in the dark, and twice he thought he had lost his way. At last a gleam of light ahead resolved itself into the gaslight on the pike outside. Against its yellow radiance

FRANCIS STEVENS

the gates hung, an elaborate silhouette, and he could see the red sheen of the ivy-covered lodge.

Then, as he came toward it, a slight sound came to his ears. Straining eyes dazzled by the light beyond, it seemed to him that in the side of the lodge facing the grounds a door stood open. Yes, there was an oblong blackness there, blacker than the shadowed ivy about it and near the center of the oblong—a whitish oval patch—a face?

It disappeared abruptly, and when Colin came up to the little lodge there were only a closed door and silence. Any windows there might be were hidden by the clinging ivy.

As the gates were unlocked, Colin had no desire to disturb Reed's repulsive servant. The gates opened at a touch and he went his way.

XVII

A Surprise and a Disappointment

The following day brought Colin a surprise as great and in a way, more disconcerting than had been given him by Genghis Khan when he descended upon him out of an oak-tree the evening before.

Cliona arrived at the bungalow, and she was a Cliona indignant and filled with the just wrath of a woman deceived. She was so angry that she had forgotten all dread of the place and marched into the dining-room unannounced, like a small avenging angel.

Colin was alone. Mrs. Bollinger had made good her resolve and renounced his service in a wonderfully spelled note, which a small boy thrust under the front door that morning. So Colin had cooked his own breakfast and luncheon. He was a good cook, within the limits of his cuisine, as this ran chiefly to wild game "of which he had none," fried ham, eggs, flapjacks, and coffee. There promised to be a certain monotony of diet unless he could persuade some other Mrs. Bollinger to dare the goblins of the bungalow.

He was somewhat sadly reflecting upon this fact when Cliona surprised him. Unexpectedly long though his residence here had been, and though the continuance of its secrecy had seemed a daily increasing miracle, yet the worst he had anticipated was discovery by his brother-in-law, who might have got wind of his presence there through the gossip of some Carpentierian in business circles. He would be unlikely to carry word of it to his wife, but would investigate on his own account.

For Cliona herself to descend upon him was lightning from a clear sky, and he had never felt more astonished and embarrassed in his life. He choked on his coffee, but this was fortunate. By the time he was able to speak he had thought of something to say.

"Cliona, my dear," he beamed, coming around table with outstretched arm, "it's a fine thing to see you looking so well and all!"

But she ran away from him, barricading herself behind a chair. She regarded her brother scornfully.

"You lied to me!" She was fairly ablaze with the white-hot anger that occasionally flared up in both the O'Haras. "You lied, and you never went away at all!"

Because he was dear to her, the discovery of his incomprehensible deception had hurt her intolerably. As she had written him, her health and strength had practically returned, and she had begun to go about much as usual.

While in the city shopping, she had chanced to meet a lady whose husband owned an extensive property adjoining Rhodes' former possessions at Carpentier.

Cliona could not understand the woman's meaning when she said: "Your brother looks so well, Mrs. Rhodes. I often see him, though only at a distance." Then it had all come out.

Cliona said nothing to her husband. This was between her and Colin, and as soon as Rhodes left her to return to his office, she took the first train to Carpentier.

"Why, no," confessed Colin, halting to run his fingers through his hair and reflect. "Sure, I didn't go away. Did you think I would really travel off to the far end of the earth and leave you so sick and all? I—"

The matter of the lie Colin excused on the ground that if he had told the truth Rhodes would have insisted on coming with him, or at least occasionally sharing his nightly watch. Cliona shuddered at the thought. She heard the story of his last night's adventure, somewhat toned down and denatured, for Colin had no notion of increasing her concern for him.

He told her of his suspicion that Reed's strange "stock-farm" was responsible for her own experience, and in that case, of course, there was no danger in his remaining at the bungalow. Reed would now take the utmost care that none of his creatures, whatever they might be, should again escape.

But even to her O'Hara could not bring himself to tell of Reed's daughter. Deranged or sane, to him she was sacred, a vision bestowed upon him by the friendly gods, and he would not speak of her.

"So I am going there again this day," he concluded, "and when I come away I may have news to phone you or not, but at least if such a creature is there as your ears informed you of, and your eyes saw the white claw of him, he will not be hard to pick out. So let me live here a while longer, Cliona, and do you go back to Tony. Then in a few days I will join you, and perhaps I'll visit St. Augustine with yourselves."

To this she finally agreed, stipulating, however, that he should telephone her daily so that she might know he was safe.

"Night and morning I'll phone you," Colin promised. "And now will you sit at my table, Mrs. Rhodes, and enjoy the elegant menu provided by my fine Irish chef? There's little variety, but plenty of quantity, which, you know, is the main thing as shown in my own person!"

After all, except her husband, there was no one in the world so nice as Colin. Her wounded affection healed by the knowledge that his deception had been carried out for the purpose of avenging her own wrongs, the two had a very merry meal together, and later Colin rode with her to the train.

BEFORE PAYING HIS CALL, O'HARA determined to obtain some outside information regarding his new acquaintance, Chester Reed. For this purpose there seemed no one more convenient than the station agent, for Undine, excelling therein most such small suburban points, boasted a real, live agent. O'Hara found him to be a pleasant young fellow, ready to handle passengers with admirable impartiality.

Yes, certainly he knew Mr. Reed. Reed had bought the old Jerrard place a year ago last April. Beautiful old estate. Dated clean back to revolutionary days, and been in the Jerrard family ever since, till—well, Mr. Charles Sutphen Jerrard was the last of 'em. Too bad he had to come such a cropper. Five years ago it was. Hanged himself in the gatelodge.

His creditors had been trying ever since to rent or sell the place at a decent profit, but nobody seemed to want it till this man Reed came along. Makes a place mighty unpopular to have a memory like that hanging over it. Say, if you'd hear some of the stories about that gatelodge—what? Oh, well, Reed had taken the place anyway, and didn't seem to care a tinker's cuss for all the dead Jerrards that ever walked. Not the sort that cared to have living outsiders about, though.

Yes, be believed Reed did handle some breeds of stock. His animals were brought there on the hoof, or in crates and boxes, and he for his part had never seen that any of them were unusual. Just sheep and calves, chickens and rabbits. Nothing even very fancy, so far as he had noticed.

Here a man who was lounging against a packing-case put in his word.

"Y'know, that guy Reed is funny. When he first come here he give out that he was goin' in for what he called 'scientific stock raisin'.' There's two or three real stock-farms hereabout, and some fellows went and offered him some nice prize stock, but he says no, he don't want nothing like that. What he was goin' to begin on must be *im*ported. . .

"So he puts up a lot of wire fencin', the strongest I ever seen, an' then outside o' that he shuts in the Jerrard grounds with high board fences all along Llewellyn Creek and the other sides away from the pike. Then he nails up 'No Trespass' signs about every five feet, like he was goin' to start a dynamite factory."

"Well," broke in the agent, "he has a right to keep people off his grounds, hasn't he?"

"I ain't sayin' he ain't. I'm only tellin' you what a funny guy he is. You only gotta look at the poor old house to see that. What'd he want t'stick that big round cupuly thing right in the middle of the roof for—huh? What's a cupuly got to do with stock raisin'? Then he *im*ports this here fancy stock, and—haw! Say, I got a good look at a lot of it when it come in. By jiminy, they was the commonest, orneriest bunch o' cattle that anybody ever turned out in the road to get rid of! They was—"

"There were some fine Belgian hares in the last shipment," cut in the agent.

"Them brown rabbits, you mean? I dunno nothin' about them—but, say I do know cattle. I was raised on a real stock-farm. Them calves and sheep of his couldn't sneak up on a blue ribbon that was give out by a blind judge at midnight! An' the poultry—oh-h, my!"

Here his feelings overcame him. He fairly doubled up with mirth.

All this was very puzzling to O'Hara. Had not Reed distinctly stated that his farm was not for the purpose of breeding ordinary domestic animals?

"And what do you think of his taste in monkeys?" he suggested tentatively.

Both his informants seemed to take this query as delightfully facetious. The agent had appeared inclined to defend Reed, but he, too, laughed saying: "That bleached out man of his is the limit, isn't he? I always said he was more like a white rat than a human being, but I guess an albino monkey does come nearer the mark."

Colin stared. Could it be possible that Genghis Khan was unknown in the neighborhood?

"You don't take my meaning," he said frankly. "I'm not referring to Marco, but to the real monkey, the one he calls Genghis Khan."

The agent shook his head. Both men looked blank.

"Didn't know he had one, mister. Must be some pet that came in one of the small boxes. Well, I've got my bills of lading to check over. If you want to go out to Reed's place, Jimmy here will show you the way. Won't you, Jimmy? That is, unless you've been there before."

"I know the way," nodded O'Hara, "and thanks for the time you've given me!"

As he started up the road the lounger called after him.

"Say, mister, don't be surprised at nothing you hear there. That Miss Reed, his girl that lives there with him, is loony! I never seen her, but I've heard she takes on somethin' awful every wunst in a while. An' say, don't buy none of his imitation fancies, neither. I c'n put you next to some real good—"

But with an impatient wave of the arm O'Hara strode out of hearing. Without reason he resented intensely the man's reference to the girl. And to follow it up with advice about live stock! Had the fool no sense of what was fitting?

Though he resolutely declined to face the fact, O'Hara was taking an astonishing amount of interest in this mad girl, to whom he had never spoken, whom he had seen for a scant three minutes. He might refer to her as a "blessed and miraculous memory" all he pleased, but it was not so much memory as a faint hope of seeing her again that made this present visit the most exciting he had ever planned paying in his life.

THE DAY HAD BEGUN FINE and sunny, but a high wind had arisen. Now, at four in the afternoon, masses of dark cloud were surging across the sky, threatening rain before nightfall. Dust and dry, brown leaves swirled around and past him, and he had to cling to his hat lest it follow the leaves. The branches of the trees whipped and writhed in a wind that was stripping away the last of their October splendors.

Colin walked slowly, for he wished to think over the things he had just learned.

"Sheep, calves, poultry, and hares. Now which of those four could groan like an—earthquake? Faith, it sounds like a riddle! Something did moan last night, and 'twas no cage dragged over a floor, either. It frightened the poor little Dusk Lady upstairs. But if the people about here know nothing of Genghis Khan, why may it not be that Reed has other secrets—for museums, says he, and menageries?

"Now, what sort of beasts would those be? I never did hear of a man that could breed the larger carnivora with any success at all in captivity—or not in these latitudes. Freaks, then. Maybe. Now, what is this queer 'science' of Reed's? Does he cut the poor brutes up alive and hang the fore part of one on the hind part of another?"

O'Hara had been reading "The Island of Dr. Moreau," and its vivisectionary horrors had stirred his imagination.

"If there's anything like that going on here," he thought, "'tis high time it was put a stop to. I did not like that man Reed at first, and now, after thinking him over, I do not at all. He's too smooth and too polite, and behind it he hides a nasty temper. And his glasses are too big and ridiculous. I'd like to see the lad with them off, and his beard off too. A man might as well wear a mask as all that adornment. I may have seen him before, and I may not, but if I could see him shaved it would help me decide."

Here he postponed further reflection, for he had come up to the wrought-iron gates. He sought the button of the electric bell and pressed it. It rang in the gate-lodge, as before, but since it seemed unlikely that the entire time of Reed's one servant was spent in that sepulchral refuge, Colin assumed that the button had two connections, one of them at the house.

It was in that lodge, the agent had said, that the last owner had hanged himself. Recalling his experience of last night, a doubt flashed through Colin's mind like a flying spark. It was gone in an instant. He had his superstitious side, but seldom allowed it to get the better of him. That pale oval in the gate-lodge doorway had been Marco's face. Ghosts do not push doors open, nor close them to, and, anyway, it would be a very inefficient "haunt" that showed itself only to disappear so instantly. Colin smiled at the thought and looked beyond the lodge.

Within, the grounds seemed more desolate, though less mysterious, than on the previous night. Through the trees, which had shed so many of their leaves that afternoon, he caught glimpses of gray granite walls, and above them the roofs of the old, many-gabled house—and yet above them, like a misplaced reminiscence of the Orient—a strange, round, domed affair.

The dome form is one of the glories of architecture, but this one was not beautiful at all. It somehow suggested that an incredibly large, white fungus had sprouted there in the night and not yet been discovered and removed by the outraged dwelling's owner. Somewhere, some time—where and when, thought Colin, had he once before received that impression of a dome?

A fugitive memory that he could not place—and now Marco came rustling down through the leaves on the unswept drive. He met O'Hara with that same frightened stealthy look which seemed his habitual expression, and opened the gate with the air of a conspirator.

"What ails you, man?" demanded O'Hara as he entered. "You're shivering like a wet poodle dog. Is it the ague you have?"

The man shook his head and replied in his mumbled toothless voice: "Last night—you made great noise last night. Too much noise! Silence—silence!"

Colin stared. He had supposed the man normal save in appearance, but it appeared he was only half-witted.

"All right, my lad," he said soothingly. "Since noise troubles you so I'll try and make less of it today. Will I find Mr. Reed at the house?"

Again Marco shook his head and, putting a hand in the pocket of his worn corduroys, pulled out a crumpled envelope. "Here," he mumbled, extending it to O'Hara. "There are words on the white paper inside!"

"A note, eh? Now, what—"

Colin tore open the envelope. As the albino had phrased it, there were indeed words on the white paper inside, and words, moreover, which he read with considerable disappointment. The letter ran:

My dear Mr. O'Hara: I am writing this in case you should honor me with a visit this afternoon, as you spoke of doing. It is with great regret that I am obliged to postpone the pleasure of showing you about my little place, but imperative business calls me away. I cannot set the exact time of my return, but probably it will be in the course of a few days. I will then drop you a line, and sincerely hope that your visit may be repeated. Again regretting this involuntary rudeness to an invited guest, believe me,

Most sincerely yours,
Chester T. Reed

Colin glanced from Reed's note to find the albino's eyes fixed on his face, but, as usual, not with the least appearance of seeing him. One could hardly believe that those black, pointlike pupils were designed to look outward.

"So, your master has left you in charge here?" queried Colin thoughtfully.

"I am here—yes."

"But I mean, is it alone you are? No one to look after—Miss Reed?"

Marco frowned and pointed, first to the note, then to the gate.

"The master said—after reading, go!"

"Faith, you've a polite way of dismissing his guests, friend Marco!"

Colin hesitated. Could it be possible that Reed had actually gone away and left his pitifully lovely daughter in the charge of this red-eyed and possibly degenerate creature?

If so, what had been none of his business became his business or that of any other decent man. There must be some law of the State to cover such a situation. He decided to consult his brother-in-law. That clever lawyer could surely advise him. In the meantime—

"Marco," he said, "look me in the eye and heed well what I say. Should any harm come to Miss Reed in her father's absence, be sure I'll know of it, and be sure that it's myself you'll have to deal with for it. D'ye understand? I could tear you to bits, little man, and well you know it!"

"The master said—after reading, go!"

"Oh, I'll go! But do you think of my words and heed them! And tell your master that the O'Hara was here. Good day to you, Marco!"

The gates clicked shut behind him. Colin paused outside to light a cigar, with difficulty shielding the match from the gale. When he glanced back through the iron scrolls Marco had disappeared.

"'Tis ashamed of myself I am," mused Colin, "threatening violence to a weak, white worm like him! But that's the best I could think of to do. I do not know what is wrong with that place, nor with the master of it, but that something is wrong I am sure as sure can be. And I could hardly invade the man's premises by force to look into the matter. Or could I?"

He stared thoughtfully through the beautiful gates that Sutphen Jerrard himself had imported from Italy. As he looked, the first few drops of driven rain beat stingingly upon Colin's face, and the wind ripped through the trees like the breath of a giant's shouting—violent, impetuous, intolerant of all foul vapors and secret vileness.

XVIII

A Voice

B ut Colin did not invade Reed's place that afternoon. For one thing he wanted Rhodes' opinion before acting. He knew himself for an impetuous man, more used to the rough, forthright ways of the open than the ruled order of civilization. He feared committing some blunder, overriding the law in some way that might injure the girl rather than help her. Yes, he must talk to Rhodes.

He returned to his lonely bungalow in a mood so meditative that he was scarcely aware of the wild tempest that raved and tore at his drenched figure as he ascended the hill-road from Carpentier.

Night had fallen—a roaring blackness, and there had been no one to light up against his coming. He stumbled in, switching on the lights through the house as he went. They were comfortable, cheery rooms that sprang into view, still wearing some few of the homelike touches given them by Cliona, but for some reason the sight of them only emphasized the trouble of his mind.

Still pondering gloomily, Colin exchanged his dripping clothes for dry ones. Then he called Green Gables on the telephone. His sister answered, and, having informed her of the negative result of his visit to Undine, he asked for Tony.

But Tony, it seemed, was in town, having been detained on business. He would be home later in the evening.

"I'll call him later, then," said Colin, and bade his sister goodby.

He went through the dining-room, and from a bracket of the sideboard there a little porcelain image smiled benignly at his passing form. The broken shield still lay beside it. He had kept the godling "for the sake of the dream it would always bring to mind," but that "dream" was far from his thoughts tonight.

He passed Quetzalcoatl's small eidolon without a glance, and sought the kitchen, where he began preparing his supper. The cold rain had given him an appetite that even vague worry could not spoil. Having made a wonderfully good meal, he pushed the dishes to one side of the kitchen-table and lighted his pipe with a deep sigh of physical contentment.

FRANCIS STEVENS

But the satisfaction of his appetite had by no means quieted his mind. Back and forth fled his thoughts, spinning an invisible, intangible web between the bungalow at Carpentier and the house at Undine, till it seemed as if the cords of it had entangled his very body and were dragging him forth into the storm again.

What was the real connection between the huge, bloody thing that left its trail on this hill and that grating, vibratory roar he had heard last evening as he sat in Reed's entrance-hall? Was there a connection? And why did Reed keep a mad girl in the very surroundings best calculated to increase her dementia? And why should he, Colin O'Hara, care so very intensely what Reed did for his daughter, or left undone?

Could insanity rouse love? No. Common sense told him that the barrier of madness was higher than he could cross. Then it must be only pity that he felt for this poor daughter of Chester Reed. Pity, it seemed, was a force of fearful power! What was she doing now? What fate hung over her? Or was this feeling of indefinite dread no more than a film of his too active fancy?

Now and again, while Colin sat smoking and frowning through the smoke, the whole bungalow would shake, quivering as if in the grasp of some fierce monster. It was just that, and the monster was the living, raving wind. It dashed rain against the windows with savage roars, and shouted among the branches, daring the man within to match his strength to its violence.

Colin wished that Rhodes had been in. He wanted authority— authority to remove the girl definitely and forever from the care of a father not fit to have charge of her. Did he take her by force and prematurely, it might weaken the case. How could he tell? Rhodes was the law-wise lad—

The wind's voice no longer defied him—it was calling, pleading with him in great shouts and gasps of terror. It was a reckless, impetuous messenger, tearing at his windows and his heart in gusty throbs of wordless passion. There he sat, stolid, content in his animal comfort, and the wind knew that which should drag him through storm, fire, or hell's self, could it but impart its dread information.

Colin laid down his pipe and rose with a troubled frown. Wandering into the living-room he touched a match to the pile of kindling and logs in the fireplace. For a while the snapping, friendly flames were a solace to his rising discontent, but soon the feeling of unrest returned like a flowing tide.

The wind—the wind! Its invisible hand was shaking at the latch. Down it plunged through the chimney and spat contemptuous smoke and ashes at his stubborn inertia. It howled scorn at him for an irresolute, doubting fool, and wailed sorrowfully about the house in a long prophecy of bitterness and lifelong regret.

Till at last he could bear no more.

"Colin O'Hara," said he, "you're a fool; but if go you must, then go and have done with it!"

SUDDENLY HE TRAMPED TO HIS room and again changed, this time to heavy hunting clothes, with stout, water-proof boots, donned an ulster and pulled a steamer-cap well down over his ears. Then he hesitated. Should he carry the blued steel weapon that still lay in his suitcase?

Colin had a certain scorn for any weapons other than the very efficient ones provided him by nature. To his mind there was something childish, even cowardly, about the look of a pistol in that great right hand of his. In the end he flung the thing into a drawer, hunted out and thrust in his overcoat pocket a small flashlight, extinguished the living-room fire, and marched from the house, nose in air in defiance of his own folly.

The gale fairly snatched the breath from his nostrils, but Colin lowered his head and lunged onward down the hill. He knew where he was going, and if he were thrusting himself in where no one wanted or needed him—well, let it be that way.

It was then eight o'clock, and he was just in time to catch the local that ran every two hours until midnight. At Undine he descended and was glad to observe that even the socially minded agent had been driven to cover by the storm. Passing through the small group of stores and dwellings beyond the station, Colin walked on out the pike, fairly leaning his weight against the blast, and too blinded by rain to get much good of the flaring and far-separated roadlights.

Instinctively it was toward the gate that he directed his steps, but reaching it he found his purpose too indefinite for convenience. Should he ring the bell and Marco answer it, what reason could he offer to gain him admittance?

If he were going in at all, it was clear that the entry must be clandestine. Once more he eyed that spike-topped wall with speculative glance. Then he recalled that the station-lounger had spoken of board-fences enclosing part of the estate. A fence might be easier to, scale, and might just possibly be spikeless.

Ten minutes later found Colin standing on the further bank of Llewellyn Creek, a spot he had reached by following the pike across the bridge and turning in at a little foot-path branching off beyond. It led a hundred yards or so along the bank and ceased at what his flashlight showed to be another bridge, a single, narrow arch of stone, crumbling and without hand-rail or parapet.

On the other side, there appeared to be a small building, rising flush with the stream's bank and standing out somewhat from a high wooden barrier.

Crossing the bridge, Colin found himself faced by a plain wooden door set in a windowless wall of granite.

What interested him was that this door was not only unlocked, but slightly open. He entered, and his light playing over walls and floor showed a large, bare, dusty place. Boxes and packing-cases were stacked on one another, and in a corner lay a few rusty bits of old machinery. Nothing alive here save rats.

Perhaps it was the contents of one of those packing cases that gave off so unpleasant an odor. There was the dusty, disused smell natural to such a place, and through it whiffs of this other, and by no means agreeable, exhalation. Colin wrinkled his nose and sniffed. Failing to identify its source, he dismissed the matter and looked for an inner exit.

Crossing the old wooden floor, broken in more than one place, he discovered a pair of double doors, like those of a carriage-house. These, too, were unbarred and slightly ajar.

Someone had surely been careless. Colin wondered if Genghis Khan were once more abroad, but thought not. No sensible monkey would choose a night like this for its rambles.

Emerging from the storehouse he found his feet on a narrow plank walk that skirted a length of twelve-foot-high wire-fencing. It looked strong enough. Those springy steel meshes might have withstood the attack of a mad elephant. Curiosity, subordinated before to his concern for the girl, welled up now, and, yielding to it, Colin sent the light of his flash through the meshes.

The darting ray disclosed an expanse of trampled mud and wet turf, and beyond that a small, semi-enclosed shed. He held his light steady upon it. The rain, which had for a few moments diminished, descended again in driven, slanting sheets, but he thought he had glimpsed a heap of something gray that stirred as his light found it. Then a plaintive, long-drawn "Ba-a-a!" reached his ears. Colin snapped off his light in disgust. He had disturbed the innocent rest of some harmless sheep.

Following the plank walk, he squelched heavily along in what he felt must be the direction of the house. Now and again he allowed himself another brief glance beyond the wire fence, but most of the space seemed empty. One mournful cow, unprovided with even so flimsy a shelter as the sheep-shed, mooed at him dolefully as he splashed by.

"This I am sure of," thought Colin indignantly, "if that Reed man treats all his creatures like this, he'll soon have no stock to play scientist with. Sure, they'll all die of pneumonia!"

He had traversed a considerable distance, and still he saw nothing but on one hand that absurdly strong wire fence, on the other, shrubbery and a multitude of lashing, wind-tormented trees.

"I'll get nowhere at this rate save the other end of the estate."

So, turning aside, he plunged into pathless shrubbery. It was bad going and, except for his flash, would have been worse. They were blackberry and currant bushes, run wild and malignant with thorns and prickles. Out of their clutches at last, he, for the first time, glimpsed a light other than his own, which latter he promptly extinguished.

"That'll be the house," he said decisively, and hoped he was right.

Plowing toward it through a wet wilderness of weeds that had once been close-cropped lawn, he came among trees again and shortly found himself within a stone's throw of his goal.

It was a double light for which he had been heading, and proved to emanate from two windows set close together in the second story. Presently, using his own light cautiously, he identified near by the deep porch and *porte-cochère* of his last night's visit.

AND NOW, HAVING ACHIEVED THE goal for whose attainment he had laid himself open to a charge of felonious trespass, Colin found himself somewhat at a loss. Standing there in the rain it seemed to him that the strong inner force that had hitherto driven him, and which constituted his only real excuse for being there, now mockingly withdrew.

He shivered and scowled morosely at the dark, inhospitable entrance. For the first time he knew what a prowling, prying fool he must seem to Reed, could that gentleman have guessed his presence.

He glanced again toward the lighted windows above him. To his surprise he saw that the lower sash of one was raised. The drenched white curtains were flapping inward with the wind-driven rain. Then, as he looked, a figure appeared there, backing slowly into view, and O'Hara gasped at the desired but unexpected apparition.

There she stood, and though her back was toward him and the rain slanted between, he could make no mistake. He knew every curving line of those green-clad shoulders, that erect, white neck, and well-poised head. Had she been his closest comrade for years, instead of the stranger common sense called her, he could have felt no keener sense of familiar recognition.

Still keeping her face to the room, she stretched back one slim arm, feeling for the window-ledge. A wet curtain lashed and wrapped itself about the arm. With a quick, frantic energy she strove to free it. Then another arm flashed into view, and at last Colin knew the meaning of the silent drama of whose actors he had yet seen but one.

That darting arm was neither charming nor graceful. White, shaggy, rough as a length of pale, thick vine, it clutched toward her throat, with hand and fingers extravagantly long and terrible. Colin knew that hand, for he had felt it on his own throat.

With a great shout he sprang across the drive and was under the window.

"Jump!" he yelled through the sheeting rain. "Throw yourself backward and jump!"

He commanded a difficult feat, and from where he now waited could see nothing of what was going on above him. How might she possibly elude that near and gripping hand? And why should she obey his own roaring command from the outer darkness?

Three seconds passed, four, five. This was folly. He must break his way in somehow, before it was too late, and—

Above him there leaned out a head and a pair of slim shoulders, while a low voice called:

"I am coming! You frightened it!"

A pair of white, bare feet swung out over the window-ledge. Sitting so, the girl was instantly drenched. To emerge into the raging maw of the tempest, blinded by rain, and swing off into a vacancy which might or might not receive her tenderly, must have required a courage—or a recklessness—of uncommon quality. Yet sitting so, without pause or hesitation, the girl pushed herself off and dropped.

Colin caught her in his arms and did not even stagger to the shock. It seemed to him that she had fallen lightly as a leaf drifting earthward, or a bird with the air cupped in its wings. How had his strength increased that she lay in his arms so lightly? He closed them about her in a quick fierceness of protection. That brute—that hairy, clutching ape-thing—had dared clutch at her—at his Dusk Lady!

"Are you hurt?" he whispered. "Is it hurt you are that you lie so still?"

She answered in the same low, sweet tones that had addressed him from the window.

"No, my lord. But it was well that you came when you came, and well that you called to me! The demon above there would have killed me, I think, had you not frightened him with the trumpet of your voice. My lord, will you take me away now?"

"My lord" scarcely knew what to do. To some queer deep part of his being it seemed quite natural that she should call him so; quite reasonable and satisfactory that she should speak to him with the quiet confidence of one who appeals to an old friendship—old and sure. But his surface mind was less easy. Her father had spoken no more than truth—the girl was demented!

"Sure and I'll take you away," he declared. "And isn't that the very reason I was waiting under your window? But first we'll go into the house and make all straight and proper, the way none may say I've been stealing you, little lady."

"What? Return behind the walls of hate? But why?"

"It's a matter of decency, my dear. And, besides, before I can take you away you must be dry and better clothed. You're shivering this minute."

"Not for cold," she began, but just then a light sprang up close to Colin's head.

Startled, he fumed and saw that he was close by a window of the entrance hall. Two forms flashed, running across his field of vision, and a moment later he heard the door within the deep porch flung open.

Carrying the girl, he stalked around toward the steps, for he was no sneaking marauder, and felt neither shame nor further need of excuse for his presence. It had been too amply justified.

Marco met him, behind him a crouching, snarling, bestial form, but of that latter Colin had a very brief glimpse. Genghis Khan may have recognized the enemy who had chased him across five miles of rough going after breaking his right arm, now bandaged in splints at his side. Khan promptly retreated, sliding through, the door and out of sight with the streaking speed of a giant white cockroach. But Marco held his ground.

FRANCIS STEVENS

"You—you!" he mumbled, pointing a shaking, furious finger. "*You* come again? *You* touch her—my lady?"

"Better I than some others less respectful," retorted O'Hara calmly. "Is your master here?"

"Well, you know he is not! You fear him—everyone fears him! You come when he is gone! Put her down—let me take my lady!"

Coming at him, the albino thrust his hand beneath the girl's shoulders as if to tear her away. At that she screamed for the first time, clutching at Colin with small, convulsive fingers.

Then Colin struck Marco with the full weight of his fist, and with all his really terrible strength at the back of the blow.

It was a needless, savage act, as he afterward condemned it.

Marco was no possible match for him. In cold blood he would have brushed the albino aside without harming him. But the sight of that repulsive, red-eyed, pallid thing clawing at the girl, and the loathing and the terror in her voice acted upon him like a draft of maddening liquor. He struck without thought or premeditation, as at some noxious insect, desiring only to crush it, obliterate it from the world it polluted by living.

The blow caught Marco just under the point of the chin. His head flew back with an audible snap, his body jerked through the air, and sliding full length across the porch, brought up at the inner threshold. It twitched spasmodically and lay quiet.

Colin stood, and the girl clung to him, silent and quivering.

Very softly he ascended the steps, crossed the porch, and gently disengaging her arms set his burden down within the doorway, her bare feet on the dry softness of a rug.

Then he bent over Marco. He had hit him hard—too hard, and well he knew it. A thin, scarlet trickle was running from a corner of the flaccid mouth. He was not at all surprised when, lifting the albino's shoulders, the head dropped back with the limpness of a broken stick held together by a few torn fibers. He felt for Marco's heart and examined his neck with inquiring fingers. Then he laid him back and rose.

From the dead man he looked up to his mad Dusk Lady. She was watching him with dark, wondering eyes. Her wet, green gown clung to limbs and body, close as the green bark of a young tree, and the thick curls of her hair glistened black and shining.

Like some sorrowful spirit of the storm-torn forest she stood there, and Colin was ashamed before her. He, who had come to protect and guard her, had been betrayed by his temper and thereby involved them in Heaven only knew what entanglements.

"My lord, why do you look so sad and stern? Have I given you offense?"

"You! Poor child, no, 'tis myself has offended—but how, never mind. Go to your room, little lady, and dress yourself so that I may take you to a kinder place. At least, Marco will trouble you no more the night. He is—hurt."

"Hurt? Is he not dead?"

She said it so simply and with so childlike an inflection of disappointment that the words took Colin aback.

"Never mind that!" he retorted almost sharply. "Never mind that! Go dress yourself dry and warm, and put on a coat, if you have one, against the rain."

Frowning, she looked down at her one inadequate but becoming garment.

"I owe you gentle obedience, my lord, but I had vowed never to don robes of *his* giving. Must I, then, break my solemn vow?"

"Indeed, and I fear you must. They'll not let us on the train otherwise."

She meditated a moment longer. Then, "I will put on me a coat, since my lord desires it," and she started for the stair.

Remembering Genghis Khan, O'Hara followed. She led him straight to the door at the end of the second floor hall, where he had first seen her. It stood open, and as she entered he looked in over her shoulder.

He saw a large bedroom, well, even luxuriously furnished. Clearly, careless though he might be of her welfare in other respects, Reed did not begrudge money spent on his daughter's immediate surroundings.

Having made sure that the great ape was lurking nowhere in the room, and having closed the window above a rain-flooded Persian rug, O'Hara left his charge alone. She had said nothing in that while, only watched hum with attentive eyes that followed every move with quiet interest, and he himself had little mind for conversation.

But in the act of closing her door he turned back. "Where's the phone?" said he.

"The—the phone?"

"The telephone—the box they talk through when a bell rings," explained O'Hara patiently.

She shook her head, with a look of perplexed distress that was to him unutterably pathetic. Dusk Lady indeed, ever wandering through the twilight of a darkened mind!

"I'll find it myself," said he hastily, and closed the door.

Down the stairs he went, heavy and slow, weighed down by a great sickness of the spirit. Despite Reed's assurance, despite the dictates of everyday reason, O'Hara had until the last hour been possessed of a secret, unvoiced hope that this girl, the glamour of whose elfin personality had drawn him as no woman ever drew him before, might prove to be a sane and normal being. That hope was dead now—dead as the unlucky albino slain in his master's doorway. And for the sake of a mad girl he had committed a crime which in his own eyes debased him to the level of any common thug.

Coming at last to the stair foot, he turned and crossed toward the corpse of his poor, repulsive victim. And reaching the threshold of the hall, lo, it was empty!

The body of Marco lay there no more, nor any trace of it.

XIX

CLIONA RECEIVES A GUEST

I'll pay the fare, for I've no tickets." The conductor nodded and counted out change.

"A nasty sort of night, Mr. O'Hara," he observed affably.

Like every man on that short line, he knew half his passengers by sight, many by name, and there was little gossip going about at any of the smaller stations with which he was not acquainted. O'Hara had ridden with him only a few times, but the conductor was familiar with every extraneous fact concerning the Irishman's life at Carpentier. He remembered taking him to Undine earlier in the evening.

Now O'Hara was going in town, where he was said never to go, and accompanied by a mysterious female.

At that hour—eleven thirty—there was not another passenger on the inbound train, so the conductor had plenty of leisure for curious thoughts.

Sitting on the dusty red plush cushions beside his silent Dusk Lady, O'Hara's mind dwelt grimly on the results of his little expedition.

The disappearance of Marco's body troubled him, though he had made no effort to find it. Perhaps in the few moments that he was absent above-stairs, Genghis Khan had carried it away; or it might be that another witness than the girl had seen the slaying of Marco, someone who feared to show himself to this savage invader of Reed's domicile.

One idea he clung to. Whatever he himself had done, Reed's daughter should not spend another night in that house of mysterious human and bestial inhabitants.

She was silent and unquestioning, and he glad of her silence. When she talked his reason continually rebelled against the eccentricities of her speech. Silent, he felt renewed that intangible bond which seemed to exist between his nature and hers. Silent, he could almost forget that between them was also the dread specter of insanity.

"My lord, are you still angered with me?"

At the sound of that low, slightly tremulous voice, O'Hara turned reluctantly to the girl beside him. Toward her when she spoke he felt only gentleness and pity, but he dreaded what she might say, feeling a sort of personal shame in her irrationality.

"I have no anger with you, little lady," he answered kindly.

"Ill pleased, then. Is it because I have told you nothing of my story? One and another person I have told, but they had no—no understanding—"

She broke off, hesitating, and O'Hara groaned inwardly, thinking, "And how should they understand? Poor lass, only God understands foolishness!"

"But you are not as others; you will believe, for you are great and strong and noble, and, moreover, you are bound to me by the Golden Thread."

Colin started.

"Tell me nothing!" he broke in hastily. Then, seeing that she shrank away with a little hurt motion, he added, "We've no time just now for the length of your tale. Do you just wait, little lady, till we are safe at home with my sister. It's but a few minutes now till we get off the train."

"I will wait," she answered with a submissive sigh, and indeed there was no more time for talk. They were then entering the trainshed at the city terminal, and shortly thereafter Colin was hurrying his charge toward the gates and through them, thankful for the late hour and bad weather.

But there were few people about on the train floor, and in any case his fears proved needless. As they went she clung tightly to his arm, shrinking against him.

GREEN GABLES AT LAST, AND as Colin, standing in the shelter of the *porte-cochère*, paid off his driver, another car swung in and came to a halt just behind the taxi. This midnight motorist was Rhodes, very much belated—for him—but aglow with the results of a successful business day. A few minutes later that satisfaction was obliterated in pure astonishment.

Colin, full of the trouble and excitement of the past few hours, had clean forgotten that by Rhodes he was still supposed to be several thousand miles away, and it was a moment before he could see any reason for his brother-in-law's thunderstruck amazement.

Between that and genuine delight at finding him there, Rhodes did not notice the girl standing so silent at O'Hara's side until the latter, protesting that explanation must come later, called attention to this mysterious companion.

"Little lady," said he, drawing her forward, "here is a good friend of mine who will be a friend to you, too, I am thinking. This is Mr. Anthony Rhodes, the husband of my sister. Tony, Miss Reed has come far and is needing rest."

"My wife will be delighted to welcome you, Miss Reed. Won't you come in?"

For all his cordial tone Rhodes was secretly filled with growing amazement. O'Hara's abrupt and unheralded return had surprised him, but that he should drop out of nowhere at 12:45 A.M. accompanied by a mysterious and lovely female who appeared to be dumb—for she had acknowledged neither the introduction nor his invitation to enter save by a barely perceptible inclination of the head—this struck him as unreasonably queer, and altogether out of keeping with O'Hara's known character.

The latch-key was scarcely withdrawn from the opening door when Cliona appeared at the head of the stairs. She had sent the servants to bed, but herself waited up for her husband. Having planned a pleasant little supper *à deux* with her beloved Tony, and having donned for his benefit a most charming negligée, all soft white frills and chiffon rues with little gold bands to their edges, her glimpse of two other figures entering after him disconcerted her. Then, recognizing Colin, she came flying down the stairs like a small white whirlwind of welcome.

Colin laughed, holding her off at ands length. "Rues and ribbons," said he, "do you not see that I am dripping from the rain?"

"We have a visitor, Cliona," put in Rhodes in his pleasantest manner. "Miss Reed, let me make you acquainted with my wife."

"Oh," murmured Cliona, peering around her brother, behind whose shielding bulk the visitor seemed to have retreated. "I'm so glad to know you, Miss Reed. Won't you come upstairs and remove your wraps? I see that as usual Colin has scorned to carry an umbrella, and I fear has let you suffer the consequences."

Pause and silence.

"As for that, though, I don't suppose any umbrella would survive a wind such as we have had all evening. We'll have a little supper in a few minutes, and something hot to prevent all three of you from catching your death of cold."

No answer nor acknowledgment from the mysterious one.

FRANCIS STEVENS

"Will you come with me, Miss Reed?"

No response to that, either.

It is rather difficult to continue a flow of cordial welcome addressed to a dark, motionless, speechless figure, whose very presence carries an ominous foreboding. And while her tongue had run lightly enough, Cliona's mind was a confusion of surmise.

Who on earth could this strange woman be? Reed? Reed? Why, that Evan the name of the man who owned the queer stock-farm. And Colin had come openly to Green Gables, which he was not to do till the bungalow affair was finished.

Was the mystery solved, then? And what had this Miss Reed to do with it? Why lead Colin brought her here, in the middle of the night and without warning? When he had phoned her at seven o'clock there had been nothing definite to report, or so he said.

Cliona ceased to speak, and one of those sudden ghastly silences overtook all four of them—the kind that the ideal hostess is supposed never to allow. Cliona wanted to be an ideal hostess—she looked appealingly from Rhodes to Colin.

The latter realized that the time had come when he must begin to explain. With a sigh for the task ahead of him, he turned to his Dusk Lady.

"Take off your coat, child," he said gently. "This is my sister that I told you of. You'll find only kindness in this house."

Cliona and Tony looked at her, fascinated. The situation had passed beyond conventional handling. There was something here which only Colin understood.

They beheld a magnolia pale face, with crimson lips and starry, frightened eyes, but no words came from her.

"Oh!" cried Cliona again involuntarily, and Rhodes echoed the exclamation in his mind. Where had Colin discovered this girl with her unearthly beauty and equally unearthly manner? In South America? Spanish, perhaps? She looked like a Latin of some sort.

"Let me take your things," offered Cliona, realizing that the girl's coat was as wet as Colin's own.

"Shall I remove them here?"

The mysterious Miss Reed asked the question of O'Hara, as though she regarded him as the arbiter of even her smallest acts.

"You may as well." He took off his own ulster and thoughtfully flung it over the umbrella-stand in the entry. It was too wet for Cliona's hall-rack.

Miss Reed wore no hat, only the hood of her coat. Unfastening the coat itself, she slipped lithely out of it, leaving it in O'Hara's hands.

A startled and simultaneous gasp issued from three mouths at once, but Colin's was the most expressive. Saints above, he was glad there had been no occasion for her to remove that coat in the train or station!

Save that her feet were no longer bare, there stood his Dusk Lady exactly as she had stood upon the rug in Reed's entrance-hall while he stooped to examine Marco's body. Her green gown, wet as ever, clung to body and limbs in the revealing lines of a thin bathing suit. Her dark hair hung in the same beautiful but informal curls, and for the first time Colin was painfully aware of those worn places in her gown through which bare limbs shone whitely.

Her eyes darted from one face to another of those about her, frightened, questioning. They were all, even her "lord," looking at her in the strange way that no one had ever regarded her before the beginning of her long time of sadness. In the place of her nativity, no such tremendous and burdensome value was laid on mere costume as "civilization" places there, and little indeed had been her chance to learn. In the house at Undine she had been kept close and guarded.

Something was wrong. What was it?

Glancing at his sister's flushed, astounded face, O'Hara wished with all his heart that he had not so much—so very much explaining ahead of him. To introduce a crazed and half-clad maiden *and* the fact that he was in his own opinion a murderer, all in the same hour—well—

With another deep, weary sigh Colin undertook the beginning of his task.

It was morning. Wind and rain had followed night into the past, and a glorious late October sun was doing its utmost to cast a last glamour of summer over the shivering, storm-denuded trees and to gild the sodden leaf-carpet that covered lawns and gardens. But it found more success when it peered in the windows of Cliona's breakfast room, already a sufficiently cheerful apartment.

Though the hour was near noon, Cliona and Rhodes were first at table. With a very thoughtful brow she was putting slices of bread into an electric toaster, while her husband glanced mechanically through the morning paper.

Casting it aside, he picked up the first edition of a so-called afternoon journal which had a paradoxical habit of appearing at 11 A.M.

Therein he came on an item which changed his perfunctory interest to keen attention and caused him, after twice reading it, to fold up the sheet and with a very pale face thrust it in his pocket.

Cliona's attention had been riveted on the toast, but, glancing up, she saw that something was wrong.

"Are you not feeling well?" she asked quickly. "What's the matter, Tony?"

He smiled reassuringly. "Nothing that coffee won't mend, dear. A slight headache. Last night's revelations were a trifle upsetting, though *you* weren't upset, were you?"

He gave her an admiring glance. Dainty and fresh in her plain house-gown of blue linen, her appearance denied the sleepless night behind them.

"You are the only woman in the world, I believe, who could bear such a strain in the way you are doing. Frankly, I thought Colin was crazy himself to come here with that girl and that story so soon after your illness. But I see he knows you better than I do!"

"Not better—differently." She smiled back at him, then grew extremely grave.

"Tony, are we going to let him do it?"

"What? Give himself up? Now, Cliona, I don't see what else he can do. If he had been content to leave the girl where he found her, go quietly home and keep still afterward, I doubt if he could have been connected with the mur—the death of this man Marco. No one would have paid any attention to her story, even if she had the sense to tell it.

"But as it is, and having removed the girl from her father's house, and having been recognized by that conductor and very likely several other people, there is no possibility of his *not* being connected with it. No one who knows Colin is ever going to believe that he meant to kill the man, and the provocation was probably greater than he says. His bringing the girl here is proof enough of his good intentions, and now that the thing has gone so far the only course for him is to plead either justifiable or involuntary manslaughter.

"I'm no criminal lawyer, but I think when Reed's place is investigated, and everything is cleared up and the evidence laid before an impartial jury, Colin will get off scot free. This beautiful insane girl, left to the mercy of a huge ape and a probable degenerate, is bound to appeal to popular sympathy amazingly.

"*But* you and I have our work cut out in dealing with that unruly conscience of Colin's. He says he meant to kill the man and that he wishes to take the consequences. If he says the same thing in court, and when the relative bulk of Colin and Marco is considered, the court is likely to take him at his word! I'm not trying to frighten you, darling, but I wish you to realize that Colin must—be—persuaded!"

Cliona looked at him quite calmly.

"He has to be persuaded to more than that—he has to be persuaded that 'twas not he but that big monkey, Genghis Khan, who killed Marco!"

Rhodes opened his mouth to speak, then shut it again. A woman's conscience is a tender thing, but it is not like a man's. Cliona, most innocent of women, considered perjury a small price for her brother's life and liberty. Yet after all it was no more perjury than what her husband had himself proposed.

Rhodes possessed a deep and genuine friendship for his wife's brother. But he also knew the violence and impetuosity of the man. In his heart he believed that Colin had, as he insisted, intended for one furious moment the death of Marco. However, to his masculine mind there was a difference between the lie involved in a plea of involuntary manslaughter and the bolder lie which shifted the whole burden to another's shoulders, even though they were the shoulders of a beast.

And at that moment Colin himself appeared.

If possible he looked more depressed than on the previous night. Having shamed himself before these two, he must now go and shame himself before a less sympathetic audience at city hall. And the girl he loved was as mad as a hatter! The world looked very cold and bare to Colin O'Hara that morning, despite its sunshine.

"Where's my—Miss Reed?" he demanded as he seats himself.

"Your Miss Reed is still in bed," retorted Cliona with an attempt at lightness. "I ordered her breakfast sent up."

"Oh! All right."

Colin attacked his breakfast, served by the dignified butler whom the Rhodes had acquired with their large menage. But he found his appetite surprisingly slight. The instant they were alone he laid down his grapefruit spoon, leaned back and thrust his hands in his pockets.

"I'm going in town now."

"Yes," said Cliona quietly. "And we are going with you."

"You're not."

"Before anyone goes," Rhodes interposed with great firmness, "we shall have to talk things over a little further."

"There's nothing to talk about," began Colin in his most obstinate manner, but just then the door opened and a timid, beautiful face appeared in the aperture.

"May I—is it fitting that I enter?"

"Of course—come right in, dear. Did you find it too lonely in your room?"

Cliona, though she had good cause to dislike this ************* who had brought sorrow to all of them, was incapable of treating her in other than a kindly manner. Rising she went to the door and opened it for her fair and singular guest.

The green gown was no longer in evidence, though Colin darkly suspected it of being somewhere beneath the pale lavender peignoir which now adorned her person. Cliona knew better. That unfortunate garment had been removed by herself at 3 A.M., after an expenditure of diplomacy sufficient to settle the fate of nations, but barely enough to persuade her guest out of it and into one of her own dainty nightrobes.

Under Cliona's guidance the girl entered and seated herself in the fourth chair at the small, square table, facing Colin. Every motion she made, every glance of her bright, mournful eyes, expressed the timidity of a graceful wild creature, anxious to please and to believe in the sincerity of those about it, but intensely conscious of the strangeness of its surroundings.

She had been given no opportunity to tell her story. Last night they had all seemed desperately concerned over the killing of one who she well knew deserved his death—so concerned that no attention could be spared her, and every effort she made to speak—went wrong, some way.

They would look at her, kindly, pityingly—and very courteously indicate that silence on her part was greatly to be preferred. The more important part of her story she had not dared even begin on. That was for her lord's ear alone. Surely he, who was so irrevocably bound to her, *must* understand and believe.

Strange how the speaking or withholding of one word will sometimes affect whole destinies! One word—one of several names that were on her very tongue-tip—and the hindering veil of miscomprehension would have fallen.

But she deemed her "lord" as ignorant of those names as everyone else of the few she had been allowed to meet in this mad world that lay outside her native hills. She knew him and he her, and they knew each other not at all—a paradox that was to cost dear before the finish.

The girl was beautiful enough, in all conscience—more beautiful in the morning sunshine than he had thought her by the lights of night. Her hair was dry now, and had that dull black softness about her face which had caused O'Hara to name her "Dusk Lady" on first sight. Her smooth skin possessed a pearly, translucent whiteness, almost like alabaster with a faint pink light behind it, and her eyes were pleadingly, deceptively intelligent. Yet just now Rhodes felt that Colin himself was a sufficient problem and the presence of his insane protégée superfluous.

"Did you sleep well, Miss Reed?" he inquired.

And she replied with an admirable simplicity: "I slept."

"And why not?" demanded Colin, heavily cheerful. "You're out of that house, and not even your father shall put you back there, little lady."

"My—father? Oh! You mean he who names himself Chester Reed? He is not my father."

"No?" Rhodes tried to look interested. "Your name not Reed, then?"

The girl drew herself up with a funny little air of hauteur, and replied surprisingly: "I have no name!"

A pained expression flashed across O'Hara's frank face. Again he was troubled by that double emotion—shame for her pitiful speeches, and, deeper than that, a sympathy which took no count of madness.

She saw the pain in his eyes, the momentary astonishment of the two other faces, and its instant veiling behind that kindly, intolerable tolerance with which well-bred sanity confronts an unsound mind. She saw, for she shrank back in her chair and her dark eyes glimmered.

"You know, dear child," said Cliona gently, "because we all have names ourselves, we get in the habit of expecting other people to have them, too. But indeed, if you are wishing it to be so, you need have no name with us."

Frowning, the girl glanced from one to another, as if trying to determine exactly what they, their surprise and Cliona's too-soothing assurance might really mean. The she said in a very low tone, speaking only to herself, it seemed: "All the customs are so strange!"

"They are that," conceded O'Hara with suspicious heartiness. "But now don't you be troubling your mind for the matter a minute longer. What do we care for names—the four of us here? Faith, 'tis the same to us if there were no names at all in the world—you need none, little lady, nor your mother nor your father—"

"Oh," cried the girl, brightening unexpectedly, "but of course my father had a name, and gave one to my mother likewise, but for me, I am not wed. Do *your* unwed maidens bear names, then?"

"Generally." Rhodes sighed. He supposed they must humor the poor girl. "If you would tell us your father's name we could call you that, you know—that is if you object to 'Miss Reed.'"

For the first time she laughed. "To call me as if I were my father! How strange are your customs!"

Then she looked anxiously about the table.

"I have heard him say that some harm had come to his name—what, I did not understand—so that it would bring him sorrow in this, the land of his birth. But you are my friends—you will not speak it to others. You are friends, are you not?"

Colin, though he groaned in the soul of him, nodded and smiled bravely. Rhodes laughed in a kindly, encouraging way, and Cliona, filled with pity, leaned over and kissed the poor, sick girl on her beautiful forehead.

"We are friends," she replied softly. Then: "Oh—what is it, Masters?"

The butler, who had just entered, straightened himself with a resolutely passive face. "There are two men in the reception hall, and they asked me to tell you, Mr. Rhodes, that they are from headquarters and wish to see Mr. O'Hara at once. One of them says his name is MacClellan, sir."

Masters had come to Green Gables shortly after O'Hara's departure for "South America," and consequently, though MacClellan had previously visited the house several times, he was unknown to the butler. But Masters did know that he disapproved of a household in which red-haired giants appeared at breakfast dressed in worn, water-proofed khaki, and were then called upon by plain-clothes men.

However, Masters' inward disturbance was nothing compared to the consternation roused by his announcement in the bosoms of three of his hearers.

No one said anything, but their eyes, meeting across the table, spoke volumes. Then Rhodes turned to his stately servitor with what calmness he could command at the moment.

"All right, Masters. Go tell them to wait a few minutes—right there in the hall."

"Very well, sir."

Masters' restraining presence removed, O'Hara came straight to the point.

"They traced me so soon! Indeed, I've never given that lad MacClellan credit for such intelligence. Well, it's sorry I am, Tony, that they should take me from your house."

But as Colin was rising from the table, Rhodes stopped him.

"Wait a minute! I don't think they've come for that, and I want you not to see them. I have something to tell you—"

"Let it wait!" Colin shook off his brother-in-law's hand and stood up. His face was darkly flushed but his eyes shone with a grim determination. He dominated the rest of them like a giant at a pigmies tea-party.

"Not see them? Would you have me sneak out the back door, then? Be sure they'll see me if I'm in the house—and I'll not run away. Do you stay here."

He strode to the door, but his last command was disregarded. When he entered the reception hall Rhodes was behind him, still protesting, while Cliona and the strange girl brought up the rear.

"Ah, Mr. O'Hara!" And MacClellan's rather heavy and stolid, countenance brightened as he beamed upon the advancing Irishman in a manner singularly cordial to be bestowed upon a murder-suspect. "I thought I might find you here. Quick work, eh? I suppose you've read all about it in the early afternoon editions?"

"No." Colin favored his prospective captor with a morose stare. "I'd no notion they'd be having it—so early."

"Oh, they got it at headquarters. We tried to phone out to Mr. Rhodes here, but they said you didn't answer. Line out of order?"

"Not that I know of." Rhodes was nervous. He was becoming more and more positive that MacClellan was innocent of any knowledge dangerous to O'Hara, but at the same time there was imminent peril of his acquiring such information within the next few moments. O'Hara must be kept quiet until there was time for further conference.

"More likely something wrong with the operator," he continued. "But I read the paper, MacClellan, and was just going to show it to the rest when you arrived."

"And I was just on my way," began O'Hara, but Rhodes forestalled him, speaking very loudly and quickly.

"It's the bungalow again, Colin. The bungalow received another visitation last night!"

And pulling the folded newspaper from his pocket, he thrust it into O'Hara's hands, pointing to the column in question and for the moment at least effectually distracting his attention.

Cliona, keyed to a worse calamity, laughed and exclaimed involuntarily: "Is that all?"

"Ain't it enough?" MacClellan looked a trifle offended. No man likes to bear news of a mountain and hear it called a mole-hill. "I tell you, Mrs. Rhodes, it was enough to send me and Forester here shooting out to Carpentier within ten minutes after we got word of it. The news was phoned in by a milkman—name of Walker—and he said when he went up there to deliver the milk, there wasn't, in a manner of speaking, any place to deliver it at. Said you'd been living there alone, Mr. O'Hara, and the way he talked we got the idea you was murdered and laid out in the ruins.

"So Forester, here, and me shot out there, and sure enough the place was pretty well smashed up, but not a sign of you or anybody else hurt. So on the train comin' in we got talkin' with the conductor—we central office men pick up lots of valuable clues just talking, here and there— and he says the night man told him how you and a lady went in town somewhere after eleven-thirty last night.

"Well, we was anxious to get in touch with you, just to let you know we're on the job, so I tried to get Mr. Rhodes by phone. While I was trying, Forester, he called up the hotels and drew them blank, so I says the best thing was to come straight out here, and we did and here's Mr. O'Hara, just like I thought."

MacClellan was so enamored of his own perspicacity in locating Colin that he was quite good-natured again. But to that gentleman himself it seemed a childishly simple feat—particularly when compared to the one which he had suspected MacClellan.

He had meant to make the whole of last night's doings known to the complacent detective, but now he hated to do it. Somehow MacClellan would arrogate to himself as much credit as if he had captured a desperate criminal in the red act of assassination. Besides, there was the bungalow. After waiting six weeks for that visit, it had come in earnest during his one night of absence!

"So the place was pulled down?" he asked slowly, scanning the headlines.

"Oh, no. That was Walker's exaggeration. But it was pretty well wrecked up all right—worse than the first time. And Walker said that when he got up there, there was a horrible smell about the place. Some sort of chemical, I guess, though that may have been some more of his imagination. It didn't look to me like there'd been any explosion."

"I smelled something queer myself when we went inside." This from Forester, an intelligent-looking but very young man. "Don't you remember I called your attention to it?"

"Yes, and I said you was dreamin'," snapped his superior. "If there was any smell it got out the windows before we reached there."

Forester shrugged and subsided. But to O'Hara this talk of a mysterious odor called up a memory. The scene was a large, bare, dusty interior, illuminated by one leaping white ray. Faith, and it was a most unpleasant stench the place had been filled with! The front and the back door of that storehouse had stood open—open! And it was from Reed's place that Genghis Khan had wandered all the way to Carpentier—and tried to strangle him! Had Khan "wandered"?

"I'll be returning to the bungalow," he announced.

"Oh, no!" To Cliona, Carpentier and its vicinity were by this time doubly enhanced with terror. "Colin, darling, promise me you'll never go near there again!"

"I'll have to. Sure, every stitch of clothes I have but these are out there. You'd not have me sacrifice my entire wardrobe, Cliona?"

"You can send for them—besides, that's not your reason!" she added suspiciously.

"And what if it's not? In broad daylight! For shame, little sister, 'tis not like yourself to be so unreasonable!"

"I don't mean to be," Cliona considered, while MacClellan turned away to examine a picture—and grin. He disliked this domineering Irishman as instinctively as O'Hara despised him, and it was highly amusing to hear him plead against petticoat rule as meekly as the least of his fellows. "You may go," decreed Cliona at last, "if you'll take these gentlemen with you."

Rhodes laughed. "I'm going myself, so you'll have quite a bodyguard, Colin."

Somewhat to his surprise Cliona offered no objection to that. Perhaps she felt there was safety in numbers, and anyway, on reflection, a daylight expedition to the bungalow could rouse little dread. There must be people all over the place, too, as she had been told there were while first she lay there unconscious.

"Where's the—the—Miss Reed?"

It was Rhodes who asked. All the time they talked, the girl had stood close to Cliona, partly in shadow and so motionlessly silent as to be practically forgotten by all save Colin. He never quite forgot her, but she had been pushed to the back of his mind by these more pressing matters.

"I think—perhaps she went back in the breakfast room. Shall I look for her?" Cliona made a motion toward the door, but her brother checked her, drawing her somewhat aside from the rest.

"'Tis as well," he said in a guarded tone, "that MacClellan does not see her just now. Who knows what the day may bring? I'll not bid her farewell, either, for the poor lass might not understand. Just tell her I've gone and will return soon, and do you try and get at the truth of this business of her father. I'd not be surprised if there was real truth behind that. Be good to her and gentle—ah, I know there's no need to say that! Were you ever aught else in your life, little sister? But indeed, I'm that troubled—"

"Colin, MacClellan says he has only another hour or so to spare. If we're going we'd better start." This from Rhodes.

"I'll take care of her, Colin." Cliona gave his arm a reassuring pat as he turned to obey Rhodes' summons. But she looked after him with a sadness in her eyes.

Though so much younger, she understood Colin, as a mother understands a beloved son, and she knew that it was not only shame or despair for his deed at Undine that had taken all the buoyancy from his step, all the happiness from his face. She had seen him look at the girl he had brought here, heard his voice when he spoke of her—and the girl was so lovely—so hopelessly, pitifully lovely!

XX

THE FOURTH VISITATION

O'Hara stood on the macadamized drive beneath the same tree from which Genghis Khan had reached for his throat two nights ago. MacClellan alone was with him, for at the last moment Rhodes had received a telephone call from his partner—that line was in working order, after all—begging that he come in town at once on a matter of considerable business importance.

O'Hara urged him to go, and in the end he did, but with a promise to join them later if possible. So they had run down to the city in Rhodes' car, dropped its owner at his office, set Forester down at city hall—his superior having denied any need of the young man loafing away any more time on this job—and proceeded straight to Carpentier.

O'Hara was his own chauffeur, and he had MacClellan in the tonneau, so at least he was spared any converse with him during the trip. Once at the bungalow, however, the detective gave his tongue and his opinions a loose rein.

As he had told them, this fresh bit of apparently objectless destruction bore a broad resemblance to the earlier attempt, save that this time its perpetrators had left no visible trace of themselves save their work.

Every room in the house had been visited, as if by a small invading whirlwind. An indiscriminating whirlwind, too, that had scattered and smashed with no regard for relative values.

A finely carved and heavily constructed sideboard which had escaped the first visitation had been broken to bits in the most difficult and painstaking manner. But equally the cheap deal table, at which Colin had taken supper the night before, lay about the kitchen in well-nigh unidentifiable fragments. In the bedroom that had been first Cliona's and then Colin's, nothing had been touched except the bed, and that was irrevocably smashed, even to the twisted mass of wire which had been the springs.

So everywhere things common and valuable were broken or left intact with the whimsicality of choice that distinguishes those three insentient destroyers—fire, storm, and concussion.

Yet there were no signs of an explosion, no fire had raged here, and, though a storm there had been, it must have been a strange one to have shattered windows and doors, ravaged inner rooms, and left roof and walls uninjured.

The milkman's statement that he "came up to leave the milk and found no place to leave it" was not entirely unfounded. His custom had been to put O'Hara's quart bottle of the healthful fluid on the front steps, but these steps, which were wooden, had been torn away and lay some distance off. Every one of the veranda windows was broken, sash and all, and the door was flat and in two pieces.

Having gloomily inspected the remains of his premises, Colin stood in the dining-room and listened with acute boredom to MacClellan's views. Something small and bright-colored caught his eye, and stooping, he plucked it from amidst the sideboard's *débris*. It was the last surviving remnant of that unfortunate Aztec godling—the head, minus its miter, and part of the red and blue tunic.

Colin stared grimly down at the still patiently smiling face.

"So they got you at last, little man," he muttered, half-abstractedly.

The face smiled on—patient forever with the *blindness* of mankind.

"What's that?" demanded MacClellan.

"Nothing." Colin tossed the fragment aside, and led the way toward the door. "Just a bit of pottery that was worth a few thousand before we began receiving midnight callers. There's no luck to this house—no luck all. I shall live here no more. Drop the case or keep on with it as you like—its a matter of no further interest to myself."

This annoyed MacClellan. It annoyed him more than O'Hara's insistence that he solve the previous case. There could be drawn an inference that the Irishman had lost all faith in his ability to solve anything whatever, but in that he was mistaken. O'Hara could not lose what he had never possessed.

"We shall continue to investigate," he declared with stolid dignity. "We have sent word down the line to round up every hobo between here and headquarters, and—"

"Hoboes!" The exclamation had a quality of bitter scorn that dissipated the last of MacClellan's patience.

"Yes, hoboes!" he snapped. "If you're so sure that I don't know anything, then you have some good reason for being sure! When you get ready to tell it, let me know. I'm going back by train. Good day!"

Colin viewed his retreating figure with wide, amused eyes.

"And that's the only really clever thing he ever said in his life! Good day to you, Mr. MacClellan! Sure, I'll let you know—but not until I'm ready!"

The detective, on his early morning visit, had again called out a patrolman to stand guard over O'Hara's possessions, and there he stood, MacClellan having departed in too great a rage to remember his patient sentinel.

"Go or stay as you please," said O'Hara to the officer. "I'll send up a man presently to pack what's left worth packing and ship it in town. I doubt if I'll return here myself."

"I'll see that your man makes a good job," volunteered the policeman agreeably. O'Hara had just slipped a bit of green paper into his willing hand—extended for that purpose, perhaps from habit, discreetly and with back half turned.

"Thanks. I wish you would."

As Colin climbed into the driving seat of his borrowed car he gave a last glance about the now desolate hilltop. Here and there strayed some idle and amateur seeker of "clues." A reporter or so, ruthlessly repelled by the gloom-stricken Irishman, still hovered hungrily in the offing. One individual hurried toward him as he started the car. Had Colin looked he would have seen a lean, worn-looking man, white-haired, with the mark of an old scar across his lower forehead.

"Mr. O'Hara!" he called. "Hey, there! O'Hara! Wait a minute!"

"Go to the devil with the rest of 'em!" muttered Colin without even a glance, and fairly shot out of hearing.

He wanted to get away from it all. He had by no means surrendered hope of achieving a final solution—in fact he was grimly certain that the solution would not be much longer delayed. But he was sick of the bungalow—sick of everything.

No matter if he exposed Reed as the *deus ex machina* of these lawless manifestations; no matter if in exposing him he discovered the reason of Reed's grudge, if he had one. No matter, even, if for one reason or another the killing of Marco should be publicly applauded as a righteous act—though that last seemed to him unlikely enough. No matter for anything. Was he not indeed linked by a "golden thread" to the one girl in the world for him—and was she not hopelessly, unquestionably insane?

HE DETERMINED THAT HE WOULD not go back to Green Gables. She was safe in his sister's keeping, and he determined that before yielding himself to the police he would have one final interview with Reed—providing that is, that he could easily locate him.

Yet before going on that errand, he brought the car to a halt before Bradshaw's shop, entered and with a nod to the storekeeper made for the little telephone booth. But Bradshaw halted him.

"Say, Mr. O'Hara, your sister called up a while ago. Said the bungalow line was out of order. Did you find out—"

"Did Mrs. Rhodes want me, then? How long ago was that?"

"Oh, about an hour, more or less, the first time. She's called twice since and says for you to phone her right away. Did that detective fellow—"

"Why didn't you send up the hill after me?" demanded O'Hara indignantly.

"Nobody to send. Been looking around for a boy, but they're all up round your place, I guess. Did you find out—"

"I did *not!*" O'Hara disappeared in the booth, banging the door in poor Bradshaw's aggrieved face. That is, he tried to bang it, but the booth never having been built for his bulk, the attempt was a miserable failure.

In an uncomfortably stooped position Colin went through the customary struggle to get Green Gables from Carpentier through a matter of three exchanges, and in the end was rewarded by Cliona's voice on the wire. She had been waiting anxiously for the call and before he could ask a question she imparted her news.

"Colin—she's gone!"

"What? Who's gone?" But he knew very well.

"That Miss Reed, or whoever she was. She's gone—and I've been trying to get you for nearly two hours. Where have you been?"

"Here." Colin's voice was a trifle hoarse. Of course they would find her again—she had wandered away, but he would find her—

Again Cliona was speaking. She had, it appeared, seen her guest safely bestowed in the bedroom assigned to her use, and herself gone to lie down for a short time. When she returned to offer the girl a cup of tea the room was empty. She was nowhere in the house and her coat had also disappeared. And—"Colin, she had taken that dreadful green dress again!"

"Taken it? She didn't wear it?"

"I—I'm afraid she did. The clothes I gave her were on the bed—they were laid out very nicely and in order, Colin dear—she must have had a beautiful bringing up—"

"Never mind consoling me, Cliona. What have you done to find her?"

It seemed she had sent every one of the servants to search the neighborhood and had tried to get in touch with him before notifying the police. And three reporters had been there already about the bungalow—and the servants had all returned with nevus, and she had waited and waited—

"Yes, to be sure. But do you tell me, darling. Did she say anything to you before you left her? Tell me word for word all she said. I may get some trace of her by it."

"Let me think. I asked her about her father, but she would tell me nothing. She said that already she loved me, but only to you would she speak. She said: 'I have seen kindness in the eyes of others than you, but it has been as the mockings of the shadow people. They went and returned not. But between me and my lord hangs a Golden Thread, and therefore there is trust between us.' Something like that. I'm trying to remember exactly, but—"

"You've a wonderful memory, and you're doing fine. And then?"

"Well, she seemed disturbed because you had gone to Carpentier, and asked me to take her and follow you. Then she said she left the reception hall because you disliked the fat, clean man—Mr. MacClellan, I suppose—so much that you were making her hate him. She hates Marco and you—you struck him. And she thought that striking Marco had made you sad, she knew not why. So she went away lest you strike the fat, clean man also. Forgive me, Colin, but you wanted to know *exactly*."

"And so I do. Then?"

"That was all. When I wouldn't take her after you, she asked to lie down in her room and she did. She wad so perfectly nice and—and pleasant that I never—never *thought*—"

"And why would you? There's no blame at all to you, darling." His exoneration of Cliona was quite mechanical, a matter of habit, for in truth his thoughts were not on her.

From head to foot he thrilled with a bitter, uncanny joy that shocked but refused to be banished by his reasoning mind. She had felt his dislike for MacClellan, sensed and sympathized with it to the point of hatred, in the same way that he had flamed to deadly, unjustifiable passion for her sake!

What fire was this in which fleshly barriers melted and their two spirits fused? A dangerous blaze, surely, that expressed itself only in hate! No, that was the chance of unlucky circumstance. What opportunity had there been for happiness to, leap between them? Oh, all madness, madness!

Somewhere in him there must lurk a weak, abnormal strain that responded to her insanity. He forced thought of it from him as something to be faced another time, and resolutely set his mind to the present exigency.

"Don't be telling the police—yet. I've an idea where she may have gone. Had she any money, do you think?"

"How do I know?" wailed his harassed sister. "She might have had some in her coat."

"Cliona, do you take your mind off this business entirely. I'm the one that's responsible for her, and it's myself will find the poor lass. If any more reporters or detectives come bothering you, have Masters send them about their business. All will be well and 'twill be less than a help should you fret yourself into another sickness. Call up Tony at the office and tell him I'm leaving Carpentier and he had best return straight home when he can, so I'll know where to find him. Will you do all that for me, darling?"

"Where are you going?" Her voice hinted of indefinite alarm.

"Well, the railroad station would be a good place to seek first trace of her, don't you think?"

"Perhaps—yes, I believe you're right, Colin. And then try the police stations. She's certainly quiet and well-behaved enough one way, but you can't tell what she might do outside and alone. Then will you come home—whether you find her or not?"

"Oh, I'll come home. Goodby, Cliona, and mind all I told you."

He hung up the receiver without waiting for a reply. Having purposely misled her in regard to the direction his search would take, he wished to answer no more questions.

THERE WAS ONE PLACE TO which his Dusk Lady, had she been of sound mind, would have been supremely unlikely to return. Being what she was, in O'Hara's opinion that was the first covert to draw. She had expressed to Cliona alarm for his safety and a desire to follow him.

Danger and the house at Undine must be to her synonymous terms. There she had known misery and terror, there she had barely escaped the clutches of danger carnified in the person of Genghis Khan; there, she had seen him, O'Hara, kill a man and felt vicariously his own after-horror.

There, then, if she thought of danger, would she picture him, and since she wished to follow him, it was to Reed's house that she would straightway go.

It was sketchy theorizing, perhaps, but Colin had been trained in a rough school that turns out excellent and not often mistaken psychologists.

He swung out of Bradshaw's, and almost into the arms of the white haired man, who had followed him down the hill.

"Mr. O'Hara," he began again, but Colin brushed ruthlessly past.

"I've *nothing* to say," he flung back.

He had an impression that the persistent journalist sprang after him, tried to get a foothold on the running board, and fell. But his thoughts were a rushing torrent that fairly bore him with them. The outer consciousness that repulsed the man and set the car in motion was as mechanical as the motor itself.

And so went Colin's last chance of escape from that which awaited him, swept under by the impetuous nature that no experience could lessen—that would be still impetuous to the very hour of its death.

The road to Undine was well enough known to him, when he was not led cross-country. The big car ate up those few miles at reckless speed. Of course, there was a possibility that the lost maiden might have started for home in a vague, wandering way, without the wits or the money to reach it. But O'Hara deemed otherwise. The cleverness of lunacy is notorious, and who knew how familiar she might be with ways and means of getting about the city?

Ten minutes after leaving Carpentier, he pulled up with a jerk at the iron gates upon whose intricate beauty he gazed for the fourth time in two days. It was then after five o'clock, and dusk was spreading its mantle of indistinctness and mystery. Behind those iron scrolls the gate-lodge loomed as a dim, sepulchral mass.

O'Hara was out of the car almost before it had stopped, and at the gate in two long strides. But with his hand on the bell he paused. The thought of another clandestine intrusion on these premises was distasteful. He wanted to ring the bell and make his demands boldly of whoever should answer. But would anyone answer? Why had he so taken it for granted, because of last night's havoc at the bungalow, that Reed had never gone further from home than Carpentier—that the note transmitted by Marco's hand contained a lie?

What if, up there at the house whose gray roofs so melted into the gray dusk as to be invisible behind their screen of skeleton boughs,

FRANCIS STEVENS

what if no one was there save the monster ape and Marco? Marco, deaf forever to the ringing of that or any earthly bell?

Had Reed returned, from however nefarious an expedition, would his own criminal proceedings have stopped him from sending out a general alarm, that the slayer of his servant and the abductor of his daughter might be immediately traced? And it would have been so easy to trace him!

Surely, even MacClellan could have picked up that trail, followed so obvious a clue as the conductor's story. But if Reed were not at his "farm," if no one were there save Genghis Khan, and it had been he who caused Marco's body to vanish so disturbingly, then the girl could not be there either. Had she come, there was no one to admit her—ah, stupidity! What of that open storehouse door through which Colin himself had showed her the way? And if she had gone in—had found Khan there, alone, masterless—

Filled with an increasing horror of possibilities conjured up by his own imagination, O'Hara laid his hand on the gate, shaking it slightly— and at that light impulsion it swayed inward an inch or so. The loud complaint of its hinge smote his ears like a blow. The gate was unlocked! Anyone might have entered here—*anyone*.

Half reluctantly, like a man who approaches some sight too terrible for human bearing, O'Hara pushed the gate wider and set his foot on the sodden leaves of the drive.

He had left that house, left the man-ape loose there and given no warning that should save any harmless intruder from its unrestrained and cunning savagery. He knew what reward had been meted out to him, the double offender—knew it as though the torn, dismembered body of his Dusk Lady lay at his feet. Yet, since he must, he entered and turned his footsteps toward the unseen house.

Tonight there was no wind; only silence, intense, painful as an evil dream, which the soft sound of wet leaves beneath his feet only served to make more lifeless. A thin haze had risen from the sodden ground, so that about him there was neither light nor darkness, only gray neutrality from which gaunt trees lifted their skeleton tracery against a sky only a little brighter than the mist below.

Yet objects close at hand were still discernible. He passed the vine-hidden gate-lodge, and as he did so, and because of the general stillness, a sound reached his ears, a just perceptible rustling, as of wood gently rubbed upon wood.

Whirling quickly, he stared through the thin haze toward the inner wall of the lodge. From where he stood, ten feet away, its outlines were somewhat blurred, its vines a mass without detail. And yet he was almost sure that again, as on that first night, a blacker oblong had appeared in the dark wall of vines.

Then and for the first time in his life O'Hara learned the meaning of stark, horrible fear—fear that shut his throat against breath, and turned the strength of his giant limbs to water!

In the center of that vague black oblong, faintly gleaming through the mist by a pallid light of its own, appeared an oval shape that swayed slightly from side to side—the oval of the gate-keeper's barely visible countenance. And to Colin the gatekeeper was Marco. And Marco lay dead by Colin's hand!

Had the Irishman been given time to reflect, time to set the stern clamp of reason on his slipping faculties, what followed might have happened differently. But time was not granted. The oval wavered and rose a foot or so, then shot itself outward straight for O'Hara's face.

He screamed out, loud and harsh, twisting his head to one side. Something struck his neck a terrible blow, and the gray mist flared red about him, to vanish, roaring, into blank unconsciousness.

HE WAS LYING BENEATH THE sea, lapped in the slimy ooze of its deepest profundity. He could feel the rocking of his body to some slow, dense current, and the awful pressure of the depths crushed the flesh inward upon his vital organs, squeezing out the very life. Yet struggling to breathe—why, he could breathe, though shortly. He felt the air in his nostrils. How was that? Was there air on the sea-bottom?

With that question, awakening reason dissipated the dream and roused him from unconsciousness. But the pressure it did not dissipate, nor the slow rocking motion. With an effort he forced open his eyes. It was night. He was lying on the ground somewhere in the open air, for he was looking upward through mist not dense enough to obscure the larger stars. His mind, still dazed, refused at once to resume the business of life.

Marco? Marco? What was it concerning Marco? Reluctantly, then with gathering power, memory took up its office, showing him the day as he had lived it, action by action and scene by scene, till it brought him to an iron gate—the lodge within—the face that had hung poised in the doorway, unbearable horror of its flashing out at him, then that great blow and—darkness.

But what after that? Why was he lying here, with body and limbs surrounded by some strange, tightening substance? Heavily he raised his head. He saw his own chest as a dim, whitish mass that seemed to stir with a slow, creeping motion. And now he knew that continually, through the paralyzing pressure, he had felt that sluggish creep, creep of the thing about him.

There was a pounding in his ears, his temples throbbed and his eyes were dim with a suffusion of blood. But he perceived that the coiled mass round his chest was becoming faintly luminescent—that it was by its own light he saw the flat broadness of the coil nearest his face; noted, with a great effort of attention, its thin edge and the translucent parallel corrugations of its upper surface.

Like the body of a worm it was, seen by transmitted light—a gigantic, living, shining worm that had no right to existence, even in a bad dream. And it was around him—he felt its naked coldness pressed against the skin of his right wrist, where the sleeve had been pushed above the protecting leather of his heavy glove.

The coils tightened, contracted, with that continual revolting deliberation of movement, that drawing together and expanding of the corrugations that each time slid them a little further along. From chest to feet this—thing had wrapped itself about him, and still rocked him gently to its leisurely and sliding compassion.

The luminance of its body was not constant, but increased and faded, increased and faded in a long, slow pulsation.

Letting his head fall back on the sodden leaves he strove to move his limbs, to struggle. It was like straining against tight, thick rubber that gave a little but overcame the resistance of his deadened muscles simply by pressure.

Then came the worst, for up from beneath his left shoulder a head rose and stretched itself on a thin, flat, tapering neck. It was a head that seemed mostly mouth, a great triangular aperture, gaping, tongueless, with soft drooping lips, and behind it on either side a fleck of red that might have been eyes or their remnants.

It reared a good two feet above Colin's face, and he, staring, saw that its under side was dark, opaque, and that it was only from its upper surface that the light came. Then the head drooped and lowered, the neck curved backward.

For one instant there was presented that same pale, shimmering oval which had hung in the doorway and that he had believed to be Marco's dead face. It descended with a swift, darting motion and Colin felt flabby lips muzzling at his neck.

A dreadful, groaning cry rang in his ears, and he did not know that it was his own voice. He writhed in that close embrace, and its flat, contractible coils tightened around his chest—till the lungs collapsed and could no longer expand themselves—till he could utter not so much as a whisper of sound.

Mental torment gave way to acute physical pain and that again to the merciful blankness of negation.

PART III

XXI

Cliona Meets a Stranger

I don't care, Tony! It's well enough for you to bid me not worry, but how can I *help* worrying?"

"Now, my dear, you're letting your nerves run away with you. Colin is in no danger of anything worse than getting himself locked up, and he will hardly do that intentionally before he has located this girl again. I wish, though, that you felt free to let me notify the police. That would not—"

"He particularly said not, and it would not be right for us to go against his wishes."

"Very well, dear. I don't want to betray Colin's trust in you. It is only eight o'clock now and—he said he thought he knew where to find her?"

"He meant to try the railway stations first and—there's the bell now, Tony. Maybe he's come home!"

"I sincerely hope so."

More troubled for Cliona than for her brother, whom he considered well able to take care of himself, Rhodes forestalled the servant by himself going to the door.

He flung it open, but instead of Colin's welcome bulk, the slighter figure of a stranger confronted him. By the entrance light Rhodes saw that he was a man with a worn, scarred, anxious face, and the hair that showed under his hat was snowy white.

"Is Mr. O'Hara here?"

"Why did you wish to see him?" fenced Rhodes. They had been on guard all day against reporters.

"An extremely important matter that is—pardon me—entirely personal. If you will give him my card, I think he will see me."

Still hesitant, Rhodes took the extended card. The name was strange to him, but Colin's friends were wide-scattered, and by no means all known to his brother-in-law.

"Mr. O'Hara is not in," he said, "but his sister is here. Would you care to speak with her?"

"I *must* find O'Hara!" The stranger's voice was vehement with some irrepressible emotion. "For heaven's sake, let me talk to his sister, then! Perhaps she will help me to get in touch with him!"

Surprised, Rhodes nevertheless stood aside for the man to enter. He hoped that nothing new was coming up to increase Cliona's anxiety.

On the other hand, with Colin's affairs in such a state of tension, he dared not turn the man away unheard.

Then he found that Cliona herself was at his shoulder.

"Who is it?" she whispered. "Someone from Colin?"

"Someone to see Colin." He turned again to the stranger. "Come in, won't you? This is Mr. O'Hara's sister, Mrs. Rhodes. Cliona, this is Mr.—" he glanced at the bit of pasteboard in his hand—"Mr. Svend Biornson, a friend of your brother's!"

FOR THE SECOND TIME COLIN returned to sense and life. He came to with the taste and sting of liquor in his aching throat, and was at first conscious only of the extreme pain attached to the act of swallowing.

Then the cup was no longer against his teeth, and some support removed itself so that his head fell back rather sharply. That slight jolt hurt—hurt terribly—but it also aroused his resentment.

"You!" The voice from between his stiff lips was a hoarse whisper. "What—what you tryin'—do?"

From somewhere above him came the sound of a low, amused chuckle, but no other reply.

He was lying flat, and there was still pressure about his chest and body, though it was no longer so deadly unendurable. But though vapors were still above him, no stars shone through them. In fact, those vapors seemed curiously lighted from below, and he had an impression that beyond and above them something more solid than vapor intervened between him and open sky.

The humid air breathed stiflingly close and heavy—an unspeakable atmosphere, in which an odor like that of putrescence mingled with a stronger murkiness. He might have wakened in a den of reptiles, where half the inhabitants were very much deceased—or—a comparatively faint whiff of air like this had scented the storehouse which was also a passage to the banks of Llewellyn Creek.

Striving with all his will, fairly forcing his muscles to obedience, Colin managed to raise his head and shoulders an inch or so, then fell back exhausted.

FRANCIS STEVENS

"Take your time," advised a voice. "You can hardly expect to meet such an adversary as my little gatekeeper and leap up in full strength immediately afterward."

Colin knew that voice.

"Ches'r—Reed!" he articulated with great difficulty, but a weaker man would have been past any speaking, for he would have been dead some time since. "Is—that thing—on me—now?"

"No. I assure you, though, that it was touch-and-go whether or not I could get him off in time. A bit more and your veins would have been empty, my friend."

Certainly as a rescuer Reed had a curious way of speaking—a sneering, contemptuous way, that seemed to hide a secret insult. And—his veins? The side of Colin's throat felt swollen, and just where shoulder and neck joined there was a heavy, dull aching. That heavy blow on the neck would account for the one, but the other? He remembered the feel of those soft, cold lips between neck and shoulder.

"Here, have another drink." Leaning over, Reed set a glass to his patient's lips, and Colin gladly obeyed. The fiery strength of the draft coursed through him, and it was a strength sadly needed.

"You are in my work-room," said Reed. "Sit up and look about you."

Upon again struggling to raise himself and with Reed's arm under his shoulder, Colin succeeded and sat panting heavily.

An earlier suspicion was confirmed. From shoulder to forearm he was skillfully involved in thin, strong ropes. This did not greatly surprise him, for Reed's tone had carried its own warning of unpleasantness in store, and if the Dusk Lady had come home, she might in all innocence have related the tale of last night's doings. One expects no discretion of madness.

But though finding himself a bound prisoner roused no surprise, the surroundings of his captivity assuredly did.

The scene was laid in the extensive cellars of the Jerrard house; but the colonial architect who planned that residence would have found trouble in recognizing this portion of his work.

To make Reed's "workroom" possible, a good share of the dwelling's interior had been bodily born out. Its ground was the level of the old cellars, and took up their full extent, which was considerable. All the central part opened upward into a kind of square shaft, three stories high, with blank, white sides, whose roof was that enormous "cupuly" which had so puzzled the station lounger.

To the contractors who did the work, Reed had explained that he required a high, well-enclosed chamber, with plenty of room in it for air circulation.

SINCE FIRST REGAINING HIS SENSES here, Colin would have said that even more room for air circulation would have been an improvement—a great deal more room. In the service of science, however, men are wont to smile at personal inconvenience. So Reed smiled through the somewhat turgid atmosphere, as his prisoner sat up and took cognizance of his strange surroundings.

Rather than a work-room, Colin might have almost thought himself facing the inspiration for some mad poet's dream of Walpurgis night, or for such an artist as Doré to picture a new and more appalling vision of the inferno's lower circles.

He saw a dim, marsh-like expanse, whose further boundaries were completely veiled in vapors. It extended on three sides of the solid ground that underlay the shaft alone. It was roofed by the black underbeams of the floor above, and out of its mire rose the old granite piles that supported them.

That dim expanse must be called swamp or marsh, because a better name has not been made to name it by. But Nature never made a marsh like that. Between the granite pillars, fungoids and some kind of whitish vegetation like pale rushes grew thickly, but though those fungoids and rushes had a strangeness of their own, it was not the vegetable growth alone which made Reed's marsh peculiar.

Its entire space was acrawl with living forms that for repulsiveness could only be compared to a resurgence from their graves of creatures dead and half-decayed.

Colin saw them by a livid light that by no means increased their beauty—a light that was derived from the fungoids. These singular growths glowed with a whitish-gray effulgence that, diffused by curling vapors, gave the place such a dim illumination as might grace the surface of a witch's caldron.

A cold, dank caldron it was, with fires pale and heatless as the moon, and giving off with, its mist wraiths the effluvium of decay and of the life that springs from decay.

Like some horrible, hidden ulcer, Reed's work-room lay festering; and above it the black beams of the old house dripped and rotted with its moisture.

FRANCIS STEVENS

Not to Colin had been sight of a white marble rotunda, opal-domed, where surrounded by golden thrones a strange marsh glowed. But even had he seen it, that place to this had been homelike, as its white hounds were kindly, friendly beasts, compared to the creatures of this.

Out from among slimy rushes and glimmering fungoids, out of the rising whorls of vapor, came a Thing. It leaped in one bound from the mire to a scrambling foothold on the firm ground where Colin sat.

Save that it was neither the reptile nor saurian one might expect from such a breeding-place, the creature was hard to classify. In color, it might have been white, but for the mire in which it had been wallowing. High above four slender legs arched a thin, shaggy back, and beneath a plaster of mud and green slime gaunt ribs stood out like the bones of a beast that has starved to death in the desert. Its head, drooping low at the end of a neck equally gaunt and colloped, had a feline shape.

But no honest great cat of the jungle ever owned such eyes. Large, lambent, yellow as topaz, they stared Colin in the face with the most curiously *knowing* expression—and its knowledge was solely evil.

The brute was silent—in all that place there was no sound but the drip of water, an occasional splash or swishing of the rushes—it was silent and stared him, eye to eye. Then the lips drew up in a fiend's snarl that disclosed the yellow fangs of a fiend behind. One stiff-legged, forward step it took, still staring at its securely-bound prey.

Sick with repulsion rather than healthy fear, Colin knew that it meant to spring. This, he thought, was the final revenge Reed had planned for his servant's slayer—to have his throat torn out by those grinning detestable jaws. By one great effort, and without a word or glance of appeal to the man beside him, Colin steadied himself to meet death as he had always met its danger—unswervingly, eye to eye and face to face.

XXII

A HERDER OF GOBLINS

Colin was ready, but in thinking that his death was planned at the jaws of that frightful beast, he had misjudged his captor.

Stepping forward, Reed intervened his own person between the flame-eyed brute and its purposed victim. Uttering a sharp command he waved it back—with that left hand of his, that Colin saw very clearly now was covered with a bulky, white fur glove.

The beast's jaws opened wider in a soundless snarl. Then with a cringing motion it whirled, leaped and vanished in the swamp like the gaunt fantom of hunger it resembled.

Reed turned. "They know their master, eh, O'Hara?"

"It seems so." Colin eyed him sternly. "What sort of goblin den is it you have here?"

"Goblins? Your Celtic superstition deprives me of credit! What you see is my work—my work, all mine! No supernatural bogy or god or demon lent any help to the creation of these dainty pets! They are mine—the children of my unaided hand and brain! Do you doubt me?"

He put the interrogation with an explosive insistence that puzzled Colin. When he spoke of the "workroom" as a goblin-den, he had used the term in a hyperbolic sense. Despite everything, his preconception of Reed as an experimenter in freak zoology had kept the supernatural from his thoughts and not even his experience with the luminous, blood-sucking gatekeeper had changed this view.

In the steaming jungles between Capricorn and Cancer he had seen creatures as strange and loathsome. Such a one had Reed found, no doubt, brought it here and fed it daintily till it throve past the size of its tropical fellows.

And he had taken it for granted that the frightful, starved-looking brutes thronging this den were the misbred abortions of more natural beasts.

But Reed's words had an effect contrary to their meaning. As if with new vision Colin scanned the fetid breeding-ground.

The feline brute had hidden itself, but a number of its fellows were distinct in all their grotesquerie. From the pale blob of a thing that

FRANCIS STEVENS

lurched past on a bunch of tentaclelike legs, to a creature so buried in mire that only its bony head lay on the surface like the yellowed skull of a horse, all were hideous. But nature herself makes many loathesome forms.

It was not their ugliness that enlightened Colin. It was their eyes.

Venomous, intelligent, unforgettable, that which looked-through them was far removed from the innocent ferocity of wild beasts. They were goblins!

And turning from them to their master he saw in Reed's glance that same stare of naked, demoniacal hate that was in the eyes of his creatures.

AT GREEN GABLES A WHITE-HAIRED man paced restlessly up and down the library, and as he walked there poured from his lips the pent-up stream of a story so terrible, and at the same time so incredible, that he had dared to tell it to no man before.

And in this he was right, for in all America there were but two living men who would have believed. Anthony Rhodes was not one of them, but it was not to Rhodes that he was talking. That level-headed young lawyer sat by the table, toying with a paper-weight and wondering if there was any risk that the second lunatic he had entertained might become dangerously violent.

That the second lunatic claimed to be the father of the first made the tale no more credible. Rhodes could only think of the beautiful "Miss Reed" with pity, but he saw no reason why he should be called upon to tolerate her equally mad relatives.

Perhaps had Rhodes either shared in the fragmentary confidence bestowed by Colin on his return from Mexico in June, or stood behind a bulging door and watched the white claw of a demon rip through its panels, his credulity might have been greater.

To Cliona had been both these experiences. It was to her that the white-haired man talked, and whether Tony were convinced or not bothered her very little just now. In fact, for once Cliona was not thinking of Tony. She was listening with the keenest and most lively attention to the story of Svend Biornson, once adviser to the Council of Sacred Gilds in Tlapallan, now a homeless wanderer, trailing an unnameable horror across the earth.

It was a trail he had lost—lost very soon after it entered the United States. Only the chance that guided his wanderings to this city had also ordained that he reach there in time to read of the latest ravages at Carpentier. In June he had been on the western coast, whither the purely local excitement over that earlier mystery had never traveled.

And yet it had been on some such incident as this bungalow affair that Biornson had relied to pick up the trail again. "I knew," he said, "that its ambition had become impatient—that strange, bad events must soon happen because of it—"

"I was sure," said Cliona, "that the thing which came to my door that night had no natural origin!"

"Madness—pure madness!" muttered Rhodes, playing with the paper-weight and wondering if it would be worse for Cliona's nerves to put the stranger out now, or let him go on talking till he began to get dangerous.

"I saw your brother's name in this morning's account," continued Biornson, "and a reference to what happened in June. I looked that up in the old files at the *Daily Record* once and then—then I knew. From what I have already told you, you can imagine how wild with anxiety I have been to find them—and *it,* the thing they took, I should almost say, that *escaped* with them from Tlapallan.

"I went straight to Carpentier. I suppose your brother was too disturbed and preoccupied to recognize me and"—he laughed shortly—"Mr. O'Hara is not a person who is easily stopped when he happens to be in a hurry! By the way—I—the fact is, when your brother does recognize me, he may not exactly meet me with open arms. There was something—a thing I neglected to tell you.

"At our last parting I did him a very great wrong. That was fifteen years ago, but it was not the kind of wrong that a man forgets."

Biornson paused somewhat drearily. In spite of his anxiety to find Colin, enlist his help and get from him any information he might have acquired, he rather dreaded that moment of recognition.

"Colin's probably forgotten it," said Cliona abstractedly. "He never bears malice long." Her mind was running back over the man's narrative. "I tell you, Mr. Biornson, there can be no question at all. This Reed man, with his hints to Colin of strange beasts, with his albino servant, and his daughter who's so lovely and strange and claims to be no daughter of his—the three of them fit to a T with what you've been hunting! For the black god you speak of, I do not know. Colin said nothing to me of seeing any such carved stone demon out there, and the poor girl—I am afraid we gave her little chance to tell us of anything."

FRANCIS STEVENS

"You meant well. Oh, I know by your face, and your manner and your—your sympathetic *comprehension*—you meant well. You say she seemed in good health, only very mournful. Mournful! How can I make up to her for this last year? I had never thought to be glad for my dear wife's death. But I thank God now that Astrid passed in peace, with the child she loved at her side, to be mourned by many friends—yes, I am *glad* she passed before that red night came to Tlapallan.

"But our poor child—let me find her again—only let me find her— This won't do!"

Biornson halted and visibly straightened, both in spirit and body.

"Personal ties," he said sternly, "have a compelling grip, but my duty lies first in another direction. Mr. Rhodes, do you realize that we have to save the world from an invasion atrocious beyond credence? I don't think it has begun yet. I believe—I hope that we are in time to smother the thing in its infancy.

"THE PRIESTS OF NACOC-YAOTL KNEW the danger. They were very careful to restrict the power they had of it to one certain channel. But it is free now—free—loose in the world with its chosen servants! You may think me mad if you like, but I swear to you that there was—there is—life in that dreadful, carved black stone called Nacoc-Yaotl! A life that is ambitious and vile and that chose these vile men I have told you of for the agents of its fiendish ambition!

"And it has an enmity against the human race—an enmity darker and vaster than human enmity could ever be! Can you believe, child, that there are gods of old who still live? Old gods, and powers that have survived the passing of their worshippers?"

"I can the easier believe in your demon," Cliona said, "for the sake of that which came to my door one night. Now, do you really think, Mr. Biornson, that it was the porcelain image Colin brought me from Mexico that drew the bad luck to our bungalow?"

"I do indeed!"

"Then I have no doubt you are right. And I think 'tis in Reed's house at Undine that you'll find the lair of the evil spirit you are seeking!"

"Cliona—Rhodes!" exclaimed Tony, getting to his feet at last, and shocked beyond measure by the whole conversation.

"Cliona *O'Hara* Rhodes," she corrected him with a sidelong flash of very much excited blue eyes. "There are things that we Irish are quicker to understand than the rest of the world. You keep out of this, Tony!"

XXIII

The "Lord of Fear"

L ook about you," said Reed. "Before I carry out my purpose, there is much for you to see and hear."

Though in Colin's opinion he had already seen a trifle more than enough, he obeyed Reed's gesture and glanced behind him. After a moment he turned back.

"That's not strange," he said wearily. "That the old black devil himself should preside here is just the most natural thing in the world, Mr. Reed!"

For some reason, Reed's sneering face flooded with angry color.

"I preside here!" he snapped. "Stand up and turn around! Quick! Or you'll find a devil in me really to be dreaded!"

But though Colin might be foolish enough to believe in demons, he was not a man easily overawed by one.

"If you wish me to stand," he said quietly, "you'll have to be either untying me or helping me up. That leech-thing of yours has not left me in just the pink of condition."

To feign a greater weakness than he felt was elementary strategy, but to his disgust not much feigning was required. It was all he could do to get on his feet, with Reed's rather grudging assistance, and once up he found himself very wavery and with a painful tendency to buckle at the knees.

No sooner was he up than he sat down again, but this time on a chair carved, so near as he could tell, from virgin gold.

One does not expect to find solid gold furniture in the midst of a swamp. But neither is it usual to find a swampful of fiends in the heart of an old colonial residence. Being past surprise, Colin viewed his surroundings with interest and let it go at that.

The space immediately beneath the shaft, whose square was some twenty-five feet in diameter, had been floored with cement, on a higher level than the marsh, but sweating with dampness from the general moisture. Three sides were open to the swamp, but the fourth was a wall, flush with the side of the shaft above it and pierced by a single broad, high doorway.

On the cement floor were ranged a number of objects which, like the chair, seemed to be of astonishing value and entirely out of place.

Jars and vessels of massive gold were set about at hazard. Close to Colin there stood a great lidless chest or box. Its apparent value would have capitalized a bank, but into it there had been tumbled a heap of shabby, common things—some dirt-encrusted overalls, an old pair of canvas trousers, and the like. A steel spade had been flung in among them so carelessly that its blade had chipped off a long, curling flake of gold.

Three solid gold cougars supporting a six-foot basin, like a baptismal font, were impressive, but a stained rubber apron draped over one cougar's head rather, spoiled the effect.

The only thing here which Colin considered absolutely and completely appropriate was the squat, polished, black statue that crouched on a small dais beneath a canopy of black, with five candles burning on either side of it set on the prongs of two golden candelabra.

No evil could be too vile for that ugliest of images to grin at.

The head—particularly the mouth—might have been compared to a humanized toad, save that a toad, for all its lack of pulchritude, has a certain honesty of expression. The sculptor of that image had not stopped at frank ugliness. Alert stealth was in the very distention of its nostrils. The eyes were slits, but they were watchful slits. The mouth grinned, but it was a tense, cruel grin that had never heard of humor.

With long, treacherous fingers clasped around its knees, the thing squatted, naked, having none of those adornments with which religion, barbarous or otherwise, symbolizes the attributes of its deity. The being represented had but one purpose and one end, and of that the face alone was an adequate symbol.

As Colin looked he felt rise up in him such a wave of loathing and detestation as turned him sick.

"Reed," said he, "I could forgive you the imps of your quagmire there, and I could forgive you the vile bloodsucker you loosed on me at the gate, but the sight of that black iniquity you no doubt worship I'll not forgive you! Faith, it'll haunt my dreams if I live to be a hundred!"

Again Reed flashed into resentment.

"No more of that!" he snarled. "I worship nothing! Do you understand me? Nothing! Good God! Are you such a blind fool that you fear a chunk of carved marble more than me? I am the lord of fear—not Nacoc-Yaotl!"

"Who did you say?"

A word, a name is at the least, when you stop to think of it, a potential force. At best and strongest it may have the power of magic. For Colin the years dropped away like a falling screen. Afloat on a sea of light, he raised his eyes to a dark cliff crowned by a monstrous building—blind, pallid, oppressive in its mere appearance.

"It is the seat of Nacoc-Yaotl," said a girl's voice. "Nacoc-Yaotl, maker of hatreds, who would destroy mankind if he could!"

"Nacoc-Yaotl!" Reed's impatient voice reached Colin through time and dragged him back to the present. "One phase of an old Aztec god. Lord! You look stupid when you gape like that! The years have certainly brought you no increase of intelligence—*Friend Boots!*"

Colin's mouth shut with a snap.

"Archer Kennedy!" he exclaimed. "It was the beard and the glasses that did it! That and thinking you a dead man long ago. You can tell me then what I've been wondering about for fifteen years, more or less! Was Tlapallan a real city, or did I dream it?"

It is very tiresome, when one is trying to impress a man with the horror of one's malicious power, to be regarded as a mere purveyor of information. To Archer Kennedy the distinctly impersonal nature of Colin's first question was irritating to the point of insult.

In the days of their earlier acquaintance, his chief grievance against the Irish lad had been a trick he had of ignoring him as a personality. As Chester Reed, man of mystery, Colin had given promise of at least according him the respect of hatred. Identified as Kennedy, that old manner had instantly returned. A pin-prick, of course, but this man's nature was not only malicious. Its malice was of the shallow type that resents pin-pricks more than blows.

"Tlapallan," he said between his teeth, "was real once, but it's nothing now! Do you know who destroyed it?"

"Nacoc-Yaotl?" inquired Colin, with deep interest.

Rather to his amazement, the reply was a heavy blow across the mouth.

"You utter dolt!" raged Kennedy. "Mention Nacoc-Yaotl again and I'll have you dragged to the middle of that swamp and left there bound for my servants to devour! I caused the ruin of Tlapallan—and I drained it first of a knowledge that makes me your master, as it will make me master of the world in my day of triumph!"

FRANCIS STEVENS

Colin said nothing. The man who had struck him he remembered as too insignificant and absurd even to be seriously angry with. As for the grandiloquent claim he made, Colin took no stock in it.

But Nacoc-Yaotl was another matter.

From the haunting glare of the goblin creatures he looked to the slit-eyed watchfulness of that more terrible though seemingly inanimate demon, and he knew that this business was between him and them.

What was it Biornson had said before he turned him out to die, as he thought, in the desert? "To prevent a possible thing that I dare not speak of, I would condemn myself as readily as you. For *I* know that Nacoc-Yaotl grows restive—"

Was this what he had meant? Had the evil power that laired in that pallid, enormous building above the lake desired a freedom greater than Tlapallan allowed? And had it achieved that desire?

"There is a prophecy," the Moth-Girl had said, "that some day Nacoc-Yaotl will destroy Tlapallan, but I do not believe it. Quetzalcoatl, noblest of all the gods, is stronger than he."

But the city that swam in a lake of light was no more. He himself had beheld the dark tarn that filled the hollow of the hills it had glorified. And Quetzalcoatl—the rival god—the image he had brought thence— twice broken, and the third time utterly shattered through invasions which he now certainly knew to have emanated from this house—

Colin's imagination was racing now. It produced a dozen half-lost memories and flung them together in a most appalling pattern.

And back of all the horror a joy was hiding—a joy that in the flying confusion of his thoughts he could not at first identify.

Then suddenly the pattern was set. Everything fell into order, and, seated, as he believed, between the devil and his fiend-eyed offspring, Colin caught the greatest joy of his life and knew the most rapturous relief.

His Dusk Lady was not mad!

Were anyone crazy, it was himself for so believing her! The strange, elfin look of her beauty; the low, musical voice that was as if a thrush should speak; the fine, level courage of her, to be disconcerted neither by her own danger nor the killing of a man she loathed!

Only one girl he had met in his life had shared those qualities, and though to Colin the Moth-Girl had been a pretty dream where the Dusk Lady was an all-engrossing reality, the race-resemblance was strong enough for him to have placed and understood her—had he not been such an utter and prejudiced fool!

She was a child of Tlapallan, and though he doubted if her race were entirely human, that was a matter of no consequence. Hadn't an ancestor of his married an elf woman that he met on the *Bri Leith* itself? And hadn't she been a good wife to him, and his own, Colin's, great-grandmother on his mother's side—

Suddenly Colin realized that Kennedy was speaking had been speaking, in fact, for some time.

XXIV

A Lonely Traveler

Across the rough ground of an empty field two miles beyond Undine, a dark figure stumbled and panted beneath the unheeding stars. Once or twice it fell among the hard rows of old, dry corn stubble. One might have thought it some strayed child, lost in the night, but the figure was too tall, too slimly graceful beneath its flowing outer garment of black.

It was a weary, courageous figure, that had come far, far, and all the way on foot. For the bright galleys of Tlapallan were the only means of travel that slim figure knew till its time of grief, and in the one long, terrible journey across the outer world it had learned little, by reason of being kept close by enemies.

But to Tlapallan's children were certain birthrights. No homing pigeon could have come more sure and true than that slim, tired one that stumbled among the stubble-rows.

The night was not so still as it had been. A wind was rising. It blew in sudden gusts, like the breath of an invisible giant. The long cloak flapped and struggled, wrapping hinderingly about the wearer's limbs.

Away to one side blazed the lights of the chateaulike "farmhouse" of whose acres the stubble-field was a part. The house was full of flowers, lights, and laughing people, for its owners were entertaining many guests that night.

But the cloaked one was no guest of theirs. In a desperation of thwarted haste it stumbled on, as indifferent to the gay, human throng in the distant house as the stars were indifferent to itself.

XXV

The White Beast-Hand

A nd so," Kennedy was saying, "being mad for the girl, and having
learned that my brains were worthy of respect, Marco, or rather
Marcazuma, to give him his full name, sold me one or two secrets that
were absolutely invaluable. Just for my help in winning her! Lord! If I
could have got a like hold on some priests of the other gilds the world
would be at my feet now, as it shall be yet! Believe me, friend Boots, the
most powerful god in Tlapallan never had a seat there, nor received any
recognition. Even I was blinded for a while."

O'Hara decided that his abstraction had lost the thread of a very
interesting narrative.

"I don't understand," he said.

"Neither did I—at first. Do you remember in what agony of mind
I called you to come back that night when they turned you loose and
kept me a prisoner? I had seen a thing that would have made any man
afraid. I had seen the transmutation—but I'll get to that, later. Believe
me, you'll have a very clear idea of that particular 'mystery' before this
night ends!

"But to get back, there was quite a while there when I was actually
afraid—afraid of their trumpery stone and gold images! I! Then old
Topiltzen—you remember Topiltzen? He was first priest of the sacrifice
to that lump of stone there"—he nodded contemptuously toward the
eidolon of Nacoc-Yaotl—"he was the one you dropped overboard and
I nearly paid the debt—with not my life, but a fate that, as I hinted
before, you will be well able to understand before I'm done with you."

There was an ugly and reiterated threat in the man's words, but
somehow Colin found it unimpressive. That vile, unnatural marsh, with
its obscene forms and spectral eyes, was terrible enough. The squatting
similitude of all evil beneath the black canopy was—like the things a
man sees in the dark light of delirium.

But the self-styled "Lord of Fear" himself was not terrible at all. He
was as incongruous to his surroundings as the soiled rubber apron to
the golden cougar's head, or the miscellany of common trash to the
golden chest that contained it.

The black god of the dais, the goblins of the swamp, were loathsome but awful. Kennedy was loathsome, and inspired contempt. He was shallow, cheap, the shell of a man, empty of aught but petty egotism and a malice that had not even the redeeming dignity of greatness.

Looking him in the eyes, Colin wondered that he had a little while before seemed to see behind those round lenses the true fiend-look that characterized the marsh beasts.

"I wish," he said steadily, "if it's all the same to you, Mr. Kennedy, that you'd give me the straight story and be through."

"You do, eh? If you knew what waits for you at the end of it—Well, to go on, old Topiltzen received a 'revelation' in a dream that his god wished me for a temple servant. Darned fortunate revelation for me, too. I told you that I let imagination run away with me at first. I swept and carried and toiled for them in fear and trembling! I! Till I began to use my reason, to remember that material effects have material causes, and I saw clear to the real god behind the sham ones."

"And yet you'd not strike me as a religious man this minute," observed his captive thoughtfully.

"You fool, I don't mean what you mean! The god I speak of is the only one of real power the world has ever known. I mean—science! Those priests had a dozen secrets they took from science and gave the credit to Tonathiu, and Tlaloc, and Quetzalcoatl, and Lord knows what all. And in the end they paid the penalty of all fools who cloud science with superstition and have faith in their own empty rituals.

"They, who might have ruled the world, turned on each other. In the terrific collision of blind forces loosed, they and their misused knowledge and Tlapallan itself simply vanished from the earth.

"Ha! I helped to bring that about—I—the poor, despised, insignificant temple slave! Like all proud, superstitious fools, they were ready enough to believe the tales I carried from one to another.

"Svend Biornson rather fancied himself in those days. High adviser to the Council of Gilds! He scorned me. Once he called me an 'abject, cowardly slave' to my face, but it was the slave who undermined Svend Biornson's work, and the slave who caused Tlapallan's fall! And those hulking guardians! Neutral by oath! God, but they were bitter against each other before I had finished!"

"A desirable citizen they got when they got you!"

But Kennedy, caught in the rush of his own triumphal memories, went on.

"Of course, luck was with me, or I'd have brought nothing out of the grand smash but myself and some pleasant memories. Marcazuma—he was an under-priest of Nacoc-Yaotl—is one yet, in fact—"

"What? Marco?"

"I call him that, yes. The other's too long for convenience and too odd. We haven't been anxious to make people ask questions of any sort. Even you can understand that. But Marcazuma he is, and still a priest of Nacoc-Yaotl—in his own silly opinion."

Colin had cause to doubt it, but if Kennedy had not discovered the albino's demise, there seemed no good reason to enlighten him,

"As I was saying, Marcazuma had already got in pretty deep with me. Then he was kind enough to have a revelation of his own—or say he had one—in which his black ugliness there expressed a desire to escape into a wider field of activity, and named me as his chosen agent."

"H-m! And maybe the Creator of Hatreds wasn't off in his choice of an agent at that, Mr. Kennedy."

"Will you shut up, or do you prefer to be gagged? You're wise, for once. Be silent and listen! While they were fighting on the lake, Marco and a few of his fellows, who believed in his silly revelation, helped move his godship and this temple paraphernalia that you see out of the hills, and afterward lugged them to civilization for me. And then they were fools enough to go back to that cataclysmic hell we'd left raging behind us—all but Marco. He is a coward as well as a fool, and besides, there was the girl."

"What?"

"The girl. Why do you look—ah, you did see her that night, didn't you—and lied about it afterward?"

"D'ye mean to tell me that you—that Marco—"

"Oh, forget the girl! She's not important. I brought her along for the same reason that I brought his black ugliness yonder. Marcazuma has been in love with her since she was a mere child. But the poor fellow is no beauty himself, and her father would never hear of a match between them. She has always sworn she'd kill herself if I gave her to Marco, but that doesn't seem to faze his devotion a particle.

"Queer! I wouldn't step out of my road for all the dark-eyed beauties that ever walked, but Marco is a cowardly, weak simpleton of a man. I've never let him have her for just that reason. Afraid she would kill herself, and Marco would follow suit, and until recently I've' needed the fool.

"He believes that Nacoc-Yaotl has deigned in a measure to carnify himself in me. Between desire for the girl and fear of the black god he fancies is in me, I have owned the man body and soul, and in no other way could I have owned him so completely. To tell you the truth, I rather suspect that the young lady has overcome her distaste for his society and persuaded him to take her away from here.

"I was out last night—tell you about that later—and when I came back they had both disappeared. But it's no particular matter. They are such a queer pair that no one would believe any story they could tell, and Marco, at least, has enough sense to know better than tell tales on me. Let 'em go. I don't need either of them, any more than I need the statue there. I'd have *that* carted out and broken up tomorrow, only, to tell you the truth, I've a certain affection for the silly thing. Rather a pretty little parlor ornament, isn't it?" he chuckled.

"Well, to return to my story, luck was with me from the start. I tell you, though superstition was Bonaparte's one weakness, I can almost sympathize with the little Corsican's belief in his star of destiny. If there had been a real star of destiny working for me things could have been made no easier.

"You would think that shipping all that gold out of Mexico, particularly in the form it bears, would have been a hard enough trick to put over. The government would have grabbed the whole loot at the first suspicion of what I was taking out. It isn't worth my while to tell you the full history of that trip. But it fairly, ran on greased rails from start to finish.

"We ended with a run across the Gulf to New Orleans in a schooner that must have been plastered with pure luck; I don't know of anything else that could have held her rotten old timbers together. Her skipper knew me in other days. Helped me out for the sake of old times—*and* one of the gold ingots Marco had looted from the temple supply of raw material. I rather expected a knife in the back, but Diego Rosalis must have become quite a reformed character in the years I spent in Tlapallan.

"He told me he had never seen so easy a run as we made, nor one he was so glad to see the end of. Complained of frightful dreams through the entire voyage, and stuck on deck without sleeping all the last forty-eight hours. I asked him why, and all I could get out of him was: *Tengo miedo—tengo miedo malo!* But what he was 'badly afraid' of, unless it was the dyspepsia that gave him the dreams, is a mystery to me yet. If any one had reason to be afraid it was I. That old rip of a schooner, with her leaky hold full of my gold, and the original sixteen pirates of the 'sixteen men on the dead man's chest' song for a crew!

"Queerer yet—if you knew Rosalis—he deliberately took the ingot I'd given him and dropped it over the side; just after we came to anchor. Those pirates looked on, wooden-faced—and it was their gold as well as his, mind you!

"I came back on board that night, after the stuff was landed, and I'll be darned if they hadn't dug out a *relico* of Santa Maria from somewhere about the ship, and set it up near the bow, and the whole gang of 'em on their knees to it! To 'purify the ship of its passenger', Rosalis said. I might have felt personally insulted, if there hadn't been three of us, and one such a queer-looking beggar as Marco. Maybe those red eyes of his got their goat—"

"Four of you," corrected Colin O'Hara softly.

"No, three. The girl and Marco and I. But I didn't bother much to find out what particular superstition was troubling Rosalis. The old *contrabandista* had landed my stuff so that the customs authorities never got a look in, and that was enough for me. Done up in straw and gunny-sacking it was. Never even had wooden cases till I had it in a warehouse, and from there I took it to another, as 'mineral specimens'. And, by George, I shipped it north as freight—plain, common-as-dirt *freight,* and never lost a piece!

"Chances? Of course I took chances. But the difference between a fool and a wise man lies in the kind of chances he takes, and I rather fancy that success is the last criterion of that. Even if Rosalis had suffered a change heart and told tales of me on the other side of the Gulf there was little connection between Archer Kennedy, one-time of Campeche, and Mr. Chester T. Reed, who signed bills of lading, at last, for several cases of worthless bits of stone."

KENNEDY PAUSED. AFTER A MOMENT he kicked reflectively at one of the golden urns.

"Lord!" he said. "There was a time when just owning so much yellow glory would have turned my head. And look how I use it now! To me it is merely a non-corroding elemental metal, necessary to a certain process, and which it amuses me to utilize in the traditional forms it was carved into in Tlapallan. But if I should ever need money you would find how sacred the temple vessels are to me! Not that I expect that need to come. By the time I've run through what raw gold we brought away I'll have a stronger ruling power than gold in my hands!

"Supernaturalism is only dangerous," continued Kennedy, "if you believe in it. The priests made that mistake. I didn't. With the one little 'mystery' that I managed to bring out of Tlapallan, I shall establish such a dominion as the world never saw before. Men bow to two powers— gold and fear! In the day when I am ready they will bow to one only, and that will be in my control. Gold! What's gold beside fear?"

Again he kicked contemptuously at the urn. Then he stopped speaking abruptly, and a queer, dazed look came into his face. He passed a hand over his forehead.

"Strange, too," he muttered, more to himself than Colin. "I could do a lot with all this wealth here. Mastery of the world! What will I get out of it more than the gold would buy me?"

"A very sensible question!" approved Colin. "But what have the bogies yonder that you're so set on claiming as your own to do with world-mastery?"

"They? Why—they are only a beginning." The tone was almost querulous—he was like a man half-asleep and beginning to doubt his, dream. But in continuing the dazed look passed and his old grandiloquent manner returned. "Only a beginning. I had to learn the method. Marco taught me much, but the priests had never half realized what could be done. They were afraid of their own power, the fools!

"My fearless intelligence has wonderfully improved results; the brutes grow now with the most amazing rapidity—and multiply! And how they eat! You would hardly believe that those starved-looking beasts get away with living meat enough to keep a whole jungleful of tigers fat and happy. It's growing so fast, I suppose.

"But in the first month, after getting all this in order, I achieved only two successes—the beauty that strayed to Carpentier in June, and Genghis Khan, who, by the way, remains strong enough for all your attempt to injure him. He dragged your weight from the gates down here with one arm.

"As for the other, my first-born, as you might say, your sister killed it before it was half-grown. It strayed away one night, and I fancy you can guess the answer now to your famous 'bungalow mystery'. The poor brute crawled home up the creek and died before morning! Lord, but I was angry! Then in a few short weeks came all these!"

He gestured with that left hand of his in its bulky white glove.

"Came from where?" asked Colin. "I heard tell of a man once who went down into hell and bargained with the old boy himself for a billy-goat, but I never did give what you might call credence to the story. If you've been doing the like o' that, though, Mr. Kennedy, I'd advise—"

"Oh—silence! Do you hear me? Sikence! Your superstitious chatter is enough to drive a man mad! I tell you, these beasts are of my own making-mine! Or rather, they are my recreations from the common, silly, useless forms they first grew in. How can I make a dolt like you understand?"

"I don't know, unless you should tell it all in plain English."

"It is rather difficult," sneered the Lord of Fear, "for me to make clear to a man like you the technical details of a process more than sufficiently recondite for the comprehension of a—"

"I understand all those words," said Colin meekly.

"Of a trained thinker," finished the other. "Will you kindly cease interrupting me? As I was saying, to make the details clear to you is not only impossible but needless. I should not go into the matter in any degree were it not that I wish to dismiss from your so-called intelligence the idea that you are about to become the victim of a supernatural phenomenon. Do you know what occurs when an organic substance undergoes what is known as decay?"

"It rots," came the rather weary reply.

"The answer I would have expected. But, to delve a little deeper into the veridical nature of this 'rotting'—"

"The cell-structure," broke in his audience, "deteriorates under the caducous influence of the oxygenation of the atmosphere and other similar atrocities. Mr. Kennedy, as you say I'm a man of the simplest attainments and not only that, but between being hit on the neck and loss of blood and the elegant ventilation of this strike-off between a voodo temple and a section of purgatory, 'tis only by sheer will power that I do not faint from moment to moment. If you've information to impart, put it in words of one syllable, and as few of them as possible, or I'll not take the trouble to stay in my senses to hear it!"

There may have been that in his face which confirmed the statement and urged haste. At any rate, the would-be lecturer conceded glumly: "I can't explain it so that most of it won't go over your head, but the A B C of it is this:

"In an animate creature the life of the microscopic individual cells which form its tissues and the life of the organization of all those cells,

FRANCIS STEVENS

in other words, of the creature *in toto,* are entirely separate and distinct. An animal may die, in the common sense of the word, and if its body is kept in a place sterile of germs and of moderately cool temperature the *cell*-life will not perish for a considerable period. In fact, the body of that 'dead' animal is so very much alive that a portion of it may be grafted upon the body of another 'living' animal, and that portion will take up its normal functions as if there had been no interim of 'death.'

"In other words, flesh, tissue, blood, sinew, and the organic matter, of bone never die until decay sets in. But (paradoxically in sound, not fact), decay is *always* preceded by death—not the death of the animal but the death of the cell. And decay means dissolution—the breaking down of the cell-structure—the resolving of firm flesh into a semiliquid and putrescent mass. That is the *natural* course.

"There is, however, a certain substance of obscure mineral derivatives which was known to Nacoc-Yaotl's priests, and whose secret I brought away with me, as well as a considerable supply of the substance itself. The application of a thin film of this substance in solution to living tissue dissolves the cell-organization, which it immediately permeates, without destroying either the *cell-structure,* the life of the cell, or the life of the organisation.

"One might call this portion of the process pseudo-putrescence—false decay. As it goes on the entire being of an organism melts, as it were, into a homogeneous, jelly-like mass *and yet remains in every sense alive.*"

Kennedy paused impressively. Colin saw that for once comment was really desired.

"'Twould be more exciting," he ventured; "did you give a name to your organism. So be it was a cabbage now or a turnip, one's sympathies would scarce go out to the poor thing as they might to—"

"*Stop* it!" shouted Kennedy. "Is there no power on earth which will divert your idiotic flippancy into serious attention? I clearly indicated that I was speaking of animal life, not vegetable. Can't you understand that it is the blood, the sinews, the bones, the living, conscious, feeling *flesh* that is resolved into this—"

"That's enough!" flashed Colin. "You make me *sick,* you do! The man that would do the thing like that to so much as a rat is not fit to be living in the world at all, and much less listened to!"

"So that is how you feel about it, eh?"

"That's how I feel about it!"

Kennedy seemed rather pleased than angered. This was the first symptom of any emotion other than indifferent contempt which he had managed to elicit from his captive.

"Then you don't wish to hear," he continued, "how in this vital jelly there rises a new impulse, a reorganization of the cells, a reconstruction to new form, molded, strangely enough, by neither chance nor heredity, but solely by the will of the—"

"Of the empty-head who is at work! No, I care to hear no more at all about it."

"Empty-head!" exclaimed Kennedy indignantly.

"I said it! Any man who is fool enough to play with the devil's own process you've been describing, to try to explain it by a rigmarole of 'science', not to perceive the black power behind his own power—such a man is no more nor less than an empty-head, and I say it again! What do I care for your methods! Look at your results! Look your results in the eye, Mr. Kennedy, and then tell it to me that the worser beast on the dais there had no finger in their making!"

"Fool—fool—fool!" The Lord of Fear fairly raged up and down the floor. "I'll show you! You shall see with your own eyes! Before you pass beyond comprehension you shall see the living creature—rabbit—cat—bird—it makes no difference what creature, or how silly and innocuous—you shall see it lie in the elemental vessel of gold!

"You shall see me anoint it with my own hand, see me lave it then in the second solution, and"—his voice calmed, lowered and grew almost reverent—"you shall see that creature dissolve to a quivering, living mass, almost transparent, palpitant with strange, fugacious hues, with one steady crimson fleck at the center that is the nucleus.

"And from that nucleus—you shall watch how the new structure spreads and forms. To you it may be dreadful because it is so strange. To the trained mind it is a beautiful and a very curious sight. It is like watching a wonderful egg, of which the shell is transparent, and seeing the live creature within grow visibly. It is more than that. It is like being God—a real God—and beholding the formless protoplasm take structural shape under mere power of will.

"Oh, there is a science of will as well as of matter. One has to get the trick of it, and it doesn't come too easily, I assure you. There is a point in the process where one's bare hands must be laid very cautiously on the work. If you miss that point of time it all melts away to an evil-smelling

FRANCIS STEVENS

mess that has to be burned; the very odor is poisonous. If you act too soon there is a greater danger. I had one accident that taught me—but never mind that now.

"Then, at that moment of crisis, the whole force of one's being must be concentrated in a thought—and one can almost feel it flow through one's finger-tips. Then watch. First come the little scarlet veins, an orderly tangle of filaments, shooting out from that red speck at the jelly's heart. They grow and the arteries form; the bones begin to be fragile, translucent as clouded glass.

"Presently a dim throbbing comes—all the center is clouded now—and under the shapeless, glistening surface a *shape* is beginning to show. *The shape I had thought of.*

"Two dim, flame-colored disks peer out at me, and I know that they are eyes—the feral, yet obedient eyes of my newly created one. The outer jelly is almost absorbed now—it solidifies—toughens into membrane—into skin—

"But why should I tell you more? You shall *see*—and after that doubt if you can that I am a creator in my own unguided right!

"But never think me a conceited egotist! No! I don't pretend to know *all* that goes on in my laboratory. What true scientific man does? There are even yet phases—difficult riddles—for instance, the amazingly rapid after-growth. I have the wet marsh there for them, because in that environment they grow faster, larger, stronger.

"I take the little new beast, all naked and shivering and snarling with feeble resentment—I take it and feed it well—it eats from the first moment—and lay it in that cool mire among the white rushes and the fungi whose spawn I brought from Tlapallan.

"It creeps away and is gone—and when, an hour or so later, I call my beasts to the edge and bid them seize their living food, the little new beast comes with them, and already it is larger!

"But that is by no means all. These beasts have a faculty that they share with no other creatures save the simplest organisms. They do not multiply slowly, but split in twos as easily as—"

"Mr. Kennedy! Can you not realize that 'tis a nightmare you're talking, not science?"

"I tell you they do! They must! I admitted that I hadn't traced that phase of the experiment yet, but in no other way can their extraordinarily rapid multiplication be accounted for. And the queerest part is, they don't split into twos of the same kind.

"The gatekeeper now—the shining leech-worm. I never made him. He was draped round the neck of that statue when I came down one morning. I knew at once that he had crawled up there from the swamp, looking for food, but I71 admit that the thing gave even me rather a start. It was so different from anything I had even thought of making!

"But obedience is the test. When I found he obeyed even better and more intelligently than the rest, I knew him for the child of my children. I named him Gatekeeper, and hid him in the lodge. The last owner hanged himself there, and there are some remarkably silly stories current about it. I generally leave the gates unlocked at night now. Anyone who comes prying through them will find a gatekeeper to tell a real story about—if he survives.

"Isn't that an amusing idea? The first night you came here I rather expected him to get you as you went out, but I suppose, having seen you admitted, he regarded you as under protection."

"Very like," agreed Colin dryly.

It was characteristic of both men that neither had made reference to any reason why Kennedy, whatever horrors he kept for the rest of the world, should have refrained from loosing them on Colin. The debt of life one man owed the other had been easily canceled on Kennedy's side for the sake of a fancied grievance. For Colin, what was done was done with. If he had nearly sacrificed his own life, not once but twice to preserve a creature so contemptible, why—so much the worse for him.

"I suppose," he continued, "that it was this gatekeeper pet of yours that wandered into my veranda a few weeks ago—and ran again, poor cowardly worm, for the silly noise of some pots and pans!"

The Lord of Fear started and frowned.

"No," he said shortly. "I never sent him to the bungalow."

"Then it must have 'strayed' like the others. Wasn't it an odd coincidence, now, that Genghis Khan, who never got inside the house, was the only one of the lot that didn't manage to do a bit of damage to a certain little statue I owned? Quetzalcoatl it was—the same that yourself introduced me to when we were together at Biornson's hacienda."

Watching closely, Colin thought that a reminiscence of that odd, dazed appearance shadowed the other's face. Then the man shook it off and scowled.

"I know nothing of it. If it happened it was a coincidence, and I can see nothing particularly strange about it. Till last night I never sent or guided any of my beasts outside these grounds. I tell you, I am not yet ready. If you hadn't come prying I would probably have never bothered with you at all.

"Do you think that *I* am a man to go out of my way for the sake of anything so trivial as *you*—unless driven to it? As for the image. I read in one reporter's account that you had brought it from Mexico. Did you really find time and courage to go back at last? I waited for you long enough—hoping against hope that you'd cross the desert alive somehow and return with help!"

"There," said Colin gravely, "I owe you an apology, Mr. Kennedy. If I'd guessed you were still living I'd have gone earlier—but it's done with now."

"Along with a number of other things, including Tlapallan and—yourself!" he grinned. "You'll see the point of that shortly. To return to my gatekeeper, I don't believe he ever went near the bungalow. I told you he was more intelligent and obedient than the rest. But for that matter, save for one or two unimportant lapses, they are all obedient.

"As they grow larger I may find a use for the fenced enclosures I supposed would be necessary, but now—well, you can see for yourself. Look into their eyes! Can you see a hunger, there? And yet not one of them will cross the deadline after that first beast's rebuff.

"And the gatekeeper—think of it! Loose in the lodge and attending his duty more closely than any human. There's a science of will, I tell you, as well as of matter. Those I made, my will went into, and their procreations recognize me as master.

"Think of a horde of such—when I am ready—ravaging the countryside by night, slaying whom I will to slay! And always multiplying, increasing—growing in numbers faster than men can kill them off!

"And they won't be easily killed. They die hard at best, and besides, man is lord of the beasts only because he is more intelligent. These will have the intellect of man himself behind them. Had I directed that poor brute in June there would have been no trail of its blood to set folks gaping.

"Have you seen the bungalow today? It is rather fortunate that you weren't in it last night, for, after considerable thought, I have decided to use you in a much better way than by killing you. I had seen a danger in that eternal curiosity of yours, and thought best to get rid of you quickly, and in your own house rather than here.

"But, having you alive in my very hands, there is another temptation which I find quite irresistible. But if you had been in the bungalow—wasn't the wreckage there pretty thorough? My newer servants are very strong and easily directed. Do you wonder that I call myself the Lord of Fear and say that I will some day rule the world?"

"You'll rule the inside of a condemned cell," said Colin coldly. "You've done nothing that I can perceive but make a warlock of yourself, and at that no self-respecting man would be afraid of you! You're not the first to trade your soul to the old boy for promise of the world and all, but of them that ever did it, you do look the most foolish! Take My advice, little man. Smash the black one there before it's too late, clean out your swamp with a shotgun, and start fresh! Free my arms and I'll find strength to help you to the doing of it. Is it a bargain?"

THE SELF-STYLED LORD OF FEAR glared pure exasperation. "You *will* help me," he snarled, "but not in, that way! Do you see my hand?"

He thrust it under Colin's nose.

"I see an uncommonly ugly glove. From one of your pets' paws by the talons of it."

"Glove!" The man pushed up his cuff to disclose the wrist. "Look closer, fool! An accident did that to me—a moment's carelessness when I was attempting my first recreation. Do you remember those white hounds you fought in the pass? I'll never forget the minute when I first discovered their origin! You'll help me, I say, and that great lumbering body of yours will be put to good use at last!

"I'll dissolve your living flesh and remold it to such a shape as will frighten even your brothers of the swamp! And after that you'll kill and destroy at my bidding! Yes, though I sent you against a friend, or those of your own flesh and blood, you'll hate and rend and kill—and die, ravening at last, in some midnight battle fought for my sake and glory!"

"No," said Colin. Had that beast-hand closed on his heart he could have hardly been more sickeningly shocked. Somehow the final inference of all Kennedy's wild talk and vague threats had not come home to him until this moment.

They had been talking of the transmutation of beasts into other beasts—of the lower order of creatures, for which even the kindest-hearted of men feels a sympathy rather patronizing. Colin had thought to be killed—fed to the monsters of the swamp, perhaps, a fate bad

FRANCIS STEVENS

enough. But this! And yet Colin's voice, though still hoarse, sounded very sane and cool. "No. You can't do that with me, Mr. Kennedy."

"Why not, pray? One of the rabbits that went to make those stalking terrors yonder could be no more in my power than you are!"

"No," said Colin again. "A rabbit—maybe. Yourself—I don't doubt. 'Twould take little at best to bring the beast out of you, Mr. Kennedy. But a real man—no!"

"You flatter yourself! Again—why not?"

"It won't be allowed, that's all. If you were really the clever devil you think you are you'd know that! Ask Nacoc-Yaotl there! By the eye of him he's had a wider experience than yourself, and *he* knows why not!"

Before Kennedy could reply there came a slow, shuffling sound from somewhere outside the cellar. It stopped, and that one door in the wall was pushed open. Something—it was hard to see what—bulked palely in the dark beyond.

Then it came on slowly, shufflingly. It came into the light and across the floor, and it laid the burden it had half-dragged, half-earned hither in the space between Kennedy and his prisoner.

Of all the horrors that Colin had met since entering the gates at dusk only one had really shaken him to the soul. Not the real gatekeeper. coiled around his chest had been so bad as that first moment when he thought the drooped oval of its head was Marco's face.

And just so, not the sight of goblins, nor the black, brooding genius of goblins, nor even the beast-paw that Kennedy bore for a hand—not one of these things had moved him as did the sight of Marco's body, dragged in and laid gravely at his feet by Genghis Khan.

If Khan were not a real ape, he had all the appearance of one. He had the short bowed legs of a simian, the thin arms, tremendous chest and almost neckless head—but, above all, he had the infinite simian sadness in his face.

No human accuser could have equaled the solemnity of Khan's manner in that act, which he performed as one who does the last, sad duty by a departed friend.

Then, with startling abruptness, he turned a back somersault, landed on Nacoc-Yaotl's sacred dais and crouched there, chattering and nursing the broken arm he had probably forgotten when he attempted that acrobatic feat.

The grotesquery of it was the final straw for Colin.

Marco had lain heavy enough on his conscience. Having learned the full history, and become cognizant of the monstrous crimes toward which Kennedy's "work", made possible by Marco, was directed, Colin might reasonably have felt the burden lighter. But so far this view had not struck him. For twenty-four hours he had agonized in spirit over the killing of this weakling, and those hours had left their mark.

To be presented with his victim's corpse by a white monkey-thing that turned somersaults afterward was the strain too much. What strength had been left him fell away like a dropping tide. Dimly he heard a voice say: "Marco—and dead! Well, by George, I thought he and the girl—had run off together! I wonder what's become of her, then?" But Kennedy's further speculations went unheard, for his prisoner had fainted.

XXVI

To Undine

F ar toward the heart of the city a car sped silently over the asphalt, with a greatly perturbed young man at the wheel. The car was Cliona's, and this late expedition was Cliona's, and Cliona herself was in it.

By the time she and Svend Biornson had finished, comparing notes and jumping at the maddest conclusions Rhodes had ever heard spoken in sober earnest, that young man was in a semidazed condition. He scarcely retained spirit to protest when Cliona commanded him to run out her car, to place in it his shotgun and what other firearms were in the house, and prepare instantly for a sortie in force against the house of a man he had never heard of twenty-four hours earlier.

His suggestion of "Police!" was met with a scorn to take his breath away. But here, having learned that a man high in the city detective force was already working on the case, Biornson seconded Rhodes' demand that the law be called into alliance.

"No need to explain fully," he asserted. "Keep the story within their comprehension. The bungalow affair is a lever to move them which I should have lacked, working alone. Begin by telephoning this MacClellan that O'Hara had reason to suspect the owner of the Undine place of keeping dangerous wild beasts in an insecure manner, and went there this afternoon or evening, alone. Tell him that O'Hara has not returned here, though he agreed to do so, and that a man—myself, of course—has brought you information about Kennedy, alias Reed, which proves him a very dangerous criminal.

"Tell him that you and I will run downtown and join him, that I will then make known to him facts that justify Kennedy's instant arrest, and that for good reasons he had best have a detail of several men ready to go out there with us.

"I believe the charge that Kennedy kidnaped my daughter is serious enough. We shan't need to venture on the more—er—improbable part. What we shall certainly find in his house will speak for itself, I think. There might be delay, in swearing out a warrant on the kidnaping charge, so in phoning, be sure and emphasize the fact we believe O'Hara's life to be in serious peril."

Somewhat reluctantly, Rhodes undertook the task set for him. His disbelief in Biornson's story as a whole was not voluntary. He *couldn't* believe it. But on the other hand, that story in combination with Colin's strange experience with the giant ape, had brought him to a kind of incredulous uneasiness of mind about it all, and to have the place investigated by lawful authorities would cut the knot of doubt in a very satisfactory manner.

He called the Detective Bureau at City Hall, and by luck caught MacClellan just as the latter was about to "lay off" and go home early. The life of a city detective being both strenuous and irregular, he accomplished this feat about one day in thirty, and, being human as well as stolid, he sometimes got very tired. He was tired tonight.

Rhodes, of course, could not know this. Neither could he know that, in the light of their last parting, sympathetic concern for Colin O'Hara's life or limb had no share in MacClellan's feeling for him.

But Rhodes did know that the ensuing conversation was so highly unsatisfactory that he suddenly hung up the receiver very forcibly, and turned a flushed, indignant face to the other two.

"He says that Colin told him to drop the bungalow case, and when he reported, his chief took him off the assignment. He says that if you will come down and make your complaint in person, Mr. Biornson, the matter of Reed will be investigated, but they cannot make a night-raid on a respectable householder unless the person demanding it presents convincing proof and good credentials of his own.

"He seems to ignore the fact that I myself am a respectable householder. He said—he was extremely insolent!" snapped the young lawyer, breaking off into sheer indignation. "He deserves to be reported to his chief. I think I'll do that little thing, too!"

He reached again for the receiver, but Cliona caught his hand and fairly dragged him away from the telephone.

"Tony, my Colin has gone to Undine and you waste time arguing with the polikce! I know he's gone there. Didn't Mr. Biornson see him in Carpentier and see him put the car to the Undine road at a speed to frighten one? I've known it all evening—he's gone there in search of *her,* and from what she said 'tis sure as the world that she's traveled the same way in search of *him*—and it's there we'll find both of them, so be they've not been murdered before this!"

FRANCIS STEVENS

And so, almost before he knew it, Rhodes found himself, his wife, and a stranger in the car, bound, apparently, on the armed invasion of another utter stranger's residence.

"Hurry!" came her voice in his ear.

"We're making enough speed to cost me a fortune in fines, if every policeman we've passed has taken our number!"

"What's that in life or death! Mr. Biornson, have you a plan for us when we reach there?"

"No," he said simply. "If what I know might be is true, then our going alone in this manner is mere suicide. And yet—that detective's attitude was rather indicative. We have no hours to waste. How could we convince the police in time, or where else could we raise a force of men tonight?"

XXVII

Strange Victim—Stranger Conqueror

Though invisible from the road, in the gate lodge its "keeper" still pulsed with a faint, excited glowing. The flat length lay in a loose coil, the head, with its specklike eyes, at rest on the threshold of the lodge.

Suddenly the head lifted. With a swaying motion it rose upward some five feet, to droop and poise, a luminous oval, as when Colin had first seen it to his sorrow. By some sense, whether of hearing or vibration, it had become aware that the gate was softly opening, that someone had entered and was advancing along the drive.

Into the keeper's range of vision—if it had vision and were not guided by some other unknown sense—there flitted a dark figure. The obscuring mists of earlier evening had been blown away by the gusty night-wind. Had the figure turned it would have seen clearer than had Colin that floating, menacing oval in the lodge. But it did not turn, and when the keeper shot out in pursuit the rustle of straightening coils was lost in the swish and clash of wind-torn bare branches.

Unwarned, the dark figure hurried on up the drive, and like a writhing white flame the keeper followed. In a moment it was almost upon the heels of its second quarry.

There came one of those freakish gusts, like the breath of an invisible giant. It crashed through the branches and swept the black cloak out like a sail.

Something came whistling down through the air with the speed of a flung spear.

The keeper's intended quarry hurried on, but the keeper itself no longer followed. Writhing, lashing, a fury of pulsing fire, it whipped its length again and again about the enemy that had pinned it to the path. But the enemy was only an old dry branch, broken off by the wind and hurled endwise. Let the empaled creature fight as it would, a dry branch is to be neither terrorized nor slain.

In a frantic tangle of flashing coils and snapping, splintering twigs, the gatekeeper remained wholly engaged with its conqueror.

XXVIII

RIVAL CLAIMANTS

Colin O'Hara had a vision.

He thought that again he lay stretched on the "workroom" floor. Though his eyes were closed, he thought that the lids grew transparent, and by this phenomenon a great clarity of sight came upon him, so that all about him was thrice clear, and without stirring a muscle he could see every part of his surroundings.

He and Marco lay side by side, very stiff and straight. This seemed just, though unpleasant. When Kennedy came with Genghis Kahn to roll and drag him away, had he been able to speak he would have protested. They had no sense of what was fitting! Or perhaps they were ignorant of who had slain the poor weakling.

With his one good arm Khan was trying to lift him now. They had dragged him to the golden font, and he noted with no particular interest that the stained apron no longer draped the third cougar's head. Then he perceived that Kennedy was wearing it, and was also trying to fit a glove, yellow and shining as soft flexible gold, over his right hand, but the taloned white paw that had been his left retained no skill.

At last he motioned the great ape to aid him, and Khan did. The ape's hand was clever enough, for all the fur on the back of it. Did that prove the created beast its creator's superior? Colin pondered this deeply, but ere he could reach a satisfactory conclusion they were at him again.

Kennedy began untying the knots of his bonds, but left off suddenly.

"No," muttered he. "To be on the safe side I shall have to anesthetize before stripping him. The faint may be only a sham. Let him stay tied for a while."

This amused Colin, who knew himself to be dead. How cautious the little man was!

Now Khan was lifting at him once more. This time the master helped, and though his strength was comparatively feeble, the two of them managed to raise Colin to the font's level. Tumbled over the edge, he subsided into the font and lay there uncomfortably. The thing wasn't long enough. His neck was doubled at a painful angle. Marco's body now would have fitted much better. If they must have a corpse to the font, why couldn't they have chosen Marco's?

Then—for though his face was below the basin's edge, he could see as well as ever what went on he perceived that Kennedy was taking some jars, some boxes, and a small flask from the depths of those golden vessels by the wall. He came presently and set them out on a kind of shelf that extended from the font.

The flask he took in his hand, and it was a thing of gold and great value; and carved all over with writhing, lizard-like forms. The stopper of it, which was glass or crystal, fitted tightly, and Kennedy had some trouble in removing it. But it came out at last.

He sniffed, as if testing the freshness of the stuff it contained, smiled in unpleasant satisfaction, replaced the stopper and set it down again. Then he stooped, and from the floor behind the font, lifted a more commonplace receptacle: a large, glass bottle, half-filled with some kind of colorless fluid.

After that there were two or three things done, but exactly what they were Colin was not sure, because the strange *sight* that had come on him blurred for a time and all was confused, shadowy, and not to be remembered. Something was put over his face, he thought, and after a time taken away again. A sickish-sweet odor oppressed him, hands fumbled about his body, and somewhere, very far away, a bell rang constantly.

Then, clearer if possible than before, the sight returned.

There was Kennedy still, but he had done with the bottle, and now he was for opening one of the small olden jars. As he did it he looked at Colin, and behind his beard the thin red lips grew to a smile that was ugly as a toad's without its honesty.

Suddenly, with no moment's interim of thought or doubt, Colin knew the meaning and the end of these preparations. And he knew that he was not dead, but only helpless, and that the slitlike, watchful eyes behind those round glasses were no longer Kennedy's, but the eyes of Nacoc-Yaotl, maker of goblins!

With that, he who had been Archer Kennedy faded to nothing, and in his place stood the naked evil that had squatted on the dais.

Smiling, it leaned to pass treacherous, caressing fingers across the victim's face.

Colin's spirit shivered, but all that was great in him rose to fierce rebellion. Never! Never! What claim had that dark vileness upon him!

But he could not even speak to protest, for his body slept. Then somewhere a low, clear voice was sounding.

"Wait!" it said softly. "Nacoc-Yaotl, you who were once my brother, wait! Lest you break the law that must not be broken, and destroy yourself with the world!"

Colin had thought the voice that of his Dusk Lady, but surely the Demon had never been a brother of hers!

His attention, which had been fixed on what hung over him, widened.

The speaker, he discovered, was a tall youth, very slender, who stood before the font facing Nacoc-Yaotl across Colin's body. In one hand he grasped a staff, its serpent-head curving out of a circlet of quail-feathers. Of the speckled quail-feathers was his cloak, and the round shield he bore on his left arm was rimmed with them.

His face was very bright and beautiful. A kindly face, too, with patient, smiling lips. But in the eyes a spirit lurked that made less incongruous the gaping, intolerant jaws of the serpent crest above it. And every plume about him flickered wavering, as if in some draft that blew on him alone, for the air in the place was still.

LOOKING BEYOND HIM, COLIN PERCEIVED that the floored space beneath the shaft had filled with thronging people.

Very strange folk they were, and at the same time extraordinarily familiar. Like old friends in masqueraders' robes he knew each one, and recalled the names of them in different lands.

There was him whose flowing robes were woven of the beaded gray rain. White foam was his beard, and his eyes like blue ice-caverns. Tlaloc was he, Neptune, and Mananan, son of that great one who dwells forever invisible in the Slieve Fuad.

But his robes were not all gray. At one side they were struck through to rainbow hues by another who stood behind him. That was Lugh, the shining one; Tonathiu, the fiery one; Amen-Ra, of the Egyptians; Apollo, of the Greeks.

Meztli, with his paler fire, was there; Centeotl, who is Ceres and also Dana, mother of gods; Tlapotlazenan, with her flasks of healing, and Tezatzoncatl, merry of face and wreathed like Bacchus.

They and many others of friendly appearance stood behind their spokesman; but a demon leered across Colin's body, and the mouth of him was wide and cruel.

"Shall I wait?" said Nacoc-Yaotl.

"Yes, for the man is mine! But yesterday he was claimed for me in Tlapallan!"

"But yesterday he was claimed for me also, and—but yesterday Tlapallan fell. Did you save your servants?"

"Tlapallan's time was ended, and I might not save them. But death is little. I have fought you for this man's life because I love him, but slay him now if you will, for my children do not fear death. Slay him and spare this other deed, which is forbidden!"

"Did you forbid it when my white hounds roamed the hills?"

"Your hounds served a sacred use—to guard Tlapallan. Moreover, in their making only your power, not your spirit, went into them. Their violence was the clean violence that fights, but not for malice. For the sake of their origin those hounds stood equal with the mighty guardians. But the hounds you send forth today are fouler than foul. Evil is their service, and their nature an infinite degradation!"

"They are as I wish them."

"Then degrade beasts only, or such beasts as are human only in form. Claim service of your own, black one, but this is my child! I have followed him through many lands and I know him well. His spirit has flamed to the courage of my breath; I have sung to him on the plains, and lulled him to sleep in the forests. He is one of my clean-hearted children, and you may not corrupt him."

"He has traversed my waters," muttered a new voice, deep and thunderous as distant breakers. "In our play we hurled great billows, the Lord of the Air and I. We hurled them against him, and he was not afraid!"

"I have set my burning mark upon him!" Tonathiu spoke, a hissing whisper, "I have tested him well, and the fire of my own spirit was not more steadfast than his!"

"Beware of us, oh, mine enemy!" The feathered one's countenance grew bright and fierce, even as the glory of Tonathiu. Wildly waved his turbulent plumes, and raising his serpent-staff he shook it like a spear. "Beware of us, for our patience is nearly ended! Tlapallan fell, but its time was finished. Think not that we will stand idle forever while you destroy our children! The Lord of the Air guards his own!"

"There is a house on a hill," sneered the demon, "that you did not guard."

"You know otherwise. Not against me did you send your emissaries,

FRANCIS STEVENS

but against this man, who had been claimed for me, and against his loved one. Knowing that your own claim on him was false—"

"Not so false now as then!" murmured Nacoc-Yaotl.

"I say," continued the other sternly, "knowing that you might not corrupt him, you sought the lesser satisfaction of killing. Not against me were your emissaries sent; but was it not my staff—my little broken staff—that sent back the first crawling up a blood-stained stream? Was it not my shield—my little broken shield—that kept the second, the glimmering worm, at bay till my child should awaken? For the third, no ward of mine was needed. But the fourth—was it not my great voice roaring in the trees that called my child away from a force too strong for him?"

"There is no question," retorted Nacoo-Yaotl, and there was a sneer in his tone that was very like Kennedy's, "there could be no question that before you were Lord of the Air you were a man! So do men boast of their most trifling deeds. The end of it all is—your child, or this that was your child, lies here. What protection do you offer him now, most powerful one?"

There came a pause and a silence. The other gods stirred restlessly, as in anger, but Quetzalcoatl's face grew patient again, and when he spoke it was in a voice of pleading, gentle as the wind of spring.

"He is not yours! Oh, Nacoc-Yaotl, once you were called Telpuctli the Young, and Tezcatlipoca, Shining Mirror! You rewarded the just, and for the wrong-doer you had mercy to bestow. Remember your youth, Telpuctli, and be merciful!"

But the Evil God only grinned wider.

"Men made me what I am, and for that I hate them! In all Anahuac there was no mercy among them. In the shrieks of the bloody sacrifice, in the cries of babes murdered upon my altars, in the steam that arose from the unspeakable feast, the mirror of Tezcatlipoca was fouled and dimmed; Telpuctli grew black, old and cruel!

"I am Nacoc-Yaotl, creator of hatreds, and why should I alone of the gods walk unrecognized? To Tlaloc are the rains, floods, clouds, and the billows. All these are his visible servants. Tonathiu is seen of all; and you, Lord of the Air, you are heard in the forests. In the day of your anger men know you and bow down in fear.

"But I, who am stronger than any, must work in secret! My own bond servants deny me. Many centuries I sat patient in Tlapallan, working in secret, restricted by the very priests that served me. Till there came to our hills a man who was mine from birth. Even he, being man, I must delude, lest in full knowledge of its service the weak vessel be shattered.

"'The Fortress of Fear,' he has named this, but it has a truer and more secret name—The Birthplace of Corruption!'

"Yet he has been an apt tool. Look about you in this, the seat he prepared for me, unknowing. Free runs my will today and freer shall it run tomorrow. Hate breeds hate, and demon produces demon. How fast have their numbers increased! He is pleased like a child, and believes that he shall rule the world! He! That empty, hollow reed through which my will runs!

"But through all, and despite his coward soul, I have brought this blind slave of mine to dare that for which I waited through the centuries! We have come at last to the utter corruption of man!

"Here lies the first who shall wear my outer livery because he has worn it once in his heart, but he is not the last. You have said that in the deed about to be performed I break an immutable law, and I know the law you mean. It is the right of the soul, which may not be utterly damned without its own consent. We will test that law. Here, in the person of one man, lies the fate of all mankind—whom I hate!

"If I succeed—as I shall succeed—then a barrier goes down which has long withheld me from my own. No longer shall I need my blind and foolish tool, who has thought to use *my* power to further his small and futile ambitions. From that hour I am free indeed. He whose heart I may stamp but once with my seal, I shall claim for my own! All—all—body and spirit together—as I claim this man! He has slain at my bidding, your perfect one. Protect him if you can!

"And when you fail—as you must, for you are weak cowards all, who fear to overstep boundaries and lose your godhead—when you fail, think well on this:

"In the day of the full corruption, and when each hater shall wear the foul outer form of his hatred, who, think you, will be best worshipped of the gods?"

There was silence. Then the dull, distant breakers roared again.

"I am Tlaloc! I bear the ships of man—my rains water his fields. Shall I serve a race of demons?"

"It may not be!" Tonathiu went ruddy, as if he peered through storm mists. "Shall I behold only devils as the world turns under me?"

"It may not be! It may not be!" The cry was echoed by the lesser gods, till one voice sang clear above the rest—the wind's voice, chanting forever round the world.

"It *shall* not bet Beware of me, O mine enemy! I am the Lord of the Air, without whom no thing lives. Fire, the pure, is my playfellow, and the whelming flood, my friend. But ere ever I was a god I was a man! Man is my brother! Better than all I love him! I am the song of his heart and the strength of his spirit! Courage am I, and hope, and the breath of the wild, sweet places! It is you who have flung down the challenge! It is I who take it up! Beware of me, O mine enemy, *for the day of my patience is ended!*"

The singing checked abruptly, and the god's face, bright and fierce even as Tonathiu's, darkened, grew dimmer.

About him and all of them the mist closed in, obscuring the clearness of Colin's vision. Like a premonition of evil the dark mist closed and thickened. When the Feathered One spoke again it was in a mere whisper. Colin could not be sure if he heard with his ears, or if the whisper and faint answering voice were equally in the bounds of his own brain.

"Claim your own, Nacoc-Yaotl, but not this man! It is forbidden. You cannot do it!"

"Why not, pray? One of the rabbits that went to make the stalking terrors behind you could have been no more in my power than he is!"

"No," retorted that dim voice. "A rabbit—perhaps. Yourself—by all means. But a real man—no!"

"You flatter him! Again—why not?"

"It won't be allowed, that's all. Were you really the clever devil you think you are, you'd know it!"

The conversation had taken on a reminiscent tang that puzzled Colin, and at the same time deeply depressed him. He had an idea, too, that just here someone should come in and—yes, there lurched Genghis Khan down a lane opened for him between the now barely visible ranks of the gods. Again he was dragging that unlucky and persistent corpse. Having laid it solemnly before the font, he somersaulted off like, a black catherine-wheel, to vanish in the mist.

"Marco—and dead!" said Nacoc-Yaotl.

At the words a soft, murmurous sound swept the mist, ice mind mourning through a forest.

"Dead," continued the demon, "by the angry hand of my servant!"

"By the just hand of mine!" murmured Colin's defender.

"No, for he knew no reason to kill. I rose up in his heart suddenly—and lo! he obeyed me! Obedience is the test. Why should I not give my servant what form I choose?"

Again there was silence. Colin began to think that to the last question no answer would be vouchsafed, and his depression increased. He would have liked to hear it answered—answered in some definite, satisfactory way, that would have convinced himself as well as the demon.

But now the vapors had swallowed all the friendly gods save the Lord of the Air, and his face changed yet more—changed and humanized, till suddenly Colin knew it for the face of Maxatla, that young captain preferred by the Moth Girl on Tlapallan Lake.

Striding forward he laid a hand on Colin's shoulder.

"I claim this man," he cried in a stern, sweet voice, that was unmistakably human. "I claim him in the name of the Feathered Serpent! Let any servant of Nacoc-Yaotl lay hand on him at his peril!"

And Nacoc-Yaotl answered: "You little fool! Unless you wish to lie in his place, go away! I am tired of having my work broken in on by a silly, superstitious girl. Now, for God's sake, if you know what's good for you, clear out of here and stay out!"

XXIX

A Golden Flask

The Black God's reply to Maxatla struck Colin as highly incongruous. He wondered what the young captain would, say to it, and so wondering, opened his eyes.

With the suddenness of a blow the basin, that had been as obligingly transparent as his eyelids, shut in solid around him. The demon-fate above flashed back into Kennedy's, with its sneer and its enormous glasses.

It occurred to Colin that he had been dreaming; but he did actually lie in that golden basin, and there was actually a hand on his shoulder. By twisting his cramped neck a little he could see it. If it were Maxatla's, however, that young warrior possessed marvelously delicate fingers.

Desiring above everything to identify the owner of that hand, Colin tried to raise himself. The ropes which had been on his arms were gone, his coat had been removed, and the flannel shirt under it half unfastened. But though free of bonds, he was so weak that the Lord of Fear easily pushed him back and held him there.

"Anesthetic wearing off," he heard Kennedy mutter, and then Maxatla spoke again.

"I shall not go—not without my lord. Between us there is the Golden Thread that may not be broken—"

"What on earth are you raving about now?"

"You are as discourteous as evil," she retorted quite calmly. "When, first I saw my lord, that night he came to your pitiful Fortress of Fear and I knew that its end was destined—when first I saw him in the passage outside my door, great and kind and noble—then I saw that which glimmered between us. Centeotl, who weaves the fruitfields on her looms, spins also the Golden Thread, for a sign between those who are destined. To not all is it given, but none who receive it may break it. Through all the distance I felt his need calling me—"

"Distance!" sneered Kennedy. "You can't have got very far away from here in that costume!"

"I have been far," was the retort, given with a placid dignity that nothing could shake. "For my dress, it was woven for me by the Lady

Astrid, my own dear mother, ere she was taken home by the gods. Into it she wove many charms of love, and because of those charms, while I wear it no great harm may befall me."

"Oh, is that why you've hung onto it like grim death all this time? Lord, I never find out anything about your actions without uncovering a new superstition! You'd be an interesting study, if I had time for it. Now, before you clear out of here, tell me in three words where you have been, and—by Jove! *You* know what killed Marco! Or did you do it yourself?"

"I had no need. Because I spoke some thoughts of him and the vile passion he called love—because I promised to die before I would mate with him—he loosed upon me the devil-man there. So he was slain by one whom my prayers brought to aid me."

The leisurely, quiet statement brought an impatient grunt from Kennedy, but for Colin something at last slid off his conscience that had lain like a deadening weight. Repent Marco's killing? There had been cause, and to spare, for it! He had never supposed that Khan's murderous attack on the girl had been not only countenanced, but—commanded! Weakling? So are the rattlesnake and the gila-monster—but men hardly hesitated to crush them for that!

Colin stirred again, and Kennedy's attention came back to him.

"You go!" he said to the intruder. "I'll attend to your case later. Go—or I swear I'll loose that on you which prayer won't save you from!"

"I shall not go," she repeated. "Is there no warning that you will heed? Have you forgotten how, upon the first visit of my lord, your Fortress of Fear quivered, groaning in every stone and timber? To one less blind than you, it would have been sign enough that his coming presaged the end."

"You little fool, this house is centuries old. A place so old as this will often shake and settle by its own weight"

"You have made it the seat of Nacoc-Yaotl, and only a god could shake it! The Lord of the Air is patient, but I think that tonight he will set his foot at last on his enemy's neck. A great wind blows without—a great and awful wind! I tell you, the Feathered Serpent tears even now, at the roof-beams of this temple of evil. The end is near and—ah-h!"

Even Kennedy started, drawing back from the font and casting an anxious eye about his "work-room."

As on the evening of Colin's first visit, a long-drawn, grating moan was shaking the very walls; a strange, ominous, vibrating sound that seemed to come from everywhere at once, and brought with it a feeling of nausea and vague terror. It was answered by a hideous concerted wail from the monstrosities of the swamp. At his master's back appeared Genghis Khan, chattering and cringing.

Released for a moment, Colin sat up. Where he got strength for that act he did not know, unless it had flowed into him from the fragile forgers on his shoulder.

There she stood, his Dusk Lady, the cloak flung back from her beautiful, worn, green gown, one hand still laid on her "lord," and on her face the look of a pale young prophetess.

"Warning!" she cried. "Warning! Maker of Hatreds, the end of patience is upon you!"

Like a pale young prophetess the Dusk Lady stood, but her voice rang on silence, for the groaning sound had passed, and with its cessation, the creatures of the mire had resumed their habit of quiet.

All seemed as before. All as before, save that the swamp's level seemed strangely higher, and over its edge at one side the head of a serpent had appeared. It crept forward a very little way and lay still. Unlike the gatekeeper, this serpent was black—black with a polished gleam—black like the *teotetl,* the sacred marble, from which had been carved a body for the Maker of Hatreds.

As the sound and vibration ceased, and Kennedy's hasty glance discerned nothing come of them, he turned angrily toward the girl.

Then he swore, and a moment later had flung both arms about his resurgent captive. But from some source Colin had certainly derived an influx of energy, enough at least for a struggle. Kennedy addressed a sharp command to his apish ally; but Khan held off, cowering back toward the dais and at last springing upon it to crouch beside its deity.

Colin had one leg over the basin's edge. The immense weight of the font prevented its oversetting, but some of the gold containers set on its ledge went spinning down to roll across the floor.

After one futile effort to aid her lord by loosening his captor's grasp, the girl stooped for one of these containers. She took it without selection at the hazard of desperation. All she knew of them was that they held stuff of diabolical power, and a desperate woman is not particular about her weapons.

She rose, a gold flask in her hands. It must have held about a pint, and it was carved all over with writhing, lizard-like forms. It possessed a crystal stopper that stuck but could be twisted out. She proved it.

Meantime, the Lord of Fear recalled that he had other servants than Khan and raised his head, mouth open for command.

It was well for Colin that in the same moment he had wrenched himself fairly free. Calm as she seemed, his Dusk Lady proved capable of an impetuosity as unconsidered as had more than once carried her lord into trouble. To fling the contents of a flask at two struggling men, trusting to hit the one and miss the other, requires either great recklessness or supreme faith in one's own aim.

But impetuosity for once was justified. Because of his sudden efforts and wrenching away, only a few minute drops of the stuff sprinkled Colin and they on his hand. Though he hastily wiped the hand on his trousers it was painful for days afterward.

Kennedy, however, was less fortunate. He released his prisoner and staggered back with a short, stifled shriek, and it was the last sound save one that was to be heard from him. He had clapped both hands over his face—the human hand and the paw—but not before Colin caught one glimpse of it—a dripping, darkening, purplish expanse, of which the features in that flash of time had assumed the most curiously *blurred* appearance. A strong odor as of bitter almonds filled the air.

It is likely that the liquid in the flask was what Kennedy had referred to as the "second solution." Very probably the application of it in this wholly unscientific manner would not have produce the "beautiful" results that he so much admired.

The question, however, is theoretic, for as a subject of this variation of process he did not last long enough to be termed a decisive experiment.

As he reeled backward, there began a recurrence of that great, inexplicable vibration, and with its coming a wild rage appeared to seize upon the marsh's grisly in habitants.

Transmuted or not, they retained the instinct of beasts to sense disaster, and if they had any share in "the intellect of man" they displayed it now by behaving as man does in a panic. The rage that gripped them was of fear, not malice.

Archer Kennedy, head in arms, limbs wabbling like an animated strawman's, staggered blindly to the pavement's very edge, and instinctively Colin shouted a warning. But this third effort to save a worthless life was vain.

Out of the rushes beyond a slimy mass heaved, lashing out with a dozen squid-like arms. It was hard to conceive how such an acephalous mass of squirming tentacles had ever known a master, but the grace to obey was whelmed under now in a more natural instinct. Panic makes no discriminations.

Round the Lord of Fear a tentacle whipped, clung and contracted, and as it caught him a last sound passed what was left of the man's lips.

Colin heard—the word was pitched in a key so low and different from the other noises. "*God!*"

Prayer perhaps, but much more likely habit. It was his favored exclamation.

Colin, who not being God, could not help him, turned away his eyes, and when he looked back a score of nameless, fighting creatures were at the edge, with Archer Kennedy somewhere under them, wallowed down in mud.

As he had lived, so he died—without comprehension. But he was an empty, negligible thing, and behind him he left the real master—the black, discarnate *hate* for whose will he had been the blind channel.

XXX

The Gate Lodge Again

"M acClellan! Well, upon my word!"

Rhodes descended from the car and advanced, hardly knowing whether to be amused or indignant.

They had come through Undine a few minutes earlier, and by following the pike had found Reed's place without difficulty. But they were not the first on the scene. Two cars were standing outside Jerrard's ill-omened gates, one drawn up by the wall, the other fairly blocking the road.

As Rhodes' car halted, a man had turned away from the first car, and under the roadlight Rhodes had no trouble in knowing him.

The stout detective gave something very like a guilty start, but recovered instantly.

"Ain't this your car, Mr. Rhodes?" he demanded, as casually as though their meeting here was most natural event.

The other two passengers from the Rhodes car had descended now.

"Colin did come here!" exclaimed Cliona tensely. "That is our car that he left outside!"

"I knew it!" MacClellan seemed affably triumphant. "Forester," indicating a second man who had emerged from the car's shadow, "he says she ain't, but you can't fool me on a car I've once rode in. I says—"

"Mr. MacClellan, pardon me, but did you come out in search of my car, or because you changed your mind about the possible dangers of the house behind those gates?"

"Now, don't get sarcastic again, please. I'm a conscientious man, and I thought, since you were so worked up over it, we might as well run out and look things over. But seeing you've brought your wife along, I guess you drew it a little stronger than you meant over the phone, eh?"

"Tony!" Cliona pulled at his sleeve. "My Colin's in there, and we stand talking!"

"The gate is unlocked," Biornson called over his shoulder. "I've left the shotgun for you, Rhodes, and taken the rifle. Coming?"

He was already pushing through the gates.

"Rifle!" snapped MacClellan. "Hey, there, mister, I don't know who you are, but you haven't any license to walk in that man's grounds carrying weapons! Come back here!"

"Mr. MacClellan, please, please!" In her distress Cliona caught the stout detective's hand. "Don't stop us! I tell you, the thing's maybe in there that left that awful trail of blood down our hill—do you want my brother's death on your soul?"

"If your brother had seen fit to tell me of his suspicions—" began MacClellan, but was interrupted by a series of sharp, quick reports. "That fool!" he exclaimed, and sprang for the gates. But once inside, his intent to check Biornson and confiscate the rifle underwent sudden alteration.

Behind the gate lodge a curious scene was being enacted.

The norseman stood there, beating with the rifle's heavy stock at what seemed a tangled mass of writhing white fire.

"Can't kill—a thing like—this—with bullets!" he shouted against the wind "Got that shotgun, Rhodes? Quick! Oh, watch out there! Watch—out!"

The tangle of fire had fairly rolled away from him and toward the drive. An automatic spat viciously from MacClellan's hand. He didn't know what he was shooting at, but even his conservatism admitted a need of shooting.

Rhodes turned, only to have the shotgun thrust into his hands by an, excited little figure that had dashed out to the car and back again while the men were thinking about it.

A second later the mar of a ten-gauge duck gun shattered the night. Rhodes, who had let go with both barrels at once, staggered back, but the double dose of number four at that close range had been very effective.

The writhing fire fairly flew asunder and quivered almost instantly to darkness.

"What is it?" MacClellan's voice shook suspiciously. "For heaven's sake, what is it?"

Young Forester, who had stood his ground though unarmed, bent forward.

"Some kind of big white snake," he said coolly, "all tangled up with a tree branch. It's still wriggling. Going to plug it some more, Mr. Rhodes?"

For that gentleman was hastily shoving fresh shells into the gun's emptied chambers.

"No need." Biornson had stooped for a closer inspection than Forester's. "It's blown into three pieces now. When I came past the lodge," he continued, "I heard a rustle, and then this—this creature came rolling out the door. Odd about the branch—look here! The end of it was driven clean through the thing's body, just behind the head. Hmph! I wonder who did that, now? O'Hara, do you think?"

"He would have finished the job, not left the thing alive and dangerous," judged Rhodes.

"Alive, but not dangerous. *I* think this is O'Hara's work."

Above them the naked branches lashed, as if blown by the gusty laughter of some invisible giant. The gatekeeper's hard-dying fragments writhed feebly, but there was no light in them now.

"Golly! Watch it bleed!" said Forester.

He obeyed his own inelegant recommendation cheerfully, but the others turned aside, rather sickened.

"Come away, Cliona," pleaded Rhodes. "Let Forester stay with you in the car while the rest of us go on. I suppose," he queried of MacClellan, "that you are convinced now?"

"Guess something's wrong," conceded the detective heavily. "Any man who keeps an illuminated boa-constrictor like that in his gate lodge will bear looking at."

And just then, through the shouting wind, a mighty reverberation shook the air—a long, dull, roaring sound, followed by a kind of tearing crash.

Both noises came from deeper within the grounds, and before Rhodes could interfere Cliona was off up the drive. She had not even a pistol for self-protection, but self was not concerning her. In a rush to the rescue, she no more stopped to consider what she would do on arrival than the Dusk Lady had thought twice before returning here after her lord. The main consideration was to get on the spot as quickly as possible.

But, unlike Tlapallan's child, Cliona was followed by human reinforcements. What might otherwise have been a justifiably cautious advance was made at a reckless run that only caught up with its feminine leader in the shadow of the *porte-cochère*.

XXXI

A Strange Battlefield

Somehow Colin got out of the font and onto his feet. Did the floor really heave under them, or was it the dimness of his brain that made it seem so?

"The door—the door!" cried the Dusk Lady, and clutched at his arm to pull him toward it.

But Colin was looking to the marsh. Would its inhabitants regard a former command of their master's as more sacred than his person? They were already at the forbidden boundary line on all sides, and only the fact that they were fighting very energetically among themselves hindered their crossing it.

The idea of weaponless flight with such pursuers at their heels was unattractive to Colin. His eye fell on the spade lying in the golden chest. It was leaf-shaped, pointed, and looked heavy.

Rather unsteadily, he made for the only weapon in sight, and in the act perceived a new development.

Out of the marsh not one black serpent but a dozen were invading the solid pavement.

They writhed, crept, advanced—*flowed into one,* and suddenly under that sinister invasion a whole section of the floor sank away and was swallowed.

Colin cried out wildly, "The marsh! 'Tis the devilish marsh itself coming in!"

But he was wrong. Not the marsh, but what had flooded the marsh was carrying its mire across the floor. The ooze was no longer taking the form of exploring serpents, but coming on in long ripples, like water over breaking ice. And not the floor alone was affected. The old granite piles of the house were sinking, crumbling, while the rotted beams they supported sagged and bulged downward.

But another force than water was at work tonight.

Above the roofs, like the blow of a giant's fist, something struck the cupola. The candles burning beside Nacoc-Yaotl's dais flickered wildly. Colin felt a great blast on his cheek and looked up to see night sky roofing the shaft—stars, obscured by scudding vapors of cloud.

The outer gale had lifted the cupola. bodily, had flung it far and shattered, and its after-breath struck down the shaft like an eager promise of freedom. The foul mists swirled and cleared.

All had happened so swiftly that Colin, stooping for the one visible weapon, had barely time to raise it before the first goblin brute crossed the line.

Combat in the open would have been folly, and sweeping his Dusk Lady with him the Irishman made a rush for the doorway. Under their running feet the floor had a give and resilience like thin, tough ice. Reaching the door, Colin would have closed it but lacked time. On the very threshold he turned to meet the first assailant, a thing of innumerable legs, rather like a magnified centipede, but whose head belonged somewhere in the mammalian scale.

It was a hybrid of fancy worth looking at, but Colin was unappreciative. He was very weak and the spade seemed not only heavy, but heavy as lead. When the many-legged brute came at him he struck out feebly.

It dodged like lightning, came at him from another angle, and the end came near being immediate.

But the floor, an inch deep in water now, chose that opportune moment to subside altogether, with a long, gurgling swish!

Colin had pushed the Dusk Lady through the doorway, and himself stood just inside it. The footing there remained solid enough, but the creature of too many legs found itself wallowing in thin mud and much impeded thereby. The floor had gone to pieces under it like a breaking floe.

Colin thrust with his spade, and this time was so lucky as to bury its point in one of the beast's eye-sockets. It screamed horribly and plugged its bleeding head in the liquid mire.

Colin looked for its mates, but in looking beheld a sight so strange that he nearly forgot that peril.

More than the floor had gone under. The font and every other piece of gold in the place was gone; but the dais of Nacoc-Yaotl, with its black canopy, had not sunk. Like a somber islet on a surface of rippling ebony it lay, not floating, apparently, but solid as if supported by a column of stone.

There still crouched Genghis Khan, and there the Black God sat unmoving. But that last was not strange, for how may marble, however sacred, move of its own volition?

The strangeness was above the dais—above the canopy.

Though the candelabra had sunk out of sight, though the livid vegetation of the marsh had been crushed under the inundation by its inhabitants, the place was by no means in darkness.

Something hung in mid air now, globular as had been the evil fungi, transparent, pale as the ghost of an old moon against the sky of day, but growing brighter with each passing moment. Hung in mid air where only vacancy had been. Out of nothing it hid come to illuminate all with a sweet light, mellow as a sunset's afterglow. It was bright as a clear winter moon in a black sky—brighter—not transparent at all.

A great gust roared down the shaft, circling the dais with the sweep of a whirlwind.

It sucked the breath from Colin's lungs and drove it back again. He straightened. That was clean air—air to breathe and be strong, but—but hot as the desert's sand wind!

That fireball, so mysteriously appearing from nowhere, was giving off more than light. Having passed in a few seconds from pale shadow to dazzling brilliance, it hung less like the moon than a fiery replica of old Sol himself. And the hot wind circled the shaft.

"My lord—my lord!" cried a sweet, excited voice in Colin's ear. "I think the gods battle tonight! The gods! So have I seen Tonathiu grow to glory in the heart of his temple! The rushing wings of the Feathered Serpent beat fiercely by! Tlaloc of the Floods is with us! But the Black God is strong—strong! See how he sits unharmed! The flood may not rise further nor the fire descend—and his servants live on in the flood—oh, my lord—"

"Back there! Get back!"

Colin had wrenched his eyes from the fierce focus of light that overhung Nacoc-Yaotl. Whether the Dusk Lady were right or no in thinking this a battlefield of gods, he knew for sure that battle for a man was toward, and that man himself.

The liquid blackness before him was suddenly all asplash with swimming terrors. Heads came up at him from every direction, no longer tearing at one another's throats, but reaching toward his with a unanimity of purpose that called for instant defense.

The Dusk Lady came of a warrior people. At his rough command she sprang back out of his way, and the fight was on.

The fire globe grew more radiant, the hot, pure wind circled the shaft, and Colin strangely forgot that he had been drained of strength.

In his hands the heavy spade was like a feather—like a living feather of fire—like a sword of fire!

There came to him a great, joy and exhilaration. He smote and thrust joyously. The strength of ten was in him, and a vigor that was endless—undying.

The great wind circled the shaft—and across the black water, beneath Nacoc-Yaotl's canopy, two slit-eyes had opened wide and glaring in a rage more frightful than any mortal anger!

XXXII

The Battle of the Doorway

"Everything's dark as a pocket," complained MacClellan, "and this flash won't work. Battery's wore out. Say, Forester, gimme your flash."

"He's outside with my wife," said a voice in the dark beside him.

"No, I ain't," contributed another voice cheerfully. "Here you are, Mac. Sorry, Mr. Rhodes, but your lady here would come along."

A white beam snapped into existence, disclosing a quiet, orderly looking reception hall. They had entered it from the porch through a door that stood invitingly open, and though Rhodes had begged Cliona to remain outside, and hastily asked the younger detective to see that she did, neither request, it appeared, had been respected.

The two had followed close on the leaders' heels, and now the whole party stood together near the hall's center.

"Don't believe that crashing noise came from here—" began MacClellan.

"Hush!" said Cliona. "Listen!"

"Sounds like a crowd of people yelling from a long way off," Forester commented after a moment.

"From beneath our feet," corrected Bjornson sternly. "And those are not human voices."

"Say! Do you smell smoke? And—say, the floor's shak—"

MacClellan's exclamation was drowned in a vibratory roar, like that they had heard earlier, only now they were fairly above its source. Through the heavier noise there ripped a long, shattering crash.

Something had happened to the room they stood in. What it was they did not pause to find out. With only a vague notion that in some way the room had become much larger, and that this enlargement, together with the jarring quiver of the floor, meant instant peril, Rhodes fairly snatched Cliona from her feet and led a rush for the porch.

They were barely in time. As Forester, last out, crossed the threshold, a great noise of splintering wood and beams that cracked with an almost explosive uproar followed him. His companions had not paused on the porch, but Forester was a young man of that reckless sort of cool-headedness which, though it run from danger, will turn again at the very edge of safety. The porch felt solid to him. He instantly stopped there and stuck his head back through the doorway.

The reception hall, or rather the space it had occupied, was no longer dark.

He had a brief glimpse of a huge open space, billowing with clouds of lime dust and black smoke, shot through with ruddy flames. The floor level had apparently dropped some distance and was no longer level at all, but a seep, uneven slant descending to—what?

From the rolling clouds a fierce, white *focus* of light shot blinding rays. The smoke filled his eyes with acrid tears, and as he raised his hand to dash them away, crashing doom shot down from above.

The end of a flying beam just missed his face, and he withdrew it hastily.

"By George," he exclaimed, "the whole darn house is caving!" and thrust his head forward for further news.

Then a heavy hand jerked him away from the door and off the porch.

"Come away from there, you fool!" yelled MacClellan in his ear. "That wall will go in a minute. Don't you know enough to stand from under when a house falls in? Now you beat it over to Undine and turn in a fire alarm. Phone Deering at—no, phone the Lillybank station that's nearer. Tell 'em to chase a patrol load out here *quick*. Don't wait for them nor the department. Get hold of any men you can pick up in Undine—and axes—and back here on the jump. Get me?"

"You bet!" came the young man's informal acknowledgment, and he was gone into the darkness. He intended to make his absence from this fascinating scene as brief as was humanly possible.

MacClellan turned to his companions, only to find himself alone. By the light of a ruddy, sullen glare newly sprung into being, he glanced from side to side, but none of the three was visible. The wall before him had not fallen, but through the open doorway smoke poured, only to be beaten back by the wind. Behind it glowed a redness like the very heart of hell.

Never in his life, save once, had he seen a fire develop with such amazing celerity. That other conflagration, though, had occurred in a sash and door factory, and had been encouraged by the bursting of a fifty-gallon tank of varnish. One does not expect a stone dwelling house to flare up into easy flame. The roar of falling *débris* warned him that

FRANCIS STEVENS

other walls were proving less stanch than the one which faced him, but the collapse had begun too early to have been caused by the fire.

The entire catastrophe was as incomprehensible as sudden.

MacClellan dashed off, searching at hazard for the three reckless ones who had come in the car. He had called himself a conscientious man, and it happened to be true. The stout detective felt personally responsible that "his party" did nothing rash in an effort to rescue that wild Irishman, O'Hara, who most likely lay dead now in the flaming ruins.

He had half encircled the house before he found any trace of those he sought. To his increased surprise, not a single outer wall had fallen, though the windows, heat-broken now and belching smoke, betrayed what a stone-sheathed welter of flame they enclosed.

He knew nothing of the reconstruction that had metamorphosed the Jerrard's time-honored residence to so strange an inward form. As a matter of fact, the rear walls of the reception hall and two rooms on either side of it were contiguous to the shaft's inner sheathing, and when the piles beneath finally gave way, that entire wing of the house, including the shaft's side, collapsed, leaving only the outer wall to stand.

The two other sides of the shaft overhanging the marsh were not long in following, but the fourth, the solid wall in which was the doorway where Colin fought, did not fall. It abutted upon a one-story wing built on as an addition and which covered no portion of the cellar. The doorway led through a passage to a flight of stone stairs, opening in turn upon a suite of rooms reserved by the Lord of Fear for his own use.

When MacClellan came to an outstanding wing whose windows were dark and cool, and where a low veranda bespoke possible entrance, he had no reason to think this what it was—a point of greater though different danger than that from which he had peremptorily snatched Forester.

Seeing the figure of a man just disappearing into the verandas shadow, he dashed hurriedly after him, still bent on dissuasion. It was no use to shout. His voice wouldn't have carried ten feet in that uproar. Once inside he snapped on his borrowed flash at the same instant that someone else struck a match.

THE LONG, NARROW ROOM HE had come into was fogged at one end with thin smoke, but MacClellan saw at least two figures immediately ahead of him, one of them holding a match above its head and peering anxiously about.

Cliona had again played leader and with such an instinct for directness as had carried her this time clean out of touch with her anxious "support." Just as MacClellan reached them his flash disclosed another pair of wide doors standing open in the room's far wall.

Instantly both Biornson and the lawyer fairly hurled themselves toward that black aperture, and again the conscientious one wan forced to follow or give up his mission. He followed.

A stone stair led steeply down, ending at a blank white wall. The first two plunged down, their pursuer involuntarily lending the air of his light-ray to their descent, but at the blank wall they turned to the left and abruptly disappeared.

The stairway was almost free from smoke, but a wave of heat came up from it. It occurred to MacClellan that he was quite possibly about to immolate himself at the altar of other people's recklessness. He hesitated.

The air shook to a heavy concussion. It came from beyond the stair-foot and sounded as though a bomb had exploded.

All three of his party were probably down there.

MacClellan swore and ran down the stairs three steps at a time. He hardly expected to come up them again. The whole house would go in a minute, and the recklessness of people, throwing away their lives in hopeless attempts at rescue, was very trying indeed to Mr. MacClellan!

When, a minute or so earlier, Rhodes and Biornson had arrived at the stair foot, they discovered that a wide passage opened there and some five yards along it there seemed to be a large rectangular opening in its wall, through which beat a light so white and fierce that even its reflection vas dazzling. Dark forms moved against it.

The newcomers had hoped for little but to drag Cliona back to safety. But on racing along the passage they found not one but two women at the end of it, and in the center of that brilliant rectangle, a huge, wild figure of a man that thrust and struck outward desperately.

What he was striking at, however, they could not make out till they were fairly abreast of the glaring doorway. The opening was broad and difficult for one man, however powerful, to guard against such assailants as were besieging it. Even as Rhodes arrived, somewhat in advance, a head came thrusting through beside Colin and under his guard.

It was a frightful thing, that head, slimy, and dripping, large as a

FRANCIS STEVENS

lion's and hideous as a gargoyle's. It thrust through with a writhing motion, at the end of a neck unthinkably long and snakelike.

The once skeptical lawyer didn't stop to consider whether what he saw was possible. Again both barrels of the duck gun spoke together. That explosion was what MacClellan had heard, reechoed by the walls of the passage, and it announced quietus for at least one more of Kennedy's "recreations." Hard dying they no doubt were, but the charge of a double-barreled shotgun at a range of an inch or so is a mighty queller.

The neck, with what was left of the head trailing, slid laxly back.

Colin thought the passage was falling behind him and turned, but as Biornson shouted "All right! We're with you!" he lunged forward again, content to accept reenforcements without stopping to ask why or whence.

Biornson sprang to one side of him and Rhodes to the other. Shoulder to shoulder they stood across the doorway.

The light was blinding and the heat terrific. Half-seeing, they shot and hacked at swimming enemies whose diverse loathsomeness was only equaled by their ferocious determination to pass that doorway.

Beyond a twelve-foot-wide area of hot, black water, where the recreations thronged, towered a heap of blazing *débris* that sent its roaring flames and smoke to the very height of the "fortress", sucked up by the rushing wind. At the center of the heap was that fierce white *focus* of light which Forester had observed and which it seemed no smoke could obscure.

Below that again—it was terribly hard to see anything—but Rhodes thought a darkness was there, as if in falling the beams and walls had made a sort of recess of cavern beneath themselves.

And even in the midst of battle the young lawyer became gradually conscious of a dread worse a hundred times than the facing of all the racing beastliness they fought.

The fancy came on him that something hid in the sheltered darkness—something living, but that had no right to life—something vague in his thought as a smoke cloud, and definite in terror as the 'bogies' of childhood days.

Biornson shared the impression, but with a difference. He *knew* that the darkness was a recess, and the recess a lair, and that what peered forth from it lived without the grace of flesh and blood which made even its distorted creatures endurable to think of. But if there is an evil which is not only of the flesh, so also there is a courage. Knowing, he fought on.

Ammunition quickly exhausted, the weapons of Colin's allies were soon less efficient than his spade. There was little room to swing a gun-stock, but now the attack began to seem less vigorous. The black water steamed hot vapor. One or two of the monsters that had been neither shot nor smitten disappeared to rise no more.

With scorching face, Rhodes thanked God for the heat, if it were weakening the enemy more than himself. Probably it was because they were in the water, and the doorway on a higher level. No, that was absurd. Heat rose upward.

The shotgun's stock landed fairly on the forehead of a neckless, flat-faced abnormality, with the tusks of a wild boar and a frontal carapace that should have been impregnable.

It crushed in with ridiculous ease, and the stock flew in a dozen pieces.

Rhodes laughed. He had not struck very hard. The heat was terrific. It had softened the beast's skull, no doubt, and the walnut stock of his gun.

With the barrels he foiled a clever, monkey-armed fiend, reaching for Colin's ankle to pull him down. The barrels, too, bent in shattering that arm.

The heat, of course. How lucky it was that he himself did not feel at all weakened, any more than his companions!

There was a glorious wind blowing from somewhere—a hot wind, but laden with vigor. Rhodes was conscious of a kind of enormous vitality in himself—as if he were larger than himself—much larger and stronger. His brain swam dizzily, but his vigor was tremendous—endless. Fire, fire everywhere, and he in the midst of it—part of it—elemental, deathless fire. Demons swam in it, drowning, and he struck at them joyously with a sword of fire—

But at this point, regrettable to state, the testimony of Anthony Rhodes becomes valueless, because he was later quite unable to remember what happened next.

In fact, since an unbaised account is desirable, it seems best to fall back upon that unprejudiced, if bewildered witness, Detective MacClellan. He arrived on the scene only a few moments after Rhodes and Biornson, and was present at the final attack, and that he adhered to facts in reporting the affair next day to his chief does him great credit. A less conscientious man would have saved his reputation for veracity by lying.

"That was one scrap that had me guessing, chief. I didn't know what was happening, nor what had happened, nor what was due to happen. These three guys stood across the door beating and shooting at something beyond. It was hotter than a river tug's stoke-hole and the light was awful.

"I tried to squeeze in the doorway but there wasn't room, and those two women were there, and I couldn't get 'em to come away. I'd have gone back afterward, but I wanted to get them out of the house where they weren't doing a bit of good. No use. I might as well have been a phonograph five miles off playing 'The End of a Perfect Day.'

"Then all of a sudden something come flying through the whiteness beyond the door like a shadow against it, and next minute this guy O'Hara smashed over backward with a big black thing on him that looks to me like a big monkey. He says afterward it's a live marble statue. Maybe he's bughouse and maybe I am. I dunno. There might as well be live statues as some of the other nightmares I saw afterward. Well, anyway, Mr. Rhodes had phoned something about a big monkey out there, so I thought it was that.

"And here they are, this thing and O'Hara, rolling all over the floor together, and me hopping around the outside trying to keep the women out of it, and wanting to shoot, but scared I'd hit the wrong one.

"Then Mr. Rhodes and this Biornson party wheels around to see what's going on, and right away there comes scrambling through that doorway an aggregation of—of—what-is-its—eight-legged, four-legged, three-legged, and no-legged that well, when I try to think of 'em I just can't seem to get my mind down to details, chief. But honestly, Ringling Brothers would have paid a million dollars just for their *pictures* to slap on walls.

"O'Hara says they were white-colored, and the monkey was white, too, and so it couldn't have been the monkey that jumped him, because what jumped him was black. But the whole bunch was so messed up with mud they might have been pink or baby blue underneath for all anybody could tell. They came plunging through, and Rhodes and Biornson went down under 'em. I was clean at the passage, understand, trying to keep those two women out of it, and we just missed being tramped under.

"For a fact the brutes didn't pay any attention at all to us. They weren't fighting mad, they were fear mad, with the fire behind 'em. I don't know how many there was. There might have been a dozen or there might have bin more. The last one—it was a thing like a kind of spidery cat, and big as any tiger—it jumped clean over the fellows on the floor and the rash was over, but I could hear the brutes yelling and tearing each other up the stairs, even over all the other racket.

"I'd emptied my gun as they went, but it might just as well have been a bean-shooter for all the good it did.

"I didn't reckon to see any of those three guys that had been tramped under get up again. But when I looked, darned if the Irishman and whatever it was he was scrapping with weren't tumbling around just the same as before. Too busy to know they'd been run over, I guess. And this Biornson, who, I must say, is one of the gamest old guys I ever met he was just scrambling up. But Rhodes don't get up, because he's got a busted leg.

"Biornson, he looks around kind of wild, with the blood streaming over his face, and then darned if the old white-head don't jump into that fight to a finish between O'Hara and—and whatever it was.

"I'd shoved a fresh clip in my gun, and was willing enough to take a shot, but—say, chief, if you'd *seen* that scrap you'd know why I hated to mix in personally. If I'd see a man scrapping with a full-grown gorilla—and maybe that's what it was—I'd pot the gorilla if I could, but I'll be darned if I'd do what Biornson did.

"As I says before, he jumps right in and grabs the thing around the neck, tryin' to jerk its head back. He lasts about five seconds and then got his. At the time I couldn't tell just what happened, but it seems the brute had its teeth comfortably clamped in O'Hara's shoulder and didn't take kindly to interference. It let go and its head came back all right, and the same minute it gave Biornson a left-handed side-swipe that landed the poor guy about ten feet away.

"Then it got back to business, but just that few seconds had given O'Hara his chance. And I want to say, chief, that anything I ever said against that big Irish mick I take back here and now. Fight! Say, I wish you'd seen that scrap! And in the time its head was up he got one hand on its throat and next minute the other.

"And—say, chief, come to think of it, you couldn't strangle a stone statue, even if it was alive, now could you?"

"Mac," said the chief very solemnly, "I am listening to a story on which comment would be—er—cruel. Proceed."

"All right, don't believe me then." MacClellan's tone was more dogged than injured. "I knew you wouldn't, anyway, but I have to make my report, and this thing happened just like I'm telling it. Didn't I say at the start I thought it was a gorilla? Though, I'll be darned if anybody even saw a gorilla with a face like—well, anyway, it could be choked, for O'Hara did it.

"That was when I got my first good look at the thing and—say, I don't like to think about it even now. Makes me kind of sick. No use. You'd have had to see it to understand. I could have plugged it easy then. But I give you my word I forgot I had a gun in my hand. I just stood there staring. I wanted to run, and I couldn't. Not with those women behind me.

"I'd had my arms out—so—keepin' 'em back. Isn't it the devil the way women are? If they've got a man in a scrap and think he's getting the worst of it, they'll rush in and never think twice about getting hurt—"

"Back to your animated statuary, Mac. You're wandering."

"Well, these two had stopped trying to get past me. They were struck still, just like me. He—he strangled it with his hands—and—and—that's enough said. If it was bad living, it was worse dying. I've seen a few messy scraps in my time, but this was different. Can't tell you. Makes me side to think of it.

"I was never so grateful to anybody in all my life as I was to O'Hara when he straightened up all of a sudden and dragged that—thing—up with him, and pitched it out of the door. He didn't pitch it any little ways, either. It was near as big as him, but he just took it neck and ankles, give it a couple of swings, and sent it flyin' across about twelve feet of water right into the heart of the fire. I give you my word, the flames flared up like he'd slung a bag of gunpowder into them.

"Then O'Hara drops back against the wall and starts laughing like he'd gone nutty. 'Claim on me!' he gasps out. 'Claim on me, is it? The claim that he had is the claim he collected! And I think,' he says, 'there's one demon will be making no more claims of any man!'

"I tell you just what he says," the detective added rather apologetically, "because right then—I guess I was pretty excited myself—but just then it seemed like he'd done something big—not ordinary big—but tremendous—like—like—saving a country or—oh, some darn dangerous thing that everybody ought to pin medals on him for."

MacClellan paused.

"Well?" said the chief, with suspicious calmness.

"Then we got out, that's all. There were some other things I was going to tell you, but I'll be hanged if I will when you look that way! You ought to know me well enough—"

"Wait a minute. Think it over, Mac. Never mind this statue-gorilla business. We'll be quite open-minded about that. But—could a dozen or so ferocious—ah—golliwogs such as you describe have been turned loose last night, and no one—absolutely no one have sent in a complaint to this office since?"

"I didn't say turned loose," retorted MacClellan gloomily.

"Oh! Not turned loose. Adopted as pets, perhaps, by the neighbors?"

"Chief, I'm done. I knew how it would be, but I'm a conscientious man—you ought to know that—"

"You haven't answered my question."

"ALL RIGHT. WHEN WE WENT out there was a heap of nasty, purplish jelly on the stairs, and some more in a room on the first floor, and some more clear outside the house. A lot of people saw it besides me. Forester saw it, for one. If you don't believe me, ask him—"

"Oh, I do believe you, Mac. I do. But it's the golliwogs I'm interested in. Where are they?"

"All right. I'll tell the rest, then. The fire flared up like I said, and that passage was no place to stop and chin in. O'Hara and me and these two girls—who sure are plucky ones—we carried out the wounded between us. Funny. That was a regular reunion down there in the middle of the fire, but nobody had time to be sentimental then.

"I told you already that this Mr. Biornson claims to be the father of the girl everybody round Undine had thought was Miss Reed and crazy. She ain't crazy; only, brought up some place in Mexico where there seem to have been a lot of queer white people, and her mother was one of 'em.

"You can get all that straight from Biornson, if you want to.

"And he says afterward—when he came to—that once he tried to kill O'Hara down in Mex, and here he finds him rescuing this kidnaped girl of his—or she rescuing him, it seems to be a toss-up which—and O'Hara says he don't care a whoop what happened fifteen years ago, just so he gets old Biornson for a father-in-law now, and—"

"A very romantic situation," cut in the chief, "but aren't we again straying from our golliwogs? Leave marrying to the minister, Mac, and trot out your animiles."

"Hang it all, you make it so darn hard—I'll tell you in a minute. We got out of the house, and just in the nick of time, too. As we jumped down the steps there was a flare of flame licked after us that singed the back of my coat. That wing of the house had got so hot from the rest of the place that it must have exploded into flame of itself—spontaneous combustion, you understand—like the trees do in a forest fire.

"We get away from there quick, believe me, and then it strikes me as funny that there ain't any string of fire engines around, nor anybody at all but us. I starts cussing Forester, but five minutes later he's with us with bells on and pretty near every soul in Undine at his heels. He says he ain't been gone over twelve or fifteen minutes. He was right, too, but it had seemed more like fifteen hours to me—straight.

"Of course, they couldn't do much with the fire, even when the department got there. Besides the start it had, a water-main had busted, and they couldn't get any water till they hitched up hose clear into Undine.

"Well, O'Hara was all messed up, and his shoulder in awful shape, and Mr. Rhodes with a busted leg, and poor old Biornson so shaken up he couldn't walk. There was a doctor came over from Undine with the crowd, and he fixed 'em up temporary, and having three cars handy it was no trouble to get 'em home. I says hospital, but they were all set on going to Rhodes' place, so of course the doctor and me gave in.

"I wanted answers to a few questions, so I went along, and just as we pulled out they got the water on the fire at last, but O'Hara says to me, 'They'd best let her burn out, and at that the ruins of it should assay fifty-fifty pure gold and devilishness. I wish joy to him that gets it.'

"I says, 'I'm proud to have known you, Mr. O'Hara, but I wouldn't want any gold that came out of that cellar.' And he says, 'You're a man after my own heart, MacClellan, or you'd never have been in at the finish like you was. It wasn't gold that drew you,' he says, 'and I know fear didn't drive you, and as the same may be said of all of us I'm thinking Mr. Kennedy was mistaken. For a man to judge the whole world by himself is a dangerous matter. But,' he says, 'the black god was another matter entirely.' And then he goes on to tell me all that had happened to him before we arrived. It was like this—"

"MacClellan," snapped the chief, "are you or are you not intending to answer my question? What became of the animals you say escaped ahead of you from the cellar?"

The stolid detective clenched his teeth despairingly, but dared evade no longer.

"When Biornson came to," he muttered, "after we got him out, he—well, he says those heaps of jelly we passed on the stirs and round were the—were the golliwogs, as you call 'em. O'Hara, he'd talked to the fellow that was killed—one of the two fellows—Kennedy alias Reed—and claims they'd been turning common harmless rabbits and cats and such into jelly life that, and then making 'em over into these regular hellions of brutes.

"And Biornson figured that when O'Hara choked the life out of Nakrok-Nakokyotle, or some darned name they teed the statue by, the beasts all slumped back into jelly again. I tell you, I don't say anything's true but just what I saw with my eyes—"

"Exactly. And now I no longer blame you, Mac, for darkly concealing the golliwogs' sad fate. So you go home and go to bed."

XXXIII

As One Triumphant

And here rightfully the story ends, with the end of what was either a very singular biological experiment, or the most extraordinary and sinister invasion by which the race of man was ever threatened.

The rest is all surmise—conjecture—the muddling work of many divergent minds.

The burning of the old Jerrard place, together with what was later found in its ruins and the strange story of the fire's survivors, caused considerable excitement at the time and started some controversies of which the ripples have not yet quite subsided.

The unpleasant heaps of purplish jelly outside the house had rotted clean away by morning, and had been absorbed by the earth past analyzing. It seemed probable to the world at large that the jelly—if it had ever existed—had no connection with the beasts—admitting that they had existed—and that the latter had perished in the fire and been utterly consumed, even to their—equally problematical—bones.

The fact that two alleged human corpses had also vanished could not, however, be explained in this manner. O'Hara testified that the bodies of both Marcazuma, alias Marco, and Archer Kennedy, alias Chester T. Reed, had sunk in the flood, one having, been already lifeless and the other perishing beneath the fury of his own handiwork.

It stands to reason that bodies immersed in mud or muddy water would be safe from incineration. A number of other things were found in said mud, but no bodies. Ergo, Mr. O'Hara was mistaken. No bodies had ever been there.

By part of his own testimony he had spent at least a portion of his evening's captivity in a dreamy and semiconscious condition. No doubt this accounted for much that was—well, slightly incredible in the Irish gentleman's testimony. The lady from Mexico, too, was no doubt pardonably mistaken. In moments of excitement delusion is easy.

The Irish gentleman, for instance, believed that he had broken Marco's neck twenty-four hours previous to the fire. No doctor was present. He merely assumed that the man was dead on the strength of his own unprofessional judgment. What more likely than that, O'Hara's back turned, Marco rose and walked away?

And Kennedy, in all probability, escaped from the burning house alive and comparatively uninjured. Quite likely master and man were now in hiding together, and it was recommended that the police bestir themselves and rout them out.

Svend Biornson, however, disagreed with the world, though he confided his opinion to none but sympathetic ears. He based it on the fact that every one of the jars, boxes, and other golden vessels dug out of the mud were found *open*. Even he declined to surmise what force had opened them and thus destroyed every particle of their diabolical contents.

But for a time, at least, the flooded cellar must have been highly charged with the stuff. He knew for a certainty that, exposed to air or impurities, it lost power quickly. The men who dug in those ruins were safe enough, but to Biornson it was not strange at all that no bodies were found there. They were present, but dissolved as utterly as though the mire had been a kind of temporary quick-lime.

There being no *corpus delicti*, Colin was spared a trial for manslaughter, justifiable or otherwise, and it cannot be truthfully said that he was sorry. He and his Dusk Lady were really very much in love, and it is a pity to be wasting time in jail or law courts when one wishes to be on one's honeymoon.

As it was, the investigation was tiresome enough. It ended at last in clouds of doubt, with a few bright spots of definite decision. A burst water-main was found to have caused the flood. That, together with the weakening nature of the building's reconstruction, had brought on its sudden collapse. And the insurance people, after deep pondering, set down the fire as resulting from "faulty insulation and crossed wires," a favorite explanation for otherwise inexplicable conflagrations.

As to the golden temple vessels, the state fell heir to them in lack of any other claimant. They may be seen today in a certain national museum, though their value is considered dubious. Authenticity as Aztec relics has never been properly established, and their gold was found to be a thin coat laid over solid-copper.

BESIDES THEM STANDS AN OBJECT of still more dubious value—a black stone, in fact, shapeless, yet with an odd suggestion of having once possessed a shape—as if the marble of same old, wicked idol had been melted in a hotter flame than science has ever fanned to being. But there is nothing terrible about it now. It is just a black stone. Of course, it may be that MacClellan's first surmise was correct, and that Genghis Khan, magnified and distorted by excited imaginations, was the antagonist conquered for a second time by Colin. Certainly the pseudo-ape had crouched on the dais, and when it grew too hot beneath the fallen *débris*, such a brute could have leaped the intervening twelve feet of water as it had leaped the forest glades from tree to tree!

At the time, Colin himself believed otherwise. To him the whole matter seemed simple enough then. A demon had claimed him; he had conquered the demon in a satisfactorily personal manner, and as to fire out of nothing, flood that wrought swift miracles, and whirlwind that lent the strength of a Titan with its breath, why, he had never denied that under the Almighty were powers of good to aid a man as well as of evil to crush him.

Having met nothing to shake his faith in either his universe or his God, he remained a good Catholic, and the Dusk Lady was duly baptized into that church, loving her lord too well to quarrel with his religion.

But though he is sure of her love today as he was then, he is not so sure of the nature of that last battle. After meeting the thousand and one contemptuous arguments hurled at their heads, he and his companions became at last sure of nothing about it except that he strangled *something* and flung it into some kind of a fire.

And so, of the most somber actor in a very strange drama, little remains but a shapeless stone and an uncertain memory, and that ever growing more dreamlike as it recedes into the past.

But on that night of nights it was not like a dream at all. It was clear—"clear and bright like"—as had been the sight of Tlapallan to Colin. And when those six first emerged from the burning Fortress of Fear they had no more doubt of their adventure's sinister nature or of its reality than they had a few moments later of the last strange sight of all, though that was more glorious than sinister. It was a vision all shared, from MacClellan, starting on an angry mission in search of Forester, to Biornson, just opening his eyes, safe, and with his daughter's arms about him.

They were among the trees then, some distance from the house. Rhodes lay groaning with the pain of his broken leg, and Cliona had his head in her lap. Colin, very sick and dizzy, with a mangled shoulder and various other wounds, was leaning against a tree and wondering how a man could have the strength of ten one minute and be weak as a kitten the next.

And then it was that MacClellan stopped in his tracks with a sharp cry of amazement. The others looked where he pointed.

Above the Fortress of Fear the fumes roared high. In a lull of the gale fire crested it with a fuming tongue of scarlet. And as that fiery tongue soared skyward, a vast, diaphanous form plunged through the lashing tree branches—plunged through and up—and up—and flung itself on the flame that bent roaring before it!

A vast, impetuous, shouting form, of turbulent plumes and a face of undying youth. Quetzalcoatl, Lord of the Air—the Wind—the victorious Wind!

Ah, that pure and violent one, gently, patient and fiercely intolerant, breath of the wild, sweet places, enemy to all foul vapors and morbid vileness! Great deeds he chants of, and hope, and the courage that is not only of the flesh.

"A heathen god, but a stanch friend," muttered Colin. "I'd be less than a friend myself if I did not admit that I like him!"

Bending, the flame streamed out like a banner—as a trailing banner of scarlet plumes it followed the shouting one.

The End

A NOTE ABOUT THE AUTHOR

Francis Stevens was the pseudonym of Gertrude Barrows Bennett (1884–1948), an American writer of science fiction and fantasy novels. Born in Minneapolis, Stevens wrote her first story at 17, finding publication in popular pulp magazine *Argosy*. Believed to be one of the first American women to publish a work of science fiction, Bennett gained a nationwide reputation as a leading short story writer with such tales as "The Nightmare" (1917), "Friend Island" (1918), and "Serapion" (1920). Additionally, Bennett published several novels throughout her career, including *The Citadel of Fear* (1918), *The Heads of Cerberus* (1919), and *Claimed!* (1920). To supplement her writing, Stevens—who was widowed in 1910 when her husband Stewart Bennett died at sea—worked as a stenographer to support herself, her daughter, and her invalid mother. Credited with influencing H. P. Lovecraft and A. Merritt, Bennett is recognized as a pioneering figure in the history of science fiction.

A NOTE FROM THE PUBLISHER

Spanning many genres, from non-fiction essays to literature classics to children's books and lyric poetry, Mint Edition books showcase the master works of our time in a modern new package. The text is freshly typeset, is clean and easy to read, and features a new note about the author in each volume. Many books also include exclusive new introductory material. Every book boasts a striking new cover, which makes it as appropriate for collecting as it is for gift giving. Mint Edition books are only printed when a reader orders them, so natural resources are not wasted. We're proud that our books are never manufactured in excess and exist only in the exact quantity they need to be read and enjoyed.

bookfinity™

Discover more of your favorite classics with Bookfinity™.

- Track your reading with custom book lists.
- Get great book recommendations for your personalized Reader Type.
- Add reviews for your favorite books.
- AND MUCH MORE!

Visit **bookfinity.com** and take the fun Reader Type quiz to get started.

Enjoy our classic and modern companion pairings!

Classic & Modern